Readers love BRANDON WITT

D1715984

The Shattered Door

"What an incredibly well written emotional story, as if you haven't already guessed HA! It really is quite a journey our Brooke goes on, one which I strongly encourage everyone to read. It'll hurt, it'll make you question, yet it will also bring home the importance of respect, decency, the good that exists and the importance of faith, whatever that might be, and importantly it brings home hope. It will also make you smile through tears and chuckle a few times too at the sarcasm and irony. It was passionate, intense, beautiful and poignant."

—Totally Booked Blog

"Wow. Need something more than that? How about… go buy this book!"

—Prism Book Alliance

Men of Myth series

"*Clashing Tempest* is a must read for anyone who read the first two Men of Myth books. And if you haven't, pick up all three ASAP!!!"

—The Novel Approach

"Men of Myth series is hands down one of the best paranormal / fantasy series I have ever had the pleasure of reading."

—On Top Down Under Reviews

"If you want to spend an afternoon reading an enthralling, entertaining, and satisfying tale, then I recommend that you check this one out for yourself."

—Mrs. Condit and Friends Read Books

"Again the masterful story teller and evil, evil, evil Mr. Witt has left us with a cliffhanger making you want to immediately pick up the next book in the series."

—World of Diversity Fiction

By BRANDON WITT

Grand Adventures (Dreamspinner anthology)
The Shattered Door
Then the Stars Fall

MEN OF MYTH SERIES
Submerging Inferno
Rising Frenzy
Clashing Tempest

Published by DREAMSPINNER PRESS
http://www.dreamspinnerpress.com

then
the
stars
fall

BRANDON WITT

Dreamspinner Press

Published by
DREAMSPINNER PRESS

5032 Capital Circle SW, Suite 2, PMB# 279, Tallahassee, FL 32305-7886 USA
http://www.dreamspinnerpress.com/

Then the Stars Fall
© 2014 Brandon Witt.

Cover Art
© 2014 Anne Cain.
annecain.art@gmail.com
Cover content is for illustrative purposes only and any person depicted on the cover is a model.
Photos by David Schmidt, http://bloomportraits.net/blog/
info@211photography.com

ISBN: 978-1-63216-258-8
Digital ISBN: 978-1-63216-259-5
Library of Congress Control Number: 2014944168
First Edition September 2014

Printed in the United States of America
∞
This paper meets the requirements of
ANSI/NISO Z39.48-1992 (Permanence of Paper).

PART ONE
AUTUMN

CHAPTER ONE

"HE'S JUST a dog, Bennett! Get a hold of yourself."

At the deep sound of his master's voice, the dog lifted his head from where it rested against the door handle and craned his neck to look across the cab of the truck.

"Just a goddamned dog," Travis Bennett muttered to himself, attempting to ignore the burn of his constricting throat. He wiped his callused hand roughly across both cheeks, the scratch of his stubble loud in his ears. He spared a glance from the road as he pulled his hand away. Dry. No tears. Their absence wasn't a surprise, but it almost disappointed him nonetheless. "Just a dog."

With a spray of gravel and a harsh lurch, the truck hit a pothole in the middle of the road. Instinctively Travis's right hand shot out and steadied the dog, keeping him from tumbling to the floor of the cab. The dog let out a long groan but remained firmly in the divotted spot he'd occupied for years.

The sight of the dog made Travis flinch. With a cursory glance at the rearview mirror, he pulled the truck over to the side of the road, keeping his foot on the brake. "Ah, Dunk. Buddy, I'm so sorry." He reached out and stroked the swollen left side of his dog's face. Even in the half hour since Travis had woken up, the dog's face had nearly doubled in size. His left eye was completely swollen shut. He was unrecognizable. If it weren't for the reddish auburn fur and white muzzle, Travis wouldn't believe it was his dog. Even so, the dog pushed his face against Travis's hand, burrowing closer.

"Sorry, Dunk. I didn't mean it. You're not just a dog. You're gonna be fine. Just fine." Without looking over his shoulder, Travis let off the brake and pulled back out onto the dirt road. His eyes burned. He swiped at them again.

Still dry.

He didn't look back at the dog again for the remainder of the ten-minute drive, only muttered words of comfort to his old friend.

"We're almost there, buddy. Soon. You'll be good as new by tomorrow."

Words uttered out of fear.

"It won't be anything serious. You're in good health. Shit, you were chasin' buffalo yesterday; can't be serious."

Some that weren't spoken.

I can't do this. I won't. The kids can't go through this again. It isn't fair. I can't do it again.

TRAVIS HAD barely pulled into the parking lot before slamming the truck into park, hopping out, and rushing to the passenger side. He refused to look at his dog's face as he swept the forty-five-pound ball of fuzz into his arms. "We're here. The vet's gonna make you all better."

He only made it a few feet from the truck before the dog began to thrash. "Goddammit, Dunk, you're gonna make me drop you." Still the dog squirmed, looking like a seal caught in a net. Travis knelt on one knee and placed the dog on the ground. He shook, as if attempting to dust away the indignity of being carried, causing his mass of fur to puff out to an even greater degree.

Despite the pain the swelling had to be causing, the dog trotted beside Travis, tiny legs hidden under his hair. If it weren't for his waddle, he could have almost pulled off the illusion he was floating. Even his floppy ears shuffled back and forth as they closed the last few feet to the vet.

The scent of cleaner and medicine stung Travis's nose as he opened the door for his dog to walk through. He hated it. Though different, it was too similar to the sanitized stench of a hospital.

"Cheryl!" Travis tried to ignore the tinge of panic his yell betrayed as he crossed the small veterinary office. Leaning over the glass counter, he tried to see down the narrow hallway. "Thanks for coming in so early on a Sunday morning. I sure appreciate it."

A door closed somewhere in the back, and the clip of shoes sounded on tile. Travis glanced down at his feet, trying to force his heart to slow. The dog gazed up at him, his tailless butt wagging in his typical adoration of Travis. When Travis looked back up, he flinched at the man standing across the counter. "You're not Cheryl."

The man let out an easy laugh. "No. Not Cheryl." He stuck out his hand. "Dr. Ryan. You must be Mr. Bennett. Nice to meet you."

Travis paused before extending his own hand to return the greeting. He didn't have time to waste meeting people. "Cheryl's not here yet?"

"No. She's not coming in. She called and let me know you were on your way. I was already here trying to get stuff ready for an appointment tomorrow. She's not used to having me around yet. She said she'd try to call you back and let you know I'd be the one to meet you."

Travis patted the front pocket of his jeans. "I guess I left my cell at home. I was kinda in a hurry." For the first time he really looked at the man in front of him. Tall—taller than him, at any rate. Lean, with dirty-blond hair, and probably in his thirties. "You're an... assistant or something?"

"No. I'm a real veterinarian." He motioned back down the hallway, pointing at something Travis couldn't see. "Got the degree on the wall for proof if you need to see it."

Travis just narrowed his eyes in response. New doctors were never good; they messed up. Didn't care about patients other doctors had taken care of.

"Mr. Bennett, if you want to go get your dog, I can take a look at him. Cheryl said there was some facial swelling...."

Travis looked at the vet as if he was an imbecile and motioned toward his feet. "He's right here."

The vet peered over the counter, meeting the dog's eyes as he turned to look up at him. "A corgi. A fluffy corgi at that! I haven't seen one of those in a long time." He glanced back up at Travis, then back toward the dog.

Travis knew the expression. People always gave him that questioning look when they first realized the short compact dog belonged with the tank of a man.

"Sorry, Mr. Bennett. I didn't have a chance to look him up in the system before you got here. I'll do that real quick before we take him back, just get a glimpse at his history. But before that, let me take a look at the little guy."

Travis bristled at the comment. He hated when people made comments about his dog's size or how he looked like a redheaded mop as his long fur dragged on the ground. Though short, the dog was nearly fifty pounds and spent several hours a week herding buffalo just for the fun of it. He wasn't a damned Chihuahua or toy poodle or anything.

The vet was already around the counter and kneeling beside the dog, allowing Dunk to sniff the back of his hand before gently scratching the top of his head. "Ouch, that looks painful, little guy."

"Dunkyn. His name's Dunkyn."

The vet didn't even look up, directing all his attention toward the dog. "Good Scottish name, or Irish maybe. Corgis always have the best names."

Dunkyn's butt began to wiggle twice as fast at the attention.

"So can we take him back and do some tests or whatever to find out what's going on with him?" There was that damned strain in his voice.

The vet must have noticed it too. He stood and quickly returned behind the counter to the computer. After a few short keystrokes, he looked up at Travis with a cocked brow. "Two T's in Bennett?"

"Yeah."

"Ah, there. There's a couple of you Bennetts in town. You don't look like a Wendy. You must be Travis or Caleb."

"Travis. Caleb is my son. He's got his own dog, Dolan. He's a corgi as well."

"See? Corgi's have the best names." A few more keystrokes, then another cocked eyebrow. "Dunkyn, spelled with a Y. That's unusual."

Travis felt his face flush. "Yeah. My wife's idea."

The vet glanced back at the screen. "Wendy, I take it."

"Nope. That's my sister."

The vet waited for more explanation, but when none came, he returned his attention once more to the computer, making a few clicking noises with his tongue, brown eyes flitting back and forth as he read across the screen. "Looks like Dunkyn's all up to date on everything. He's about ten years old. Ten is up there, but not too concerning for a corgi." He motioned for Travis and Dunkyn to follow. "Let's head on back to the examination room."

In all, it was less than fifty feet around the counter and back down the hallway, but Travis's feet were made of lead, each step more laden than the next. Each step closer to bad news, to death. Heart monitors beeped in his ears. The tang of anesthetics wrinkled his nose. Empty platitudes echoed in his mind.

"Mr. Bennett?"

He could see the indent of a head on the pillow, strands of long red hair caught in the folds of the fabric.

"Mr. Bennett?"

Dr. Cahill's voice sounded in a whispered shout, *I'm sorry, Mr. Bennett, there's nothing else—*

"Travis?"

"Huh?" The veterinary office snapped back into focus. The vet stood in the doorway of the exam room, a hand outstretched, suspended between them, nearly close enough to touch him. "Sorry, Dr.... Um...."

"Dr. Ryan. You can just call me Wesley if you want. Everyone does."

Travis nodded absentmindedly and looked past the vet to where Dunkyn was sniffing around a metal chair in the room, continuing his never-ending hunt for forgotten food, as if nothing were wrong.

"Are you okay, Mr. Bennett?"

This time Travis met the man's eyes, straightening his spine to his full five foot ten. Still a couple of inches shorter than the vet. "Yeah. Can you take a look at Dunkyn now?"

Dr. Ryan opened his mouth as if to inquire some more, then, to his credit, reconsidered. He turned, walked over to Dunkyn, and knelt on the floor, closer to the dog's level. He ran his hands over the dog's long body, nimble fingers moving with graceful confidence.

"Dunkyn is in great shape, Mr. Bennett. A little chunky maybe, but he's got excellent muscle tone and is as strong as a dog four times his height. You must walk him a lot."

Travis gave a vindicated grunt. Not such a little guy after all. "He goes everywhere with me. Dunk's favorite thing, besides eating, is heading out to the ranch and chasing the buffalo."

The vet glanced up, his brow seemingly caught in a quizzical position. "Buffalo?"

Travis couldn't suppress a pride-filled grin. "Yeah. He loves it. Caleb's dog, Dolan, is too crazy to do any good, but they all know Dunkyn's the boss as soon as he shows up."

"I've heard of corgis herding sheep and cows, but that's a first. Buffalo." He turned back to the dog, then looked up at Travis again. "Are those the buffalo out by Carman Road? I can't imagine there are more buffalo than that in a town the size of El Dorado."

"That's them."

Dr. Ryan nodded appreciatively. "They're beautiful animals. Your house is fairly impressive as well."

"Oh, no. They're not my buffalo. I'm just a hired hand for Mr. Walker. I don't live there. I live out on...." He let his voice trail off, suddenly unsure why he was giving any details to this stranger. He motioned toward the aluminum examination table on the other side of the room. "Want me to lift Dunk up there for ya?"

The vet shook his head. "No, I don't like doing that unless we absolutely have to. Most dogs don't like being on something so far off the ground. If you just want to join us down here, that would be great. Maybe hold him while I try to look in his mouth and see if we can figure out what's causing the swelling. You told Cheryl, um, Dr. Fisher, that you first noticed it this morning, correct?"

"Yep." Travis sat down on the floor, his back against the wall. Dunkyn waddled over to him, plopped down between his legs, and rested his head on Travis's lap with a satisfied grunt. Travis scratched the red fur on top of Dunkyn's head, then put both hands on either side of the corgi's body and turned him around to face the vet. With his long hair splayed out around him as he was spun over the floor, he really did look like a mop.

Dr. Ryan knelt on both knees in front of Dunk and Travis. The room stayed silent as he inspected Dunkyn's ears, eyes, heartbeat, and temperature. Dunkyn groaned uncomfortably at the insertion of the thermometer into his rectum, offering the doctor a condemning glare, but otherwise putting up no resistance.

The dog whimpered when Dr. Ryan inspected his teeth. He tried to flinch away, but Travis had his head cradled between his hands. The vet remained focused on Dunkyn as he continued his inspection. "Any chance Dunkyn had some sort of impact to his face? Herding buffalo could be a pretty dangerous game. Of course, I would assume if there were any injury from one of them, there'd be a lot more trauma than a swollen face."

It took a moment for Travis to answer. Longer than it should have. When he did speak, he had to stop, clear his throat, and start over. "No. He's always with me. Nothing's happened, not so much as a yelp of pain. It's not an injury." The vet's gaze flicked up, the concern in his brown eyes sending a shot of irritation through Travis. "Can we just do some tests and find out what's going on with my dog?"

A soothing hand stroked over the smooth side of Dunkyn's face as Dr. Ryan inspected Travis. "Is there something specific you're worried might be wrong, Mr. Bennett?"

"His face swelled overnight. There's gotta be a growth or tumor or something." Travis preferred the anger he heard in his words now. Much better than the quavering weakness. The answering smile that appeared made him want to smash a fist into the vet's face.

"Actually I'm not concerned about that at all. Growths don't normally appear that quickly. If you're certain you haven't noticed a gradual swelling, I'd say the chance of it being cancer is one of the last things I'm worried about."

The anger swept out of Travis, leaving in its place the kernel of hope. He would rather have the anger. Again his throat constricted. "Yeah?"

Another fucking smile. "Yeah. There's some sort of infection, which should be easy enough to take care of. When I was inspecting Dunkyn's gums, I could smell it. You'd be able to as well, if you got your nose down here. My guess is there's a dental issue. Maybe a cracked root or abscess. I'll have to do X-rays to be sure, but that's almost always what these signs indicate. I'm not concerned about cancer at all."

Travis's eyes burned. He knew there were no tears, but it felt like there were. He pulled Dunkyn closer to him. The dog grunted, and Travis released his grip some.

"It's just a simple operation, and the little guy will be as good as new in no time." The vet smiled.

Travis pulled the dog tighter, this time ignoring Dunkyn's protest. "No. No surgery. What else can we do?"

Confusion crossed the vet's expression. Clearly he'd thought this had been good news. He looked at the dog held tightly in Travis's arms. "Well, we can try antibiotics to kill the infection. If that's all it is, then that will take care of it. However, if a root is cracked or something is wrong with Dunkyn's teeth, the infection will keep coming back and be more detrimental if nothing is done. If it comes back, he really needs the surgery. Again, I'd need to do X-rays, but I've seen this enough that I'm nearly 100 percent certain what's going on, and I think he requires surgery."

Travis shook his head emphatically. "No. Absolutely not. No surgery."

"Mr. Bennett. There's no real concern with an operation such as this. It's very routine, and Dr. Fisher will be there with me. Dunkyn will be in the very best of hands. He'll feel much better after."

"While choriocarcinoma is fairly rare, with chemotherapy, the cure rate is nearly 95 percent. And you've opted to do the hysterectomy, which may be overkill, but I don't blame you for wanting to be certain. There's nothing to be concerned about. I assure you, I know what I'm doing. She'll

be back to normal within a year. As young and healthy as she is, maybe less than that."

Her grip tightened as their fingers intertwined. Their gazes met and held. Though scared, hope shone through.

He raised a questioning brow at her.

She knew him so well she rarely required him to use words. "Of course we do the chemo. I'll do whatever it takes. The kids need their mother, and Lord knows what you'd get up to without a wife to keep you in line." The forced humor left her voice and a tear slipped down one of her cheeks. "Will you still love me if I lose my hair?"

"No surgery. Dunkyn's not having surgery. We'll do the antibiotics." Travis stood before the vet could say anything else. Not that the man would dare, if he knew what was good for him.

DESPITE DUNKYN'S protests, Travis carried him from the vet's office and deposited him gently into the truck from the passenger side. He tossed the white paper bag containing the antibiotics and pain pills onto the floorboard.

Making his way around the front of the truck toward his door, he paused when he noticed the lemon yellow Mazda Miata. It was the only other car in the parking lot. How had he missed it on the way in? The thing stood out like a pink flamingo in a flock of mallards. A car like that shouldn't have the nerve to drive through El Dorado Springs, let alone hang out in the veterinary parking lot. And what was that sticker by the rear license plate? He took a few steps closer, narrowing his eyes.

A rainbow decal, shaped like a dog. A fucking rainbow sticker. Here!

It was proof of the morning's stress that it took the few seconds required for him to walk back to his truck and open the door before two plus two added up to its correct sum.

He looked from the vet's office to the Miata, then back again. What had Cheryl Fisher brought into town?

CHAPTER TWO

WESLEY RYAN tugged on his sage green cashmere scarf, loosening the knot. It had been colder when he'd gotten dressed that morning, but the day had warmed up to the midfifties, and between the leather jacket and scarf, he was starting to feel a bit claustrophobic. He'd parked by the hardware store at the south end of downtown on Main Street; he wished he'd taken the time to shed some of his layers before walking through the park.

This was exactly what he remembered from when he was a kid and would spend the occasional weekend with his grandparents. He'd loved Mom and Pop Mitchell. It hadn't hurt that he'd been their favorite grandchild. It wasn't his fault, or theirs. His older brothers had loved their mom's parents, but they both preferred staying with Grandma and Grandpa Ryan in Kansas City.

By the time Wesley had been in high school, he would come down at least one weekend a month to stay with Mom and Pop. Those weekends were memories he held on to with every fiber of his being, especially lately. However, those memories weren't the ones that made him love El Dorado Springs.

His most loved memories were from much further back, when Mom and Pop would bring him to the park and watch as he played on the rickety play set and gigantic slide. The fiery orange of the oaks and brilliant yellows of the black walnut trees would blend together in a watercolor smear as he zoomed down the dipping slide.

Wesley's disappointment over the playground's updating had surprised him, as had his relief when he'd discovered the rejuvenation had only fixed the massive slide instead of replacing it. He hadn't realized what comfort and happiness he'd associated with the spot until it was nearly gone. Now, with the trees turning their reds, oranges, and golds, he felt ten again. He could feel Mom and Pop watching over him, just out of sight, maybe unpacking the basket on the old picnic tables under the wooden shelter. He could almost hear Mom's voice as she called him from his playing, announcing the chicken salad and grape sandwiches were ready.

The sensation offered only a momentary melancholy, which quickly gave way to peaceful relaxation. This had been the right decision. Maybe not forever. Actually he was quite certain it wasn't forever. He was a city boy, just like his brothers. Just like his mother, who couldn't believe her youngest son wanted to live in the childhood home she'd been so desperate to leave.

But for now? It was perfect. He had no bad memories here. He looked around at the small-town beauty, just able to see the top of the bandstand from where he stood at the apex of the hill. How could there be bad memories in such a place? He was smack dab in the middle of a Norman Rockwell painting. Able to see them or not, he was certain Mom and Pop really were watching over him.

Peace. He needed some peace. His brain hadn't had a moment's rest in years. Let alone his heart. As soon as his convertible Miata had passed the El Dorado Springs, *population three thousand and something*, city limit sign as he sped down Highway 54, a calm settled over him. He'd taken a deep breath. He hadn't been able to remember the last time he'd breathed. Not really.

He whispered a barely audible, "Thank you," as he turned from the playground and began walking down the steep sidewalk into the heart of the park. He wasn't sure who he was thanking. Maybe Mom and Pop. Maybe God. Maybe the trees.

The feeling of gratitude intensified the lower he descended, stepping deeper into the picturesque park. Hope. Not just gratitude, but hope. A laugh escaped him at the realization. He'd given up on that particular emotion.

Pausing just for a moment, he looked at the panorama of the park and the stretch of the old buildings of Main Street behind the rock wall. In his mind's eye, they appeared in the sepia tones of an ancient postcard he'd seen as a kid. It had been a photograph from the very perspective he currently occupied. The circular domed bandstand off to the right, the steps leading down to the spring near the center, an elaborate gated fishpond over to the left. Each structure covered in hand-sized round stones. Masses of trees dotted the sloping hills. Peering through their branches, he could see the lavish stores lining Main Street over the rock wall and people milling about in a blur. Almost out of frame on the left side of the postcard stood a slender brunette woman, her hand resting on the wrought iron bar as she peered into the fishpond. She wore a long white Victorian dress, dripping in lace, and a matching hat.

The image faded, returning Wesley to the present, where the trees shone in their mid-October hues and the buildings in the background looked worn and unloved.

Home. He was home. Even as the sensation hit him, he thought it odd. This had never been home. Not really. At least not in name.

Barely able to refrain from skipping, Wesley walked the rest of the way down the sidewalk, then paused by the curved steps leading down to the spring. He looked down and saw the two rusted pipes from which the orangish water still spouted before rushing down a small stream covered by a narrow grate and disappearing once more somewhere under the park. He started to descend and take a drink, like he had a hundred times before, but suddenly the pleasant feelings began drifting away and the melancholy that had threatened earlier began to set in.

Picking up his speed, he passed between the fishpond and bandstand and made his way up the sidewalk that led to the opposite side of the park and through the iron arch marking the entrance into downtown.

Three elderly men sat on the edge of the sunken rock wall, feet firmly planted on the sidewalk, oblivious to the dangers of falling backward to the park nine feet below. Wesley lifted a hand in greeting and smiled toward them. The men only stared, as if trying to figure out what sort of creature had just emerged from the park. One of them even turned to look back over his shoulder toward the bandstand. Wesley had heard some sort of cave was under the park. Maybe the old man thought Wesley had crawled up from its depths. He knew his designer clothes didn't blend in with the town, but he didn't think he deserved quite the reaction these men gave him. Finally, long past the time it would have been appropriate, the most wrinkled of the men lifted his chin in a minuscule greeting.

Wesley almost stepped closer to speak to them, then thought better of it. If they couldn't even wave in his direction without such a reaction, trying to start up a conversation could have disastrous results. Better to simply let things be.

Though Wesley had been in town a couple of weeks and had visited the park before the leaves had started to turn, he hadn't walked along the storefronts. He'd been nervous for some reason. Judging from the men's reaction, maybe the concern hadn't been misguided.

On his visits with his grandparents, they hadn't spent much time downtown outside of the park and the annual Founder's picnic each July. For three days Main Street was overtaken by food trucks, carnival rides, and B-list (more often than not, C-list) country music stars. Other than that, the downtown wasn't much more than a worn-out backdrop.

The melancholy that had started to nip at him as he left the park sank its teeth in deeper with every store he passed. Most of them were closed up long ago, windows covered or broken. A couple of the lots were empty, the buildings burned down in a fire some time ago. Wesley couldn't remember if they'd still been there when he was a kid or not. A relatively new gun shop took up half of the block, and considering the downtown was basically two blocks long, four if you counted the east and west sides of the street separately, that was a large percentage of ammunition. A sign bigger than himself stretched over the doorway—Mark's Gun Emporium.

Wonderful. Just what every town needed.

Wesley hated guns.

Across from the gun shop—oh, *emporium*—on the east corner of Main Street and Spring were three stores in a row that appeared in good shape. Two of them Wesley remembered, though he'd never been in them, and both seemed to still be in business—Mei-Lien's jewelry store and Rose Petal's Place. Both of these seemed to have recently been updated, each with a fresh coat of paint. The jewelry store was done in tasteful, neutral tones, but Rose Petal's Place nearly hurt his eyes. The combination of red, pink, purple, and silver paint came together in a truly terrifying effect. If those old men sat on the rock wall across from this eyesore every day, it was a wonder they were able to see at all, let alone pass judgment on his appearance.

The presence of those stores lifted Wesley's spirit slightly. At least something was left of his childhood. He darted across the street, thinking he might go into the stores. He wasn't sure what he'd say if he went into the jewelry store; it wasn't as though you could just browse around for wedding rings. He'd played with Mei-Lien's daughter a couple of times as a child, but that was over twenty years ago. No way Mei-Lien would remember him.

Though jewelry wasn't an option, he might come back another day to get flowers, maybe for Cheryl for giving him a chance to run her veterinary office. Moving on to Rose Petal's Place, he angled for the doorway but couldn't make himself go in. He glanced through the window; the colors on the inside were even worse than the exterior, and he was fairly certain he saw an entire wall of fake flowers. He didn't even try to suppress a shudder.

The third store had a different feel. Even the large front windows were welcoming. It looked clean, cheerful, and bright. He glanced up at the massive wooden sign above the door. The Crocheted Bunny was carved in scrolling script—the words painted in cornflower blue over a white background. Wesley wasn't sure what he would do with crochet supplies, but he was going to buy something. This store was the one positive spot that wasn't trying to ruin every childhood feeling he'd had.

His eyes grew wide as he stepped into the store. The place was almost an assault on the senses. He wasn't sure where to look first.

A warm laugh floated out from behind the long wooden counter. "That expression never gets old. Although it's rare to get new people in here, so I don't get the pleasure of it often anymore."

He wasn't sure how he'd missed seeing the woman the minute he'd walked in. She was a spray of color in an already vibrant store, but she managed to stand out. Long rich auburn hair hung in a tangle of spirals nearly to her waist. Ropes of turquoise stones hung over her puffy teal blouse. Dangling silver earrings grazed the tops of her shoulders.

Wesley couldn't help but smile at her. She radiated kindness. He liked her instantly. "I think I might have just stumbled into Willy Wonka's chocolate factory. Just without the chocolate."

She laughed again, louder this time. She had one of those voices that infused the listener with a sense of calm. "You just look around, hunny. There's chocolate in here. I promise."

"Thanks. Your store is charming."

"Isn't it?" The woman nodded in agreement. "Would you like a chai tea or anything? I just got a little coffee station from a new vendor and have been using everyone who walks in as guinea pigs."

"No, I'm fine. Thank you, though."

Her face fell slightly, and Wesley rushed to correct his error. "Actually that sounds really good. I for sure haven't had enough caffeine today."

She shone again. "Wonderful. You go explore, and I'll bring it to you as soon as I remember how to work the darn thing."

The Crocheted Bunny was much more than just a yarn store. The mother of all gift shops, it had a little bit of everything. Wesley felt as though he were in a huge garden, each new portion another patch of produce. The sensation was intensified by the little paths darting back and forth, forcing the shopper to meander about—not to mention the massive amount of clean, homey decorative choices. The effect reminded him of a Cabbage Patch coloring book he'd had as a child. The store had sections of jewelry, greeting cards, T-shirts with quippy sayings, a case filled with unicorn, fairy, mermaid, and dragon statues, a wall of crosses and Christian icons, arts and crafts supplies for kids, a corner full of candies and party mix packets, and a display of incense and crystals. Even a bin of pet toys. Sparkly Halloween decorations, all cheerful and fun, nothing grotesque, were spread throughout the store.

All remnants of his gloom evaporated, leaving him feeling somewhat like a child again. When she'd told him to go exploring, she'd chosen the right verbiage. Everywhere he looked he found a new discovery. While it was a bizarre mishmash, it all worked somehow. Quite well.

Behind a massive display of handmade aprons, knitted scarves, and mittens, a large rectangle of the floor was sectioned off by a miniature white picket fence. Wesley knelt to inspect closer. It was a tiny farm, complete with a red barn next to the wall, some type of fake lawn covering the ground, a small crate of real alfalfa sprouts, a bin of actual grass, and a clay water bowl that had been fashioned to resemble a shallow pond.

Wesley gasped when a movement from the barn caught his eye. From out of the darkness of its interior, a tiny lop-eared white bunny with large ginger patches shuffled out.

"Hey, little guy." Without thinking, Wesley stretched out his hand and laid it on the fake turf.

Whiskers danced as the bunny sniffed the air, then trotted over, passing between the pond and the crate of hay, and rubbed up against Wesley's fingers.

"Ah! Nutmeg likes you! That's a good sign. She's got a perceptive discernment of character."

Wesley glanced up from his crouched position, taking in the shopkeeper. From this angle, she was truly larger than life. Even as he stood, and she proved to be shorter than him, his perception of her didn't alter. She was fuller figured, well over two hundred pounds, but wore her curves well. Now that she was out from behind her counter, he could see her teal blouse was accompanied by a floor-length white broomstick skirt. Pink and white cowboy boots peeked out from under the hem. On a lesser woman, the outfit would have looked garish, or possibly like the conglomeration of insanity. Somehow, she pulled it all together, looking rather bohemian chic.

Wesley returned to his senses when she extended a large paper cup in his direction. He took it, the warmth pleasant against the palms of his hands.

"Thanks. That's sweet of you." He motioned toward the rabbit with his chin. "She might be the cutest bunny I've ever seen. Nutmeg, you said?"

"Darlin', she is most definitely the cutest bunny you've seen." She bent, the full skirt billowing around her, and scooped up the tiny animal. "She's the shop's mascot."

"And, hands down, this is the best rabbit pen of all time."

She nodded, her smile beaming even brighter. "My oldest nephew, Caleb, made most of it for me. I just did the painting. He's a sweet boy." She shifted the bunny to one hand, resting it on her left breast, and stuck out a ring-incrusted hand. "The name's Wendy, by the way. Don't think I properly introduced myself when you came in. Sorry 'bout that."

"I'm Wesley. Nice to meet you." The calluses of her hand surprised him. She had such a soft, feminine appearance. He couldn't help but be intrigued by her.

"It's good to meet you too, Wesley. What brings you to El Do? I haven't seen you 'round before. You just passing through or you got family here?"

"My mom's family is from here. We're all in Kansas City now. But I just moved back into my grandparents' old house. Dr. Fisher is having me take over the veterinary clinic."

Wendy's blue eyes grew wide. "Kansas City! Have you eaten at Houston's, there on the Plaza? They have *the* best chicken strips and cheesy bread I've ever had."

He chuckled. "I knew I liked you. That's one of my mom's favorite places. Anytime there's something special in the family, she makes a reservation. I don't think she'd order chicken strips, though. She's more of a prime rib kinda gal."

Wendy's long curls shimmered as she shook her head. "Well, she doesn't know what she's missing. They are just the best...." She furrowed her brows and titled her head as she inspected him. "Did you say you're taking over for Cheryl Fisher?"

"Yes. Well, it's not final yet. More like a trial period, on both our parts. It will probably just be for a year or two. I love it here, but I'm not really a small-town kinda guy."

"You're not what I expected at all."

Suddenly Wesley felt as though the old men on the rock wall were scrutinizing him once more. "Oh? You've heard of me?"

She laughed, the cheerful sound making him feel at home once more, almost. "If you've spent any time here at all, you know that El Dorado is abuzz with wondering who the new person in town is." She shrugged. "You took care of my brother's dog, Dunkyn, a few days ago. Don't judge me by my brother. He can be kinda gruff sometimes, and he was a little stressed when he met you."

"Oh! Wendy, that's why your name sounded familiar. Wendy Bennett. I saw your name in the computer next to him. You must have brought Nutmeg to Dr. Fisher at some point."

"Yep. She had an awful case of ear mites a while back. Poor baby." She dipped her head and nuzzled the rabbit before looking back to Wesley. "Dunkyn's swelling has gone down quite a bit. It looks like the medicine you gave him helped."

"Good. I'm glad. I hope it does the trick. I'm pretty convinced Dunkyn will need surgery, but I could be wrong. We'll keep our fingers crossed."

Wendy's eyes clouded, and her smile dropped away for the first time since he'd come into the store. "I sure hope not. I don't know if Travis could take that." She raised her free hand in a surrender gesture. "Not that you're not a good vet or Dunkyn wouldn't be fine or anything."

"No need to explain. Like I said, I'm hopeful Dunkyn will be all right. He's such a sweet old boy. It can be scary to have your pet be sick or realize they're getting older. They're such an important part of our lives."

"Yes. They are. Especially for my brother. I don't think I've ever seen a man love a dog so much. Or need one so much." Her voice trailed off, her thoughts drifting somewhere out of Wesley's reach.

Wesley hadn't been able to get Travis and Dunkyn out of his mind since they'd come in the past Sunday. He'd almost called to check up on the dog. He did that with all of the animals he saw. He'd had the number half dialed before deciding against it. It wasn't the first time he'd seen people upset about their pet being sick. It wouldn't have even been the first time he'd seen some muscle-bound tough guy melt into a sobbing heap of tears, not that Mr. Bennett had shed a single tear. But there was something different to the pain he saw in Travis, about the anger that was barely contained. Wesley had been sort of worried the man was going to lash out and punch him if he'd said the wrong thing. He was willing to bet the dog would need surgery, and typically would have pushed for quicker action. Healing the animal was only part of the solution when dealing with pets, though. Travis Bennett seemed to be in as much pain as his dog. Maybe more.

Wendy bent and placed Nutmeg back in her miniature barnyard.

Wesley took a long sip of chai, and the warm spice of the drink pushed away some of the stress that shot up every time he thought of Travis Bennett. At least, he chose to believe stress was the feeling that thoughts of Travis brought up in him.

"Is the chai all right? The mix came with instructions, but I like to add a little bit more than it calls for."

"Oh, yes, Ms. Bennett. It's delicious. Just hitting the spot."

She shook a finger in his face. "None of that business. I can't be much older than you. What are you, thirty-seven?"

"Thirty-five."

"Well, see, I'm only three years older. You cut that Ms. stuff real quick."

"Yes, *ma'am*."

"You! You are cheeky." She gave him a flirtatious wink. "I like you."

Oh hell. He hadn't been thinking. It'd been a while since a woman had mistaken his easy-going manner for attraction. The first friendly face he'd seen all day, and he'd already messed it up.

"Travis mentioned you had a cute little car. A yellow something 'r 'nother. At least he thought it was yours."

Wesley highly doubted the burly cowboy had referred to it as a *cute* anything. "Yep. That's me. It's a Miata."

"Convertible, right?"

He nodded.

"Believe it or not, I've never ridden in a convertible before. Wanna take me for a spin? I did give you a free chai...."

How did he get himself into these situations? "Listen, Wendy, I didn't mean to—"

She cut him off. "I'd actually heard about your car before Travis saw it. People are in and out of here all day, and a car like that doesn't drive around El Dorado often. People have mentioned you have a sweet little dog sticker on the back. Makes sense since you're a vet and all."

Was she alluding to what he thought she was?

She smiled at him like he was a child. "Wesley, just because I'm a small-town girl doesn't mean I haven't been to the big city, hunny. When I get a hankering for chicken from Houston's, sometimes I take myself dancing afterward at Missie B's. I got divorced five years ago, praise

Jesus, and don't have any desire to ever marry again. And while I don't announce it all over town, I sure do enjoy spending a night dancing in the city with all the pretty boys."

It took several moments for Wesley to realize his jaw was hanging open as he stared at Wendy. Missie B's was a gay club less than fifteen minutes from the Plaza. Dancing, karaoke, drag shows—about as far away from El Dorado Springs as you could get. For the vast amount of time he'd spent there, he hated that he'd missed the nights Wendy Bennett waltzed in with her cowboy boots and turquoise jewelry.

She patted his hand, making him spill a bit of chai in the process. "I can close up for half an hour or so. How about that ride?"

Wesley hadn't planned on hiding any aspect of who he was, but he wasn't naive enough to believe it would be a nonissue. His insides warmed up in a way that had nothing to do with the chai. He beamed at her. "You bet! Probably wouldn't bring Nutmeg, though. That breeze wouldn't be good for her ears."

"Glad you mentioned that. Let me go get something to tie up my hair. I have a lot more important things to do than unrat this mess for hours this evening."

CHAPTER THREE

"I'M TELLING ya, I'm gonna sue your ass off, Bennett."

Travis let out his breath in a long exhale through his nostrils, doing his best not to roll his eyes and intentionally infusing his voice with boredom. "What are ya wantin' now, John? Another free fifty-pound bale of alfalfa or maybe just a six-pack of Miller Lite?"

"Not this time. You think you can just waltz into town and learn how to take care of cattle, buy a feedstore, and all us yokels won't care you're nothing more than a city boy." John pulled up on his silver belt buckle, hiking his Wranglers higher on his skinny hipbones. "You don't know nothing about taking care of a farm. I'm done with this shithole. I'm gonna take my business over to Stockton."

Crossing his arms across his chest, Travis leaned back, resting his hip on the edge of the counter. He'd never liked John Wallace. Something about the man just gave him the willies. Years ago, John had been one of the best-looking men in town, and if you used your imagination, you could still make out a bit of the attractive residue. Two decades of a diet consisting of nothing more substantial than fried catfish and endless bottles of cheap beer had left him with an aged and pot-bellied exterior. Typically John's ranting did little more than provide comic relief in Travis's day. However, he wasn't in the mood. He'd been on edge all week, even snipping at the twins. And he never did that.

He felt his cheeks flush, which just irritated him more. The last thing you let John Wallace see was that he was getting under your skin. The little leech would just wriggle in deeper. "You're more than welcome to take your business over to Stockton, John, if they'll have you. Course we both know you're too much of a cheap son of a bitch to drive the twenty miles it would take. And, *for the last time*, I've lived in El Do for twenty years and have worked here for just that long. And owned the damned place for over a decade."

The bang of the front door of Cedar County Feed made both men look over from their bickering. A tall, wiry man silhouetted in the doorway slipped off his ball cap as he walked through. "Not to mention,

John, you wouldn't have anything to do with farming, or any of us *hicks*, as you liked to call us, until you blew out your knee senior year and lost your dreams of playing pro ball." The man crossed the room and tossed his hat on the counter beside Travis, lowering his voice in a mock whisper. "Of course, I've heard tell that the severity of that particular injury was greatly exaggerated. Could be due more to not catching the eye of any recruiters than it was to torn ligaments or joints, or whatever it was." He cocked a brow toward John, who was seething. "What'd you say happened to it again?"

John took a step toward the men, spittle flying from between his lips. "You always were too full of yourself, Jason Baker. And yer still mad I stole yer girl."

Jason's laugh was loud, large, and genuine. He reached out and slapped John on the arm, causing John to have to steady himself. "You keep telling yourself that, John. You just keep telling yourself that." He looked over at Travis. "You were saying something about giving Mr. Wallace here a fifty of alfalfa? Make it a hundred. I owe him big-time for stealing Missy Wilson away from me. You seen how fat that heifer has got?"

"Fuck you, you faggot. You can't talk about my wife like that!"

Travis stepped between the two men, put an arm over the smaller man's shoulders, and steered him toward the door, his anger at John overtaken by the sense they were one insult from a complete brawl in his store. "He didn't mean it, John. Calm down. Missy's a swell woman."

Jason called after them, not even trying to keep the laughter from his voice. "Did you say swell or shrill? Lord, just hearing that woman hum could give ya a headache."

"Shut up, Baker!" Travis glared over his shoulder, then refocused his attention to leading John out the door. "I'm still sticking to that you got yourself a case of foot rot, and you need to get that looked at quick. Still, you come back and pick up a fifty tomorrow? That work?" He should just take care of it now, so he wouldn't have two days in a row of John Wallace—but he couldn't take another minute with the man at the moment.

"That cow don't have nothing wrong with its feet. It's the shitty quality of the crap you sell here that—"

"I'll throw in that six-pack as well." Travis had him to the door of his old Chevrolet. "Tomorrow."

John continued to grumble but gave a curt nod and slid into his truck.

Travis barely waited until John's extremities were inside before shutting the door and smacking the bed of the truck as if it were a horse getting ready to race. "See ya tomorrow, John."

Without looking to make certain John was in fact driving away, Travis headed up the short sidewalk that led to the front door of the metal building. He paused just long enough to glance up at the huge tin sign on top of the roof—Cedar County Feed—painted in barn-red letters. It had been years since he'd touched it up, and the sign was beginning to look shabby. Walking the last few feet, Travis shook his head and let out a huff. "More trouble than it's worth."

"If you mean John Wallace, I've been telling you that for years. We need to kick his ass outta here."

Travis narrowed his eyes at Jason, which only prompted the man's smile to widen. "I was talking about the store, but now that I think about it, it's you who's more trouble than you're worth."

Jason clamped both hands over his heart and staggered backward, running into a cardboard display advertising a new chicken feed. "Your words wound! Is that any way to talk to your best friend? Your blood brother? Your brother from another mother?"

Even though he rolled his eyes, Travis wasn't able to keep a grin from cracking over his face. "You're an idiot." He walked to the side of the counter and knelt down, peering behind it, and slapped his hand on the concrete floor. "Come here, boy. He's gone."

From out of the shadows of the counter, Dunkyn padded forward, floppy ears even lower than normal, eyes darting this way and that. When he reached the end of the counter, the dog peeked out, taking in the rest of the space. Once certain the coast was clear, he pushed his head against Travis's outstretched hands, allowing himself to be soothed.

Travis rubbed Dunkyn's ear between his thumb and forefinger. "I tell ya, something is wrong with that man. Dunk doesn't respond to anybody like he does John Wallace."

Jason snorted. "You're telling me? I grew up with the fucker. At least now his outsides match what he's like." His typically cheery face darkened. "He really did steal Missy Wilson from me, you know."

Travis grinned up at his friend. "You wanting her back?"

An irrepressible shudder passed over Jason, causing Travis to laugh. "Not hardly. Still, not the point. The guy is nothing but sleaze. We really should ban him from CCF."

"CCF? Seriously, you're back on that kick? It sounds like a cross between KFC and the WWF. And banning John Wallace really would be more hassle than it's worth. He makes me nervous, but I'd rather keep him where I can see him."

"Why did you make me the general manager if I don't got a say? CCF needs to stay updated and cool."

"Which is exactly why we're staying away from CCF." Travis stood and walked behind the wooden counter, swiped up Jason's hat, and hung it on one of the metal hooks on the pegboard behind the cash register. Dunkyn plodded along at his feet, still glancing back every few steps. "Welcome home, by the way. How was Colorado?"

Jason sighed, walking over to the counter. Putting his weight on his elbows, he leaned toward Travis. "Man, I love that place. It's so beautiful and rugged. You just feel like… I dunno… a man."

"You don't feel like a man here? Is there something you wanna tell me? Should I start calling you my *sister* from another mother?"

"Fuck off, dude. You know what I mean. Just the mountains and wilderness. It's amazing. You should go with me next year."

"You know I don't like hunting."

"You could just go to hang out and drink some beers. You haven't gotten outta town since—" Jason's words dropped off abruptly, and he began inspecting a knot in the slab of lumber that made up the countertop.

Travis had to tell his shoulders to relax, and he unclenched his fists one finger at time. When he was able to speak, his words were strained. "So did ya get anything?"

Jason circled his forefinger over the knot. "Nah. No luck this year. Paul, one of the guys I meet up there every year, he got a buck. Not a great one, as far as elk go, but decent. Nothing you'd mount, but enough meat to eat on for a bit. He's gonna send me some steaks once he's gotten it butchered."

"You didn't do it for him?" Travis almost sounded normal again. He cleared his throat.

"Hell no. The guy got the elk and I do the work? I don't think so. Besides, I had other huntin' to do."

Travis groaned, but a smile crept back in. He shoved Jason roughly on the shoulder. "I bet you did."

Jason finally looked up from the countertop, all grin and puffed-out chest. "I might not have proved myself a master elk hunter, but I got the pussy hunting trophy, don't you worry about that!"

"God, you're vile."

Standing, throwing his shoulders back, Jason lowered his voice to a gravelly decimal. "And virile."

"I think I need to quit having you around my kids. You're not a good influence."

Jason glanced around, exaggerating every motion. "I don't see any kids now. We can talk about all the pussy you want. You wanna hear about the blonde pussy, the brunette pussy, or the bald pussy?"

"I'm gonna pretend I didn't hear that." Travis glanced at his watch. "I gotta get Caleb from school in a bit. I need to run by the hardware store and get some new stuff. Dolan ran through the screen door again."

"Again? I swear Caleb dropped that dog on his head when he was a pup. He's the most retarded animal I've ever seen. And that's including John Wallace's mutt."

"I swear you do that on purpose."

"What?"

"You try to be offensive. First with the pussy and now with saying retarded. Caleb would kill you if he heard you call Dolan that. And if he didn't, Avery would."

Jason looked around the feedstore once more, this time with more genuine intent. "Trav, your kids aren't here. What's got into you?"

For just a second, though probably not that long, Travis nearly told him. Just nearly spilled his guts about the dark places his mind seemed to be stuck in. "Nothing. Just in a mood I guess. You cool to handle the store for the rest of the day?"

"I was only gone two weeks, Travis. I can run this place in my sleep."

"That's what I'm afraid of." Travis slipped into his brown canvas jacket.

"And I'd still do it better than you." Jason grinned and stooped down. "Come here, dog. I haven't even said hi to you yet."

Forgetting about the threat of John Wallace, with his short front legs springing in little hops, Dunkyn bounded toward Jason, snorting and nipping at his fingers.

"That's good, old boy. You take care of your dad tonight, Dunk. Try to get him to lighten up a bit. He's...." Jason leaned closer to the dog, tilting his head to the left, then looking up at Travis. "What's wrong with Dunkyn? His face is kinda swollen."

Travis didn't meet Jason's gaze, instead fiddling with the keys in his jacket pocket. "You should have seen him Sunday. I had to rush him into the vet. He's a lot better now, but he's still got six more days of pills left."

Jason returned his attention to the dog, moving his hands in circular motions over Dunkyn's sides, eliciting a long, contented groan. "Glad you're better, big man. You're a vital part of CCF."

"Let it go, Jason. If I die tonight, you can call it whatever the hell you want. Not that I'm leaving the place to you at any rate."

Giving Dunkyn a final pat on the rump, Jason stood back up, his voice lowered to a secretive tone, as if there were others in the feedstore who might overhear the gossip. "Did you talk to Cheryl Fisher when you took Dunk in?"

"Actually she...." Travis paused, suddenly knowing where this was going. "Why?"

"Well, Mom took her dog in to see Cheryl the day before I left for hunting. That damned poodle has a constant case of diarrhea. Nastiest thing. Anyway, Mom said Cheryl wasn't there. That some gay guy took care of Daphne—prescribed her some fancy, new expensive food. Mom said she nearly left, but she was so tired of cleaning up after that damned dog she didn't want to have to wait for Cheryl."

"Really?" Travis still didn't meet his friend's eyes. "Why'd she think he's gay?"

"Well, let's just say that expensive dog food wasn't the only thing fancy in there. Plus, she saw his girly, yella car in the lot. It's got some kinda rainbow sticker on it."

"What the fuck's that supposed to mean?" Travis mentally kicked himself. Who didn't know what a rainbow sticker meant anymore?

"Shut up, Travis. Everybody knows only queers get rainbow stickers on their cars. It's how they know each other." Jason leaned forward. "So Cheryl was there? You didn't meet the fag?"

"I swear, Jason, you sound more like a gossipy old woman every day. If I left for a week, I'd come back to find you'd turned this place into a beauty parlor."

Jason shrugged, unconcerned with the criticism. "Course, Mom said there'd always been rumors about Dr. Fisher being a carpet muncher. Well, she didn't say it like that. Thank God. She and Cheryl were in school together. I guess there was talk of it even back then."

"Dr. Fisher was married to Jack for probably thirty or forty years before he died."

Another shrug. "Hey, don't blame me. I didn't make it up, just passing along the word."

Travis smacked his upper thigh once, and Dunkyn trotted over, waiting as he opened the shop door. "Like I said, beauty parlor."

"Whatever, Bennett. You're the one who's offended by the word pussy all of a sudden." Jason closed the distance between them and slapped Travis on the shoulder.

Travis sighed. "Good to have ya back, bud. Thanks for covering the place for me."

"Good to be back. Can't stay gone from El Do for long." He started to turn away but then paused. "Dunk will be fine, Travis. You'll see."

Travis nodded, his throat tight. Maybe Jason *could* see where his brain had been stuck lately. "Thanks. I promised the kids and Wendy I'd pick up hickory burgers from Simone's later tonight. I'll get ya one. Wanna come by?"

"You bet. Pick me up an order of curly fries too."

CHAPTER FOUR

CLOSING HIS eyes, Wesley concentrated on not vomiting. He released his hold on the hoof, stood, walked a couple of feet away, then took a shallow breath through his mouth. Even that caused him to gag. The smell had permeated his senses, seeming to coat his tongue and throat. Rookie mistake. He took a few more steps away from where the cow stood secured in the chute. The rotten stench blocked out all other thought. Grasping the wooden plank of the fence, he leaned against it, determined to keep his breakfast inside his body.

"Well, what do you think, Doc?"

Wesley didn't respond verbally, only raised a finger asking for another moment and squeezed his eyes shut tighter. When he was relatively certain he could open his mouth without incident, he turned toward the man. "Sorry about that. I should have known better than to take such a deep breath."

"Is it bad? I can't afford nothing expensive. Just bought the wife the new TV she's been wanting. We're strapped."

His eyes watering, Wesley looked over at the man. A little shorter than himself and a strange combination of a skinny, nearly malnourished frame, with a protruding potbelly. He'd thought the smell of alcohol radiating from the man had been bad enough, but it was nothing compared to the unfortunate cow. "Mr. Wallace, when did you say you first noticed symptoms?"

"Um, the dumb bitch started limpin' two or three days ago, I'd say. Yesterday she wasn't putting any weight on that leg at all." He raised his hand and swiped out his left nostril with the tip of his little finger. After inspecting, he brushed the finger against the leg of his jeans. "I know what it is. It's that shit food I get at Cedar County Feed. Charges me a shitload and it ain't worth shit."

Wesley grimaced, this time more from the man in front of him than from the smell of the infected animal. His gaze wandered over to the cow. He'd always thought Limousin cattle were one of the prettiest breeds, especially the red-golden variety. From what he'd seen of Mr. Wallace's small herd, their hide was more a sad blonde color. None of them looked like the picture of health.

"I'm not sure what type of feed you're getting, but it's not what's causing this." Wesley intentionally let his gaze drop to the ground at Mr. Wallace's feet, glaring at the length of barbed wire sticking out from a clump of manure. "Your cow sliced the skin between her hooves on something; then infection set in."

"So what does that mean? Just need some stitches or something?"

Wesley looked back up at the man. Was this guy for real? Even though Wesley was a city boy, he'd spent enough time with livestock as a kid to find the idea of giving the poor animal a few stitches nearly laughable—and that was with or without a doctor of veterinary medicine degree. He tried to keep the judgment out of his tone when he responded. "No, I'm afraid this is well beyond stitches. You've got yourself a case of foot rot. I'd say we're right on the edge of it being critical. It's a good thing you called, Mr. Wallace."

The man spit a stream of brown toward his feet. "My name's John. And it ain't no foot rot. That's what the fucker at that shit feedstore said." He motioned toward a bale of alfalfa sitting outside the barn. "I decided to call Dr. Fisher and have her come look."

Wesley wasn't sure what the alfalfa had to do with it. "Mr. Wallace—John—there's no doubt she's got foot rot. You can see it if you look at the skin around the hoof, and you can for sure smell it. I'd say if you'd waited another day, she'd be lame. Might still get that way, but if we start antibiotics today, we can probably get it under control before it gets much worse."

"How much is that gonna cost?" John glared over at the cow, a sneer curving his upper lip, revealing sickly yellow teeth.

Wesley managed to refrain from grimacing. A part of him was tempted to step closer in an attempt to determine if the man had a horrible case of gingivitis or displayed signs of meth use. He decided he wasn't curious enough to find out. "I can call you once I get back to the clinic. I want to do a little checking to make sure I go the best route, and I'll call Dr. Fisher just to get a second opinion on what she'd do, but I'm fairly certain of the route she'd take."

"It might just be best to put her down. I was gonna wait a few more months before I butchered another, but no reason to wait." John nodded like the decision was already made.

Wesley grimaced. "John, I think you called in enough time to save her. If we start today, she should be fine. I don't think there's a reason we wouldn't be able to save her leg."

The man's laugh was loud and harsh. "You are a city boy, aren't ya? Who ever heard of cutting off a cow's leg? If a horse breaks its leg, ya shoot it. No reason to pay to have a three-legged cow. Steak's a bit too pricey if you do it one leg at a time."

"Mr. Wallace, I wasn't suggesting an amputation, but even if her life wasn't savable, you wouldn't want to consume her meat, not when she's got this type of infection."

He waved Wesley off. "Listen, Dr. Ryan. I don't know how they do it where you're from, but we don't waste the good gifts God has given us."

It took effort for Wesley to keep the disgust from his expression. From what he'd seen of John Wallace, there was nothing but waste. The small field was a mud pit, filled with trash and debris. All twelve of the cows he'd noticed were malnourished and sickly. He was willing to bet the only reason the man still had cattle was that he lived at the end of a long dirt road and no one was ever here to witness the state of his animals. "Foot rot is highly contagious. I'd like to come back out this afternoon with the medicine for this cow and inspect your others while I'm at it. If it starts spreading, you'll have a lot bigger expense."

Distant thunder rumbled to the east, causing them both to look toward the horizon. Dark clouds were gathering, promising that the brightness of the morning was going to come to a wet, gloomy end.

Looking away from the upcoming storm, Wesley visually inspected the cow once more, anger building at her condition. "I won't charge you for inspecting the rest of your herd. If we catch it in time, it'll save you a lot of money."

John scowled, considering. "Well, I can't butcher my whole herd. We depend too much on 'em for that. And I don't have enough deep freezers to handle it." His watery blue eyes jittered as he inspected Wesley's body, then returned to his face once more. He grinned suddenly. "On the upside, we are supposed to go to Missy's folks' this afternoon for dinner. Looks like I got reason to cancel." Another brown stream hit mud.

A cool wind swept over them, stirring up the smell of the field. Wesley grimaced. John Wallace didn't seem to notice.

"Whelp, I guess that does it until you get back here in a bit." He turned and started walking toward his house.

Wesley glanced at the cow still secured in the corral, then at John's retreating backside. "Aren't you gonna move your cow into the barn?"

John paused, glaring back at the miserable-looking cow, then at Wesley. "You'll be back in a couple hours. She'll be…." His voice trailed off, something in the vet's expression making the man change his mind. He let out an exasperated sigh, then began walking toward the animal.

WESLEY AND John had nearly reached the house when a large woman with a cloud of frizzy blonde hair stepped out onto the concrete slab of a porch, letting the screen door slam behind her. The hue of her hair matched the chipped, faded yellow paint of the house, almost giving the illusion she was somehow part of the structure, maybe even being consumed by it.

At the woman's appearance, John paused momentarily in his steps, appearing almost startled.

After hesitating a moment, Wesley stepped toward the woman, extending his hand. "Hi, I'm Dr. Ryan. We were just taking a look at your cows."

The woman's attention darted between the vet and her husband before she accepted the handshake. "Missy Wallace. I know who you are."

It seemed everyone knew who he was. He tried not to read into the woman's cold tone. It might have nothing to do with him or what she may or may not know about him. She looked nearly as forlorn as the sick cow. A limp sack of a woman, she was all sagging curves—jowls, breasts, belly. For some reason, it struck Wesley that she wasn't that much larger than Wendy Bennett if you put the women side by side. But Wendy glowed. She was beautiful, larger than life, and looked as though she could handle any storm that might come her way. This woman appeared as if she might crumble in a stiff breeze, despite her size.

John stepped up even with Wesley. "Missy, Doc here says he's gotta come back out and take care of the cows this afternoon. Guess they're a bit sick. You and the kid go on to yer folks. It's gonna take a bit."

Again her narrow gaze flitted between the two men. "Cain't we just butcher her?"

John stepped up and joined his wife on the slab porch. "Would you let me worry about this shit, Missy. I wasn't asking for your input."

The woman's flinch was miniscule. So much so that if Wesley hadn't already been furious over the cattle's condition and open to finding more reasons to despise the man, he might have missed it.

John hadn't noticed or, more likely, didn't care. "The vet's gonna get whatever that dumb cow needs and then take care of it." He turned away from his wife, giving a dismissive glance toward Wesley. "How long till you think you'll be back?"

THE SUN set in an inglorious lack of color. The hours Wesley and John spent doctoring the sick cow and inspecting the rest of the herd had transitioned the gray afternoon to a wet, dark evening. The last couple of cows were examined by the glare of a flashlight.

Missouri thunderstorms were nothing new to Wesley, but he'd forgotten how different they felt away from the lights and massive buildings of Kansas City. They brought back memories of the late summer storms he'd experienced when staying with his grandparents, the humid evening thick with lightning bugs giving way to torrents of rain and the walls of their small house seeming to shake with the crash and flash of the sky. He'd never been afraid of them, instead sitting in his grandmother's lap staring out the large window of the front room. "God's fireworks" his grandpa had always called them. He hadn't been an overly religious man, but always equated everything in nature to God.

Ankle-deep in mud and manure, the evidence of neglect mounting with each cow Wesley inspected, the flash of lightning felt ominous, the crash of thunder only increasing the fury building within him. The vile man grumbling and cursing beside him became more loathsome. Where John Wallace had seemed ignorant and possibly abusive earlier in the day, he now had a sinister edge to him. Of course, Wesley reminded himself, his mom had always said her youngest son was prone to be the slightest bit dramatic.

Three other cows had signs of foot rot. With each new discovery, John Wallace's mood darkened, his curses growing more fervent.

Wesley had to keep biting his tongue to keep from commenting about the state of the cattle and their living conditions. Wallace was already upset and on edge. It wouldn't do any good to try to address the improvements that needed to be made. Wesley would come back out the next day, both to check on the cow and stress the importance of improving the quality of the cows' environment. Regardless, he was going to call and report the man to the ASPCA. It would probably be a good idea to speak to Dr. Fisher about how to address the issue with Mr. Wallace. It might make sense to ask her to come with him. He wasn't sure who John would respect less, him being new to the town or Dr. Fisher being a woman. Of course, if the man knew as much about Wesley as his wife seemed to know, he probably would value Wesley less than he did a woman.

SCRAPING HIS shoes over the gravel of the driveway, Wesley groaned. It was useless. He was drenched and covered in filth. He cursed himself as he looked at the Miata parked a few feet from the front door of the house. How had he not thought to bring a change of clothes and shoes, or at least a towel to drape over the seat? He had no way to get into the tiny car without dripping mud and manure all over the driver's seat. Maybe if he stood in the rain for a while, most of it would wash off. Right….

"Come in. You can rinse off in the shower and borrow a pair of pants if you need to."

The offer took Wesley by surprise. He turned and looked at John Wallace standing on the porch. He was barefoot, his boots already cast off to the side. For the briefest moment, the man looked younger and handsome, the yellow porch light washing away the pockmarks over his face, the curtain of rain softening his features.

A flash of lightning sliced overhead, destroying the illusion. The transition left John Wallace seeming more haggard than before.

Wesley looked back at his car, then again at the man. It showed how much he disliked the man that he was even debating getting into his car in such a condition. "I can just rinse off with the hose." He motioned toward the spigot that protruded from the house.

"No way you'll get clean enough to not get shit all in your car, unless you showered out here naked."

He was right, Wesley had no doubt, but he recoiled at the thought of going into the man's house. Another glance at his car, then the spigot.

"You too good to come into my house, *Doctor* Ryan?"

The last thing he needed was to get a reputation of thinking he was better than everybody else. He had no doubt John Wallace would take every chance he got to trash his name. Grudgingly he walked toward the house and joined John on the porch. Every instinct he had was screaming for him to get into his car and speed away, mud be damned. He pushed them aside. He was being ridiculous. It was just a shower. Bending, he pulled off his shoes, his fingers sinking through the thick layer of sludge in order to get a grip.

John motioned through the doorway. "The bathroom is down the hall, first door on your left. There's a towel hanging on the back of the door."

He lifted a foot to step into the house, but John caught his arm.

"Why don't ya take off your pants? Missy will have my hide if we get shit all over the carpet."

"Actually it's okay. I'll just drive home real quick and—" Wesley's words died in his throat as he turned and looked at the car once more.

"You'd rather ruin your car than come into my house, huh?" Disdain filled Wallace's tone.

"No, it's not that. I just…." Wesley sighed and let his words trail off. He unbuttoned his jeans and slid them over his legs. The wet denim pulled on his leg hairs, but he managed to yank them off without falling over. Beside him, still propping open the door, John Wallace pulled off his own jeans. From the corner of his eye, Wesley realized the other man had gone commando. Averting his gaze, and trying not to vomit for what felt like the thousandth time that day, he let his jeans fall to the porch and stepped through the doorway. He'd make this quick.

Even in the dim light and his rush to the bathroom, the filth of the place astounded Wesley. How did people live like this? It wouldn't have made the place much worse if he had worn his bedraggled jeans through the room.

After locking himself in the bathroom, Wesley flipped on the light and gaped at his reflection in the mirror. He was covered. He'd even managed to get crap in his hair, brown streaks running over his face and dripping off his jaw. He'd told himself he would just wipe up and be on his way, but it was clear that wouldn't be enough. As uncomfortable as the situation was, he was doubly glad he hadn't gotten into his car. He would have had to burn the thing.

Realizing he was dripping filth all over the cracked linoleum, Wesley stepped into the shower, not bothering to remove his shirt or underwear. He turned on the shower, and freezing water sprayed him in the face. The clean water felt good, and the coldness didn't even bother him. Within moments, the water had heated and he'd stripped out of the rest of his clothes. He wrung out his shirt and underwear several times under the shower's spray. The shirt would never truly be clean again, but he'd gotten enough of the grime off that he could at least wear it home, if Mr. Wallace would give him a trash bag or two to cover the driver's seat.

After a couple more minutes, Wesley was clean enough that the water running over his body was clear and free of grime. He turned off the shower, reached across the small bathroom, and pulled the towel off the hook. Once mostly dry, he wrung out his wet clothes and used the towel to wipe up the floor where he'd left a trail of dirty water. Hesitantly he stepped back into the wet briefs and pulled the T-shirt over his head. At least he'd had enough sense to change into old clothes before coming back to Wallace's farm. The dampness of his clothes against his skin brought back the chill the shower had eradicated. Before opening the bathroom door, he wrapped the dirty towel around his waist.

The man was standing by the sink in the kitchen, waiting for him. He'd removed his clothes and held a dishrag in front of his crotch.

Wesley was certain there was a glint in the man's eyes as he looked Wesley over. Wesley thought he'd picked up on a certain energy while he'd been inspecting the cattle, but he'd ignored it, explaining it away. He was worked up about the mistreatment of the cattle. He'd lost even more respect for the man seeing how he spoke to his wife. He was just on edge and was imagining things. However, the leer on John's face from across the room was undeniable. He shouldn't have come into the house. He'd known better. Fucking stupid.

"I put your jeans here in the sink with mine. I was just rinsing them out. Let me hop in the shower real quick, and we can throw them in the wash machine."

John crossed the space toward the bathroom. Wesley stiffened, expecting the other man to touch him as he passed. He didn't.

"I called Missy, told her and the kid to stay at her folks'. This storm isn't showing any sign of letting up." He stepped into the bathroom, not bothering to shut the door.

The sound of the water turning on was accompanied by the shower curtain closing and then a long groan. Wesley hurried over to the kitchen sink, reached in, and separated his jeans from those belonging to John. He turned on the faucet, sticking his jeans under the warm flow. Quickly he pulled them out again, found the front pocket, and stuck in his hand. He pulled out the key ring and lifted it for closer inspection. Washing them probably wouldn't have made a difference—with as wet as his pants had been from the rain, the keyless entry button was certainly already fried. Still, he set the keys on the side of the sink and shoved his jeans under the water once more. Just a quick rinse to get the majority of the grime off and he'd leave. Car seat be damned. He'd get it professionally cleaned. Hell, he'd get a new car.

Wesley wrung out the jeans for the second time, undid the knot in the towel around his waist, and laid the towel on the counter. Somehow, left in his wet underwear and shirt, he felt no more clothed than if he were naked. He'd just lifted his left leg to stuff it into the wet jeans when a hand gripped his shoulder over the damp material of his shirt. He hadn't heard the shower quit running, not that he could hear anything over the pounding of his heart in his ears. He turned, keeping the dripping jeans in his hands, using them to shield his body.

John stood less than a foot in front of him. Naked. Wet. Thin arms and legs. Hairless protruding belly. Substantial erection jutting toward Wesley.

Wesley stepped sideways, closer to the front door. "I… uh…. Thank you for the shower, Mr. Wallace. I should get going."

John's voice was gruff and low, altered with a panting quality that hadn't been there previously. "No reason to rush, Doc. Like I said, Missy and the kid are staying with her folks. We got time."

"I think there's been a misunderstanding. I'm sorry if I gave you the wrong impression."

The grip on Wesley's shoulder tightened. Though smaller, Wallace was stronger than he looked. John's breath was warm as he spoke, smelling exactly how the yellowing teeth promised it would. "There's no misunderstanding. You're a fag. Ain't no secret."

Fear shot through him. He'd been called a faggot many times in his life, but never with the intonation he heard now. The usual disgust and hate were there, along with something more this time—a desire of some sort Wesley wasn't familiar with. Typically that particular label brought anger, but Wesley felt no anger, just fear, which only made the sensation increase. Gooseflesh rose over his skin. He tried to think, form a thought. Nothing came, just flashes of white behind his eyes. The crashes of his heart beat away any image that started to form in his mind.

His hand still clamped on Wesley's shoulder, John reached down with his other hand and clasped the base of his own dick. He shook the appendage, stepping a bit closer so its head thumped against Wesley's leg, just below the hem of his briefs. "I've met other fags like you. You're gonna blow me, and then you're gonna let me fuck your ass, like the pussy you are. You're gonna beg for it."

For a moment the pressure on Wesley's shoulder lifted, releasing him. Then it returned, clamping over the muscles between his shoulder and neck, trying to force him to his knees.

He didn't want this. Not like this. Never like this. Not this man. Never with this man.

He didn't want this.

"Come on. Get down and get my cock in your mouth. I won't hurt you unless you want me to."

Wesley glanced down, observing the man stroking his dick as if watching some fucked-up horror movie.

"Get down, Doc. You'll like it, my cock's big. I bet you like it big. Just keep your fucking mouth shut about it. When we're done, keep it to yourself or you'll bleed. I promise you that. Keep your mouth shut, and I'll give it to you again. If you're any good at any rate."

Suddenly the world came back into focus, then narrowed to a pinprick, so all that existed was this filthy room, this vile man with a purple cock banging against Wesley's bare leg, and the hand clamped over his shoulder.

Then John Wallace was slammed against the wall of his kitchen, Wesley's large hand tight around his throat.

"If you ever touch me again, it won't be me who's bleeding."

He'd never heard his voice sound like it did. A stranger spoke through him. A stranger who scared him a bit, but one he was glad had arrived. He'd always known his strength, but he'd never felt as strong as this.

Never like this.

Wesley's gaze traveled from John Wallace's bulging eyes and watched his fingers tighten and press into the stubble-covered neck. He could crush this man. It would do the world a favor. If nothing else, it would help the cattle just beyond the walls, help the man's used-up wife, probably even the kid.

A stranger's voice. A stranger's thoughts.

He forced himself to look once more into Wallace's newly terrified blue eyes. The smell of ammonia rose to meet Wesley's nose, and he was aware of a warm spray against his leg.

"I'm going to leave. If you follow me, it will be the last thing you do."

With a final squeeze and another shove against the wall, Wesley released the man's neck and took a step back.

John Wallace slid against the wall, descending into the puddle on the kitchen floor.

Only then did Wesley realize what he'd felt against his leg. Another shot of power flooded through him. Promptly followed by shame. He shoved it aside. He noticed the block of knives by the sink and reached out, pulling out the largest one.

The man on the ground began to whimper.

With his other hand, Wesley retrieved his jeans and keys. Keeping the knife pointed at the man on the ground, he backed toward the door. Once there, he nudged it open with his heel.

He turned and ran toward his car, ignoring his shoes by the porch and the gravel digging into his bare feet, ignoring the rain that still fell in sheets over the dark night. The screen door slammed, and Wesley wheeled around, knife outstretched once more. Nothing. No John Wallace. Just a closed screen door, the dim light of the bathroom visible within.

Wesley threw the knife over to the side. He heard it bang against something metallic, but didn't bother to inspect what it had been. Turning back toward the car, he ran.

The keyless entry worked.

Flinging open the door, Wesley dove inside, slipping the key into the ignition before his legs were fully inside the car.

Gravel sprayed against the walls of the house as the yellow Miata did a U-turn, spinning out before tearing over the dirt road and disappearing into the darkness.

CHAPTER FIVE

THE GROUND was still damp from the previous evening's thunderstorm. The knees of Travis's jeans soaked up the moisture as he knelt on the wet grass. He'd remained in the position so long his legs were numb, and the chill was starting to creep into his bones. The sun beat down, warming his hunched back.

He barely felt the soggy earth or the unclouded sun. Only the rough edge of the marble headstone registered as he rested his weight on his left hand. That, and the smoothness of the etched letters his right index finger traced.

Shannon Avery Pope Bennett
Beloved Wife and Mother

Only four years had passed and already the edges of the carved letters of her first name were smoothed out slightly. The tip of Travis's finger had developed a new callus within weeks of her death. Even when he was not in the graveyard, his callused finger shaped the letters of her name on the pad of his thumb.

Travis had never been the kind to enjoy cemeteries. They were lonesome, desolate places. Void of hope, destroyers of life. Even on days like this. Even with the towering trees spreading their vivid-colored boughs over those eternally at rest, the birds yet to leave their summer homes singing overhead, the still-green grass seeming to sparkle over the gentle swells of the hills lined with markers. Travis had never found the beauty or peace some claimed cemeteries offered.

He still hated the place. Raged at it. Wanted to destroy it. Even so, outside of his home and the feedstore, regardless of his feelings about the graveyard, Travis spent more time here than any other place.

Four years had passed to the day. Four years since her blue eyes had closed. Four years since he'd run his fingers through her thick red hair—more than that, actually. She'd lost her hair long before she'd passed. Four years since he'd heard her low laugh. Yes, Shannon Bennett had laughed to the end. She'd always been quick to laugh, quick to explode as well, but it had been her laughter, not her temper, that had sounded during her last few days. Tears as well, of course—fast and furious as she'd said her good-byes to her parents, torrents as she had embraced their three children, slow and heavy as she'd kissed Travis that last day. But it had been laughter that had been her last sound. After the tears were gone. After the promises she'd elicited from Travis. After the endless *I love yous.* Her last utterance, her laughter, still resounded in Travis's brain, always loudest when he was here in front of her marbled name. Maybe if she'd transitioned with crying, or yelling, or regrets, Travis wouldn't seek her grave, wouldn't need to hear her voice so often. But none of those were ways Shannon had chosen to leave. She'd laughed. For the life of him, Travis couldn't remember what he'd said through his tears that had made her laugh so hard. So fully. He could almost believe he'd imagined it. Almost. If only he couldn't still hear it. She'd laughed. The sound he'd loved the most from her was her final gift to him—a laugh gone from this world for four years, yet as clear to him at her graveside as it had been at her deathbed.

"I thought he was dying. I thought he had cancer." Travis's voice was low, barely audible to his own ears. Definitely not loud enough to disturb the birds' songs above him. "I thought it was cancer. Shannon, *cancer.* I can't go through it again. The kids couldn't do it again." His index finger traced the *S* three times. "I know I promised to be strong for them, my love, but I can't be strong if he has cancer."

How angry Travis had been the day Shannon had brought Diamond Duncan home from a shopping trip with Wendy. She hadn't even called to ask if he was okay with her getting a dog, let alone some long-haired corgi. It might have been okay if she'd gotten a golden or mastiff. Even a full-sized poodle, for crying out loud. But a corgi? Named Diamond? Like hell.

She and Wendy had stopped on their way home from Springfield at some no-name spot on the map. There'd been a painted cardboard sign stuck next to the highway beside a gravel road. Shannon had said it was Wendy who wanted to see the puppies. They weren't going to get one, just wanted to see them.

It wasn't the puppies that caught Shannon's eye. It was the two-year-old dog covered in matted dirt, locked in a crate several yards away from where Wendy had sat, laughing as she was covered in puppy kisses.

The breeders had told Shannon that corgis have a recessive gene that could pop up every few generations and cause their typically short, coarse hair to be long and fluffy. The dog wasn't show quality. They hadn't even bothered to pin his ears as they would have any of their other corgis born without the typical fox-eared perkiness.

Shannon had offered a hundred dollars on the spot for the dog. They'd accepted, and less than two hours later, the newly named Dunkyn Diamond had entered the Bennett family. Shannon said she'd thought six-year-old Caleb needed a dog, a companion. He was so quiet and shy. A boy needed a dog, she'd said.

It hadn't been the child the dog bonded to. Not even to Shannon. Despite Travis's feelings about small dogs, the corgi had padded up to him, let out a series of Chewbacca-like vocalizations, and shoved his head against Travis's shin.

Grumbling about the new "dog," Travis bathed Dunkyn and introduced him to his young son. Dunkyn and Caleb got along, but as soon as Travis walked out of the room to get a beer, the dog followed him. It wasn't until two days later, when the corgi accompanied Travis to Emmitt Walker's farm and started herding the buffalo, that Travis fell as in love with the dog as Dunkyn had with him.

"I won't be able to handle it, Shannon. I can't lose you both to cancer. I know he's not you, and I know he's just a dog. But I can't do it. Not if it's cancer. I need you to fix it, Shannon. Anything but cancer. Please." Again his fingers traced the *S*. Travis had never prayed, never been the praying type, until Shannon had gotten her diagnosis. Suddenly Travis was a convert. He was certain he'd prayed more than any man before him. Ceaselessly he'd prayed.

Shannon died.

Travis never stopped praying—the prayers just changed directions. They were no longer addressed to the unhearing God who had taken his wife, but now to the mother of his children. A silent prayer to her was always on his lips. Only at her gravestone were his prayers audible.

He'd already been at her grave a couple of hours. Wendy and the kids had come with him. Caleb had cried. Avery and Mason had as well, but mainly because their big brother was crying. They'd been too young when Shannon had left. They knew her from pictures and stories, nothing more.

After they left, Travis did his normal routine, filling Shannon in on all she was missing, not that much had happened since he'd visited her the day before. Still he told her everything that had transpired. Things he'd already told her. Jason Baker's return from his hunting trip. Dolan busting through the screen door again. Wendy considering starting an online business for homemade bunny clothes—he swore he could hear Shannon laughing at her sister-in-law. He told her everything—that he missed her, that he loved her, that he ached to hold her. He told her things he'd told her a thousand times before.

He didn't mention the new vet in town, not him or his yellow car. He didn't mention one of the many promises he'd made to her four years ago.

He told her about Dunkyn and about his own fear. He made requests of her, as he had every day since Dunkyn's face had swelled.

No tears fell. They were gone. He told her about that as well. Again.

"We thought we'd find you here, son."

Travis looked up, though he'd know the tired voice anywhere. "Hi, Glen." He stood, having to use Shannon's gravestone to help get his tingling knees to straighten. He shook the man's hand and leaned beside him, giving the frail, sickly woman a hug. "How are you, Patsy?"

The old woman pulled back to look in his eyes, one wrinkled, spotted hand cupping his cheek. "How are you, my boy?"

Travis shrugged but didn't look away. Much like Shannon's mother, he ignored the question. "The kids and Wendy were here earlier. They left a bit ago. I'm sure Wendy's getting lunch prepared for the kids. I've gotta go back to the feed shop, but I know they'd love it if you dropped by."

Patsy glanced over toward her husband. He nodded and smiled gently at her.

She turned back to Travis. "You sure you can't leave the store a bit longer?"

"No. I need to get back to work." He tried to smile but failed. "Idle hands, you know."

Glen gave a knowing nod. "We'll see you soon, then, son. You're coming to the retirement party they're throwing for me out at the factory, yeah? You and the kids?"

"Fifty-five years you've given to that place. They'd better throw you a party. We wouldn't miss it."

"Good thing." Glen patted Travis's shoulder, then turned toward his daughter's grave. He bent—a struggle over his sizable belly—and laid a large arrangement of white flowers in front of Shannon's headstone.

Without any more exchange, Travis left them. He walked quietly through the graveyard toward his truck, parked outside the iron gates. As always, he paused by another gravestone, glancing at the inscribed name,

Dionysus Durke, and patting its bumpy edge. "Miss you too, Donnie." Though a few years younger than Travis, Donnie had often helped him around Cedar County Feed when he'd first taken it over years ago, helping update and get the place into shape. He had died in some sort of car wreck right after Shannon had been diagnosed. They'd not been able to attend his funeral—Shannon had already been in the hospital, her first of countless times, and Travis wouldn't leave her.

Even at the time, Travis had feared Shannon was going to leave him. When he'd heard about Donnie's death, he hadn't been able to keep from feeling jealous. What an easy death. A car crash. Instant. Maybe even painless. Nothing like what Shannon was going through. Nothing like he was going through watching her slipping away.

What he would have given for a car crash.

Or anything.

Anything but cancer.

"DADDY, YOU left some of those strings in here. It's gross." Irritation laced Avery's accusation.

Travis retrieved the small pumpkin from her outstretched arms. "Sorry, princess." He took the pumpkin to the edge of the driveway and scooped out the offending innards he'd left behind.

Taking the pumpkin back to the six-year-old ruler of his heart, Travis sucked in a breath as she looked up at him. Her blue eyes flashed with irritation. "Did you get it all this time?"

He couldn't answer for a moment. The little girl had inherited her grandmother's and mother's eyes. Her temper she'd inherited fully from her mother. She was the spitting image of Shannon, except that his daughter's long straight hair was strawberry blonde, not her mother's fiery red. Maybe it was just his extended time beside her grave that morning, but Shannon seemed to shine out of her daughter even more than usual.

"Well? Did you?" She stamped her sparkling silver shoe on the concrete, bringing his attention back to the present.

"Avery Bennett! Stop that attitude, young lady. You might be as spoiled as an actual princess, but there's no reason to act like it." Wendy swept over and took the pumpkin. "You can have this back when you can speak nicely."

Avery's bottom lip stuck out and began to quiver. Travis looked away, knowing he'd cave, even if he knew she was doing that face for his benefit alone. He could never tell her no; she looked too much like her mother. Thank God for Wendy, or he'd have a complete terror on his hands when she became a teenager.

A cool breeze blew a few fallen leaves across the driveway. Travis walked over and knelt beside his two sons. Avery's twin, Mason, sat in his older brother's lap.

"Caleb, why don't you let me help Mason. You go start your own pumpkin. As cold as it's starting to get, we'll need to wrap up soon. You'll run out of time."

Caleb didn't even look up at his father, and his quiet voice was nearly lost before it got to Travis's ears. "It's okay, Dad. Mason's wanting his pumpkin to look like Dolan."

Hearing his name, the dog bounded from where he'd been resting and jumped at Caleb, resting his front paws on the boy's arm.

"Chill out, Dolan." Caleb pushed the dog gently from him. "Go sit."

The dog's eyes bugged out, his tongue lolling in excitement.

"I keep telling you that dog is retarded." Jason Baker laughed from where he sat carving his own pumpkin.

Caleb looked up, his eyes flashing. "Uncle Jason, I've asked you not to say that word. It's mean."

Jason laughed again but had the courtesy to look remorseful. "Sorry, kid." He patted the concrete by his lap. "Come here, Dolan. Come here."

The dog tore off across the driveway at full sprint. He didn't even try to slow down before running into Jason's side.

Jason wobbled but got his balance before he lost hold of his pumpkin. He looked over at Caleb. "What would you call that?"

Caleb grinned. "Just happy. He's excited to see you."

"Uh-huh. *Sure* he is." He patted the driveway again. "Sit, Dolan. Sit."

Dolan did, eyes still rolling and following every movement of those around him.

"Is he sitting the way you need him to so that you can carve him?"

"Yeah, that's great. Thanks, Jason." Caleb nodded, then turned his attention back to the pumpkin. He whispered something to Mason, who shook his head, then broke into one of his shy smiles.

You should see them, Shannon. We did good, you and me. Can you believe Caleb will be driving in two years? I wish you were here. Travis would have sworn he could hear her whispered response in his ear.

He smiled as he took in his family. Only Jason stood out as different. His best friend's tanned skin and dark hair was a stark contrast to the other five of them. All had fair skin and varying degrees of red hair. Even Dunkyn and Dolan were redheaded, at least mostly. Wendy's damned bunny, nibbling away on grass in her fenced area beside the driveway, even qualified with her ginger spots. People around town called them the *red-family*. When Wendy had moved in, they'd just traded one redhead for another.

"Sorry, Daddy."

He hadn't even noticed Avery until she pulled on the leg of his jeans. He was really out of it. "It's okay, hunny. Just remember to speak nicely to people. Did Wendy say you could start carving your pumpkin again?" He glanced over at his sister, who nodded, her long silver earrings flashing in the evening sunlight.

"Travis, would you mind helping Avery real quick? I just need to go in and check on the roast."

"Sure, sis." Travis walked toward her, stretching out his hand for the pumpkin. "I forgot to ask, did Shannon's folks come out here for lunch today?"

Wendy narrowed her eyes. "Yes, they did. I meant to call you and thank you for the heads-up about company coming. Luckily we were just doing grilled cheese and tomato soup, so it was easy to compensate."

"Oh, sorry about that. I wasn't thinking."

She dropped the small knife into the hollow pumpkin before handing it to him. "You know I'm just giving you a hard time. Besides, Patsy is barely eating anything these days." She chuckled. "Can't say the same for Glen, though. I think he had three grilled cheeses, and I lost track of how many times he went back for soup."

"Five."

Wendy and Travis looked over to Caleb, who was grinning at them. "He had five bowls. I bet Mason and Avery that he'd have four. They won."

Mason glanced up, a huge grin plastered on his typically serious face. "Avery said six, but I bet five."

Travis gave the six-year-old boy a thumbs-up. "You know your grandpa. He likes to eat, that one."

"Amen to that. And, speaking of, I really need to get in there and add more broth, or that roast is gonna be about as flavorful as if Jason made it." Wendy patted Avery's head before turning and walking through the open garage door.

"Don't even try to pretend you could cook as bad as me, Wendy. Not even on your worst day could you take away my worst-chef-in-America title." Jason didn't even look up from where he sat beside Dolan, carving away on his own pumpkin. Travis was pretty sure he was carving the outline of a beer can. Always the classy one, Jason Baker.

Wendy had already reached the door that led into the house, but she stuck her head back through. "No argument from me there, Jason. You can keep that title, as well as the one naming you town drunk!" She laughed and shut the door behind her.

Jason yelled after her, "You bet I will! I worked hard for that honor!"

"Why do I let you hang out with my family again? I should protect my children from your influence." Travis knelt down on the concrete between Jason and Caleb and Mason. No sooner had he pulled Avery onto his lap than Dunkyn lay down beside him, his back resting against Travis's thigh.

"So your kids won't be boring. Left to you and Wendy, they wouldn't develop a sense of humor." Jason stuck the handle of the knife between his teeth, then reached into the cooler behind him and pulled out another can of beer.

Travis started to make a comeback, but Mason's small voice cut him off. He glanced back toward his sons. "What'd you say, bud? Couldn't hear you."

Caleb didn't look up, keeping his full concentration on carving his dog's likeness into the side of the pumpkin. "He asked if you'd turn up the radio, Dad."

"Oh. Sure." He was thankful for Caleb, but ached at how quickly his oldest son had had to grow up. He was as much of a dad to the twins as Travis was himself. Travis reached over and turned the volume dial on the portable radio. He cringed. "Seriously, Mason? You wanted to hear this crap?"

Avery glared up at him from his lap. "It's Taylor Swift, Daddy. Not crap."

Travis grinned down at her. "You too, princess? This doesn't even sound like country music."

"She's pretty good, Trav. I took a date to one of her concerts last year. I got way lucky after...." Jason's voice trailed off, his dark eyes darting from Travis to Caleb, then back. "Uhm, she's a good performer."

Travis glared at him but was pleased to notice a dark blush rising to Caleb's cheeks. He'd had *the talk* with him when he'd turned thirteen last year, and from how shy the boy was, Travis was pretty sure he had nothing to worry about—yet. That was fine with him. He didn't need to be an accidental grandfather anytime soon. Forty-two was too young to even think about such revulsion. "Still, doesn't sound like country music. Not like it did back in the day."

Jason held up his pumpkin, closing one eye as he inspected it. Yep, definitely an homage to a can of beer. "We know, Travis, we know. You'll never get over Garth Brooks retiring."

"No, I won't, if this is what country music keeps sounding like. He's going out on tour again, though, so all will soon be righted." Travis brushed Avery's hand away from the pumpkin. "Sweetie, you've got to move your fingers. I don't want you to get cut."

Avery's tone was indignant. "Well, you're doing his smile wrong. I only want him to have one tooth on top. Not two."

"That's easy to fix, princess." He angled the knife, slicing the offending left tooth off from the jack-o'-lantern's grin. "Better?"

Her hair caught in Travis's stubble as Avery moved her head from side to side, inspecting her father's work. Satisfied, she clapped her hands, stretched up, and gave Travis a kiss on the chin. "Perfect! Can I let Nutmeg out now?"

"Sure, Avery. Go ask Wendy for the leash. The last thing we need is that rabbit running off or getting eaten by an owl." He helped the little girl get up off his lap and watched her run through the garage and into the house. Then he leaned back, turning toward Jason. "Hey, Jase, throw me a can, will ya?"

Jason grinned wickedly at him. "Oh sure, Jason's a drunk and a bad influence. The worst of the town, until Travis Bennett wants a beer, then he's just fine to mingle with."

"Shut up and throw me the damned beer."

Jason did.

"I think the beer can you carved looks a little crushed."

"Oh, really? This coming from the guy who just made the most inbred-looking jack-o'-lantern I've ever seen. The thing looks like my Arkansas cousins' kids."

Travis was about to offer back another insult when he heard Caleb chuckle. He looked over at his son.

Caleb shrugged. "Jason has shown me pictures of those kids, Dad. He's kinda right." Embarrassed, he returned to carving the pumpkin. In his lap, Mason's brows were knitted together in concentration, as if he were the one wielding the knife.

Travis loved hearing his children laughing, especially his sons. Avery was so much like Shannon, one fiery emotion after the next. Either furious, ecstatically happy, or laughing louder than any six-year-old should be able to laugh. His sons were more like him, quiet and reserved. Well, Mason was like him, had been ever since he was born. Happy to let his twin make all the noise. Caleb had been loud and animated, almost as much as Avery, until Shannon got sick. For months after she died, the only people the boy would speak to were his little brother and sister.

Caleb noticed Travis staring at him. His laughter died instantly, but he offered his father a slow smile.

Travis flinched as Dolan started barking. The dog bounded from his spot by Jason and rushed to the end of the driveway. A low growl emanated from where Dunkyn lay beside him.

Jason laughed—snorted, actually, spewing beer out of his nose. He raked his forearm across his face, wiping away the spew. "Well, I'd heard about him, but I never would have believed it."

Travis followed his friend's line of sight down to where Dolan bounced up and down at the end of the driveway. His bark was ecstatic. The dog had never met a person he didn't think wanted to pet him.

A few yards away, running toward them, was the new vet. All six foot whatever of him, all lean muscle and sinew, clad in neon yellow running shoes with pink laces, purple-and-yellow running shorts, and an equally loud tank top. His blond bangs bounced as he slowed to a jog when he got closer to them.

When the vet—what was his name? Dr. Ryan something. Oh, right. Wesley Ryan. When Dr. Wesley Ryan reached Dolan, who was near to a frenzy by this point, he stopped, knelt down, and began scratching the dog's head. Travis could hear the warm inflection of the vet's words to the dog but couldn't make out what he was saying.

Travis leaned forward, whether to hear what the man said or to get a better look, he wasn't certain. At that exact moment, the vet looked up, and their eyes met.

Wesley Ryan's eyes widened with recognition, and he stood up quickly. He raised his hand in greeting and opened his mouth. Then, without saying anything, he closed it and took off jogging again. Within a few feet, the vet was running down Airport Road like the devil was chasing him.

Travis stared after him. His heart was beating hard in his chest.

Just a reaction to Dolan's fucking barking.

He felt Shannon whisper something in his ear.

He was going crazy.

Jason laughed, able to do so without wasting beer this time. "I'd heard the new vet was a fag, but wow! I'm surprised there's not a trail of glitter behind that one."

"Uncle Jason!" Caleb's voice was unusually loud and sharp. "You can never say that word. That's as bad as the other one you said."

Jason recoiled at the rebuke, not used to Caleb ever raising his voice. "Sorry, Caleb. I didn't mean anything bad by it."

Caleb's words didn't soften. "Well, don't say it. There's a kid at school who gets called that. I can see how much it hurts him. You shouldn't...." His voice trailed off, distracted. His brows knitted in confusion, and then his gaze flitted up to Travis, concern etched across his face. "Dad, you're bleeding."

"Huh?" Travis glanced down, almost expecting to see a bullet hole in his chest like they show in the movies. Stupid, but that's how the kid's voice had sounded. No gaping bullet wounds. The blood was coming from his closed right fist. He'd been gripping the knife blade so tightly, he hadn't even felt it cutting into his palm. He looked from his bleeding hand to the silhouette of the vet disappearing in the growing dusk.

CHAPTER SIX

AFTER KICKING off the fluorescent yellow tennis shoes, Wesley stepped through his front door and glared down at the offending footwear. *Pink? I just had to go with pink laces. Thought I was so cute!*

He wasn't sure what made him angrier—being stupid enough to wear such outlandish clothes in El Dorado or being embarrassed about it. His ex had always given him a hard time about dressing *too gay*. Whatever that meant. Well, he supposed he knew exactly what it meant now. While Kansas City wasn't the most liberal place to live, it had nothing on a small country town. What exactly was he trying to prove?

Walking down the hallway, he had to pause to pull the equally garish compression shorts over his legs. Once in his bedroom, he tossed them in the corner of his closet, promptly followed by the tank top. He caught his reflection in the full-length mirror, naked except for the white ankle socks. *I should have jogged like this. Wouldn't have been any worse.*

Why had he run exactly? Travis Bennett had looked surprised to see him. There hadn't been any hostility or judgment there. Not that Wesley had stayed long enough to find out.

One minute he'd paused to pet the cute, hyperactive corgi, and the next thing he knew he was looking up at the burly red bear of a man he'd not been able to get out of his head. Dammit! He had to quit thinking about the guy like that. That was part of the reason he'd come to El Dorado Springs—to be man-free. No romance. No relationship drama. No sex. Just a chance to start over, get a year or so of private practice under his belt. Time to heal. Time to focus on himself, on Wesley Ryan, on who he was without a man to distract him. At least he was lusting after someone who wasn't an option, not in the slightest, as evidenced by the kids he'd seen in the background.

Why had he run? Sure, maybe he'd had a wide assortment of lustful thoughts in which Mr. Bennett *might* have had a starring role, but they were just that. Nothing more than fantasies. The man wouldn't have been able to read his thoughts.

Why had he run? He let out a frustrated growl as he admitted it to himself. An actual growl. *Him. Growling.*

He was embarrassed to be so damn queer that he'd gone jogging looking like a one-man gay pride parade.

Embarrassed to be gay.

Oh. Hell, no. His feet made slapping sounds as he strode back down the hardwood hallway and threw open the front door. Bending down, he scooped up his running shoes. He would not hide who he was. He wasn't going to tone it down a bit. He hadn't done it for Todd, and he sure as hell wasn't going to do it for the random people of El Dorado.

Not that they'd asked him to.

Well, good! They'd better not. He was here. He was queer. They'd better get used to it! He had nothing to hide.

Wesley nodded emphatically, agreeing with the thoughts in his head. The evening breeze blew over his porch, chilling him.

He let out a yelp, backed up, and swung the door shut.

Good thing he didn't have anything to hide, since the only part of him covered was his feet. He slammed his back into the door and slid down onto the floor. What if someone had seen him? What if they called the cops, if he got a ticket for indecent exposure? Panic began to well up, and then laughter broke through.

Wesley Ryan, thirty-five, with his doctorate degree in veterinary medicine, with his fancy clothes and sports car, sat naked, long legs spread on the floor, and laughed. Laughed until the tears rolled down his cheeks. Thank God there weren't many neighbors around his grandparents' old house.

As quickly as the laughter had erupted, it faded away. He was embarrassed about being gay. Ashamed. But the source of the shame floated before his eyes, adding a wash of rage.

John Wallace.

He hadn't been ashamed of being gay or hidden it since he'd come out in high school. Never. Until two nights ago.

He'd replayed the events of the day over and over in his mind. When he was able to look at the situation in a completely objective manner, which took considerable effort, Wesley thought he might have overreacted. He'd never been in any real danger. Not really. The man had threatened to make him bleed if he told anyone about it, but nothing more. It had been an empty threat. Wesley hadn't really told the man no. He'd frozen. He'd just stood there, that gross dick slapping against his thigh. He'd not moved a muscle… until he did.

Where had that come from? He'd never been physically aggressive with anyone, not in his entire life—no playground fights, no drunken brawls at the bars, and never with Todd, not even when it had ended.

He'd nearly choked a man. He could have killed him. The first time he'd thought that, it seemed overly dramatic, but it wasn't. He could have. He was pretty sure he'd wanted to. But why? He should have said no, turned, and walked out the damned door.

The stupidest thing was that he'd gone in the man's house at all.

Something about the memory bothered him, though. He couldn't name it, couldn't say why, but every time he put himself back into that memory, when he didn't bother to attempt objectivity, fear seeped into him, as fresh at it had been in the moment. Every synapse in his brain, every fiber of his body screamed, "Danger!"

So what did that all mean? Why was he suddenly embarrassed about being gay? What did that say about him?

From the bedroom, the buzzing of his cell phone broke through his thoughts, freeing him.

After another buzz, Wesley pushed himself off of the floor, his body feeling unusually stiff.

By the time he made it back into his bedroom and realized his phone was on the closet floor, tangled in the purple and yellow spandex, the ringing had stopped. He peered at the screen. His mother.

Good timing as ever. He started to call her back, then paused. He was not going to call her while he was naked. No reason to add more weirdness to the situation.

He threw on his sweatpants and a T-shirt. Both navy blue. *See, I can butch it up, thank you very much.* He left his bedroom, walked through the kitchen to get a glass of water, and went to the small office his grandmother had used to pay bills. He flicked on the desk lamp, and soft yellow light filled the room. Wesley leaned back in the chair, taking a moment to settle in before he called his mother back. He loved the small house. Always had. It needed updating. It screamed sixties, and not in a good way. He'd spent many evenings planning what he'd do to improve the place while keeping the spirit of his grandparents. The past day or so, that seemed pointless. His days in El Do truly were limited. Even changing the color of his shoelaces wouldn't fix all that was wrong.

A long sigh escaped, leaving him feeling gloomy. At the press of a button, the cell phone lit up. With a swipe over the missed call, he held the phone up to his ear.

It didn't even make it to the second ring. "Darling! You called back! How are you, dear?" His mother's smooth alto voice seemed to fill the room through the earpiece, instantly chasing away some of the sadness.

"Hi, Mom. I just got in from a run. How are you?"

She didn't miss a beat. "What's wrong, Wesley?"

"Nothing's wrong, Mom."

Her tone turned sharp, protective. "Don't you give me that. I know when something is wrong with one of my boys. What is it? Are people giving you a hard time? I told you once you were there for more than just a visit with your grandparents, you'd see what that town was really like. Why I couldn't get away soon enough. I am so angry at Mom and Dad for leaving that house to you. What did they expect to happen? Why don't you just come back—"

He cut her off. "No, Mom. Things are fine. The people are really nice." He never could lie well, especially to her. He'd learned long ago, if he was going to successfully lie to Anne Ryan, he needed to weave in some threads of truth. "I'm just stressed is all. I had to call Animal Protection this morning to report one of the farmers."

She hesitated momentarily, possibly waiting for him to crack. "Is it going to cause an issue? Are you worried about him trying to get back at you?"

He hadn't even thought about that, though how he'd missed that possibility he wasn't sure. Maybe that was why he'd taken over a day to make a report, subconsciously feeling a threat. "No, nothing like that. I'm sure there won't be any fallout. I just… I just didn't want to get down here and stir up trouble."

"Well, I'm sure you did the right thing, Wesley. You wouldn't have taken such measures if you hadn't felt it right. That's what it takes to own a business. Do what has to be done. Period."

How many times throughout his life had he heard that sentiment in one form or another? Over a forty-year career, and still going strong as the head art director for Hallmark, Anne often spoke of simply doing what you had to do, what was right and what was honest, regardless of how unpleasant it might feel. Firing someone, layoffs, and "going another direction" were all ways of doing what had to be done.

"I know, Mom. The guy's cattle were in horrible shape. It's just not pleasant to have to make that kind of report."

Another hesitation.

Oh, crap.

"Your father and I were talking. We were thinking, now that you've decided to get your head back into the game, that we'd like to invest in a veterinary clinic here in K.C. Somewhere near the Plaza or close to work. Nothing lavish, but something nice, tasteful."

Charles, Wesley's father, was also a big name within the Hallmark Company. Money to invest in a new clinic wouldn't be an issue. Money was never an issue. Wesley could imagine what his parents' view of "not lavish" would consist of. "No, Mom. Thank you. Tell Dad thanks too. I just need to do this on my own."

"Well, dear, if you tried to work things out with Todd, you wouldn't have to do it alone. Maybe—"

Irritation flared in his voice. "For the last time, Mom. He left me. For some twink. He. Left. Me."

"No need to get snippy, dear. I was merely suggesting—"

"I'm not moving back home. I need to be here in El Do right now." He drummed his fingers on the top of the desk. "For now, at least." Crap! He hadn't meant to say that out loud.

His mother's voice sounded hopeful again. "Well, if it's just for now, I'm sure we can manage. Your nieces and nephew miss you, you know."

Wesley glanced at the framed photo that sat under the desk lamp. It was all of them. The whole Ryan clan. Charles and Anne and their three sons. Both of his brothers' wives and all of their combined offspring. Four girls and one boy, ranging from three to fifteen.

"I miss them too, Mom." He really did. "They can come down some weekend to visit. Well, maybe not Marley, she's too young."

His mother let out a laugh. "Can you really see Jack in El Dorado Springs? He spends more time shopping in the malls than you did at that age! He'd be miserable."

Guilt sliced through him as he looked at the kids' faces. He'd done a pretty pathetic job of being an uncle during the past couple of years. "Well, mention it to them. I'd love to have them. I'm sure we'd find something fun to do."

Anne paused once more, concern in her voice more than prying. "Are you sure you're okay, darling? You already sound... different."

THE GINGER bear galloped beside a pond, his reflection a red blur. Behind him bounded an orange dog—short legs, long hair, flapping ears. Something seemed to be chasing the dog... or maybe the bear. He could almost make it out. It was still too far away. Something pink. Maybe yellow. Something that... sparkled?

A loud buzzing cut through the chill in the air.

The reflection of the scurrying trio distorted in the water's surface.

Another annoying buzz.

Wesley groaned and stretched out a hand, partly tangled in the sheets, and slapped at the air.

More buzzing.

More groaning.

Sitting up, Wesley leaned toward the nightstand and finally smacked the offensive alarm clock.

Another buzz.

His eyes narrowed, and he glared at the clock's red numbers. 4:30 a.m. That made no sense at all. He smacked it again.

Still more buzzing.

Oh for crying out loud. Moron. Twisting, he thrust his legs out from the covers, pushed himself off the bed, and stood on the cold floor. Rubbing his eyes, he padded over to the bathroom, where his phone was plugged into an outlet by the sink and vibrating over the tiled countertop.

If his mother had talked his dad into calling in an attempt to convince him to move back to Kansas City....

Without looking at the ID, Wesley swiped his thumb across the screen and lifted the phone to his ear. "Hell—" His voice cracked. He cleared his throat and tried again. "Hello?"

"Where is Dr. Fisher? I've tried her home phone a billion times already."

Why did his dad want to know where Cheryl Fisher was? And why was he so angry about it? "Uhm, what?"

"Where the fuck is Dr. Fisher? She's not answering her phone, and her message said to call this number if there was an emergency." There was something familiar about the voice.

Emergency? Oh, right! "Sorry, just trying to wake up. Dr. Fisher went out of town for the week. This is Dr. Ryan. Is there anything I can do for you? What's the emergency?"

"I know who this is. Why do you think I kept calling Dr. Fisher? You're the one who didn't fix the problem to begin with. You said it wasn't cancer."

The puzzle pieces fell into place, the click of their joining loud enough to finally wake him up. Red Bear. Right. "Is Dunkyn's face swollen again?"

"Yes, I woke up—" The growl went from accusatory to suspicious. "How did you know that?"

Wesley returned to his bedroom and retrieved his pants from the floor. Despite the anger in the other man's tone, talking to Travis Bennett when he didn't have clothes on was exactly the type of thing his imagination didn't need. "Mr. Bennett, remember that I was worried the swelling might return if the infection was greater than we hoped."

The fury from the other end of the line sent a chill down Wesley's spine. "You said it wasn't cancer."

Hot or not, the guy had an unhealthy obsession with cancer. "Mr. Bennett, Dunkyn doesn't have cancer. It's just the infection from the abscess. The antibiotics simply didn't take care of it, and he needs surgery. The procedure is routine and common for dogs."

There was a pregnant pause, and then the voice returned, fear replacing the anger. "Surgery."

It was strange to hear the desperation in the man's voice. He didn't look like he would be afraid of anything. "Yes. I tried to mention it the other day. It's simple. I'd just start with a couple of X-rays to determine which tooth has damage, and the surgery would remove that tooth and clean the infected area. It wouldn't—"

"No. Surgery." Back to the anger.

One of his first clients, or the owner of one of his first clients during his internship, was an elderly woman who'd lost her husband. Her little dog had seemed nearly as old as the woman herself. She never stopped crying from the time she brought in the tangle of white fur to the time Wesley returned the dog to her. The surgery had been a success, although the dog died of other age complications less than two months later. The old woman's pain had been nearly enough to cause Wesley to rethink all his years of preparation and applications to get into the program. As impossible as it seemed, he heard the same note of terror in Travis's voice as he had in the old, frail woman.

Wesley lowered his voice, doing his best to be soothing without sounding patronizing. "Mr. Bennett. Travis. You seem like a man who likes to be told the way things are, a straight shooter." He didn't wait for a reply. "This surgery is simple and routine, as I've already told you. However, without this surgery, Dunkyn will die. The infection will become too great. Maybe another round or two of antibiotics would hold it off for a bit, but it wouldn't solve the problem."

No sound came from the other end of the line.

Wesley waited a full twenty seconds. "Mr. Bennett?"

"Fine." The word was barely more than a croak.

Wesley sighed in relief. "Dunkyn will be all right, Mr. Bennett. I give you my word. Just bring him by the clinic later this morning, maybe around—"

"No. Now. If Dunkyn needs surgery, then he will get it now." The anger was back, but the fear was still audible underneath.

The image of the old woman rose in Wesley's mind, cutting off his objection, erasing the need for more sleep. The dog might not need the surgery this very hour, but the human did. "I'm just going to hop into the shower to make sure I'm fully awake, and I'll meet you there. Half an hour at the most."

The pause led Wesley to believe the man was going to argue about the shower. "Fine. We'll be there."

WESLEY WAS fairly certain he saw Mr. Bennett scowl at his yellow Miata when he drove up. Maybe it was just the sweep of headlights hurting his eyes in the still-dark morning. Maybe, but he doubted it.

The man had beaten him to the clinic and stood by the front door, holding the squirming Dunkyn. He followed Wesley in, making impatient sounds every time they paused to turn on a light, power up the computer, or flick all the switches on all the different machines and tools that would be needed. Still, they were only noises. Just irritated vocalizations.

Wesley tried to concentrate on that. On the scowl. On the dislike radiating from the man. He was only partially successful. Travis Bennett had apparently been asleep not too much before he'd called Wesley. Baggy sweatpants were stuffed into worn-out cowboy boots—sweatpants that were well-used and clung to places that kept beckoning to the vet. A dirty tank top highlighted the massive cords of muscles that wound up forearms, heavy biceps, triceps, shoulders, and spread under a bulging, furry red chest. Even the way the thin material hugged the hard small belly was tantalizing. Although a few inches shorter than himself, the bear of a man, holding the large ball of fur, was a compact mass of testosterone. Wesley had to make a concerted effort to keep from getting close enough to attempt to smell Travis. Literally.

Despite his inability to corral the lustful thoughts, and Travis's endless string of irritated noises, everything was going relatively smoothly, right up until the moment Wesley put the surgery release form on the counter for Travis Bennett to sign. Even as he rushed through the explanation of the risks, he knew the explosion would come. Knew the precise moment when it would arrive. He almost skipped over the form entirely in order to avoid it.

Travis Bennett's large white teeth seemed to gnash through the man's sneer and did little to lessen his likeness to a bear. "That's exactly why I said no to this fucking thing! You said there was no risk. That it's a common procedure. That it's simple. Now you want me to sign saying I *acknowledge* that I've been informed of the risk of death? That the surgery might fucking kill my dog?" The growling Wesley thought he'd heard on the phone was nothing. *This* was growling. Low, quiet, and filled with venom. More terrifying than if the man had been screaming. "No surgery. I'll wait till Dr. Fisher gets back." Travis turned away from the counter and started walking toward the door. "I want a real vet working on my dog. Not some fucking faggot."

Twice. Twice in less than three days. That word! This time it didn't fill him with terror like it had dripping from John Wallace's lips. This was different, but it made him mad just the same.

"Mr. Bennett!" Wesley raised his voice but managed to keep it from sounding like he was yelling. Though it wasn't filled with the same rage he'd heard during the thunderstorm, he couldn't help but wonder where this new person had risen from within him.

At his name, Travis wheeled around, ready to battle, but paused when he saw the vet's expression.

Wesley walked from behind the counter and stepped up to Travis. Even though he stood taller, even with this new anger or whatever it was, it didn't keep him from feeling like he was walking up to a grizzly. "Most importantly, Dunkyn needs this surgery. There is risk with any surgery, and I'm sure you know that. You've probably signed that form any time you've had a minor procedure. Your dog needs this. Is there risk? Yes. Will he die? *No.* I won't let him. I'm a good vet, and outside of some bizarre fluke, there is no risk, despite what that form says."

Travis started to open his mouth.

"I'm not done." Wesley was pretty sure he stamped his foot. *God, I hope I didn't stamp my foot.* "Regardless of the stress you are under because you love your dog, never call me that word again. *Never.*" Wesley thought he was done, but that new voice just kept going. "I would suggest you never use that word again, period. However, that is your choice, ignorant though it may be. Either way, never use it in my presence." He felt like there needed to be a threat, an "or else." It didn't come.

Travis simply stared at him, blue eyes wide and pupils contracting. At last he nodded.

Although the man didn't say anything, Wesley could have sworn a swarm of emotions flowed behind Travis Bennett's eyes. He was fairly certain one of them was shame. He also thought he saw desire.

That one he knew was his own imagining.

"I want to stay in there with him during the surgery."

Wesley started to say no.

"Please. I won't get in your way. I just need to be with him."

There were no tears in the man's eyes, but Wesley heard them in his voice—heard the fear, heard the hurt. Suddenly he understood, as if someone had whispered it in his ear. Travis Bennett loved Dunkyn, there was no doubt, but his fear was only partially for his dog. The pain was about something more. Something much more. So had been his anger.

CHAPTER SEVEN

"IT'S JUST a precaution, Mr. Bennett. I'll have the best anesthesiologist with me. He'll be there with Shannon the entire time, monitoring her vitals, making sure everything is perfect. He won't leave her until she wakes up. Like I've told you both, the hysterectomy is a massive surgery, but routine. I could do it in my sleep." The surgeon's lips curved into a self-satisfied smile. He actually smiled.

Travis stuffed his fists deep into his pockets to keep from slugging him. He looked at Shannon, doing his best to keep his anger at the doctor hidden from her. He wasn't sure why he even tried. She wouldn't have to see his face to know he was furious. Likewise, in spite of her raised chin and clear, dry eyes, he could tell she was terrified. Suddenly all anger toward the doctor swirled around and engulfed him. Shannon was more afraid than he'd ever seen her. His wife's life was in danger, and here he stood, nothing more than some hick, trying to understand the implications of choriocarcinoma, chemotherapy, hysterectomies. Trying to comprehend why this cancer was deadlier if it occurred after a child's birth.

After the twins' births.

He couldn't understand. He'd been trying for weeks. Months. He couldn't understand. Couldn't do a thing. His wife sat beside him, holding his hand, refusing to cry, refusing to let her fear show. He couldn't do a fucking thing.

He looked back at the surgeon, glaring once more, though the doctor was too caught up in his own glory to notice.

"Then why do we need to sign any forms saying we acknowledge that one of the risks of anesthesia is d—" Shannon's hand clinched in Travis's grip, cutting off the word. He doubted she even realized she'd reacted.

The smile never wavered. "Just procedure. Nothing more than hospital and legal protocol. Trust me. Shannon will pull through without a glitch. She will wake up from this surgery and be cancer-free. Even the chemo will be just that—protocol, a safeguard." His narrow eyes brightened, focusing on Shannon. "And, there'll be little scarring with all the technical advances. You'll be back in a bikini in no time, Ms. Bennett."

Travis's fists nearly tunneled through the pockets of his jeans.

The doctor had been true to his word. Anesthesia hadn't killed Shannon.

TRAVIS STROKED Dunkyn's muzzle, his large hand moving tenderly. He'd tried to leave the dog alone, but he had to keep touching him, assuring himself the dog was really there, that he'd made it through the procedure. It wasn't bothering Dunkyn anyway; he kept right on snoring.

Travis pulled the covers tighter around Dunkyn. Without shifting his weight too much, trying not to shake the bed, he scooped up another pillow and stuffed it under his head, allowing himself to curve his body around his dog.

All in all, Travis thought he'd done pretty well. During Dunkyn's surgery, he'd kept one hand clinched in his pocket, the other resting over Dunkyn's hip. He would have placed a decent-sized bet that the veterinarian had no idea how many times he'd almost gotten punched in the face.

There hadn't been much blood. Dr. Ryan had removed two teeth. Both were damaged, but the molar had been the main cause of the infection. Even the root had been cracked right down the middle. Travis was willing to bet it had been one of the times Dolan had smacked right into Dunkyn's face. Jason was right. That fucking dog was getting dumber each and every day. If he didn't mean as much to Caleb as Dunkyn meant to him, Travis was certain there would be one less corgi in the world that night.

Truth be told, Dunkyn was doing better than Travis was. Other than being tired and slower than normal, the dog didn't seem any the worse for wear. The vet had even said Dunkyn could return to his normal routine in a day or so, as long as he stayed away from chasing the buffalo for a few weeks.

Dunkyn Diamond was all right.

Travis Bennett was not. He told himself that he'd managed just fine, that he'd acted normal. He knew better.

Even Avery, who typically never stopped talking, was as quiet as Mason at dinner. Only Wendy had managed to keep a steady conversation going, but her tone had been tentative, as if she was worried the wrong word would send her brother over the edge and cause a torrent of screams—or worse, tears.

He'd done pretty well. After the twins had gone to sleep, Wendy had set the large cardboard box of beer beside Travis's recliner, kissed him on the head, and retired to her room. He hadn't even gotten halfway through the twelve-pack by the time Caleb had gone to bed, Dolan pounding after him like the brainless bulldozer he was.

He wasn't sure if he would have gotten through the past four years without Wendy. Actually he knew he wouldn't have, and neither would the kids. His sister had been the one to hold the family together, not him. She had faced his fury when his drinking had gotten to be too much a few months after….

She'd been the one to make him see his children had lost their mother and father.

She was the one who knew when it was all too much, when her brother wouldn't be able to find any other way through the darkness than to get lost to it, if just for a night.

It had been a long time since Travis had had more than two or three beers in one sitting. Sure, on the weekly bowling nights, it would do no one any good to make an attempt to count all the beers he and his buddies put away, but that was with an equally endless supply of pizza, hot dogs, and nachos.

Travis had only made it through eight cans before realizing he wasn't going to last much longer. Using the wall to make sure he was balanced, though he probably hadn't really needed to, he carried Dunkyn to his bed.

To their bed.

The night Shannon had died, after Travis had to be forcibly removed from the hospital, he had walked into their bedroom and stared in horror at their bed. He was supposed to get in that thing? Then his eyes found Dunkyn already asleep on the floor beside Travis's side of the bed, as always.

Travis slept on the floor with him for the next three nights. After Shannon's funeral, he'd picked up the dog, placed him in the bed, crawled in beside him, and drifted off around sunrise. Within the week, he'd made a wide set of steps that the short dog could easily maneuver, allowing him to come and go from the bed as he pleased.

The night after Dunkyn's surgery, Travis got the dog safely into bed. He had one more beer after he got in beside Dunkyn, buzzed nearly to the point of sleep, but stopped just before it took away his choice. He needed to stay up and watch over the dog. Just in case.

Protocol.

Procedure.

Simple.

No big deal.

I know what I'm doing.

He couldn't lose him. Dunkyn was his last link to Shannon. He couldn't lose him. Sure, he saw her every time he looked at Avery. Every time the little girl lost her temper or fell into fits of laughter. They could be twins, save for the girl's inheriting his softer strawberry blonde hair instead of her mother's curtain of fire.

Shannon was there in the compassion that always shone out of Caleb's eyes, in his constant fight for the underdog.

Shannon's habit of biting her lower lip was evidenced each time Mason was deep in thought, which was nearly all the time.

Shannon was everywhere, always, in each of their children.

But Dunkyn was his friend, his companion. Dunkyn was always by his side. He was loyal, no matter what. He was Travis's friend.

Shannon had been beautiful. Stunningly beautiful. Looks that matched her temper, her laughter, her love of life. She had been his first love, the mother of his children. She'd been his friend. More than anything else, Shannon had been his best friend.

He couldn't walk through this alone.

Wrapping an arm around the dog, Travis pulled him closer, spooning him. Dunkyn issued a low, contented grunt, then shifted, readjusting himself against his master.

As long as Dunkyn was there, the dog Shannon had unintentionally given him, Travis could feel her beside him every night. Closing his eyes, he felt the warmth against his skin, and she was there. His best friend hadn't really left. As long as Dunkyn was there, he would still be able to hear her whisper.

His head nodded, his eyes drooping before he flinched, forcing himself to stay awake. Maybe that last beer had been too much.

Nine beers? That barely used to make his teeth tingle.

The dog let out a sigh, followed by a whimper.

Travis grinned. He loved it when the dog dreamed. He closed his eyes.

The dog sighed once more, his body relaxing against Travis again.

Travis's smile widened. He heard her laugh: soft, close. He could see her beautiful blue eyes and the even more beautiful light that seemed to gleam from them.

She whispered in his ear.

Travis wasn't sure what she said. He listened closer.

You're safe, love.

Behind his eyes and with Dunkyn's warmth in his arms, he could see her brilliant red hair spread over the pillow as she looked up at him.

Her warm brown eyes.

Travis's head jerked as his eyes shot open. Brown eyes?

His heart began to pound. Brown eyes.

She was gone. She was gone!

He slapped his hand against Dunkyn's rib cage, holding it with unintentional pressure. The dog huffed at the abrupt movement.

Travis didn't hear.

There was a whisper next to his ear.

He didn't hear.

Only his heavy breathing. Only the panic. Only his own panting filled the room.

Then he felt it. The slow and steady beat under the fur. Travis kept his hand there, not believing. He felt it again.

Two more times.

Three.

Brown eyes?

Four.

Five heartbeats.

Dunkyn was there. He was alive and fine. He was going to be fine.

Another whisper at his ear.

This time he heard.

You promised, love. Remember your promise.

CHAPTER EIGHT

A ROLL of thunder rattled the windows, reverberating through The Crocheted Bunny, echoing off the pressed tin ceiling high overhead. Wendy grinned up at him from under her tall witch hat. "Perfect weather for Halloween. So creepy."

"Perfect unless you're a kid who wants to go trick-or-treating." Wesley stuffed the presorted felt pieces into another plastic black and orange treat bag. "So the kids are supposed to glue the pieces together and they make a bunny?"

She nodded, long auburn spirals bouncing, hiding her face as she continued to remove paper cups and napkins from the grocery store bags. "They make Nutmeg, to be more precise. And don't you worry about the weather. El Dorado folks are tough. Halloween will continue with or without the aid of umbrellas."

"And, you're a what again?" Wesley eyed the enormous wings made of wire, yarn, ropes of fake pearls, and colored plastic wrap that stuck out from the back of Wendy's lacey black robes.

She looked up at him again, her blue eyes sparkling in delight—blue eyes that were the exact shade of her brother's.

Dammit, he shouldn't even think that. He also shouldn't have noticed that her brother's face had few freckles, whereas Wendy's nose and cheeks were filled with starbursts of them.

"I'm a witch fairy, obviously!" She twirled, her hair, black robes, and long strands of what had to be Christmas tinsel spinning out around her. Her pink, yellow, and white cowboy boots were revealed in the process.

"How long did those wings take you to make?"

She shrugged. "Just a couple of nights. Not much at all. Especially compared to last year. That outfit took forever."

More felt bunny pieces into a gift bag. "Dare I ask?"

"I was a vampire mermaid. It was glorious." She looked down at her costume, her face twisting in a critical expression. "Better than this year's."

"You look great, but a vampire mermaid? That makes no sense. Have you been checked for your sanity? By a professional, I mean?"

Wendy laughed, the sound a bright dissonance against the thunderstorm outside. "Sweetie, I'm a Gemini." She gestured around, encompassing the store. "Take a look. There are many aspects to my personality. Things people say shouldn't go together. But they do. And wonderfully, I might add."

Wesley wondered if Wendy's brother's eyes ever lit up like hers. He'd love to see that. "The store is quite a mishmash, but I agree, it's rather wonderful."

Her eyes narrowed. "What were you thinking there? Something good, I can tell."

"Nothing. Just about the store." He felt his cheeks grow warm.

"Your blush would say otherwise. But I'll let it go." She grinned. "For now."

He didn't respond, just kept assembling the gift bags.

They continued in amicable silence. Wendy finished first and moved on to opening massive bags of candy.

This was only the third time Wesley had spent time with Wendy, and that was counting the impromptu drive about town. Still, he already counted her a friend, which was unusual. A part of him felt like he used to, back before the breakup. Todd had always told him the term social butterfly didn't begin to describe him—he was the entire swarm of butterflies bursting out of their cocoons. That had changed. Everything had changed. The only socializing he'd done the past couple of years in Kansas City had been an endless string of hookups and one-night stands.

That had been part of his decision in coming to El Dorado Springs. There wouldn't be an opportunity for hooking up. He would have to focus on his career. He'd worked hard enough to become a veterinarian; it was time to act like it. He needed to focus on remembering who Wesley Ryan used to be, and hopefully figure out who he was now. He hadn't really expected to make a friend, not this quickly anyway.

As they worked, the storm outside lessened, and the late afternoon sun began to filter through the windows. "Well, it looks like your fears are groundless. There will be dry trick-or-treating. Which is good, I suppose. Though the other was much more Halloween feeling, if you ask me."

"You're a peculiar woman, Wendy Bennett."

She gave an exaggerated curtsey with one hand and flourished the hat off her head with a dramatic sweep of her other hand. "Thank you, good sir! As I've said, I am a Gemini and an artist. You will find none better."

He chuckled. "I believe you. And I would agree, thus far. You're quite extraordinary. Still, a bit odd."

"And don't you forget it. I'll give you my ex-husband's number, and he can tell you some stories, if you begin to doubt the validly of my originality claims." She gave him a wink.

Wesley paused in his gift bag assembly, inspecting his friend. "That's the second time you've mentioned being divorced. Tell me about the kind of man who let you go. He must be an idiot."

"That he is! Charles Smith is nothing more than the three B's. A bore, a brute, and a bully, as I like to say. And he doesn't deserve any more explanation than that." She smacked her hand on the countertop, as if driving home her point.

It was Wesley's turn to narrow his eyes. "A brute and bully? Was he abusive?"

Wendy looked over at him, momentarily sobered, as if surprised the conversation was still happening. "No. Not physically, at least. Though I wish he had been. I would have had the gumption to leave a lot sooner. And it wouldn't have been such a sinful travesty to my parents." She let out a sardonic chuckle, her expression darkening. "Although maybe not even then. A wife should be devoted to her husband. And let's not forget remain subservient." She finished the last word with her fingers in the air making quotation marks.

"Is that what he'd tell you? You had to be subservient?"

She laughed again, somehow darker than before. "No. Well, yes, he would, although not in that verbiage. Charles was never religious. My mother, on the other hand, well, let's just say there is little her Gemini daughter does that meets her approval. Including referring to herself as a Gemini."

"Your and Travis's folks are Bible-thumpers, huh?" Wesley and his family went to church on Easter and Christmas. And even those days weren't completely guaranteed.

Wendy shrugged. "They are just a product of their culture and their time. I hate that term, by the way. Bible-thumper. It seems discriminatory in a way, not that it isn't well earned. I go to church. I take the kids. I can't say I believe everything they say from the pulpit. Well, actually, I can say that I don't, but there are good things to be found there. Just as there are almost every place."

She was larger than life. Her sturdy size was accentuated by her vitality, and on this occasion, by her massive costume. Wesley couldn't picture her sitting in a pew. A demure Wendy made no sense, not that he knew her all that well. "And your nights dancing at the gay bar in the city?"

She waved him off. "Details. Insignificant fluff." She turned the full weight of her gaze on Wesley, propping both hands on the countertop as she leaned toward him, as though she was getting ready to let him in on life's big secret. "To put it in a way you'd understand, and that retains the spirit of this All Hallow's Eve, life is nothing more than vampire mermaids."

Wesley waited, expecting more. When nothing came, he raised his hands in surrender. "That's supposed to be a way I understand? Vampire mermaids?"

She almost looked disappointed in him. Like she'd expected a kindred enough spirit that no more explanation would be required. "Dr. Wesley Ryan, haven't you figured it out by now? After all of your years of school? After the rather privileged life you've led in Kansas City—"

Wesley started to interject, but Wendy held up her hand, cutting him off.

"That's not a judgment, just an observation. Life is nothing more than a vampire mermaid. Nothing more than a Gemini. Nothing more than contradictions. To really take part in this life, you have to open yourself up to all things. Don't cement yourself to one side or the other. Then you are nothing more than my parents, who think I'm going to hell for getting a divorce. Or Charles, who thought a wife was nothing more than someone who cooked, cleaned, and fucked. Nothing more than those who only see your sports car, rainbow dog sticker, and designer clothes. Truth is not found on one side or the other; it is spread out. Truth must be found in all places. Whether those places are a Kansas City gay dance club, The Crocheted Bunny, the driver's seat of a yellow Miata, or a church. We simply must find the pieces that are made up of the truth and put them together."

Wesley just stared at her, openmouthed. He wasn't certain if what he'd heard was brilliant, sacrilege, or nothing more than rainbowed smoke.

"Close your mouth, dear. A spider might crawl in." Wendy pulled a heavy mass of curls over her shoulder and let it fall over her back. `

He did. "You're kinda strange. I like it."

She beamed. "Of course you do, you big fairy."

"Hey! Be nice!"

"Oh, I am. However…." She looked down the length of his body, then back up. "As the only genuine fairy in the store right now, despite my wings, you should be a little more dressed up, dontcha think?"

Wesley looked down at his clothes, another flush rising to his face. "What? I've got on an outfit."

Wendy crossed her arms. "Hmm-hmm. If you wear it to work, it's not an outfit."

"I'm a vet for Halloween. If anyone doesn't understand what I am, I'll just pick up Nutmeg and give her an examination." He looked over at the rabbit's farmhouse. "She'll be out there with us, won't she?"

"Yes, and so not the point! Are you really expecting me to believe that this"—she uncrossed her arms and waved an accusing finger toward him—"this *outfit* is the best you can do? That if you were going out tonight in the city you'd wear this?"

"Not all the gays dress like drag queens on Halloween." His defensiveness was a little too loud in his own ears.

"You might not be one of the drag queens, but you are not one who wears his work outfits to go clubbing on Halloween."

"We're not clubbing. We're handing out candy and gift bags to all the kids who come to Main Street."

She cocked an eyebrow. "This is as close to clubbing as we get here. And you know what I mean."

He did.

Halloween had always been one of his favorite nights of the year. The chance to dress like anything you wanted to be. To be as outrageous, as over-the-top, and as slutty as you never dared to be the rest of the year. When Wendy asked if he wanted to help her pass out candy to the families that started off their trick-or-treating by walking up and down Main Street, he'd jumped at the chance—even before she'd mentioned that it could help him meet more of the people who lived in El Do, maybe give him an opportunity to talk about the changes he was making to the vet clinic. Not just for all those legitimate, genuine reasons, but also to simply have fun, dress up, and be silly. He needed a break, a chance to just have some fun.

Then John Wallace came into his mind, and the wary expressions on the old men's faces when they stared at him from their perch on the rock wall. He remembered the tone in Travis Bennett's voice when he'd called him a fag.

He looked at Wendy, refusing to flinch at her too-knowing expression. "What do you want me to do, Wendy? Put on a tutu?"

"No. Although I'd kill to see your legs in something like that, especially if we stuck you in a pair of stilettos. And *don't* pretend you've never worn a pair." Her teasing grin grew serious. "What I expect of you, Wesley, is that you be you. Don't worry about the town. You're right; El Do probably isn't ready for a drag queen, although maybe on Halloween. But you, be you. Plus, you're not really giving us a chance. You say you loved it here when you were a kid. That you have wonderful memories from the times you stayed with your grandparents. Well, remember those. Do you really think you'd love this place as much as you did if the town was full of mobs with pitchforks?"

Shame flooded him. Not so much for his thoughts of the town or its residents, but that after so few weeks he was trying to hide who he was. No one had asked him to. He'd been called a fag before. Why was he hiding now? Just because a closeted asshole and some beefy corgi-daddy had called him a fag?

"I don't have a spare tutu to change into, Wendy. Or an extra pair of stilettos, no matter what you might think."

She glanced at the clock, then motioned to her wings. "Look at me, hunny. You think I can't fix you up in a matter of moments? You've got more of those ugly-looking scrubs at home to replace these, right?"

Within fifteen minutes, as they carried rectangular folding tables out the front doors to set up on the sidewalk, Wesley was a full-fledged zombie veterinarian—shredded green scrubs, with lipstick bloodstains. Mascara smudges over his pale, powdered skin. Sparkly red eyeliner— *"To make your brown eyes pop and look a little sinister—win, win!"* The entire outfit was completed with Wendy's signature wire-and-duct-tape wings, because this was apparently the year of the fairy.

Other merchants were setting up along the street as well. Mei-Lien's red-and-gold clothed table outside of her corner jewelry shop looked more like an homage to Chinese New Year than it did Halloween. Across the street, Mark's Gun Emporium had a huge spread of tables running the length of the store. It looked as though they'd even set up some game stations, all gun related, of course. Wesley was pretty sure one of them had targets with zombie faces painted over the bull's eye. Perfect. Farther north up Main Street, other stores were setting out tables, but they were too far away for Wesley to discern any details.

Directly across the street, on the corner across from the park, rock-like Christian music blared from an old-fashioned boom box. Wendy just rolled her eyes. "It's the youth group building of the Holy Church. I'd ask them to turn it down, but that's the church the kids and I go to. And this is their first year in their new location." She turned, inspecting the kids setting up across the street. "Actually I tried to talk Caleb into joining them this year, now that he's a freshman. He didn't want to leave the twins, though. I hope he does. It would be good for him to build a social life that didn't involve taking care of his family."

Wesley placed a doll-sized scarecrow in Nutmeg's makeshift graveyard-inspired pen set up beside the table. The tiny rabbit shuffled over and began eating the straw sticking out the scarecrow's pant legs. With a jerk of his head, Wesley motioned toward the small CD player Wendy had placed outside the store's front doors. Creaking, clanking of chains, groans, and screams could just be heard over the Christian rock, and only if you were right in front of The Crocheted Bunny. "I can ask them to turn it down, if you want. How do you say no to a zombie with wings?"

"I did a stellar job on you, if I say so myself. Granted, if you'd given me advance notice, I could have done your wings with the designer patterns of duct tape at least." Wendy nodded at him approvingly. "Much better than a boring old vet in any case. And no, let them be. I'm the new kid on the block. No reason to make waves. Especially if there's a chance my nephew might grow a social life. It's one of the main reasons I go to the Holy Church."

"What do you mean you're the new kid on the block? Your store looks like it's been here forever."

She scowled at him. "I'll try to take that as a compliment. I just opened the store last year. Before then, I was too busy helping Travis take care of the kids, but they're more independent now, and the twins have their own spot in the store that we converted to a playroom." Her voice grew quieter, almost impossible to hear over the blare of the music, and her eyes grew unfocused as she got lost in thought. "Those first three years after I moved here were rough. No time to think about myself, what I wanted, you know?"

Despite how close Wesley already felt with Wendy, he was reminded how little he really knew of his new friend. "When you moved here? You haven't always lived in El Do?"

She gave him a surprised look. "Huh, I guess I just assumed you already knew all of that. I'm so used to everyone around here already knowing everything. Travis and I grew up in Neosho, about an hour and a half away. Our folks still live there."

For some reason this heartened Wesley, making him feel like he wasn't the only outsider. "You moved after your divorce?"

Wendy gave a half shrug, half nod kind of motion. "Yes, kind of. I got divorced a year before I moved down here. I was already planning on setting up The Crocheted Bunny there, in downtown Neosho, but then Shannon died, and Travis needed me here. So I moved."

"Who's Shannon?"

She gave him that look again, the one that said he was supposed to already know everything, like everyone else. "Shannon was Travis's wife. She died of cancer four years ago."

"Cancer—" Wesley sucked in his breath. Cancer. Cancer. He'd known there'd been more going on than Travis Bennett worrying about his dog's health. The anger that had built up over the past few days since the corgi's predawn surgery began to crumble. Cancer. *Shannon was Travis's wife. She died of cancer....* No wonder the man was such a mess over thinking his dog had cancer. No wonder he was so quick to call names.

"Wendy Bennett? Who you got over there?"

Wesley and Wendy simultaneously looked toward the voice. He was fairly certain he heard Wendy groan.

"Hi, Iris." Wendy walked toward the woman, motioning Wesley to follow. "This is Wesley Ryan. He's the new vet in town. He's working out at Cheryl's."

"Ohhhhhh, yeeeees. I've heard about him."

Wesley left Nutmeg's pen and walked over to the woman. Where Wendy's size portrayed feminine strength and vitality, this woman was more like John Wallace's wife. She was a mass of soft tissue. Two huge breasts magically set atop and hung on either side of a substantial belly, all covered up with a large-scale flower print muumuu consisting of enough fabric to upholster a couch. Wesley couldn't keep his gaze from wandering over her body, pausing at the two white-socked feet stuffed into orange sandals that stuck out from under the hanging flower garden of a dress. A huge calico cat weaved between her cringeworthy shoes.

It took considerable effort to look into her eyes instead of allowing himself to become hypnotized by the purple flowers billowing over her body.

Wendy, to her credit, continued the introduction as if she'd noticed none of Wesley's reaction. "Wesley, this is Iris Linley. She owns Rose Petal's Place." She motioned down to the cat. "And that is Horace."

He stuck out his hand. "Nice to meet you, Ms. Linley. I've been meaning to stop into your store for a while now."

Iris stared at his hand like it might contain a flesh-eating disease. Her gaze flicked up to meet his—she was older than he'd first realized—then back at his hand. Right when he was getting ready to let his hand drop, she stuck out her own, clasping his fingers in her pudgy grip.

"I've met your kind before. I can honestly say…." She paused again. "It's… nice to meet you as well, Mr. Ryan."

He almost made a comment about her knowing Dr. Fisher, then realized she wasn't referring to him being a veterinarian. "Um. Thank you, I think." A simple thank you would have been more helpful.

She smiled, then almost beamed at him. Maybe she really had been trying to be nice.

He could do that too. "I love your Halloween costume. It matches your store." From his periphery, he saw Wendy bug her eyes and give a tiny, frantic shake of her head.

Iris looked at him in confusion and lifted her hand to finger a small pink fabric rose stuck behind her ear that he hadn't noticed. "Oh, I'd forgotten I'd put that there. I was doing an arrangement earlier and just shoved that in my hair without thinking. I guess it is a perfect outfit for tonight."

Wesley was so confounded by the woman, he didn't even have to remind himself not to laugh. Before he could think of what to say, Iris leaned closer to him, her lowered voice still not a whisper.

"Do you wear that red eyeliner all the time, or is it just part of your costume, whatever it is that you are?"

Wesley shot a glare in Wendy's direction. "No, the eyeliner is just part of the costume. Wendy thought I needed to be a little more festive for the occasion. She turned me into a zombie veterinarian."

Iris leaned back, giving him space once more, and inspected him. "Hmmm. Now that you say it, I guess I can see where you get that." She looked like she was going to bring an end to the conversation, then brightened once more. "Does your... I'm not sure of the word I'm supposed to use... your husband or partner, or lover, or something, have family in town? If so, I've discovered that the gays like to give a snake plant to their in-laws. It's also called a mother-in-law's tongue, you know."

Wesley had to force himself to respond instead of simply staring at her with a mix of bafflement and horror. "No. I'm single, actually. My grandparents lived here, and I inherited their house. Leo and Virginia Mitchell. They passed a couple of years ago."

"Oh! Of course! They were fine folks. They had a girl, didn't they? She moved to Kansas City to be some artist or something?"

"Yes, Anne. That's my mom. She's an artist for Hallmark. Good memory, Ms. Linley."

She waved off the observation. "Fancy. Very fancy. Yes, Leo and Virginia were good people. Always kind to me. Even brought me a casserole when my boys passed." A shadow fell across her face, making her look even older. With a visible shake of her head, she smiled at Wesley. "Well, I should get back. The kids will be coming any minute. If you do want a snake plant for your in-laws, just come on by. It'll be on the house." She looked toward Wendy before Wesley could reply. "You making that hot cider tonight?"

Wendy motioned back toward the percolator on the table in front of her store. "Sure am. Would you like me to bring you a cup when it's ready?"

"That would be sweet, dear." She turned to Wesley once more. She reached out a hand, looking like she was going to pat Wesley on the shoulder, then apparently thought better of it. "Are you going to try to get a job at the church?"

What the hell? "No, ma'am."

She patted his arm. "Very good, then. If anyone gives you a hard time, you just let me know."

She turned away then. Wesley gaped after her before looking over at Wendy and whispering so it was barely more than mouthing the words. "What the hell was all that?"

Wendy shrugged. "I have no idea. Typically she's pretty grumpy. That's the nicest I've ever seen her. She must like you."

He looked back at Iris Linley, her large rump in full floral glory as she bent down, getting something below her minimally decorated table. "I don't think that's what she was feeling. I don't even think that was about me at all."

A FEW people stared at Wesley's eyeliner, but fewer than he'd expected. Most of the time, the introductions were brief as the horde of families descended on Main Street at the exact same time. Even when Wendy introduced Wesley as the new vet taking over at Cheryl's, there were only a handful of people whose eyes widened and who inspected him with knowing eyes. Maybe not as many people had heard of him and his rainbow-clad car as he'd been led to believe.

Wesley realized that after John and the fag comments he'd become somewhat afraid of the people of the town. Wendy was right; he hadn't been exactly being fair. Within twenty or so minutes, he was beginning to feel like he had when he'd visited his grandparents. While there weren't carnival rides or the smell of funnel cakes, with the lights and cheerful noise of the crowd, the downtown felt much like it had during the annual July picnic.

This was what he'd wanted. Exactly what he'd wanted. The very thing that seemed to drive his mother crazy about this place. He was an outsider, no doubt. Even if he lived here a decade, he'd probably still be considered an outsider. Even so, he could feel it. There was an ease here he'd never felt in the city. He'd only experienced it with his grandparents. For better or worse, everyone knew one another in this little town. Even if some of them really didn't like one another, they were kind. You could hear them greet each other on the street, carry on over their kids' costumes, ask about parents and sick family members. They'd inquire about seeing one another at the midweek church service on Wednesday night, laugh about some joke they'd heard a billion times or the retelling of some scandalous event that had happened two decades ago. This was their town and, for many of them, had been for generations. The sound of it all, the sight of it all, made Wesley relax, offered him some comfort, and at the same time, made him sad. He wanted to be part of it, to be surrounded by that much history, that much knowing.

He'd handed out bag after bag of felt bunny pieces and candy bar after candy bar. He introduced himself time after time and asked about people's pets or livestock. He answered question after question about why

Cheryl Fisher was retiring and how he had ties to El Dorado. The majority of people had known, or at least known of, his grandparents, and all offered a kind word about them or condolence for his loss. Wesley could almost pretend to be part of the town.

Then there were blue eyes. Eyes that met his, widened in recognition, held his gaze for long enough to be uncomfortable, then darted away.

Wendy rushed around to the front of the table, hugged all three of the kids, and smacked her brother's huge shoulder. "Travis Bennett, what took you all so long? The night's over halfway done."

The redheaded teenager answered for his father, pointing down at the ground. "We couldn't get the hat to stay attached to Dunkyn's hair just right." He gave the little girl by his side a pat on the back. "You know Avery."

Wendy tapped the girl on the nose. "Yes, I do. My kinda gal. A woman who knows what she wants!" She raised her hands in a flourish, once again sending the flowing aspects of her witch fairy outfit fanning out around her. "I almost forgot! Speaking of Dunkyn, kids, let me introduce you to the man who made him well again."

Wendy motioned for Wesley to come out from behind the table. He did, but moved rather awkwardly, for some reason feeling nervous and a bit guilty. Wendy didn't seem to notice. "Wesley, this is my oldest nephew, Caleb." The boy gave a shy smile and a nod, but didn't speak. Without waiting for any response, Wendy moved on, touching the girl beside Caleb and then the boy partially hidden behind his father's legs. "And these munchkins are Avery and Mason."

Wesley couldn't believe how nervous he was. He was never nervous, especially around kids. Kids and animals, better than adults any day. "Hi guys, nice to meet you all." He focused in on Avery, who was the farthest away from Travis. "I love your outfit. You're a fairy, like your aunt, huh?"

The girl's face twisted in annoyance. She pointed to her wings and then the bun on top of her head, as if she needed visuals in order to explain to the idiot in front of her. "No. Wendy's a *witch* fairy. I'm Tinker Bell." She then pointed to the sidewalk at her father's feet. "He's Peter Pan."

For a moment, Wesley caught Travis's gaze again and quickly glanced away, following to where Avery had pointed. He let out a genuine laugh and knelt, stretching out to pet Dunkyn, who had a green felt hat with a red feather stuck in the brim and a long green swatch of fabric covering his back. Before he could touch Dunkyn, a dog dressed like a skunk collided with his outstretched hand and began licking and whimpering in a crazed manner.

Wendy spoke from above him. "That's Dolan. You haven't met him yet. He's the yang to Dunkyn's yin."

He supposed Travis hadn't filled Wendy in on his and Dolan's first meeting or that Wesley had run away like a scared child—a child wearing Easter-colored spandex. Some miracles existed. "Hi, Dolan. You're a friendly guy, that's for sure. And you make a pretty cute skunk too."

Avery huffed exasperatedly beside him. "He's not a skunk. He's a Lost Boy. Just like Mason."

Wesley looked over, finally really looking at the shy boy. It was like seeing a six-year-old version of Travis. The serious face peered down at him, raccoon ears poking out through his red hair and painted black circles around his eyes. He chewed on his lower lip but stuck out a little hand, giving Wesley a tiny wave.

"Avery and Wendy pick out our outfits every year." Travis's voice was quiet and low. The sound made Wesley relax and get more nervous all at the same time. Travis didn't sound furious like he had the last time they'd seen each other. "She's been obsessed with Peter Pan lately. It seems she's decided that he's gonna fly in from Neverland to come to her next birthday party."

Wesley stood, again marveling that even though he was taller than Travis, he always felt small around him. Travis pointed over at his oldest son, then at his own head. "Caleb is a skunk like Dolan, and I'm a bear, apparently."

Sure enough, skunk ears stuck out of Caleb's messy hair, and a headband with two round red bear ears attached had been shoved over Travis's large head.

"Dad! You're not a bear! You're a Lost Boy! Stop messing up!" Avery's voice rose so she was almost yelling.

Wendy shook a finger toward the girl. "Avery, you don't speak like that. If you keep that up, you'll have to go inside and take a time-out."

Tears welled up instantly in the little girl's large blue eyes. Caleb knelt down and whispered something in her ear. She nodded, then wrapped her arms around her brother's neck and rested her head on his shoulder.

"Oh, hold on. You all keep talking. I'll be right back." Wendy whirled and dashed back behind the table to get candy for a new family that was approaching.

The five of them stood awkwardly, the only motion the skunk-clad Dolan lying on his back pawing both of his forepaws in the air, trying to get his belly scratched.

Wesley complied, kneeling once more and rubbing Dolan's exposed tummy. The dog's swimming motion only intensified. "Wow, he's a little intense, isn't he?"

Travis laughed. It was the first time Wesley had heard the sound. He liked it. "He's more than a little retarded. I'm betting he's the reason Dunkyn's tooth was cracked."

"Dad. I've told you not to say that word." Caleb didn't raise his voice at all, but did have the hint of lecture that only a teenager can master.

"Sorry, bud. I forgot. Old dog, new tricks." Travis actually did sound sorry, and maybe a little embarrassed. It wasn't a sound Wesley would have associated with the man.

With one hand still scratching Dolan's belly, Wesley reached out and rubbed behind Dunkyn's ear. The dog tilted his head, pushing into Wesley's hand. Dolan, realizing the human's attention was split, increased the ferocity of his "swimming." Wesley forced himself to look up at Travis. "How's Dunkyn doing? I should have called to check on him." For the second time, Wesley hadn't been able to force himself to call Travis's number.

Travis offered a small smile, though his tone still sounded embarrassed, as if he'd just gotten reprimanded by Caleb again. "He's doing great. No problems. I'm not letting him chase Mr. Walker's buffalo, just like you said." He paused and cleared his throat, though he hadn't sounded hoarse. "Thank you for coming in early to help him."

Typically Wesley would have offered some smart-aleck remark, like that Travis hadn't given him much of a choice. "No problem. I'm just glad Dunkyn's doing well. He's in great shape for a dog his age. I can tell you really love him and take care of him."

Travis looked flustered and didn't reply.

"It says a lot about somebody. How they treat animals." Wesley wanted to kick himself. He was flirting. What was wrong with him? Right in front of the man's kids! The *straight* man's kids!

"Dad takes really good care of animals."

Wesley followed the sound of Caleb's voice, but the boy wasn't looking at him. He was staring at his dad, unadulterated pride on his face—an atypical teenage expression, if Wesley's teenage nieces were to be trusted.

Avery looked at him, her previous mood forgotten. She looked from Wesley to the still manically wriggling dog. "Dolan! Get up! You're going to ruin your Lost Boy outfit!"

Dolan scrambled to an upright position and shuffled into Avery. Caleb pushed him back and uttered a soft whisper. Dolan sat down, then crossed his front legs over Caleb's shoe.

Wesley eyed the boy. So similar, yet so different from his father. "You've got quite the touch. With animals and kids."

"He sure does. I always say he reminds me of Dickon from *The Secret Garden*. Caleb is kinda magical." Wendy was back, washing away any remains of awkwardness between the men. Or at least overpowering it.

Caleb flushed at his aunt's words, but the hue was nothing compared to what she elicited next.

Wendy motioned across the street. "Caleb, hunny, why don't you let Avery take care of Dolan for a bit and you go see what the kids at the youth group are up to?"

Caleb peered over his father's shoulder, inspecting the growing group of teenagers like they were an alien species. "No. I'm okay."

She tried again. "It sounds like they're having a good time."

He grimaced. "That doesn't sound like a good time, Wendy. Can't you hear that music?"

Travis laughed, triggering another rush of warmth from somewhere inside Wesley. "That's my boy. If it ain't country, it ain't music."

Wendy rolled her eyes. "You're a lot of help." She turned her attention to Wesley. "I was just talking to Mei-Lien. She said her granddaughter is over at the youth building tonight. Weren't you telling me that you knew Mei-Lien's daughter when you were a kid, or something like that?"

"Um, yeah. I doubt we'd even recognize each other, though. Why? Do you think she's over there too?"

Wendy gave him an exasperated look that was nearly as withering as if it had come from Avery. "I doubt that Mei-Lien's thirtysomething daughter hangs out at the youth building, but you can check if you want, Wesley."

"Dad?"

Travis stopped messing with Mason's raccoon ears and looked over at his oldest son. "Yeah, bud?"

Even in the dim light, Caleb's increasing blush grew more visible. "Can you watch Avery? I think Dolan might need a walk."

"A walk? We're walking all over downtown. Don't you—"

Wendy reached across the circle they'd formed and grasped Avery's hand. "Come here, Tinker Bell. You can play with Nutmeg and help me pass out candy while your skunky Lost Boy gets some exercise."

"Yay! Can I have some candy too?" Tinker Bell clapped her hands.

"Of course, dear." Wendy made a shooing motion toward Caleb, who promptly took off down the street, Dolan at his heels. She waited until he was several yards away, then turned to her brother. "Seriously?"

Travis looked at her in confusion. "What'd I do?"

"Haven't you realized how nervous Caleb gets anytime Ashley's name is brought up?"

His confused expression only increased. "Who the hell is Ashley?"

"Mei-Lien's granddaughter, you idiot."

"Well what does she have to do with—oh!" Travis craned his neck to watch Caleb's and Dolan's retreating forms, then looked over at the group of teens at the youth building. "He's going the wrong way."

Wendy rolled her eyes again. "Of course he is, with us all watching him. Mark my words. By the time you're ready to go home, you'll have to swing over there to pick him up, whether or not they're playing country music. And you have the nerve to talk about Dolan."

"Ashley's nice. I like her hair." Mason turned shy eyes up to his father.

Travis smiled at the boy. "Even *you've* met Ashley."

Mason nodded, but offered no more reply.

"She and Mei-Lien come into the store sometimes. Ashley always plays with Mason and Avery."

Travis turned back to look at the crowd past Rose Petal's Place, apparently trying to locate Caleb. "Huh."

Without warning, Wendy turned to Wesley. "So I was thinking. I'm making tacos tomorrow for dinner. You should come over and join us."

Travis's head whipped around, his eyes wide as he stared at his sister.

Wesley had a similar reaction, and it took a couple of tries before he found his voice. "Oh, I don't want to be a bother. You'll have your hands full."

"Nonsense! It's the least we can do for how you helped Dunkyn and all the help you've given me tonight. Plus, it's not any harder to make tacos for six than it is for five."

Wesley shook his head, refusing to look in Travis's direction. "No, Wendy, I don't want to be—"

"Come over around six, or earlier if you want. Bring a six-pack. Travis would like that. We're not taking no for an answer." She looked over for confirmation. Glared over, actually. "Are we, Travis?"

Travis managed to croak out a response. "No. It's the least we can do."

CHAPTER NINE

BY THE time Wendy turned her old Ford Contour off Airport Road and into the garage, it was past midnight. After pulling the keys out of the ignition and opening her door, she caught her reflection in the rearview mirror. She leaned closer, the lighting from the yellow bulb on the car's ceiling harsh against her skin. With stubby, ring-encrusted fingers she smoothed out the lines around her eyes. "You're getting too old to stay up this late, girl. Time to get some heavy-duty night cream." In the back of her mind, she could hear her mother's voice preaching about the sin of vanity. Wendy smiled at her reflection. "And maybe some new eye shadow while you're at it. Something with glitter."

Turning from her reflection, keeping the car door open by pressing one cowboy-boot-clad foot against it, she twisted, reached into the backseat, and picked up the small carrier. She peered in at Nutmeg. "Come on, sweetness. We've had a big day. Let's get to bed."

Once out of the car, she shut the door carefully, lest she wake one of the kids. The pile of Halloween crap in the backseat called to her through the window. She paused, considering. It was either unload it now or in the morning before she took the kids to school. Screw it. Morning it was.

Wendy trod quietly from the garage into the dark house, silently making her way through the hallway, kitchen, and living room, stepping around the maze of furniture she knew like the back of her hand.

If it hadn't been for the warning of Dunkyn's snores, she would have yelped at the hulking silhouette in the recliner. "For crying out loud, Travis. What are you trying to do, give me a heart attack?"

Her brother grunted.

Dunkyn woke at the sound of their voices and padded over the carpet to sniff noses with Nutmeg as Wendy set down the carrier. "I thought you'd be back down to help me clean up stuff after you got the kids to bed."

"Figured you had your new best friend to help with that."

She paused at his tone, for once not really certain what it meant. She'd expected some resistance over inviting Wesley for dinner, but

Travis sounded more than irritated. His words rang of accusation. "If you're talking about Wesley, then, yes, actually. He did stay and help put everything away, and he even helped Iris Linley with a couple of things, if you can believe it. He's a nice man."

Another grunt.

"He is. I'd think you'd think so too, seeing as he saved Dunkyn's life."

"Nothing Cheryl Fisher couldn't have done if she'd been there. Probably would have fixed him the first time—*without* surgery." Travis pushed off his knees, letting out a groan as he stood.

In the dim light, he looked so much like their father, like a bull trapped inside a man's body. Though their dad would never wear a tank top like Travis had on—much too indecent, according to their mother. Wendy had a moment of déjà vu as she looked at him. He used to be more gentle, not so angry. Before. "If we're gonna talk, let's turn on a light or something. I feel like I'm talking to Dad. It's freaking me out."

"We'll do dinner tomorrow, Wendy, just so we won't be rude. After that, though, stay out of it."

Even in the shadows, she could see his eyes flash. He'd never spoken to her like that. It reminded her of her ex, with all his demands, all his chauvinistic mannerisms. Coming from Charles, all it would have done was elicit a fight, which described the last ten years of their marriage. In her brother, it was too new. An unnamed guilt whispered to her. "Travis, I'm sorry if you're angry. That wasn't my intention. I just thought I saw—"

"I don't care what the fuck you think you saw, Wendy. Mind your own damned business." He slapped his thigh. "Come on, Dunk. Time for bed."

She stood statue-like as she watched him go. Her feelings stung; she was angry at herself for not fighting back at the way he'd spoken to her. She'd sworn no man would ever treat her in that manner again. She'd never expected it from her brother.

Travis turned slightly toward her just before his shadow disappeared into his bedroom. "It's fine if you need a new best friend, Wendy. You do what you need to do. But just because you want one, doesn't mean I do." Then he was gone. He and the dog.

Her tentative anger vanished at his words. She should have realized. As soon as Travis had introduced Shannon to the family when they'd met in high school, she and Wendy had become like sisters. Wendy had been one of the few never to feel Shannon's temper. The only disagreements they'd ever had were around Shannon pushing Wendy to leave Charles.

New best friend. Of course. No wonder he was mad. Most days Travis seemed as if Shannon had just died the day before. Since he wasn't moving on, he would take it as a betrayal if she did.

Wendy let out a sigh and picked up Nutmeg's carrier before starting down the hall to her room. How she ached for her brother, for the kids—for all of them, herself included. She'd lost a sister. She silently patted her brother's door as she walked by, whispering a soft prayer. Still, if he ever spoke to her like that again, she'd kick the big oaf in the balls and tell him it was from her *and* Shannon.

She could almost hear her sister-in-law laughing.

BY THE time lunch rolled around, though she'd started off the morning angry at her brother, Wendy had hashed through her feelings and once more separated Travis's words from those of her ex-husband's. She'd called and invited Jason over for dinner as well, as much a peace offering between Travis and her as any real desire to have Jason there. She loved him, almost as much as a brother, so he was always welcome, but if she'd been right about what she'd noticed the night before, Jason's presence wouldn't help the situation.

By the time Travis and the kids bustled into the house, both dogs crashing after them, Wendy was back to being angry. Well, not angry, she decided. Determined. True, Travis might not want her interference, but that was just too bad. Too *fucking* bad, to steal one of her brother's favorite words. If he was being stubborn, too much of a hardheaded man to pull his head out of his ass, then she'd do what she felt needed to be done.

By the time the seven of them sat down to dinner, Wendy had moved from feeling simply determined to a certainty that she was justified in her involvement in pushing Travis to stop living on pause. She'd made Shannon promises, and she intended to keep them.

"So that running outfit doesn't itch?" Jason managed to make his words clear, despite the huge mound of taco in his mouth. "What do they call that again? Spandex? Looks like it would make your junk itch."

"Jason Baker, shut your mouth. We've got kids at the table. One of them a little girl, if you recall." Wendy glared at him, cursing herself for inviting him for the hundredth time since he had arrived. Wesley had shown up just a few minutes before Jason, and it had been awkward enough, but when Jason arrived, an unnamed tension she didn't understand filled the house.

Jason looked at her, unabashed, intentionally taking another huge bite of his taco before addressing her. "So what? Avery was there. She saw it already."

At her name, Avery's red head popped back up above the table line from where she'd been sneaking food to Dolan. "What'd I see?"

Jason motioned toward Wesley with his taco. "The vet's junk bobbing up and down as he was running."

Travis glared at his friend. "Jason, for fuc—for crying out loud, shut up."

"*What'd* I see?" Avery looked back and forth between the men, on the verge of a fit at not being let in on whatever the secret was.

Wendy looked away from Wesley's scarlet face and patted Avery's arm. "Nothing, hunny. You know Uncle Jason sometimes doesn't make any sense."

Jason leered at her. "Hey now. You don't have—"

Avery cut him off. "What's junk?"

Jason howled with laughter.

"I'm going to kill you, Baker." Travis's voice sounded like he meant it.

Caleb kept his eyes on his plate when he spoke, his voice barely a whisper. "Avery wasn't out there, remember? She was inside with Wendy."

Jason wiped tears from his eyes. "Oh right. It was just us boys witnessing the good doctor's junk flop—" Jason stopped speaking abruptly, flashing a glance toward Wesley, then following Caleb's tactic and finding something fascinating on his plate, his face growing scarlet.

Wendy looked at the faces around the table. All three men staring down in shame. Avery growing closer to outrage every moment she wasn't answered. Only Mason looked up at Wendy. His voice was barely more than whisper. "Dr. Ryan ran by and met Dolan while we were carving pumpkins."

Wesley looked up, first at the little boy, then at Wendy. He let out a humiliated sigh. "You can imagine what my running clothes look like, Wendy."

She hesitated for a moment, looking around at Wesley, Mason, Jason, and back again at Wesley before it finally clicked. Unconsciously she covered her mouth as she began to chuckle. "Oh no. Spandex? Really, Wesley? Spandex?"

Forgetting his earlier embarrassment over talking about Wesley's junk, Jason waggled his eyebrows in her direction. "Not just spandex, Wendy. Purple-and-yellow spandex. And little pink shoestrings too."

Wendy gaped at Wesley. She tried not to laugh. She really did. Maybe it was the trying to hold it in that caused the massive snort she issued before throwing her head back in laughter. Within moments almost everyone at the table was dying with laughter, even Caleb. The twins weren't sure why they were laughing, but they laughed. Only Wesley and Travis remained silent.

When she was finally able to breathe again, Wendy shook her head at Wesley. "And you're worried about the Miata? Oh, sweetie. Good thing you're cute. I'd pay good money to see that, though." She paused, considering. "Actually if you've been jogging around town like that, I'm surprised I haven't heard anything about it or seen pictures."

"I only run in the evenings." Wesley's sheepish tone made her start laughing once more.

"Bud, with as bright as your running getup is, it ain't ever gonna be dark enough outside to keep a lid on that." Jason rose up and leaned across the table to smack Wesley on the shoulder.

The gesture surprised Wendy. From Jason, of all people. He was not unkind, but he was about as enlightened as the livestock he tended. Travis met her gaze from across the table, then looked away. It seemed she hadn't been the only one to notice.

Jason scooped up the plate of butter-fried flour tortillas as he sat back down. "Just don't wear 'em when you come pick up the feed for Cheryl's next week. I don't think the old-timers could handle it."

Wesley finally looked the other man in the eyes. "When I what?"

"When you pick up the feed. Cheryl always swings by the first week of the month and gets all the pet food she sells at the clinic. She didn't tell you about that?"

"Yes. She did, actually. I have it on the calendar for Tuesday. Pick up the food from Cedar County Feed. I just didn't know it was your place."

Jason nodded, his expression proud. "Yep. Sure is. Mine and Travis's." He shrugged. "Well, I guess it's Travis's. I'm just the manager, but same diff."

Wendy thought she saw accusation in Wesley's eyes when he looked at her. "What? I thought you knew Travis owned the feedstore. It's hard remembering you don't already know everything about El Do."

Travis spoke up, his voice hopeful. "Is that a problem? If you want, I can bring it to Cheryl's for you. You don't have to come in."

"Now, you stop right there, Travis!" Jason waggled a finger toward him. "I've changed my mind. I think having the good vet here show up in his purple skivvies would be exactly what CCF needs. No such thing as bad press, isn't that what they say? Can you imagine if Jeff Sherman or John Wallace happened to be there? They'd have the whole town talking about it for months!" A piece of ground beef flew out of his mouth as he began laughing once more.

When Travis joined in the laughter, Wendy was suddenly glad she'd invited Jason at the last minute. Leave it to Jason to make her brother less serious. Maybe this dinner could work out after all. Then she noticed the expression on Wesley's face. Whether it was fear or anger, she couldn't tell, though she didn't think it was directed at Jason.

Travis wiped his mouth with the back of his arm. "That would be quite the picture, and stop calling it CCF, for crying out loud."

"Get down, Dolan!" Wendy swiped her napkin across the table beside where Avery sat. In all the commotion, the dog had propped his front feet on the girl's chair, and his head was darting back and forth between all of his humans, tongue dragging on the table.

"He looks like his eyes are about to pop out of his head. You still think I'm wrong about him being an idiot, sis?"

"Dad!" Caleb shot him a glare.

Wendy couldn't suppress a smile. Maybe Travis had decided not to be angry at her after all. Not that it changed her plans, either way.

"Your house is beautiful. It's a great combination of country charm and modern." Wesley's voice grew more confident as he spoke, as if it had taken nerve for him to speak up again. "My grandparents' house is in desperate need of updating."

Wendy grinned at him. "Well, thank you. Everything you see is because of Shannon or me. Travis couldn't decorate a barn if you hung paint-by-number clues everywhere." She gestured to the kitchen. "Shannon was adamant that the kitchen and living room be open concept. Luckily, though Travis can't design, he's good with his hands. She had him tearing down walls the same day as the closing, if I remember. The wall of windows over there was my idea. The chickens all over the kitchen were hers. I'd have chosen rabbits, obviously."

Everyone at the table looked around, following Wendy's motions, as if they didn't see it every day.

Wesley pointed out the window, the sunset painting the field and barn a wash of orange. "Well, it's beautiful. Good call on the windows. It makes the place really homey."

"Mom had you tear down the walls? I didn't know that." Caleb looked toward his father, a wistful expression on his face.

Wendy mentally kicked herself. She hadn't even been thinking. The last thing Travis needed was to be reminded of Shannon.

The soft smile that crossed her brother's face made her think it was going to be all right after all. "Well, bud, that was way before you came along. You know your mom, she wanted things to be exactly the way she wanted them." Travis smiled at his oldest son a bit longer, then looked over at Avery. "Just like you, missy. Always having to have everything *just* right." He gave her a wink.

Mason's soft voice sounded hopeful as he piped up again from behind a towering plate of diced tomatoes, lettuce, and onions. "Did Mom tear down walls in my room, Daddy?"

"No, Mason. She didn't want you to be cold in there without walls. But she was the one who picked out the green in your room and the yellow in Avery's."

Wendy's hope increased at the peaceful tone in Travis's voice, which made it sound like he was enjoying talking about Shannon instead of finding it painful.

"Of course, she had me do all the painting. Said it would splatter in her hair and take forever to get out." His smile faltered then, a cloud seeming to pass behind his eyes.

Wendy tried to think of what to say to salvage the moment but couldn't come up with anything besides bringing out dessert, which would be too obvious, since people were still eating the tacos. To her surprise, Jason came to the rescue. Miracles did happen.

"Can I get the picture, Trav?"

It took a moment before Travis's eyes focused on his friend. "Hmm?"

"The picture. You know the one. The vet needs to see that thing of beauty."

Travis rolled his eyes, a cautious smile returning. "You're a moron, but, yeah, sure. Go ahead."

Letting out a chattering laugh that reminded Wendy of the movie *Gremlins*—she hated that movie—Jason pushed back from the table and nearly frolicked across the living room before pausing in front of the built-in bookcases beside the fireplace. Within moments he came back, already laughing, a large framed photo in his hands.

Wendy groaned. "Oh, that? You're insane, Jason. There's nothing wrong with that picture."

Jason ignored her, instead kneeling down beside Wesley's chair and holding the photo toward him, then pulling it back to hold it against his chest. "Before I show it to you, I gotta know, are you a *South Park* fan, Dr. Ryan?"

Oh crap. And here Wendy had thought they might actually bond over something. There was no way Wesley would watch such filth. Even Travis didn't join in on his friend's love for that garbage.

"Are you kidding? I love that show! I took a trip a few years ago to see the real South Park in Colorado." Wesley's excited tone made him sound like a kid. Wendy was floored.

For the second time that night, Jason smacked the other man on the shoulder. "No shit! Dude, I am so jealous!"

"Jason, what's *South Park*?"

Jason turned and looked at Avery like he'd forgotten anyone else was even in the room. "What's *South Park*? Why, Avery, it's the best show ever made!"

"Can I watch it?"

Jason started to nod, but Wendy cut him off. "You wouldn't like it, hunny. It's a dumb show for dumb adults. I'm surprised Dr. Ryan would watch such things."

"I wanna watch it!" The little girl's voice began to rise.

"Avery, don't start. Be polite or there won't be dessert."

Avery looked over at her father, lower lip puckering.

Travis looked like it was taking all his effort to keep from smiling at her. "Don't look at me, girlie. You do what your aunt tells ya."

She let out a huff but said no more.

Once certain a tantrum wasn't coming, Jason turned back to Wesley and kept going, his excitement unhampered. "Well, you remember the episode about the ginger kids?"

Wesley nodded his head in astonishment like he'd just been asked if he remembered what a french fry was. "Uh, yeah. They have no souls."

A third smack on the arm. "Right you are, man!"

Wendy exchanged wondering looks with Travis. It seemed he was as blown away by Jason's reaction to the gay veterinarian as she was.

Jason's eyes grew wide and he made his voice sound like a game show host announcer. "Well, Mr. Spandex-Wearing Vet, take a look at this!" He flipped the photo around and held it out with both hands, arms straight in front of him. "I swear this is where they got the inspiration for that whole episode!"

Wesley gawked as he looked at it and then let out a laugh that only made Jason laugh harder.

Wendy had to bite her lip to keep from tearing up when Travis began to laugh along with them. She smiled at Caleb, who looked lost but was clearly enjoying seeing his dad looking happy as much as she was.

Jason continued to howl, but managed to keep speaking in little barks between breaths. "I mean… seriously! Look at them. All five of them… and Dunkyn to top it all off…. Have you ever seen so many gingers in one picture?"

Even Wendy found herself chuckling. The picture was of Travis and Shannon and all three kids. Caleb would have been around nine and the twins a little less than a year old. She'd been the one to take the photo. It had taken her several shots to get one where Dunkyn was looking at the camera. "That's just stupid, Jason. There are pictures with me in them as well. We all have red hair."

She didn't dissuade him in the slightest. "True, but there's just something about this picture. It's just so big, and they're all on the picnic blanket, and the sun's hitting just right. Shannon's hair is so long and red, it looks like she's on fire. Even Dunk looks like he just stepped out of *South Park*." Jason let out another howl. "It's the scariest picnic I can ever imagine. I still say we should send in to the writers of that show. I bet they'd make a whole episode out of it."

Wesley had stopped laughing abruptly in the middle of Jason's spiel. He leaned in closer to the photograph, raising a finger to touch it, but stopped before it made contact with the glass. "That's Shannon?" He spoke more to himself than anyone else. "I wasn't even thinking about it being all of you."

All laughter had left Travis's voice. "Yeah, that's Shannon."

Again Wendy couldn't think of what to say or how to distract. She never had that problem.

Wesley turned around in his chair, away from the now-still Jason and the photo, and looked directly at Travis. "She was beautiful."

"Yes. She was." Travis turned from Wesley to Jason. "And she'd have kicked your ass for laughing about it." He sounded like he'd tried to be funny but failed.

Though Jason's voice was soft, there was still humor in it. "Whatever. You know that's not true. She laughed nearly as hard as I did the first time I saw it after you had it framed." He addressed Wesley. "Shannon was gorgeous, and a hell of a lot funnier than her stick-in-the-mud husband over there."

Travis chuckled, a real one this time. "That is true, as well."

THERE WERE no more outbursts during the rest of dinner, and no more awkward conversation about Wesley's choice in clothing either. Wendy was pleased. Dessert went without a hitch. Although, really, pumpkin gingerbread with a hot caramel sauce was a no-brainer. She knew what she was doing.

For once, she didn't give Jason a hard time when he got up from the table abruptly after a text message. Nor did she point out that the girl he was rushing off to hook up with probably had a vast assortment of STDs. The booty call's timing was excellent.

After dessert was over, Travis put on a movie for the twins and came back into the kitchen to help her clean up.

"Don't worry about all of this. You go out and help Caleb give Wesley the tour of the barn." Wendy tried to shove him away from the sink.

"Nah, it's good for him to have to talk to someone other than family. Besides, with his love of animals, talking to a vet could make Caleb think about becoming one. It would be nice to have a doctor in the family." Travis picked up a hand towel and began drying the stack of plates dripping on the edge of the sink.

"Wouldn't hurt you to talk to him either, Trav." She had to be careful, and she knew it. It was a fine line with her brother between pushing just enough to drive him into action and shoving him over the edge into stubbornness.

"Wendy…." He gave her a warning growl. "I thought I made myself clear last night."

She turned to him, her anger momentarily flaring, and shoved a wet finger at his face. "I wasn't going to say anything, but since you brought it up. You will never speak to me that way again. You hear? I didn't take it from Charles, and I won't take it from you." She should stop. She should. "You know Shannon would have helped me kick your ass if she'd heard you talking to me like that."

He had the grace to look sheepish. He looked at the floor for a minute before looking at her again. "I'm sorry, Wendy. I didn't mean to sound like… *him.*"

Wendy knew Travis hated her ex more than anyone, except maybe the doctor who had been overseeing Shannon's treatment. She expected him to stop, not offer any more explanation, but he did.

"You can't think that just because he shows up, the first gay guy in town—"

"You know there are other gay men here."

He gave her a look. "Not the same thing. But fine, just because the first *noncloseted* gay guy in town shows up doesn't mean that—"

She cut him off again. "He's a good guy, Travis. A really good guy. And handsome and kind. And I know what I saw last night."

He growled again. "You have no idea what you saw or what you didn't see, Wendy. You're just making up shit."

"Travis." Wendy wiped her wet hand on her yellow broomstick skirt and then grabbed his bicep when he wouldn't look at her. "Travis."

His blue eyes met hers, and the trepidation in them nearly broke her heart. "Please don't say it, sis."

"I have to. Shannon—"

He looked away. "Don't. Say. It."

She squeezed his arm tighter. "Shannon would be happy."

"Wendy...."

His tone had a warning, but she ignored it. "Well, she would. You know it, and I know it. There's no reason to pretend differently. It would be insulting to her if we did."

He flinched, then met his sister's gaze.

Wendy lifted her hand and gently placed it on his cheek, his red stubble scratching her palm. "Just go out to the barn and finish the tour with Wesley and Caleb. I'm not saying you have to say anything. Just be there. Just... I don't know. Just try to breathe, okay?"

CHAPTER TEN

"FUCK!" TRAVIS managed to remain standing as he rebounded off the door and crashed into the opposite wall of the dorm hallway. He inspected his hand after lifting it from his throbbing nose. Blood. Made sense—it sure felt broken.

His temper rose, but he shoved it down. Losing it was the last thing the situation needed. If he got through the evening with only a bloody nose, he'd be lucky.

With his unbloodied hand, he reached out and twisted the knob.

Nothing.

She never locked her door. He stuffed his hand into his left pocket, his fingers grazing the keys. Before he'd even withdrawn them, he let them fall back into place. Using his key if she'd locked the door would guarantee more than his nose would be bleeding.

"Shannon! Open the door. We gotta talk." Though he was loud, Travis tried to keep the anger from his voice, as well as the panic that was mounting every second.

He couldn't lose her. He couldn't.

Life wouldn't be right without her.

What if she left him?

What if she told?

There was no reply, no responding yell. She really was mad.

He knocked on the door. Firm, insistent, but not angry, not desperate. A calm knock. "Come on, Shannon! Let me in!"

A click of the door latch sounded, and Travis stepped back, giving her room.

The door didn't open. The handle didn't so much as jiggle.

Then a creak.

Travis glanced down the hallway, three doors over. Sarah Peterson poked her head out of her doorway.

"I think if Shannon wanted to talk, Travis, you'd already be in her room."

God, he hated that nosey bitch. He ignored her and knocked again. Maybe pounded a little bit this time.

Sarah's squeaky voice called out to him. "I'll call campus security if you keep harassing her."

He bared his teeth at her. "Shut up, Sarah. Mind your own fucking business."

Her eyes bugged, but her chin jutted forward in indignation. "You can't tell me what to do just because you have a penis. There's such a thing as women's rights, you know!"

Shannon's voice startled Travis. He'd been so focused on Sarah Peterson he hadn't noticed Shannon open her door. "Oh, shut the hell up, Sarah! You know you're only here looking for a husband. Which is why you've slept with the entire male population of Blaine Hall and your GPA hasn't risen above a 2.5 in four years!"

"Bitch." One final squeak from Sarah, and her door closed.

"God, I hate her." Shannon's tone was vicious.

Travis made a mental note to drop a box of chocolates off at Sarah's door. She'd gotten Shannon to come out a hell of a lot quicker than he would have.

Shannon threw open her door the rest of the way and whirled on Travis. "As far as you, I have no desire to see...." Her blue eyes flashed from fury to concern in an instant. "You're bleeding."

"Yeah. I smacked into your door."

She laughed. Actually threw back her head and laughed.

Things would be okay.

Travis let a small chuckle escape.

Bad move. Her gaze returned to him, the angry gale dark in her eyes. "Go away, Travis." She turned again, long red ponytail spinning around her, and slammed the door shut. She'd swung it with such force, it bounced back open.

Travis hesitated a moment to see if Shannon was going to shut it again. He had no desire to lose a finger. After a moment or two, he cautiously stepped into her dorm room.

"I don't want you here, Travis." She was sitting on the edge of her twin bed, legs pulled up and resting on the footboard, arms wrapped protectively around her knees. The sadness in her eyes was worse than the anger.

Much worse.

And he'd put it there. There seemed to be more to it as well. She looked... scared. If anyone had cause to be scared, it was him.

Ignoring her command, Travis stepped farther into the room and shut the door behind him. His glanced at Peggy's twin bed. Gone, good. No roommate. They had some time to themselves. "Shannon, please, let me—"

"What? Let you what, Travis? Explain? Make promises? Tell me you love me?" The anger was back. Though she wouldn't meet his eyes.

"Shannon, I'm a little confused. You said that I—"

She almost sprang from the bed, rushing toward him. She punched his chest with the heel of her fist. "I know what I said. Don't throw it in my face."

He waited for her to hit him again. He'd let her. He deserved it.

She didn't, his submission draining her of her fury, leaving only sadness once more.

They stood in the middle of the dorm room, less than a foot apart. Travis could swear the cinderblock walls were shaking, getting ready to crumble.

They didn't.

All of Shannon's trophies and ribbons stayed perfectly still. The photo of her blue ribbon Dutch Booted Bantam didn't crash from the shelf above her bed. How she'd cried when that rooster had died their freshman year of college.

When Shannon spoke again, her voice was barely more than a whisper, lacking all of her typical strength and grit. "It was different than hearing about it. It was different seeing it."

His face burned, and he felt tears roll down his cheeks. Tears of sadness or shame, he wasn't sure. Not that it mattered. "I'm sorry. I didn't want to hurt you. If I'd have known it would hurt you...." Was that true? Would he have stopped?

"Don't. It only makes it worse." She turned from him, took a few short steps, and sank onto the bed. She reached back and yanked at the band holding her hair captive. The long strands fell around her face, giving her shelter.

What was he supposed to do? How could he fix things? There was so much he didn't understand. So much he couldn't figure out. So much he'd never been able to figure out. But he knew he loved her. That wasn't a question. If she weren't in his life, he didn't want a life at all.

Travis kneeled in front of her on the woven oval rug that took up the space between Shannon's and Peggy's beds. He wiped the drying blood from his face with his sleeve. When she didn't move, he dared to reach out and place both hands on her knees. "I love you, Shannon."

Her blue eyes rose and looked at him through her shield of hair. "I know you do. I love you too."

"Then we'll figure this out. Right?" His voice cracked and more tears fell.

She dipped her head. "I don't know how we can. I can't give you what you need."

"Yes, you can. You do! My God, Shannon, I love being with you."

"Then why him? Why were you with him?" She still didn't look back up, but he could hear the tears in her voice as well.

"You said you didn't mind. That since it wasn't a girl, it wasn't cheating."

"So it's my fault?"

Travis slipped his hand beneath her hair, cupping her cheek, lifting her face to look into his. "No. That's not what I'm saying, Shannon. I just thought it was okay with you. You seemed to understand when we talked about it last year. I'm always careful, always. I'd never put you at risk."

Shannon gave a disgusted groan, but didn't pull away. "I hate myself, Travis. I swear I do. That is what I should be worried about, I know. But I'm not. Just seeing him under you. Seeing you do to him... what you do to me. I guess I didn't know it would look like that. You're supposed to be mine."

"I am, Shannon. I am yours. Completely." He was going to lose her. He'd known it had been too good to be true. The fact that she hadn't left him when he'd confessed his attraction to men a year ago had been a miracle enough. When she'd given him permission to explore those feelings and get them out of his system, he'd known she couldn't possibly mean it.

"Are you? You're mine? And what are you to that man?"

"Nothing, Shannon. Nothing. I'm nothing to him, and he's nothing to me."

"What's his name?"

Travis considered lying, making up something. "I don't know. I didn't ask."

She gaped at him. "You didn't ask? You don't even know his name?"

He shrugged, shame seeming to pour cement over his shoulders. "It's just sex."

"Like with us?"

"No. Not at all. It doesn't mean anything with another guy. It's just sex. That's all it is. I love you. When I have sex with you, it's because I love you."

Shannon didn't speak, just searched his eyes. Whatever she was looking for, he prayed she'd find it.

"I hate myself for feeling this way, Travis, but I believe you, and I wish I could say that I didn't. That you are a liar. That you don't love me." Shannon pulled back a section of hair, tucking it behind her ear, exposing more of her face to him. "I can't believe I'm shallow enough to think that I can live with it as long as you don't love someone else. As long as it's just messing around with other guys. I'm weak. I have to be. If I weren't weak, I'd leave you."

He'd made her feel this way. He wished she'd claw his eyes out. "I'll stop. I don't have to do it. I can—"

"You're attracted to men. You can't stop that." Shannon interrupted him, her voice filled with frustration, but still lacking anger. "You're bisexual. I've done some reading about it since you told me. You're bisexual."

Travis grimaced. "No, I'm not. I'm straight. I just am attracted to guys sometimes."

She laughed, actually laughed, albeit bitterly. "Well, what do you think bisexual is, stupid?"

Hope pricked at his heart. She'd called him stupid. She hadn't left him yet. "I don't want to be bisexual, Shannon."

She sighed and tentatively reached out and stroked his cheek. "I don't think it matters what you want. It's just what you are, Travis. You can't change that, and neither can I. Though I wish I could."

"I'll go to church. My folks always said prayer changes everything."

Shannon scoffed. "Yeah, right. We both know better. And I thought you said you'd already tried that."

"Yeah, my whole life. But now that you're here—"

She cut him off again. "No. No lies. And I've been here for a while now. I'm not the miracle, Travis."

"Shannon, I'm not lying."

"I'm not saying you are. At least you're not trying to. It's a lie that you can change something like that. And, I guess it's a lie that I don't care if you fuck guys."

He grimaced again.

She laughed once more, a more genuine sound this time. "You don't like it when I curse, but it's okay for you to have gay sex."

"Come on, don't say that."

She grew serious again. "I don't ever want to see that again."

"I'm not going to do it again, Shannon. I promise."

She lifted a hand between them. "No. No promises. It will hurt that much more when it happens again. I'm not asking for that. I just don't wanna see it. I don't want you to tell me about it. Just do it as you need to, and I'll be fine. And, yes, be safe."

"Shannon, I promise."

Her eyes flashed. "I said don't! Don't! I can't take it—"

He grabbed her hands. "I. Promise. Only you. Even with guys who don't wanna... well, you know, ones who don't feel the way I do... they want to sleep with other women. Other than their girlfriend or wife. And they don't. Same thing. I promise I won't sleep with anyone else. Even if you say you're okay with it."

"It's not the same thing, Travis."

"I. Promise."

They quit speaking for a while. Just sat there in silence, looking into each other's eyes, a few more tears gradually making their way down their faces. After a bit, Travis rested his head in Shannon's lap, and her fingers grazed through his hair.

His knees began to ache, and then his legs fell asleep. Still, Travis didn't move. He was afraid to. He'd almost lost her. They'd already been together six years. He couldn't explain how he'd fallen in love with her at first sight any more than he could explain his attraction to other men. Both would be hell to live without, but only one lack would make him want to die. As melodramatic as it sounded, even in his own mind. He would not be able to live without Shannon Pope.

After a while Shannon spoke once more, her voice betraying her exhaustion. "There was a reason I came to your dorm today."

At first he didn't dare move, anxiety spiking. When she didn't speak further, he lifted his head off her lap and looked up into her beautiful face.

"I skipped class today." Shannon's gaze flicked away, a mannerism she only betrayed when she was nervous. "I had to go to the doctor."

Travis was beside her on the bed in an instant, though his numb legs nearly gave out from underneath him. "Are you okay? Shannon, are you okay? Why didn't you tell me? I would have gone with you."

Bitterness painted her words. "You had other things you needed to do it seems."

He flinched, unable to respond.

"Travis, I'm sorry." Shannon reached for him, an unusual pleading in her voice. "That wasn't fair. I know that."

He tried to smile at her. He doubted he succeeded.

"I should have asked you to come with me. I just needed to go on my own for some reason."

Travis sat perfectly still and kept his tone soft, afraid of making the wrong move or saying the wrong word. "Babe, are you okay?"

Shannon nodded, at last pulling the remaining hair away from her face and looking at him fully.

She was terrified. Travis had never seen her look like that.

"I'm pregnant."

He stared at her. Her words could not cut through the layers of his fear.

"I'm pregnant." She leaned toward him this time. "A little over six weeks."

Travis narrowed his eyes, trying to get her to stay in focus. "You're pregnant? Like with a baby?"

Shannon's sharp laugh cut through some of the fog that was trying to suffocate him. "Yes, you moron. I'm pregnant with a baby. Our baby."

It clicked. Travis grinned, his smile so wide it hurt his cheeks. Then it fell away. "Is that okay?"

Shannon looked at him nervously. She was showing him so many expressions he'd never seen her wear before this day. "That's what I wanted to know from you."

"Yes. It's okay with me. Is it with you?"

A smile began to cross her face. "Yes. I was so excited to tell you. Then I walked in and—"

Travis cut her off before she could finish, though he was never certain if it was so she couldn't finish or due to his own excitement. "We're gonna have a baby!" He wrapped her in his arms so tightly Shannon had to push against him to get a breath.

A week later they eloped, much to their families' resentment.

Two weeks later, they graduated from Missouri Southern State University.

Another week after that, they moved back to Shannon's hometown. Travis got a job at Cedar County Feed. Shannon applied for a teaching position at the high school for the upcoming school year.

One week later, Travis noticed Shannon was beginning to show. Finally.

Half a week later, Shannon miscarried.

CALEB'S VOICE drifted from inside the barn. Travis halted, remaining just outside the door. He motioned for Dunkyn to sit. The dog plopped down at Travis's feet, his side resting against the wall.

"The chicken coop is through this door. There's an inside and outside section. I'd show you, but I don't wanna wake them up. They're real pretty. They're show-quality Cochins. Have you seen them before?"

Wesley's voice was easier to hear than Caleb's. "Oh yeah. They're beautiful. I'm kinda surprised, though. I had your dad pegged for more of a meat breed of chicken. I'd think he'd prefer a Cornish or Jersey Giant. More practical."

"He probably would, but Mom liked these. She showed chickens in high school. That's how Mom and Dad met. They were in FFA. They met at some FFA event. I don't remember where.... You know what FFA is, right?"

Wesley laughed. It was the first time Travis had heard the man laugh when he wasn't feeling nervous. "Of course I do. Future Farmers of America. It's a great organization. Are you in it yet? You're a freshman, right?"

He could hear the pride in his son's words. "Yep. Sure am. We have a herd of Limousin cattle. Dad gave me three of my own a few years ago. I'm breeding them, hoping to get a prized bull from them one day." Travis couldn't believe how much Caleb was speaking. Most of the time it was like pulling teeth to get him to say more than a sentence or two. Of course, he had always been most comfortable around animals.

A cool breeze swept across the night, bringing the smell of earth and hay to Travis. It was a clean smell, fresh and wholesome. It smelled like home. There was something so peaceful about this time of day, when all the animals were sleeping, and everyone was fed. All at rest. It was peaceful, but also one of the lonelier times, only surpassed by the wee hours of the morning, before sunrise, when he could no longer pretend that Dunkyn was more than a dog.

Wesley's voice sounded forced, but just for a moment. "Lots of people here have Limousins it seems. Are yours the red kind?"

Caleb sounded cautious. "Because we all have red hair you mean?"

Another laugh. "No. I didn't think about that. The red Limousins are my favorite. You've got a point, though. All of your family has red hair, and Dunkyn and Dolan too. That is a lot of red if you've got red cattle too. Are the Cochin's red?"

"Some of them, but not all. And, yes, all the cows are the red ones." Travis could hear the scraping of metal—he wasn't sure what they were doing—and then Caleb spoke again. "Have you ever had to scare an opossum outta the chicken coop at night?"

"Good God, no! Have you? Those things have vicious teeth. They're nothing but huge rats." Not often, but sometimes, the vet's intonations gave him away as much as spandex and pink shoelaces.

Caleb laughed. Loudly. Dolan barked, laughing with his master. "You bet. They're kinda scary. Nasty things, huh?"

At the sound, Travis slumped against the wall of the barn with a small thud. He didn't remember the last time he'd heard his son laugh, at least not like that, not like he'd never known pain.

Nearly refusing to believe, Travis lifted a hand and wiped his fingers across his eyes. He pulled them away, inspecting them in the dim starlight. Sure enough, they were damp. Well, goddamn.

"Did you hear that?" Travis heard Caleb's voice, followed by footsteps.

Dolan popped around the corner of the door with a yip of greeting. He jumped, pushing his forepaws against Travis's leg, and then slid off to pounce on top of Dunkyn, who let out an annoyed grunt.

Travis wiped his eyes again and pushed off the wall, standing on his own before his son rounded the doorway.

"Dad!"

"Hey, bud. Dunk and I were just coming out to see how you two were doing." He patted Caleb on the shoulder. "You giving the lay of the land?"

Wesley emerged behind him, his tone more guarded than it had been mere moments before. "You've got quite the animal expert on your hands."

Caleb's smile was shy but bright.

"He should be. He's been obsessed with animals since before he could speak." Travis couldn't help but feel the tension that passed between the three of them, tension that hadn't been there before. It didn't take a rocket scientist to determine the cause of that.

Wesley looked away from him, seeming to find it easier to make eye contact with Caleb than Travis. "If you ever want to come spend the day at the clinic, just say the word. You could shadow, even see a surgery or something, if you'd like. If it's okay with your dad and Wendy, of course."

Caleb turned excited blue eyes toward him. "Can I, Dad? That would be awesome!"

Travis looked at Wesley, inspecting to see whether he was serious. Even as he did so, he wondered why. It was obvious the two of them had bonded. It was him who made them uncomfortable. "Yeah, of course. That would be great. Thank you, Dr. Ryan." The man flinched at being addressed so formally. It was subtle, but Travis had seen it. He looked back at his son. "Why don't you and Dolan head back in? Would you help Wendy with the twins before bed?"

"Yeah, I always do." Caleb looked nervously between the two men, like he was afraid his dad was going to beat up the vet or something.

Travis tried to make his smile as gentle as possible. "I'll pop in and say good night before your bedtime, okay?"

Caleb didn't look convinced all was okay but nodded nonetheless. "All right." He patted his thigh. "Come on, Dolan."

They watched the boy and his dog until they disappeared into the house. Travis searched desperately for what to say, but he needn't have bothered.

"I'm sorry if I overstepped my boundaries, Mr. Bennett. I should have asked you first before inviting Caleb to come to Cheryl's."

And didn't that just make him feel like shit. Wesley seemed to force himself to meet Travis's gaze.

"No, no reason to be sorry. I was actually just telling Wendy inside that I hoped Caleb might get interested in being a vet from talking to you."

Dunkyn padded over to the entrance to the barn and nudged Wesley's leg with his nose.

Wesley knelt, his fingers sinking into the dog's long fur. "Hey, old man. It's good to see you doing so well."

"I haven't properly thanked you for that, Dr. Ryan." Travis cleared his throat. It didn't help. It was his heart beating in his ears, not a frog in his throat. "Thanks for helping Dunkyn so much."

Wesley looked up from where he knelt, a forced smile on his lips. "No. You thanked me. And it's my pleasure. You've got a really good dog, Mr. Bennett."

How he hated hearing the vet say his name like that. Damn Wendy, he probably wouldn't have even noticed if it hadn't been for her putting thoughts in his head. Yeah. It was her fault. "There's one more thing I've been meaning to say to you."

The vet's brows rose. "Oh really?" His voice sounded nervous. Travis hated that too.

"Yeah. I just wanted to tell you—" He stumbled for words, waving his hand in the air as if searching. "Can you stand up? It's hard talking to you with you down on the ground like that." He heard the gruff tone of his voice. Why did he sound like that? He tried to adjust. "Would you mind standing, Dr. Ryan? Wesley?"

"Of course." Wesley stood, his expression of trepidation increasing with the use of his name.

With him standing so close, Travis had to tilt his head up to look Wesley in the eye. "I, uh…." *Dammit, why was this so hard?* "I just, um… wanted to say I'm sorry for…."

Wesley's brows rose even farther, almost disappearing under his sweep of dark blond hair.

The words burst from Travis in a rush. "I want to apologize for calling you a fag the other day. I was just worried, and it was Dunkyn." Again his hand seemed to flail about in midair on its own accord. He stuffed it in his pocket. "There's not an excuse. I just…. Well, I'm sorry."

"Mr. Bennett, it's oka—" Wesley broke off, then shrugged. "Thank you. I appreciate that. It's forgotten. People say stuff in those moments. It happens."

"Well, it shouldn't. At least not from me." His gaze darted away, but he forced it back, looking at the vet's brown eyes. *Brown eyes.* "And enough with the Mr. Bennett stuff. Just Travis, okay?"

A smile played at the corner of Wesley's lips. "Okay."

And there was that awkwardness, again. What came next? What was he supposed to say? Wendy would know. He could almost hear Shannon laughing at him—almost.

"You've got the most decked-out barn I've ever seen." Wesley took a step away, lessening the tension, and made a sweeping motion over the barn's interior.

"Yeah?" *Nice one, Bennett. Nice.* The man provides you with a conversation starter and you simply say *yeah. Dumbass.*

"Yeah, it's beautiful. And spotless. If I didn't know better, I'd think it was all for show and you just used the place for wedding receptions or something." Wesley looked away from the log timbers Travis had used instead of support beams. "You don't, do you?"

"I don't think too many brides want the sound of chickens clacking during their ceremony. They're quiet now, but you should hear those biddies in the daytime." Travis motioned overhead to the pulley system that ran to the midpoint of the ceiling and then angled over to the opening to the hayloft. "Plus, that probably wouldn't look good in wedding pictures."

Wesley followed his motion. "Are those skylights?"

"Yes, but I was talking about the equipment I use for the hayloft."

"I've never seen a barn with skylights before." Wesley walked over to the trough, folding his arms over the top rail and looking out into the dark field. Half of one of the barn's walls was open to the outside, forming a large lean-to, and a wooden trough ran the length of the interior corral. "I assume there are doors outside you can slide shut when you don't want the cattle to come and go from here as they want, or to keep the snow from blowing in?"

Instead of answering, Travis walked to the wall between the door to the chicken coop and the opening of the lean-to. He pushed one of two buttons. There was a click and an electronic whirr, and then the doors from either side of the opening to the field began to slide closed, meeting in the middle with a soft thump. There was a questioning squawk from a sleep-disrupted chicken in the other room, then silence.

Wesley turned toward him, and Travis couldn't tell if the look in his eyes was impressed or accusatory.

"You know, you all can tease me about my fancy clothes and running gear all you want, but I've got nothing on you. I feel like I'm on the farm version of MTV's *Cribs*."

Travis couldn't suppress a grimace. "I never watched MTV."

"Can't say that surprises me. I'm just saying that you're the fancy one."

"Actually most of this stuff, the *fancy* stuff, at any rate, was all given to me from the companies we deal with at the feedstore. I guess they figure if they give me their products and I like them, I'll tell the folks that come in the store."

Wesley glanced at him, then turned his attention back to the barn. "Well, whatever the cause, it's pretty amazing. I can't imagine that there'll be that kind of throwback from the suppliers of vet clinics, but I guess I'll find out. Maybe some free pet food or something."

Travis hit the button once more. This time a greater number of chickens let their annoyance be heard. "It's too pretty a night to have those closed. Another week or two, and we wouldn't be able to be out here without bundling up first. Kinda chilly already, actually."

"I like it—makes me excited for Christmas."

Travis could feel Wesley watching him but didn't look away from the dark horizon showing through the trough. "You shoulda brought your dog with ya tonight."

Wesley took a moment in responding. "I, uh, don't have a dog."

Travis turned toward him. "You don't got a dog? Please don't tell me you're a cat person."

Wesley laughed. Not in the same way he had with Caleb less than ten minutes ago, but laughed nonetheless. "No. No cat. No pets at all."

"You're a vet. How do you not have a dog or something?"

"I had a dog a couple of years ago, I just...." Wesley suddenly looked nervous. "I don't think you want to hear this story."

"Oh. Did he get sick like Dunkyn?" The night seemed even colder suddenly. "Cancer?"

"Oh no. Nothing like that." Wesley reached out and gripped Travis's shoulder, then whipped his hand back when he realized what he'd done. "Ah, sorry about that. And, no. No cancer. Nothing like that. My ex, Todd, and I had two dogs." He paused again. "You sure you don't mind hearing this?"

"Just because I said fag doesn't mean I'm a homophobe." Travis shrugged. "I'm just an ass sometimes."

Wesley's laugh was a little more like the one Travis had heard before he'd interrupted the vet and his son. "Point taken. But, not even because of that. Sometimes, it's one thing to know a person is gay in abstract, and a different thing when you hear details."

Travis forced a smile. "I'm not sure about all the abstract or not. Wasn't trying to get into psychology or anything. Just tell me the damned story already."

Wesley inspected him, as if trying to determine if Travis was irritated or not.

"Like I said, I'm an ass. Don't read into it. Tell me why you don't have a dog, Dr. Ry—Wesley."

"Okay, then. Like I said. Todd and I broke up about two years ago. We lived together. He took the house. It had been his before we started dating. And he took the dogs, Gucci and Prada. The breakup was hard enough, but losing the dogs too.... Losing all three of them at once. I guess it was good that he kept the dogs. I, uh, well, I wouldn't have been that good a daddy to them afterward."

Again words failed Travis. What was the right thing to ask? Was he supposed to say he was sorry, see if Wesley was okay? "What kinda dogs?"

Wesley peered at him, maybe trying to see if he was serious. "Toy poodles."

Travis grimaced again. "I thought you said they were dogs."

Wesley laughed. A real laugh. Travis almost looked around to see if someone else had entered the barn to elicit such a response. When Wesley settled, his brown eyes met Travis's, and they held on—longer than they should have, long enough that Travis should have looked away, long enough that it should have made things uncomfortable.

It didn't.

And then, it did. Wesley's eyes widened in surprise, and he looked away, a flush rising to his cheeks.

Travis searched for words once more, trying to fix it. *Help me, Shannon. You're the one who made me promise. Fucking help me.* "How long were you and your ex-boyfr—how long were you and Todd together?"

"A little over nine years. We were together the whole time I was trying to get into veterinary school, interning at the zoo, all the way through to where I was getting ready to open my own clinic close to our house." Wesley's face darkened. "All the way through till our life was supposed to settle down, really start."

"Why'd he leave? Was there cheating?"

"Yes and no. We were open, so not cheating like that, but he found someone he wanted to replace me with, I guess you could say."

Travis scowled again, though he tried not to. He was trying to not pass judgment. "You and he were open? As in, you were dating other people?"

"Are you sure you want to hear all this?"

"Sorry, Wesley. I wasn't trying to pry. You don't have to explain." Travis began to turn around. It was time to bring this to a close anyway. What the fuck had he been thinking?

Wesley reached out and grabbed his arm once more, this time not releasing his grip until Travis looked back. "Actually it's fine. It feels good to talk to someone else about him. And, as far as your question, I wouldn't say we *dated* other people, just messed around if the need arose, as long as we were safe." A bitter laugh escaped. "Although I guess dating around was exactly what Todd was doing."

"I can't imagine that. If anyone had ever touched Shannon, I'd have killed them." Even the thought of that, with her gone four years, caused anger to flow through him.

Wesley relaxed, leaning against the boards of the trough once more. "How long were you and Shannon together?"

The question surprised Travis, making the anger leave in an instant. When was the last time anyone had asked about Shannon and him? There were endless questions about how he was doing and how the kids were getting along, but never anything about her.

"You don't have to answer that. Sorry. I know a breakup and what you went through aren't the same thing."

Travis reached out, fearing Wesley might walk away. He tried to ignore the desperation he felt in the gesture. "No. It's not that. I just haven't talked about her in forever. At least not like this."

"You want to?"

"Yeah." Travis nodded and felt his eyes burn. Luckily he didn't cry anymore. Outside the barn door had been a fluke. "We were married for sixteen years, but we'd met way before then. Just like Caleb told you, I met Shannon in high school. We were juniors." He realized he'd just outed himself, that he'd admitted he'd been eavesdropping. Wesley didn't let on. "We got married when we were twenty-two, same year we graduated from college, and moved here. She wanted to be near her folks."

Wesley waited when Travis stopped talking. When Travis didn't speak again, Wesley spoke softly, barely more than a whisper. "Do you want to talk more about her?"

Travis nodded again, feeling stupid at not being able to just keep speaking.

Maybe understanding what Travis needed, Wesley only waited a few more moments before beginning to learn about Travis's wife. "How long ago did she pass?"

"Four years." That fucking burning in his eyes. Did his voice just tremble?

"How long was she sick?"

Travis's brows knitted. Had he said something? Maybe during Dunkyn's surgery?

"Wendy told me."

"Oh." Travis took a deep breath, or at least tried to. "Two years. Kinda. The cancer came right after the twins were born. They said they got it all. Said she was good. Clean. She wasn't. Shannon died right before their second birthday." More burning. And was his throat clenching up?

Travis looked toward the barn doors, suddenly realizing how much he'd said. No one there. He glanced back to the house. Only the kitchen and living room lights were on, and Caleb's.

The twins were asleep.

He looked back at Wesley. "The kids don't know that. Not even Caleb. I don't want them to ever think it was their fault."

Wesley didn't even look confused, understanding the unspoken. "I will never say a thing. So the cancer…. Shannon's cancer was caused by the pregnancy?"

"Choriocarcinoma." Big word. He hadn't even been able to say it correctly at the beginning. Ugly word. Now it spun around in his brain when he slept, the dark letters forming, swirling, then reforming in his mind. Fucking word. "You know about it?"

Again Wesley's voice was so soft. So warm and kind. Like Shannon's, but nothing like Shannon's. "No, I don't. I'm sorry. But it's okay. I understand what it means, for the most part."

"She lost her hair." Why had he said that? What the fuck did that matter?

Silence.

Painful, but not awkward.

"What was she like?"

Travis almost flinched at the question, but didn't. How could this man not know what Shannon had been like? The whole world should know, should feel her absence. To this man, to Dr. Ryan, to Wesley, it was like Shannon had never even existed. How was that even possible?

The burn went away as he spoke. The hands around his throat loosened. The whispers in his ears increased. "She was…. Shannon was so… alive. She was so many things—beautiful, funny, smart. But mostly, she was alive."

Travis met Wesley's gaze, and the vet didn't look away, only nodded in encouragement.

"She was like her hair. She was on fire. All the time. Either laughing loudly or mad. Man, that woman had a temper." Travis laughed. The whispers laughed with him. "Everyone loved her. Everyone. She was the town sweetheart. She'd grown up here. She taught Ag at the high school, at least up to that last year. Helped out with the babies at church too. At the church where Wendy takes the kids now. I never went. Still don't."

What could he tell the man so that he'd see her? So that he'd know Shannon? So that he'd miss her too? "She was strong. Brave. She'd fight with everything in her. Always looking out for the loser. Caleb got that from her. Always looking out for me. No matter what I did or what I was. She fought with me and for me."

Why was the barn still standing? Why weren't stars crashing around them outside? Why was he still here?

"She was my best friend."

A tear fell from the brown eyes that looked at him, slowly making its way down the recently shaved cheek.

Travis always got angry when someone outside the family cried about Shannon. Sure everyone had loved her. But she'd been his. She'd been the kids'. No one else's.

He felt a tear tracing a path down his own stubbled cheek, or maybe it was just a ghost tracing the path he saw on the other man's face.

"She gave me Dunkyn."

They stood less than two feet apart, the modernized barn bright around them and the glow of the house Shannon had redesigned visible through the wide doorway of the barn.

The roosting chickens were tucked away for the night. A herd of red Limousin cattle was sleeping in the tree-speckled field.

The early November evening wind swirled the browning leaves.

A grave with a smoothed-out moniker lay at peace across town.

Whispers soothed, just out of earshot. Two more tears fell.

The stars remained in their places. The barn stood strong.

Four-year-old promises came due.

"You made Caleb laugh."

Wesley didn't respond, the shift from mother to son too abrupt to follow.

"He laughs, of course. With Wendy. With the kids. Sometimes with me. But he sounds like a man when he laughs. Like a man who has to hold his family together. Who lost his innocence too long ago." Travis couldn't deny the tear that fell this time was his. It was definitely his. "He laughed like a child tonight. I heard my boy laugh. It sounded like hope, like he might believe there is more for him than just the twins and this town. More than opossums in the chicken coop. More than his fucked-up father."

Travis grabbed both of Wesley's arms, squeezing his shoulders so tight it probably hurt.

Wesley didn't flinch; nor was he startled. He just looked into Travis's eyes.

Travis held him still. He didn't inspect Wesley's face, didn't let his gaze wander over the man's body, didn't ask for permission—neither Wesley's nor his own.

He pulled Wesley to him, one hand traveling up Wesley's shoulder and around the back of his neck, pulling the man's face nearer.

Travis felt Wesley flinch when their lips met, but only for a moment before he gave in.

There wasn't electricity or fire. Only pressure and warmth. He held Wesley there, their lips pressed together.

Wesley's fingers grazed over Travis's shoulders, touching, darting away, then returning. They slid up his neck, and then a hand held his cheek. Fingers long and smooth and strong rested on either side of his ear. A warm palm pressed against his stubble.

A groan broke the silence. It sounded of surprise and sadness. It sounded of relief. It was gone before Travis realized it had come from him.

The hand still held his face while an arm passed over his shoulder and down his back, pulling Travis closer.

At the pressure of Wesley's body against his, Travis released his hold on Wesley's neck and shoulders, wrapping his arms around the other man's back, crushing Wesley to him.

Then the kiss was more than pressure. More than warmth.

They pressed up against the planks of the trough.

Another groan. Maybe more than one.

Travis felt his own strength as he held Wesley's hard body to him, and was surprised at the power of the arms that encircled him.

For just a moment, Travis's eyes flitted open, as if he had to be convinced this was real and not another delusional dream. It was real. And though he could hear her whisper, it was not Shannon kissing him back. He'd known it wasn't, hadn't expected it to be.

He let his eyes close again. He didn't pull away as he felt himself harden against the other man. Against Wesley.

Wesley's lips parted, and Travis let his tongue caress the opening before deepening into the kiss.

His fingers sank into soft hair, short at the base but longer as his hand rose on the back of Wesley's head, desperately pulling him closer.

They kissed.

Animals slept.

They kissed.

The barn continued to stand.

They kissed.

Maybe a few stars fell.

CHAPTER ELEVEN

IRIS LINLEY'S cat, Horace, had taken up most of the morning. Wesley loved all animals, and cats were no exception. However, this cat, like his owner, was abrasive, making the experience less than enjoyable. Granted, Horace had something in his throat obstructing his breathing, but he'd still managed to leave a deep cut on Wesley's hand, which he'd have to treat later.

Wesley had lied to Iris Linley. Not a habit he typically engaged in with clients, but he thought it prudent in this case. After he pulled the long silver string of tinsel out of Horace's throat, Iris's eyes had narrowed in suspicion. Wesley quickly stuffed it into a biohazard bag and commented that cats eat the darndest things and that yarn and string tended to be a favorite. Luckily there was enough gunk from Horace's throat stuck to the tinsel that it could have passed for yarn, if he'd moved quickly enough. From Iris's expression, Wesley doubted his duplicity had been successful. He would have to call Wendy and warn her to expect fallout from her witch fairy costume.

He couldn't figure out Iris. One moment her expression suggested she found him revolting, but then it would shift, seemingly with effort, and she would smile. Not a pleasant expression on her, either, but preferable. Maybe. She again told Wesley to let her know if someone gave him a hard time while he was in El Do and that she approved of his profession, that working with animals was a better choice for him than working with children. Wesley didn't even attempt to try to understand, and he couldn't imagine what she would do if he did report any problems to her. Maybe sic Horace on the offending party. He was halfway tempted to tell her about John Wallace. He'd like to see the calico work his magic on that particular man.

The good thing about Wesley's time with Horace and his mistress was that for a few hours he couldn't obsess about the events from a couple of nights ago. It was the first time in two days his brain had focused elsewhere. However, as he and his little yellow Miata were heading out to Cedar County Feed, Horace was forgotten, save for the occasional rub over the already itching parallel lines on his left forearm.

It had all been so fast. On the one hand, Wesley felt like he should have realized it from the beginning. He prided himself on having excellent gaydar. Of course, Todd had always told him that since Wesley always thought everyone was gay, the times he was accurate didn't really count.

But Travis Bennett? Really? He'd replayed the events on a continuous loop. He would convince himself that he'd made it up or dreamed it. However, the stubble burn over his skin attested differently. That had faded quickly. Maybe it had been a dream too.

Travis Bennett. Gay.

Totally hot, in a Dad-I'd-like-to-fuck kind of way. Sure. Check. Double check.

Massive shoulders, chest, and arms. Check. Oh, yes. Check.

Sexy, manly belly. Check. Wesley could feel its hard pressure on his lower back as Travis shoved into him. Or at least he wanted to.

Travis Bennett. Gay. Gay enough to kiss the breath out of him.

What *was* that?

Actually the kiss wasn't what led Wesley to think the father of three was gay or at least something besides a zero on the Kinsey scale. He'd received… kisses, let's say, from plenty of straight men. Especially over the past two years.

It was the look in Travis's eyes. He'd held Wesley's gaze just a moment too long. Wesley had seen inside and realized who stood in front of him. Straight men just didn't get that look. Not even during *kisses*. It was a look that couldn't be mistaken.

But he had to be mistaken. Right?

And so what? Even if he weren't mistaken. Even if Travis Bennett had signed up to throw out purple confetti and pink shoestrings on the next gay pride float to wander down the middle of Main Street, so what?

He was a father. He was mourning his wife. He was a fortysomething man who lived in a small town. A fortysomething closeted man, apparently. Yeah, sign him up for that mess. Just what he needed after Todd.

Wesley wasn't here for a hookup, not with John Wallace, Travis Bennett, or anyone else. He was here to be Wesley, to get his life back to being his own. He didn't need a hookup. Or a relationship.

Relationship? God, his brain loved to screw him over. How did he jump to relationship?

Gay or not. A Kinsey one or six, or not. A hookup or relationship, or not. It didn't matter. It was beside the point. Travis hadn't made contact at all since that night—no call, no dropping by the clinic, nothing. Not even Wendy had called, which was strange.

There was not going to be a hookup with a closeted father, nor would there be a relationship.

Relationship, *really? My God. Let. It. Go.*

Travis Bennett was off-limits. He was nothing but confusion, nothing but pain, nothing but blue balls. Nothing but…. Nothing. Travis Bennett was nothing.

But that kiss. *That* kiss.

Wesley had never had a kiss like that before. Never. He kept replaying it over and over, each time feeling like he was watching some stupid Disney cartoon. Kisses like that didn't happen.

He knew. He'd done more than his share of kissing. For the past two decades, he'd done extensive kissing. He'd had every kind of kiss—hot and heavy, romantic, in love, in lust, forced. He'd ordered the sample platter of kisses and had turned it into an all-you-can-eat buffet. He'd had them all.

It seemed there'd been a kiss that had been left off the menu. Maybe it was one that wasn't supposed to exist.

More like one that didn't exist. It screwed with your perception and mind, but it was disguised like that mythical kiss. Ah, yes. The deceitful, fooled-you, chewed-on-your-heart-for-a-long-time kiss. He was familiar with that one.

This one had been different.

Kissing Travis Bennett was different.

There'd been just pressure and warmth, a simple connection.

There was also sweetness, something he would never have guessed would reside in Travis Bennett.

There was sadness. That one made sense.

There was desperation. That made sense too. But Wesley had had desperate kisses before. Many times. This was a different kind of desperation. There was something else there with it. He couldn't name it.

There'd been a promise in that kiss. It made absolutely no sense, so he'd thought that was the lie within it, the deceit of it. But a promise had been there. It *had* been there. Fuck him, but he knew it. If that kiss really was more than just a messed-up fantasy from too much leftover Halloween candy, then a promise had been there. He wasn't sure what the kiss promised, but it was something.

Then there were the moments after their lips parted, when their faces were inches apart. Travis's breath—smelling of caramel and beer—was warm against his skin. Travis's blue eyes held his gaze, and the man's rough thumb moved gently under Wesley's eye, over his cheekbone.

Yeah. Not real.

Not. Real.

Maybe in a Disney cartoon where two dogs find love over extralong spaghetti. Maybe. In real life? No. And if, by chance, if by miraculous, messed-up chance, that actually could be real in this life, it wouldn't be here. Not in this small town. Not with a father, in a barn.

It wouldn't be with the man whose wife was buried in the same graveyard as Wesley's grandparents.

It wouldn't be in the same town where he'd been called a fag twice in a week.

It wouldn't be for Wesley Ryan. That wasn't in his cards, even if it were real.

There was no possible way it was real.

WESLEY PULLED up to Cedar County Feed, impressed by the size of the massive steel structure, and already looking for a reason to turn the Miata around and zoom to safety. Like he needed another reason. Travis Bennett was reason enough.

And, behold, ask and you shall receive. There was his second reason—the beat-up truck parked in front of Cedar County Feed, its left rear tire resting uncomfortably on the sidewalk. He knew that truck, and the sweat that dampened his brow had absolutely nothing to do with kisses, Travis, or puppies sharing spaghetti.

John Wallace.

What were the chances?

Wesley turned the key in the ignition, and the engine purred to life. He shifted out of park before he paused again. No. No way was he going to turn tail and run. Because of what? Some redneck who gave rednecks a bad name? Some closeted asshole who had scared him more than made sense?

He turned off the car, slid out, and shut the door gently. Horace wasn't the only thing that could drive Travis out of Wesley's mind. He made it up the sidewalk, past the truck, and took the stairs one slow step at a time. He paused and took a deep breath at the front door.

Drama queen.

Did he really have to wear the plum-colored shirt? Today?

Then he was through the door. The earthy smell of grain washed over him.

Jason Baker looked up from the paper he was reading, his feet propped up on the counter. No one else seemed to be in the store.

Good. He could handle Jason. He actually kinda liked the guy. Crisis averted. He raised his hand in greeting.

Jason did not. He craned around in the opposite direction, looking back into what appeared to be a storeroom. Towers of stacked feedbags arranged on wooden pallets could be seen through the doorway. After he turned around, Jason put the paper down on the countertop, popped off his chair, and hurried toward Wesley in a tiptoed shuffle. "Hi, Wesley. Listen, now's not a good time. Why don't you come back in a couple hours? Maybe we can bring the pet food to ya. Will that work?"

Wesley looked past Jason, trying to see whatever it was Jason was trying to hide. It couldn't be that bad; Jason had been lounging, eating a burger. Dumb question. John Wallace. "Ah, sure, Jason. No problem. Just give me a call when—"

Too late.

"It's not gonna do a damn bit of good if you give me more of the same shit." Wesley knew the loud voice before the pockmarked face turned the corner from the back room. "You're all saying the same shit. You're in cahoots, and don't think I don't know it. You got some scheme to get my land. You and that faggot-ass vet. I don't know why you got it in your craw to—"

John Wallace's voice broke off as he saw Jason and Wesley in the doorway.

"You!" John lurched toward them, barely missing the corner of the counter in his haste.

The potbellied, skeletal man elicited the same primal fear in Wesley that he had the night of the storm. He looked like a zombie. Like he wouldn't stop until he'd eaten Wesley's face off. This time no new anger-filled voice rose to Wesley's defense. His fists didn't clench. He didn't see red. He just wanted to run.

"Who the fuck you think you are, calling the animal control on me?" He was less than ten feet away. "I know it was you, cocksucker."

There was a massive red blur rushing from the back room. Travis wasn't going to get there in time.

John's hands were thrust out in front of him, fingers curved like claws, ready to wrap around Wesley's throat. "I'm gonna teach you to fuck with my family."

Then a body stood between them, and less than a heartbeat later, John Wallace lay sprawled on the concrete floor.

It was a moment before Wesley realized the man in front of him was Jason—his left fist clenched at his side, the right one just pulling back from colliding with John's face.

John started to push off the floor, strings of expletives filling the room. Jason took another step forward, a leg raised like he was ready to kick. "Don't you get up off that floor, Wallace."

"Fuck you. I'm gonna sue you for assault." Despite his venom, he stayed where he was, ass and elbows on the ground. He looked up to where Travis now stood behind him. "And you. I'll fucking take this shit store from you. First for getting in cahoots to steal my land, and then for taking part in having me beat up." He flinched as Jason's shadow moved over him.

"Jason! Enough!" Travis's voice was a bullhorn, stopping Jason and silencing John's rant. "Get up, Wallace."

John glared at him but didn't move.

"Get up."

John twisted, looking like an overturned insect trying to right itself. "I'll make sure to put in my report that you didn't even offer to help me stand. Just stood there while your thug and his boyfriend assaulted me."

Jason laughed. A genuine laugh from the sound of it, but not masking his anger. "Boyfriend? Now you got me and the good doc here bumping uglies? What *you* been thinking about? Missy not giving ya what you need? Too much of a woman for ya?"

"Jason! Shut up!"

Jason glanced up sharply at Travis, looking like a wounded puppy.

John Wallace glared at the two of them, first Travis, then Jason, then Travis again. "I'll ruin you, Bennett. Mark my words." He turned toward Wesley, and Jason sidestepped, blocking him. John didn't spare him a look. "Don't worry, sweetheart, I'm not gonna damage your little cocksucker." His watery eyes locked on Wesley, and his rotting teeth showed through his snarl. "Not yet. But I will. I'll ruin this shop, but you? I'll do more than ruin your fucking vet clinic. You'll pay for what you did. You'll pay."

"Get the fuck out." Travis grabbed John by the back of his collar, partly lifted him off the ground, and shoved him out the door, almost hard enough to send the man careening down the stairs. "Shoulda kicked you out years ago. You're nothing but trash. Show yourself again around here, and there'll be nothing left of you to make a report." Then, as an afterthought he added, "And that also goes for showing up at the clinic."

He didn't wait for a response, just turned back into the feedstore and slammed the door.

The three men just stared at one another, Travis's back against the door, Wesley and Jason breathing heavily only a few feet away.

It was Wesley who finally broke the silence. "I'm sorry I froze. I didn't know what to do." There was that shame again. It was new to him. Just another fag who didn't know what to do when a bully showed up.

Travis straightened, moving away from the door. He faced Wesley angrily. "Don't you dare apologize for that asshole. I was serious. I should have thrown him out years ago. All he's ever done is bitch and complain and try to get stuff for free."

"Did you really turn him in to animal control?" Jason squinted at Wesley skeptically.

So much for the possibility of having a friend in Jason, and for having whatever it was with Travis. As much as they might hate John Wallace, he was one of them. Wesley sighed in resignation. "Yeah."

"Why?"

Wesley answered Jason's question, but looked at Travis. "He called me out there the other day to check out his cattle. The conditions were horrid, and the animals all but completely neglected. And a bad case of foot rot was starting up." He paused, not really sure he wanted to know the answer. He wouldn't be able to look at Travis Bennett the same way if he'd seen the condition of the cattle and not done anything. "Have you been out there?"

Travis shook his head. "No. I haven't, but I told him myself that what he described was foot rot."

Wesley let out a breath he hadn't realized he'd been holding. That was good. He looked between the two men. "I didn't know I'd get him mad at you all. Of course, I didn't even know you owned this place, but still."

Travis closed the distance between them and grabbed Wesley by the shoulders. For an instant, he thought Travis was going to kiss him. "I said, don't apologize. I'd have turned him in myself if I'd have realized. Quit fucking apologizing because of that little bitch."

As suddenly as he'd grabbed him, Travis let go, quickly taking a step back.

From the corner of his eye, Wesley noticed a confused expression pass over Jason's face. He wiped it away when he realized Wesley was looking at him, and his charming, carefree grin returned. "Besides, this is all gonna work out great. Knowing that bastard, he's gonna go all over town telling everybody I'm the fag that's doing the vet."

Travis stared over at his friend. "How's that good for you?"

Impossibly Jason's smile widened, and he winked. "Give me a chance to make the rounds again. Tell those girls they gotta do what they can to turn me back."

Wesley couldn't suppress a laugh, and his nerves lessened somewhat. Maybe he hadn't just ruined things after all.

"I swear, Jason Baker. You are one retarded son of a bitch." Travis grinned. "And Caleb already told ya to quit saying fag."

Jason shrugged. "Yeah. Well, he also said to quit saying retarded."

"I ALMOST feel like I fit in here, riding in this big truck. Maybe I should think about trading in my Miata."

Travis glanced at Wesley from across the cab, then focused again on the road, turning left from Main Street onto Highway 54, which cut through the heart of town. "As long as you're wearing that shade of purple, I don't think it will matter what you drive, and if the look on your face means anything, I don't see that happening. You looked like you were offering up one of your children to be sacrificed."

"Yeah, probably not gonna happen. I'm not a truck kinda guy. Though riding in one is kinda fun." Wesley smoothed out his shirt and glanced over his shoulder, taking in the huge backseat and the extended truck bed. The shifting of his body caused Dunkyn to snort in annoyance and adjust his position between the two men. "You've almost got a limo here."

"Right, me in a limo." He patted the dash of the F-350. "With three kids, Wendy, and two dogs, it was either this or a van. And I'm not driving a van. Plus, it technically belongs to Cedar County Feed, so it's all a tax write-off."

The silence was abrupt and awkward, and it arrived about every ninety seconds. Considering the drive from the feedstore to the vet clinic was about ten minutes, there shouldn't have been many of them, but they seemed to keep coming. They made Wesley nervous. They made him want to ask things—things about kisses, wives and families, and more kisses. Stuff he shouldn't ask. "So, uhm, have you named her?"

Travis spared him a brief, quizzical glance. "Who?"

"Your truck. Don't all cowboys name their trucks?"

Travis let out a dismissive puff of air. "No. No name. I love my truck. It's great. But no names, and it definitely doesn't have gender. Though I've thought about getting those big balls to hang off the rear hitch. Wendy says that's not appropriate when you're driving around a six-year-old girl." He shrugged. "And I agree actually. I don't need Avery asking those kind of questions." Travis peered over at Wesley again. "And I'm not a cowboy."

"Really? You look like one. The boots, the Wranglers, the big cowboy belt buckle. You own a feedstore, you have livestock. You take care of buffalo."

"Nope. Too many people call themselves cowboys. It's disrespectful and lessens the real thing. Cowboys herd up their cattle on horseback, do rodeos, all that shit. I've never done any of it."

"So you're a farmer?"

"Not the kind you're thinking. Don't have a field or crops or anything."

"Rancher?"

Travis paused as he turned right onto Carman Road, then inspected the vet momentarily. "Why you trying to put a label on me, Wesley?"

Wesley felt heat rise to his cheeks. Surely Travis was aware of the double meaning of that question. "I wasn't trying to. Just making conversation. And sometimes labels help. I'm a veterinarian. Pretty easy."

"Well, I'm Travis Bennett. That's my only label. I'm a Missouri boy who owns a feedstore and tends Mr. Walker's buffalo. That's it."

Again that horrid silence. It lasted until Travis pulled into the clinic's parking lot. Travis backed up the truck to the front door, turned off the ignition, left the keys hanging, and stepped out of the truck. He patted the edge of the seat. "Come here, Dunk."

With a groan, Dunkyn stood, taking his time to stretch before closing the short distance between him and his master.

"Always a production with you, isn't it?" Travis swept him into his arms and placed him on the ground, then rubbed the top of the dog's head affectionately.

Wesley had the clinic's doors open and lights turned on in less than a minute, and then he returned to help Travis unload the twenty-five bags of pet food out of the back of the truck.

They worked in silence, each lifting one or two of the heavy bags onto his shoulder and carrying them into the clinic. Dunkyn paced back and forth, always two steps behind Travis. Wesley watched Travis, though he tried to be discreet, which was fairly easy with the bags over his shoulders. The man truly was a bear, all muscle and girth as he lifted a new bag of feed onto his massive shoulders. Wesley couldn't remember ever seeing a porn that was set in a veterinary clinic, but would he ever love to change that.

He had to quit thinking of Travis that way. He had to. It wasn't why he was here. It was the exact opposite of why he was here. And the man was straight—well, obviously not completely, but straight enough it would be nothing but drama to think otherwise, no matter what Kinsey number Travis Bennett fell on.

Despite the tense silence in the truck, the silence that settled on them as they moved the feed was comfortable and easy, maybe because they were working together, no matter how mundane or small the task. If only Wesley could keep his mind from drifting to places it shouldn't. But still, Travis had kissed *him*. Wesley hadn't started anything.

All too soon they were done. The truck was empty. The pet food display was refilled, and the extra bags were placed in storage. The silence in the front office once again grew palpable.

Dunkyn began rummaging through a basket of large rawhide bones by the front door. He rooted through them with his nose, searching for one that met his approval. Wesley had been meaning to move them. He wasn't sure why Dr. Fisher had placed them there within easy access of all the dogs that came through the door.

"Dunk, knock it off." Travis nudged the dog with the side of his foot, scooting him away from the snacks.

Dunkyn huffed in exasperation and grabbed the nearest rawhide between his teeth, whirled quickly, and waddled off to lie at Wesley's feet. With a satisfied exhale, he began to chew.

Travis glared at the dog. "Sorry. I'll pay for that one."

Well, that answered his question. Smart woman, that Dr. Fisher. The treats would stay where they were. "No, it's okay. Just consider it payment for having to deliver the feed. Not sure why I thought I could get all that in the Miata." Wesley bent down to scratch Dunkyn's ear but then stood up quickly. "Oh crap. The Miata. I wasn't even thinking. We loaded up your truck, and you said to hop in and I did." Was his heartbeat increasing because he was nervous or excited? "Do you mind driving me back out to the feedstore so I can pick up my car?"

Travis pulled his phone from his pocket and peered down at it before looking at Wesley. "It's nearly eleven. Do you have anyone coming in soon?"

"No. Slow day. The only appointment I have is at two."

"Good. Let me text Jason and let him know I'm bringing him a hickory burger. You ever had Simone's?"

"Not since I was a kid."

"Well, then, it's settled. We're getting lunch. Miata and purple shirt aside, you're never gonna be a true El Doradian if you're not eating at Simone's."

"Travis, you don't have to do that. We can just get my car." *Shut up!* Why was he trying to get out of eating with Travis? The insta-sweat that ran down his spine might be the reason.

"Consider it payment for that bone." Travis gestured toward Dunkyn chewing happily at Wesley's feet.

"I thought that was the delivery fee."

Travis shrugged, his expression unreadable. "Well, I want Simone's, and there's never a day Jason doesn't want a hickory burger, and it's kinda on the way back to the lot, so if you wanna get something too, great. Just warning you, though; if you're gonna sit there and watch me eat, I'm not sharing."

Wesley hesitated, though he wasn't sure why he did. Actually he was completely sure why he hesitated. "Well, okay. I guess anything that will help me get grafted into this town will help the clinic." He grabbed the keys off the counter. "And this shirt is plum, not purple."

Travis cocked an eyebrow at him. "Seriously?"

CHAPTER TWELVE

AT THE rear of a rectangular lot of potholed, thin cement, Simone's was nothing more than a twenty-by-twenty whitewashed cinderblock square, half of which consisted of windows. A thirty-foot-long carport stretched out in front of it, turning it into a makeshift Sonic wannabe. A narrow red strip of paint wrapped around the perimeter. If you weren't a local, you'd take a quick glance at the shabby building on Highway 54—if you noticed it at all—and then keep going another half mile until you came to the actual Sonic.

The carhop brought the food-laden red plastic tray and slipped it over the F-350's partially rolled-down driver's window.

"Here ya go, Mr. Bennett."

"Thanks, Krissy." Travis handed her two twenties over the pile of food. "Hey, wait a minute. Why are you here this time of day? I only see you in the evenings."

Krissy's sallow cheeks flushed. "I had to drop out."

"Why? Your mom sick?" Travis chided himself—not every kid's mother got cancer. Still, Krissy's mom, Paula, had been in Shannon's class. Krissy was the second-oldest of five, most with different fathers. If Paula got sick….

"No, Mr. Bennett. Mom's fine."

Travis felt like he was intruding, but he couldn't help it. Krissy had worked at Simone's since she'd been a freshman. She was there nearly every evening and all day Saturday. She was one of the hardest working kids he'd ever seen. There was something so fragile about her. "You've only got till May, Krissy, and then you're done. Don't drop out now."

He was horrified when her eyes filled with tears. "I'm pregnant, Mr. Bennett. Gotta earn more money. Sarah's barely four, and it's all we can do to make ends meet now." Sarah was the youngest of Paula's brood.

Travis had no idea how to respond. His heart ached for the girl, an image of Shannon at her age superimposing itself over her face, then morphing to an older Avery. Dear God.

Unaware of his inner turmoil, Krissy looked past him, eyeing Wesley on the other side of the F-350.

"Hi." Wesley's little wave caught Travis's attention.

"Oh, Krissy, have you met Dr. Ryan? He's taking over for Cheryl at the vet clinic."

She jerked a little, like she'd gotten caught staring at something she shouldn't. "Hi. Nice to meet you." She glanced away quickly, a knowing look in her eye.

Wesley waved again. "Nice to meet you too, Krissy."

Krissy dug through the pockets of her hip apron, then extended a large wad of change toward Travis.

"Keep the change, Krissy."

She gave him a slight nod and began to walk away.

"Hey, Krissy." Travis called out to her, without thinking through what he was getting ready to say.

She glanced back, partly turning. "Did I forget something, Mr. Bennett?"

"No. I just, ah…." Again Shannon stood before him. "Jason and I have been kinda swamped at the feedstore lately. If you get tired of serving food, hit us up. It'd be nice for someone to run the register or something so we could focus on all the other stuff we have to do. We could set you up on our insurance plan. You and the baby."

Her tiny hand rose to settle over her flat stomach. "Really? Even without me graduating?"

"Well, we'd figure that out too. You'd need a diploma to work at Cedar County Feed. Maybe you could do some GED classes or something. Something online."

Krissy's face fell. "We don't have a computer, Mr. Bennett."

"We got one at the store. You can do it while you're working. In between customers or something."

She looked at him as if he'd lost his mind.

"Talk to your mom. See what she thinks."

Krissy nodded slowly, then turned away again.

Travis watched her until she entered the glass door and stepped back up to the counter. Jason was gonna ream him out. Well, fuck it. CCF was his business. He could hire who he wanted. *Cedar County Feed*, goddammit. He was gonna kill Jason for getting that fucking acronym stuck in his head.

The scent of grease cut through his thoughts, making his stomach rumble. He angled toward Wesley. "If you haven't had Simone's since you were a kid, you're in for quite the—" The expression on the vet's face cut him off. "What?"

A grin played at the corner of Wesley's lips. "You need a high school diploma to run the register at the feedstore?"

"Well, I.... Ah...." He ran a hand nervously across the stubble of his jaw. "Gotta keep the place reputable."

Wesley looked as though he was about to say something— something gushy or sweet or... something. Travis wasn't sure he could handle that. Krissy had left him feeling a little exposed. The extralarge truck cab seemed to be crushing in around him. He gestured out Wesley's window toward a rusted metal picnic table on the edge of Simone's property. "Why don't we eat over there?"

After following Travis's motion, Wesley looked back with a raised eyebrow. "Won't Jason's food get cold?"

"He don't care. Jason would eat a Simone's hickory burger if you'd left it standing out for three days." Without waiting for more discussion, Travis opened the door, careful to not spill the suspended tray of food on the window. "Will you help Dunkyn out?"

To Travis's surprise, when Wesley patted the seat after getting out of the truck, Dunkyn padded over to him and allowed the vet to lift him from the cab. He also noticed how Wesley checked for cars circling into Simone's lot before placing the dog on the ground.

After settling on either side of the picnic table, Dunkyn contentedly gnawing on his rawhide bone beneath them, Travis began to divvy up the food. He left Jason's portion in the bag but pulled out his and Wesley's burgers and bags of wavy french fries.

No words were spoken as greasy parchment was folded back, revealing the burgers, thin grilled onions, and melted cheese dripping down the sides.

Travis watched as Wesley sank his teeth into his burger and let out a long, contented groan. He was a strange mix of a man. Though much leaner than Travis, Wesley was long and solid—he looked sturdy. The cut and angles of his face were masculine, yet Travis wasn't sure of the correct label.... Refined, maybe? Even the cut of his dark blond hair, just starting to gray at the temples, was a similar blend of masculine but moneyed. That was it. Wesley Ryan looked moneyed. Kinda fancy, with his clothes and well-groomed brows. At first glance, the vet almost came off feminine, but Travis decided Wesley just looked citified. Then the image of Wesley jogging past his house flitted through his mind. Well, maybe he was a little feminine, with the pink shoelaces and all. He was handsome, though. He was attractive.

Handsome. Attractive. Travis didn't want to be thinking these things. He hadn't until that night in the barn when Wesley made his son laugh. He could still hear that voice, warm and soft and low. He could still see the horizon of stars lighting up behind him. Travis had gotten carried away. He'd lost his mind. He'd touched a man in a way he hadn't in nearly two decades.

It had rocked him. The feel of Wesley's lips. The firmness of his body. So different from anything he'd felt for so long.

The warmth, though…. That was the same. That he recognized.

After that, he'd gone through two days of inner turmoil and barely contained guilt and terror. Even Wendy hadn't asked questions, which was unheard of. She was never afraid of Travis's moods.

He'd told himself he was going to stay away from Wesley. Nothing good could come of it. The kiss had been a mistake. A stupid, reckless mistake. One that had kept him up the past couple of nights. One that kept him returning to the cold shower. One that kept him away from Shannon's grave, and that had never happened.

"Are you okay?"

The world suddenly returned into focus—a pinpoint focus that narrowed in on the brown eyes inspecting him with concern.

Travis steadied himself with a hand on the edge of the table. *Fuck.*

"Travis? Are you all right?" Wesley leaned across the table toward him, one of his hands cautiously stretching out to touch Travis's arm.

At the contact, Travis flinched away. "Yeah. I'm fine. Sorry." He glanced down. There were several bites missing from Wesley's burger. "How is it?"

Wesley's brows knitted in confusion, and then he followed Travis's gaze. "Oh. Amazing, actually. Takes me back to eating these with my grandparents. I don't know how I'd forgotten." He motioned toward Travis's burger. "You haven't even tasted yours."

Travis lifted the burger and took a huge bite, then looked away from Wesley's inquisitive eyes. As he did, he noticed Krissy watching them through the wall of windows. Behind her, the old cook peered at them as well.

He forced the bite down his throat, the unchewed lump nearly getting stuck. He took a swig from the large Styrofoam cup. "I guess we should probably get back. You're probably right. Jason would want his burger to be at least partially warm."

Wesley's eyes flicked from him to where their observers continued to stare at them. "Oh." He lowered his burger to the paper he'd been using as a placemat and began to wrap it up. "Probably a good idea."

Goddammit. "Wesley, listen. I'm sorry."

"No. Don't be. It was nice of you to, ah, deliver the feed and get me lunch. I really appreciate it." Wesley's voice was cool, a tone Travis hadn't heard from him before. Not that he'd heard all that much. Still, he didn't like it.

"Wesley, really… never mind. Let's finish eating here, and then we can go. Jason will be fine."

Wesley eyed him for a moment, then let out a long breath, a determined posture squaring his shoulders. "Listen, Travis. It's okay. Not my first rodeo. There's no reason to say anything else. I'll rent a little trailer or something every month to pick up the feed, and we're good. I'll even call Mr. Wallace and let him know you and Jason had nothing to do with the report. I'm not sure he'll believe me, but I'll do my best." Wesley looked away. "Everything else will be… forgotten. No big deal."

John Wallace. That fucker. He'd nearly forgotten the events of the past couple of hours.

Travis had decided he was going to do what Wesley was now suggesting—forget all of it. The kiss hadn't really happened. He hadn't really felt any attraction to Wesley. He hadn't desired the feel of the man's body pressed against him again. He hadn't actually felt the hint of passion in their kiss.

It was a blip. Nothing more. Just a small, meaningless blip.

The kiss was nothing to him. Meaningless. After a while, he'd even forget the vet's name.

Then… John Wallace.

The fear had spiked through him as he'd rounded the storeroom door and seen John Wallace tearing toward Wesley. The fury. He'd known he wasn't going to be fast enough to intercept John before he hit Wesley. He'd also been certain he was going to kill the man, until Jason had stopped Wallace cold.

Then John Wallace had called Wesley that word. That word that sounded so different from the vile man's mouth than from his own.

There hadn't been time to understand where that need to protect had come from. There certainly wasn't time to name it. All he knew was that the man had threatened something important. Something that was his.

"Don't you dare call that fucker."

Wesley flinched at the sound of Travis's voice, looking back at him in surprise. "What?"

Travis felt the muscle of his shoulders and arms tense as he leaned forward, like they were ready to rip someone apart. "Don't you contact John Wallace. He's nothing but a fucked-up piece of shit. You stay away from him."

A range of emotions warred over Wesley's face, but Travis didn't attempt to identify them. "I can take care of myself, Travis. And it's obvious tying your name up with mine isn't going to help you any." He glanced meaningfully toward their audience at the drive-in's window, then back.

Travis nearly glared at Wesley, his earlier desire to flee forgotten. "I don't give a fuck. Let people think what they think." Even as he said it, he wasn't certain the words rang true.

Wesley inspected him. And though he didn't jump to words like Shannon would have, there was something familiar in the way he looked at Travis, something that left Travis feeling vulnerable. While he couldn't say he liked the sensation, he didn't shy away from it, either.

"I don't understand what you're getting at, Travis."

"I just don't want you involved with John Wallace. He's no good. And I don't trust the piece of shit farther than I can throw him." Travis realized his fingers were squeezing into his burger, a greasy mixture of catsup and mayo starting to run down his forearm. He'd never liked the man, but the thought of him being in contact with Wesley brought an edge of panic he normally didn't associate with Wallace. He wasn't sure why, but it was there.

Wesley glanced around and leaned forward when he was certain they couldn't be overheard. His gaze was direct, his words firm but not angry. "You know that's not what I'm talking about. The kiss the other night. Then this morning, driving me to the clinic, bringing me here. Is this some kinda game?"

Travis's throat constricted, a sheen of sweat breaking out over his skin despite the chill of the fall day. What was he supposed to say? He didn't know what he was doing either.

Wesley continued to stare at him. Waiting. The firm set of his jaw and the determination in his expression seemed anything but feminine. After several more tense moments of silence, he pushed himself up off the bench and began to turn away. "Fine. Like I said. Let's forget it. None of it ever happened."

"Wesley, wait." Travis's teeth were clenched so hard the muscle of his jaw tingled.

Wesley turned back.

"Just wait a second, okay? Give me a minute."

The resolve in Wesley's expression softened slightly, and he returned to the table and sat back down across from Travis.

Again, Travis had no idea what to say. Or think. Or feel. A static buzzing grew in his brain where thoughts were supposed to form.

This time when Wesley spoke his voice was gentle and soothing, like he was speaking to a wounded animal. Travis heard pity in his voice as well. He didn't like it.

"Listen. Travis. It's really okay. No harm, no foul. Okay?" Wesley nodded encouragingly. "We really can just move on. We don't have to talk about it. We don't have to see each other. Not a big deal."

Not a big deal? His first kiss with someone other than his wife in the past twenty years wasn't a big deal? The static was nearly deafening.

The past two days of him constantly wanting to do it again were not a big deal?

"You'd had a few beers at dinner that night. It happens. It doesn't mean anything. It happens to every guy every once in a while. It doesn't mean anything's wrong with you. You're not turning gay. It doesn't make you a fag." Wesley looked away from him then, his voice losing some of its firmness. "Or whatever."

Again the protectiveness rose up in Travis. Similar to when John Wallace had begun tossing around the word. "Stop it."

Wesley's eyes flashed toward him, a spark of irritation clear in that moment.

Travis tried to keep the anger out of his voice but failed. He wasn't sure who he was angry at—himself, John Wallace, or Wesley. "Don't insult me like that. Don't insult yourself."

"I don't know what you want from me, Travis." Wesley seemed to shrink inward. "It's clear I make you uncomfortable. I'm giving you a way out." He sighed. "From everything I can see, you're a good man. A good father. There are no hard feelings. Let's just let it go, okay?"

He should. He should let it go. God knew he wanted to. He wanted to launch himself from the picnic table and run. Leave the truck, leave the dog, leave the vet and just run. Run until things were normal. Run until Shannon was back. Run until these feelings didn't mean anything again. Run until he remembered who he was, who he'd made himself to be. Run until Shannon's whispered requests of promises were drowned out.

"What if I don't want to let it go?" Travis wasn't sure if he'd said the words out loud. Wasn't sure he'd meant to.

The wide-eyed expression on Wesley's face told him Pandora's box had been opened.

CHAPTER THIRTEEN

THE BUSTLE and commotion of the crowd at Gringos felt like a soothing blanket over Wesley's nerves. He'd only come to the Mexican restaurant once since he'd moved to El Dorado. The first time he'd eaten there, the crowd had been so sparse Wesley had felt as though he was on display. Of course, he'd been eating lunch at two in the afternoon, which wasn't done. When Dr. Fisher had suggested meeting at 7:30 p.m. on a Sunday evening, Wesley hadn't even considered the rush as people got out of their Sunday evening church services. Hell, he'd forgotten there even were services twice on Sunday. If he'd remembered, he probably would have suggested a different time for dinner. But now that they were seated in the middle of the restaurant, Wesley was glad she had suggested the time. He almost felt like he blended into the crowd. Almost. There were a few glances here and there, but no more than curious looks. Most people were too busy with their families and friends to pay them much attention.

Gringos was pleasant—bright, clean, and homey. There was nothing about it that would lead anyone to guess it served Mexican food, other than the name and a few strings of dried chili peppers hanging above each doorway. The rest of the place was country chic, from the chicken coop with the fake eggs hanging in the vestibule, to the checkered plastic tablecloths, to the paintings of cowboys hanging on the wall. Maybe chic wasn't exactly the right descriptor, but it was a pleasing, safe effect, nonetheless.

"Here ya go, Dr. Fisher." The waitress slid a steaming plate of cheese-covered enchiladas in front of Cheryl.

"Thank you, Shelly." Dr. Fisher leaned back, making room.

Shelly transferred the plate balanced in the crook of her left arm to her right hand and plopped it down in front of Wesley, hitting the edge of his fork, knocking it to the ground.

With a frustrated sigh, she bent down and retrieved the fork from where it had landed under their table. She smacked it down beside Wesley's burrito.

He flinched and peered up at her in surprise.

"Oh." Shelly looked down at the fork, then back to Wesley. Her right eyebrow slowly rose. "Would you like a new fork?"

Wesley was fairly certain he could hear the implied, *you big Nelly*, finish off her question. Maybe not, but he definitely was able to read it in her expression. "Ah, no. I'll just wipe it off. I'm certain it's fine. Thank you."

Shelly's expression didn't waver.

What had he done to piss her off? She'd waited on him the other time he'd come in. He'd left her a decent tip. Or at least he'd thought he had.

"Do you need anything else? A *Diet* Coke, perhaps?"

Wesley shook his head and hoped his voice didn't sound as scared as he felt of the woman. "No, cherry Coke is fine, and I don't need another for a bit."

Seemingly satisfied, the waitress finally looked away and patted the other side of the table before walking away.

Cheryl's green eyes sparkled as she addressed Wesley. "What in the world did you do to her? Kill her dog?"

Wesley shrugged. "I have no idea." He glanced down and lifted the edge of his burrito with his fork. "You think she spit in this?"

Dr. Fisher chuckled. "I doubt it, but you forgot to wipe off your fork first."

Wesley yanked the fork away from his food. "Oh dammit." He lifted the green cloth napkin off his lap and scrubbed the offending fork.

Dr. Fisher cut into her enchiladas, scooped up a bite, and extended it toward Wesley. "Here, taste this. It's the best thing on the menu."

He tried to not make a face. "I told you. I hate blue cheese. And the thought of it in enchiladas…." He shuddered.

"Oh, just try it. At least it's on a clean fork." She waggled the fork in front of his face.

"Fine." He leaned forward and gingerly removed the morsel off her fork with his lips. After biting into the cheesy mixture, Wesley couldn't suppress a grimace.

A hearty laugh sounded from across the table. "You look like you just bit into a lemon."

Wesley forced himself to swallow, then took a long swig from his cherry Coke. After a moment, he was certain it was going to stay down. "I hate to be rude, but that is disgusting. And blue cheese enchiladas? Really? Could they get less authentic?"

Dr. Fisher seemed to ponder the question, as if it had never occurred to her. "I think one of their chefs is Chris Sanchez. He's Hispanic."

"Well, if he was, after making that, he isn't anymore." Wesley took a huge bite of his shredded chicken burrito, accentuating his point.

"Why don't we ask Shelly when she returns?"

Wesley spoke over the food in his mouth. "You're trying to get me run out of town, aren't you?"

"From what you've told me, it sounds like you're doing that yourself. At least, if John Wallace has anything to say about it."

He swallowed his food sooner than he should have, and it burned going down. "I'm sorry, Cheryl. I wasn't trying to cause problems for your business."

She waved him off, the smile never leaving her thin, sun-worn face. "I was just kidding, you know that. You did the right thing. Exactly what I would have done if I'd been here myself. Shoot, probably a helluva lot nicer than me, actually. More than likely, I'd have gone out there with my shotgun and raised a ruckus."

And that was without her knowing of John Wallace's other actions that night. Wesley wasn't planning on telling anyone about those events, least of all Dr. Fisher. Although the thought of John Wallace, wiry little Cheryl Fisher, and a shotgun made an appealing mental picture.

They each took a few more bites of their meals, settling into an easy rhythm, matching the relaxing buzz of conversations around them.

Wesley was nearly half done with his burrito, which was actually tasty, when Cheryl spoke again, this time a leading tone in her voice. "So how are you enjoying the clinic?"

"It's great, actually. It feels good to be back in the swing of things. I was afraid my slacking off since graduating a couple years ago made me forget everything, but it's all coming back."

Cheryl nodded. "Not surprised at all. You're a natural. I could tell that much the days we worked together. You just seem to get animals. And they get you."

Travis flitted through his mind. "Well, animals are a lot simpler than people."

She gave a sympathetic smile. "Have you heard from him?"

How had she known? "No. It's been three days. Not a word since he dropped me back off at my—" Wesley sucked in a breath and stopped short. "You meant Todd, didn't you?"

"Yes." Cheryl narrowed her green eyes at him. "But, *you* didn't. Who are you talking about? Someone here in El Do?"

He felt his cheeks flush. "Oh, never mind. It's not going to go anywhere. Just some straight guy who had too much to drink." Travis hadn't had anything to drink when they'd eaten at Simone's. Although he might as well have, as much sense as he'd made.

"Please, *please,* tell me you're not messing around with one of my married clients."

"Oh God, Cheryl! No! I wouldn't do that." Actually he had been with married men before. Plenty of wedding ring wearers had been at the bathhouses in Kansas City. It was different in a small town, though, and sleeping with a married client was a really bad idea. He pushed the thoughts aside, focusing on his friend. "Part of the draw of coming here was to focus on me. And my career. Start fresh. I don't want a relationship or anything."

Her brow rose in accusation.

"Seriously I don't."

"Okay, if you say so." She didn't look convinced.

"I promise, I'm not going to do anything that will mess up the clinic or its reputation."

Again, she waved him off. "I don't give a shit about that, at least not for the reasons you mean. Now, if you start doing a half-assed job on the animals, then we'll have an issue. But I'm not worried about that. Not with you."

He appreciated the vote of confidence.

"As I've told you before, your call asking for an internship came just at the right time. It was an answer to a prayer. Or it would have been, if I was the praying kind or thought anyone was up there listening." Using one of the chips from the basket between them, Cheryl scooped up a clump of melted cheese off her plate and popped it in her mouth. "Actually gave me the courage to do what I've been wanting to do for a couple of years now."

Wesley tried not to shudder as she slipped another chip into the mess of blue cheese. "Well, it worked out perfectly for both of us. I'd already decided I needed to spend some time in El Do to get my shit back together. Be at my grandparents' house. I just hoped you'd bring me on part-time, but I'd doubted you'd even do that." When he'd cold-called her asking if she could use a newly graduated vet, Wesley had needed to ask her to repeat her resounding yes, he'd been so certain the answer would be no.

"Actually, Wesley, you're making the transition to the next topic perfectly easy for me." For once Cheryl looked nervous, going so far as to glance around to see if anyone was listening. Satisfied, she looked back at Wesley but lowered her voice. "This past trip was more than just a vacation. It was more like a finalization of plans." A smile played on her lips. "A dream maybe."

Wesley started to speak, but she cut him off.

"Just let me get it out, *Dr.* Ryan." Another glance. Still satisfied. "I think I told you my husband died about ten years ago." She waited for Wesley to nod, then continued. "Well, what I didn't tell you was that I met someone else at a conference in Chicago three or four years ago. This trip was just a formality, actually. Just dotting some i's and crossing some t's."

Wesley couldn't suppress it anymore. "What's her name?"

Cheryl's eyes grew wide. Her mouth worked, but it was a few moments before words came out. "How did you know?"

"Any refills on anything?"

At Shelly's return, Cheryl jumped in surprise and looked up at the waitress like she had just accused her of trying to dine and dash.

"Goodness, Dr. Fisher. I'm sorry. Wasn't trying to startle ya none." Shelly eyed Cheryl's mostly cleared plate. "You done with that?"

Cheryl lifted her hand and rested her fingers on her throat. "Oh. No, dear. I'd like to finish. And I don't need anything else for a while." She glanced at Wesley. "Do you?"

He did, actually. His cherry Coke was gone. "No. I'm fine, thank you."

Without so much as a nod, Shelly was off to another table.

Cheryl watched her go, finally returning her attention to Wesley when she was convinced the waitress wasn't going to return. Her voice was lower than before. "How did you know?"

Wesley grinned and shrugged. "I just suspected. Gaydar, you know. You knew about me, after all."

"That was because I knew your grandparents. They told me about you and Todd having a house together. They were so proud when you finally got accepted into vet school."

"They told you I was gay?"

"Well, not quite as directly as labeling it, but they spoke of you and your partner living together."

His grandparents had never said a negative thing to him about being gay when he'd come out as a teenager. They'd never addressed it, either. They just kept on loving him and treating him like they always had. For some reason, Wesley had assumed they'd kept it a secret from those they knew. Don't ask, don't tell. His throat constricted, and a nearly tangible desire to see them flooded through him.

"You okay, hun?" Cheryl reached across the table and laid a hand over his forearm.

Wesley nodded, and it took him a second to speak. "Yeah. I just... I just miss them." A little of the newfound shame that kept rearing its head for the past couple of weeks melted away. With effort, he refocused on Dr. Fisher. "So, her name?"

"Gale." The moony smile on Cheryl's face made her look decades younger. "She lives in Seattle, where her kids and grandkids are. I'm going to move up there."

"Oh. That is so great, Cheryl! Seattle? I love that place. And you're moving in with—" The math added up. "Wait. You're moving? As in, moving?"

Cheryl looked nervously over her shoulder again, but her smile didn't fade. "Yes. I'm moving. I've wanted to retire for a while now, as you know. And there's nothing holding me here. Jim died years ago. And while I miss him dearly, I'm excited to start this new life. I've always known about these feelings, but back then, you just didn't acknowledge them. They'd go away. Or at least they were supposed to."

"You're moving?"

She nodded slowly, looking at him as if his brain capacity wasn't as superior as she'd been led to believe.

"What about the clinic?" Wesley's heart began to pummel his ribs. He knew what Cheryl Fisher was going to say just like he'd known she was a lesbian. He was nervous—the kind of nervous that was both excited and scared.

"Well, that depends on you. Obviously I need to sell the place." She started to glance around, but stopped herself. "I know this part is sudden, and for sure a lot sooner than we'd talked about, so we can do it at your pace. I'd like you to buy it."

She must have seen the panic in his expression, because she reached out and placed her hand on his forearm again, this time leaving it there as an anchor.

"Now, there's no rush. If you're not certain, then I'm fine with you renting the place for a while." Her grip tightened. "A long while, if that's what you need to make a decision. If you choose to not stay here, then give me a couple months' warning, and I'll put it on the market. Maybe someone will buy the whole business. If not, surely someone would at least buy the building and plot of land. Of course, I'd make more if they bought the business as well."

"You want me to buy it? Now?" They'd spoken in the abstract of him taking over, but it had been clear that the current arrangement was on a trial basis. He had not really thought he would stay more than a year or two. The past week or two had made him think it would be an even shorter amount of time than that.

"Not now. Just rent it for a bit, or we can split the profit like we do now, either way is fine. Take your time in deciding. I wouldn't want you to rush into anything." She looked as though she was finished speaking, but then spoke again. "I will say, if you do decide to buy it, I will sell it to you for less than I would ask someone else. I loved your grandparents, and I like you to pieces. I'd love to leave the clinic to someone like you."

CHAPTER FOURTEEN

"SHHH! YOU'LL wake up the kids." Travis hissed and glared at the offending keys. Placing a steadying hand on the doorjamb, he bent and swooped the fallen key ring off the garage steps. He slipped the keys into the pocket of his jeans before he could drop them again, then swung open the door and took the final step into the house.

As ever, Dunkyn was there waiting for his return, bouncing his front paws off the floor in greeting, making himself look like a bounding sheep.

Travis knelt and ruffled the dog's head. "Shhh. Be quiet, Dunk."

He made it halfway into the living room before glancing back the way he'd come. He'd forgotten the case holding the ball and shoes in his truck. Fuck it. He'd get them in the morning. Without looking where he was going, he took another step and tripped over Dunkyn, who was traveling alongside him, as always.

Travis managed to regain his balance without knocking over a lamp or careening into a wall. He glared down. "Goddammit, Dunkyn. Get the fuck outta the way."

Dunkyn lowered his head, and his floppy ears pulled back toward the rear of his head.

"It's not his fault you've had one too many beers."

Travis looked up to see Wendy standing with her hip resting against the kitchen counter. As she came into focus, he saw her arms crossed under her buxom chest.

"Maybe more than one too many."

Travis had the awareness to not argue with the accusation. He walked toward her, doing his best to keep his voice low while simultaneously avoiding Dunkyn, who maintained a cautious place beside him. "Would you get a water, Wendy?"

Even with her being slightly blurry, he couldn't miss the cocked eyebrow.

He pulled out his chair from under the kitchen table. "Please and thank you."

"How about I put on a pot of decaf too, while I'm at it."

"Thanks." Now that he was sitting, his sister came into full focus, though the bright yellow of her skirt made him squint once more. "I'm not old enough you have to do decaf, though."

She laughed. At the warm sound, his shoulders drooped from their tensed position. "Like hell you aren't. You'd be up till sunrise if I brewed the good stuff. You and I both."

"The kids asleep?"

"No, I thought it would be a good idea for the twins to have an all-night slumber party. I'm sure their teacher would love that. Monday morning's bad enough without having sleep-deprived first graders."

"You know what I mean."

"Of course they're asleep. And Caleb went to bed about half an hour ago, but I bet he's not quite drifted off yet if you wanna poke your head in."

Travis turned his attention toward the wall of windows framing the kitchen. He'd noticed snowflakes when he'd driven home. From the look of them sparkling under the light over the barn, it appeared they were going to have their first snow of the season. "No. I'll let him be. I'll see them before they go to school tomorrow." He didn't say he didn't want Caleb to see him buzzed, but the thought hung there, clear enough; he was certain his sister could hear it too.

Within a few minutes, during which the gently falling flakes turned into more of a blowing swirl, the sound of the steaming coffeemaker filled the whole space. After adding some clanking noises to the mix, Wendy slid a plate and fork in front of him. "Mason helped me make a cherry pie earlier this evening while Caleb took Avery to play outside with Dolan." She pulled out the chair beside him and sat down, partially blocking his view of the end of fall. "We had chicken casserole for dinner, if you'd like some."

He shook his head and spoke with a mouthful of cherries. "No. Thank you. I think I probably had three hot dogs. Not sure how much pizza."

"Hmmm. And you're still buzzed. You must have tied one on." Somehow, she managed to keep her tone judgment-free. Almost. "Did y'all win?"

Travis finally looked away from the window, grinning at her. "What do you mean, did we win? Old Bulldogs always wins." *Had* they won? It worried him that he couldn't remember any aspect of the final score. He had a clear image of packing away the bowling ball and shoes in the rear of the truck's cab, so at least there wasn't a complete blackout.

The coffeepot beeped from across the kitchen. Wordlessly Wendy got up, allowing Travis to get lost to the pie and the snow already building up around the barn walls. After some clinking and soft noises, she returned with two large mugs steaming the air between them.

Travis took a sip and sighed in contentment, even as the liquid burned the roof of his mouth. When he felt a hand slip over his own, he met his sister's blue-eyed gaze.

"I'm worried, Travis. You haven't done this in a couple years. I haven't been worried on bowling night in forever. You shouldn't have been driving. You promised me. You promised Caleb. Jason should have brought you."

"He went home with Belinda. And I'm fine, Wendy. Quit stressing." Travis focused on the remaining crust of his cherry pie. Guilt warred with anger. "Don't blow things out of proportion."

Wendy lowered her voice so it was barely more than a whisper. "You cursed at Dunkyn. You never do that."

Guilt won. He looked down beside his chair. Dunkyn peered up at him in adoration, his ears falling back, making them look fox-like. Goddammit.

Reaching down, he cupped the dog's face in his large hand, rubbing his thumb against Dunkyn's cheek like he would have one of the kids. Like he'd done to Shannon countless times. "Sorry, buddy."

"Wanna tell me about it, Travis?"

He looked back up, returning his attention to Wendy. Already the pie and coffee were working their magic. She was completely clear. He hadn't been that buzzed. Sure, probably enough that he shouldn't have driven, but not trashed. Not like he used to get.

Slippery slope, Bennett. Slippery slope.

"I'm fine, Wendy. Really."

She nodded, long red curls bouncing, then stopped abruptly. "No. No, Travis. You're not fine. You've been a mess ever since Wesley came for dinner, since you went to the barn. And I don't know what happened earlier this week, but whatever it was messed you up even more. I haven't seen you like this in a long time. And you need to talk about it. If tonight is any indication, you need to talk about it sooner rather than later."

"Quit pushing, Wendy. I'm fine."

She leaned closer, her words firm but not unkind. "No. You're not. Tell me about the barn."

He loved his sister, but damn, she drove him crazy sometimes. Always pushing, always wanting to talk. She was his sister, not his fucking wife. "You're the one who pushed me to go to the fucking barn, Wendy. You're the one who started this shit. Let. It. Go."

As she studied him, he nearly pushed away from the table and walked out of the room. He wanted to. He should. It was his damn house. It had just been a few beers. He hadn't had too much to drink in years. She'd said it herself. Fuck her.

Guilt again, shouting just a bit louder than his anger. For once.

Yeah, fuck her. Fuck the one who held the family together, who was strong enough to kick your ass to make you start being a father to your kids again.

Yeah, fuck her.

"Are we finally going to talk about it? Really talk about it?"

She sounded nervous. Wendy never sounded nervous. Travis looked at her, his heart pounding harder than if he'd drunk two pots of caffeine.

She was nervous.

They'd only touched on it once. Shannon had confided in Wendy after the miscarriage. She'd told him she was going to tell his sister. Wendy was her best friend, after all. Wendy had asked him if it was really true and then never asked anything about it again—until she'd hinted at it the other night.

Until now.

"What happened in the barn, Trav?"

It was his house. He could just get up and leave. He could sleep in the barn.

Fuck that! *She* could sleep in the barn if she was so goddamn curious about it.

"I kissed him." Travis's voice cracked as he said *him*.

To her credit, real or faked, Wendy didn't let her expression change in the slightest. She waited to see if he said anything else.

He didn't.

"Did he kiss you back?"

Anger, again. "Like you don't know. I guess you two are fucking best friends now too."

She didn't respond to his anger. "We've only talked once since then, and it was strained. I didn't ask. Wesley didn't offer."

He flinched at the man's name.

Wendy's hand, which had remained on his arm, slid down so she took Travis's hand in her own. "Travis? Did Wesley kiss you back?"

"Yeah." Travis glanced back out the window, then looked Wendy straight in the eye once more. "And what the fuck does that prove?"

She ignored the question. "Do you like him?"

The anger was starting to grow, burning away any remaining buzz that might have been lingering. "I don't even know the guy, Wendy. How could I like him? Not to mention he's a guy!"

"Are you worried what I'm going to think about that? If you like another guy? Or worried about what *you'll* think about it?"

He didn't answer, only glared. Just what he needed, a psychology moment.

"I doubt it's your chief concern, but I'll put it out there anyway. If you're worried about what I'll think about it, then don't. I couldn't care less. And I do know Wesley, and I like him. He's pretty great. If you're going to have feelings for someone, a girl or guy, you chose well."

For a second the anger vanished, and he almost told her about how Caleb had sounded when he'd been talking to Wesley. How the man had checked to make sure there was no traffic when he'd placed Dunkyn down in Simone's parking lot—such a small thing. How gentle the vet had been as he operated on the dog.

How he'd thought he was going to lose him when John Wallace had rushed toward him at the feedstore. Ridiculous, but still.

"I'm not gay, Wendy."

She considered her words.

He wanted to take the chance to run.

"I didn't ask that. I asked if you like him."

Travis's teeth were clinched so tight his jaw popped. "I love Shannon."

Once more, his sister considered. As always, she cut to the chase. "Remember the night I sent you to the barn I told you I made Shannon promises too?"

He didn't answer.

"Can I tell you what one of them was?"

Again Travis didn't answer. He knew what it was. He hadn't known Shannon had spoken to Wendy about the matter before she died, but he wasn't surprised.

"I promised her that—"

"Don't!" Travis pulled his hand out of her grasp. "That was between you and her. Respect that."

"I promised that I wouldn't let you be stubborn. That I'd help you be brave. That I'd make sure—"

The tears burned as they made their way down his cheeks. Dammit. He'd give anything to return to having lost that ability. He glanced over his shoulder, expecting to see Caleb staring at the weak man who was his father.

The hallway was dark. Empty.

Travis turned back to Wendy. "I love her, Wendy. I will always love her. It doesn't matter if Wesley is a guy or a girl or… whatever. I. Love. Shannon. Period."

"I know." Tears were pouring down Wendy's face, faster than those of her brother's. "I know you do. And she knew it too. I bet she still does."

"Exactly. So that's it. I love her. And that's it. I'm done. It's done."

Wendy shook her head. "That's not it. You're not done, and you know it. Because she loved you. She loves you, and you owe it to her."

Travis flinched. "I owe it to her? To kiss some fag in the barn? I owe that to her?" Even as he said it, he hated himself. He hated himself even more than he hated John Wallace. He might as well have been the one running, ready to bash in Wesley's face.

Wendy didn't so much as grimace at his words. She only kept hold of his hand and followed through on the promises she'd made to her sister-in-law.

"Yes. You owe it to her, Travis. You made her promises too."

THE HOUSE was silent at two in the morning. Despite the flood of emotions he'd brought home only a few hours ago, it was a peaceful silence. Travis had woken clearheaded and clear-eyed, even with less than three hours of sleep, even with the beers he might as well have ingested through an IV. Maybe Wendy and Mason's pie was magic.

Even with a clear head and eyes, Travis felt weighted down, as though his thick muscles were too heavy for his skeletal system to support.

Still, he was clear enough that all his thoughts were too transparent, all the warring emotions sharp and loud in the void. Maybe the pie had been too magic.

At least five beers were left in the fridge's cooler drawer. Nothing else worked quite as effectively at blurring what life had become.

He found it surprisingly easy to push the compulsion away, considering the turmoil. He would not send his children off to school with drunken, slurred *I love you*s. Not ever again. But he had to get out of the house and out of the bed where Shannon was not.

The late-night wanderings weren't new, but he couldn't consume his usual medicine. He couldn't talk to her, not the way he was at the moment. And she was under all that snow. He would need to warm her somehow. He would need to trade places.

Any trepidation left over from Travis's earlier scolding had vanished, and Dunkyn padded along noiselessly beside the man he loved, moving from door to door.

Travis pulled the covers over Avery. She was a restless sleeper, had been ever since the day she'd come into the world, always twisting and turning, arms and legs flailing. Even as an infant, her dream-filled kicks had nearly been able to knock the air out of Travis as he'd napped with her. At the moment she was still, only the soft rumble of her snores breaking the silence. It had been one of Shannon's favorite aspects of her daughter, often having to leave the room so her giggling wouldn't wake the girl. Even in his current mood, Travis had a similar reaction. She looked so much like an actual princess as she slept. Catching the moonlight from the window, her strawberry blonde hair spread out in tangles over her pillow, and long lashes lay over her full cheeks. Beautiful. She was going to be nearly as gorgeous as her mother. But with that snoring, she'd fit in better in the barn than under her pink canopy bed.

As in nearly everything else, Mason was the antithesis of his twin. Only the gentle rise and fall of blanket as he breathed hinted that the boy lived. Two night-lights, one on either side of the bed, watched over him. Of all his children, Travis worried the most about his youngest boy. While Caleb hurt the most over the loss of their mother, Mason was the one who seemed to have a core of sadness. Wendy insisted it was just a calm and loving nature. But there were moments when Travis would meet his son's gaze and swear he was looking into the eyes of a man who'd lived a century or more and knew all too well the realities of life. The small boy was the one who felt everyone else's emotions. At times he reminded Travis of Dunkyn, being able to sense what his father needed—steering clear when Travis felt he might explode on the next person to cross his path, crawling into his lap and silently resting his head on Travis's chest when Travis wasn't certain if there was anything that could secure him to the life he'd been left with. It was only in moments like these, when Mason was free of those around him and all was still, that Travis acknowledged the fear that part of what set Mason apart was the very thing that had caused Travis's own inner turmoil, though it seemed to be more present and identifiable in Mason.

Travis and Dunkyn's final stop was Caleb's room. As he pushed open the door, a low, vicious growl emanated from the darkness. As soon as Travis and Dunkyn were visible in the doorway, Dolan's warning broke off, a stupidly happy, tongue-lolling grin ripping across his face. The dog didn't leave his post, though. Despite his constant need for attention, Dolan had never cuddled with Caleb—even as a puppy, he'd squirm free—but he always stayed within touching distance. Even now in sleep, the young teenager had one hand dropped over the side of the bed, the tips of his fingers in constant contact with his dog. Travis had noticed the physical changes that were starting to happen to his son a few weeks ago. Even with the shadows across Caleb's face, the thickening blond down over his upper lip was visible. He would need to teach Caleb how to shave soon. He'd known it was coming. Caleb was actually a little late to the party, compared to the classmates Travis had seen. Caleb still appeared somewhat childlike, where so many of the other freshmen looked like they should be picking up chicks in bars. Pride and sadness comingled in Travis's chest. His boy, his strong, animal-loving, mini-father-figure of a boy would soon be gone. Travis would check in on him in the middle of the night and find a man in his bed. Then, one day, there would be no one at all.

Most of the time, it felt as though this life would continue forever—Shannon absent and three children to raise. However, he could feel the future sneaking up already. The twins would be tall and grown and then gone. Three lives out making their own way. Three parts of him and Shannon living, keeping their mother alive with every breath. As they left him, she would finally be gone, fully and completely out of his reach.

He touched Wendy's door in thanks as he and his dog walked by. If it hadn't been for her, he would have missed so much more of his children's lives. Maybe all of them. He wouldn't have followed through on his promise of living for and loving their children if his sister hadn't been the powerhouse and whirlwind she was.

Whether it was the snow covering Shannon's bones or his lips' desire to feel a man's kiss, he would not get lost again. He would not take such a risk with those three parts of Shannon's soul. His children would not lose him too. He would keep that promise to his wife, that promise to himself.

THE NIGHT was a wash of deep blue, the edges of the sky nearly purple. The hue spread over the newly fallen snow. Only the thick masses of stars in the crystalline sky broke through the cool air, their swirls of bright white lighting up the silent world. Just outside the dark expanse of trees, the small herd of buffalo slept in a spread-out oval, each a mound of snow, occasional twitches of shaggy hide causing small avalanches to career down their muscular sides.

Only Jarrod, the bull and ruler of the herd, lifted his horned head and met Travis's gaze as he and Dunkyn quietly exited the truck and took their place by the wooden fence. Even across the stretch of snowy field, Travis could see the intelligence in the creature's eyes, the question, the challenge.

Twin rushes of steam exited the bull's nostrils, and Jarrod turned away, satisfied, lowering his head back down to rest in the dense fluff.

After dusting the snow off the top rail, Travis folded his arms and rested his weight against the fence. At his feet, Dunkyn let out a whimper. Travis looked down, grinning at the dog. "Not yet, bud. Later this week. I think you're well enough."

Dunkyn let out a huff, gave another longing glance toward the resting herd, then plopped down in the snow, his back resting against the side of Travis's leg.

Travis returned his attention to the herd. Outside of Shannon's grave, this was the place he felt the most at peace. The place where the world was quiet. Actually his favorite time here was anything but quiet. He loved standing in this exact spot in the late evenings of summer, with sunset newly dead and the Missouri humidity starting to break. The lazy croaking of toads and frogs on the edge of the pond mixing with the frantic electronic buzz of the cicadas made it nearly impossible to think. If he closed his eyes and gave himself over to the sound, it brought him to the edge of enlightenment and insanity. Not a clear thought could get through. It was deafening. It was perfect.

This kind of night was nearly as good, the flawless silence as riotous in its own right as the chaos of summer. It was moments like these, though, that Travis wanted to escape the town that held so many memories, that he couldn't imagine leaving. Maybe the bustling noise of a city, the crash of ocean tides, the bugling of mountain elk, maybe those could silence the clamor in a man's head and heart. Maybe. But not like this place did for him. This was his haven. With Mr. Walker's huge house dark and invisible at the top of the hill, the small forest of trees in the middle of the field gave the illusion that a soul could wander in and never worry about being found. The pond, calm and flat, steamed in the newly frozen night. Creatures of myth and magic slept only steps away. Snow crunched as it settled under his cowboy boots. His dog's warmth against his leg radiated through the worn denim. This solace was similar to what endless cans of beer offered, but it wouldn't steal a part of him away.

Shannon's pregnancy with Caleb had been rough. Strangely it was more fraught with complications than that of the twins so many years later. They'd been so terrified of another miscarriage. If they'd only known. When the twins were conceived, the nine months went without a glitch. They'd finally figured out how to have children. They'd been wrong, it turned out. As agonizing as Caleb's pregnancy had been, the silent killer that grew alongside the twins had been what they should have feared.

Hindsight and all. It was a bitch.

Neither of them slept for nine solid months as Caleb grew in Shannon's womb. At least that's what it had felt like. Turned out, they discovered what no sleep actually felt like for the next year, as the boy never seemed to close his eyes. Caleb had been so much like his boisterous little sister—how Shannon's departure had changed him.

Still, they hadn't known things would get so much worse. Many late nights, he and Shannon had stood watching the buffalo, just as he and his dog did now, Shannon's hand resting on her twisting child inside, and Travis's arms wrapped over her shoulders as she rested her back against his solid chest and stomach.

At the time, Jarrod had just reached his maturity, only having one breeding season behind him. They both would become fathers around the same time.

Like him, Shannon found comfort in the late-night serenity of the land. They hadn't come to the buffalo during the twins' pregnancy, not with an eight-year-old boy asleep at home, and not when the pregnancy seemed so easy in comparison. Maybe if they had—if they'd stood by the sparkling pond, made eye contact with the mystic native animals, breathed deeply of the clean Midwest air—maybe that would have been her cure. All would have been well.

Travis didn't really believe that. He'd never been religious or spiritual in the slightest. Life was what it was. He was a true child of the Show-Me State. If you could touch it, see it, master it, then it was real. Everything else was just fluff and lies.

Still, what if there were more?

What if there had been a God watching them, waiting for Travis to trust in him?

What if there was magic in Jarrod's huge beastly eyes?

What if the cicadas' call brought healing?

If so, they'd missed it, he and his Shannon.

That was stupid, of course. There was no truth in any of it. They could have stood by the field every night as the twins' cells split, divided, grew, and made two beautiful copper-headed babies. They could have prayed louder than the amphibians' mating calls by the pond. Hell, they could have waded into its cool depths and baptized themselves in its pure density, even caught a catfish for breakfast while they were at it.

She'd known. His Shannon had known, even when he hadn't.

There wasn't magic in the buffalo, but she'd seen the future revealed in Jarrod's dark eyes.

There was no power in the screams of the cicadas, but she'd heard what would arrive sung from their frantic wings.

There was no eternal being, but she'd felt the whispered truth from God's lips next to her ear.

Promises to be strong. Brave.

He wasn't those things. He'd thought he was. Before he found out what life was, Travis Bennett had thought he was strong and brave.

Hindsight. That bitch.

No, he wasn't strong. *She* had been. Shannon had been strong in her love and her willingness to see and accept everything the way it was.

The promises she'd elicited had been strong.

Even her whispers to him, loud against the blue frozen night, were strong. Her warmth seeping into his skin through the dog's touch was strong. She was still strong and brave.

He would be too.

"Fine, my love. Fine. Only because you ask it of me." No tear fell, but his heart ached. "Fine."

Though Jarrod could not have heard his whispered resignation, the buffalo lifted his head once more and met Travis's gaze.

Travis nodded toward the beast. Far from strong, his whisper was nothing more than a cracked submission. "Fine."

Though there were no sounds or movements over the snowy surface, there was a reply.

She answered.

The purple edges of the sky began to lighten, the death of moon and the birth of sun commencing. A star fell. One solitary star streaked across the night and disappeared into the horizon.

IT HAD all seemed so clear while staring out on the snow-covered predawn morning. All the promises he'd made to Shannon were coming due. Though it terrified him, it had felt nearly unquestionable.

Travis hadn't been able to fall back to sleep after returning home from watching Mr. Walker's buffalo. He had been nervous—beyond nervous—but he'd also been excited, like he was standing on the edge of a cliff and could feel feathers beginning to sprout from his arms. He was getting ready to leap and soar.

By the time Wendy and the kids were awake, Travis had breakfast on the table, coffee brewed, orange juice poured, and sack lunches for all three kids ready to go. He'd even been whistling, until he'd noticed Wendy's questioning brow.

He felt alive—or almost, at any rate. More than he had in years.

A change was coming. Maybe the change had already arrived, and he just needed to grab it. He didn't need to overthink it. He just needed to do it. Whatever it was, the bottom line was that he felt something. As abstract as it might be, it was the first time in years that he'd felt more than sadness, depression, and loneliness. Granted all those were still there, as much as ever, but something else had been added.

In a matter of hours, Travis had torn through the basics that typically would have taken all day at Cedar County Feed. Jason kept looking at him strangely, but never asked, thank God. As the minutes ticked by, the adrenaline rush of the snow-covered dawn and the decision he'd made began to cool from a nearly frantic giddiness to frozen terror.

Those brief hours of excitement left him tired and lost. Shannon's closeness as he and Dunkyn watched the buffalo felt like a hangover dream, a momentary delusion, a promise spoken in the heat of the moment that would cost his soul.

Without any other explanation to Jason than that he had to get out of the store, Travis nearly raced to his truck and drove to the cemetery. He was in such a state, he wasn't able to drive all the way to her grave. He pulled the F-350 over to the side of the road and ran. He rushed to Shannon's grave like a man lost in the desert seeing a spring in the distance. Those damned tears that had found him again erupted the moment his fingers traced her name.

He sobbed.

He didn't speak. There was nothing more to tell her.

Then she was with him again, as surely as Jarrod had been sitting out in the field of snow that morning. She had to be. The weight of her presence was simultaneously heavy and comforting.

Travis thought he needed to hear her, needed to make sure he was doing the right thing, what she wanted.

He didn't. He didn't need her permission or direction anymore. He knew what she wanted. With that realization, Travis had to admit it wasn't just what Shannon wanted. He wanted it too.

Still, he just needed to be near her once more, to grieve yet again, to gain enough strength to follow through.

And he found it. It might have taken five minutes, or he might have knelt there for over an hour. Travis wasn't sure and didn't care. By the time he stood, his snow-soaked knees popping at the effort, he'd found the strength. He wouldn't take another moment to consider. He was certain his eyes were red and puffy. He was also certain he looked like shit. Between the beers the night before, the ten seconds of sleep, and the interminable arrival of tears, there was no way he looked halfway presentable. He didn't look in the visor mirror after he came to a stop in the parking lot. If he gave in to a second's hesitation, he'd dash away and wouldn't have the courage again. It was time to pull the trigger. He just needed to get it done.

Chapter Fifteen

At the sound of a car door slamming and feet crunching across the frozen gravel, Wesley closed the browser window. The last thing he needed was a client catching him browsing for scarves at Neiman Marcus. He'd just found the perfect gold and brown cashmere. Dammit. With another click, he brought up the appointment schedule screen.

The front door of the clinic banged open, smashing against the wall.

"Oh, sorry, Wesley." Travis gave a sheepish shrug and closed the door with extra caution.

It took a second for Wesley's mouth to catch up with his brain. He'd not heard a word from Travis in days—not since Simone's.

"Is Dunkyn okay?"

Confusion crossed Travis's expression, then cleared. "Yeah. Dunkyn's fine. About ready to start playing with the buffalo, I bet." He took a few steps toward the counter, dripping snow and water over the floor. His jeans were soaked from the knees down. Actually the man looked like a complete mess. His complexion was blotchy and his face was kinda puffy. His eyes were bloodshot and appeared painful.

Maybe if Travis had looked like this when they'd first met, Wesley wouldn't be as smitten with him. He looked a bit homeless, and maybe a little crazed.

"Are *you* okay?"

Travis ignored his question and placed both of his hands on the counter like he was bracing himself. He sucked in a ragged breath and held it for a second. "Go on a date with me."

Then it was Wesley's turn to hold his breath. Choke on it, more accurately. "What?"

"Go on a date with me, Wesley." Travis closed his eyes, then opened them again, staring directly into Wesley's eyes.

Travis looked desperate, near a panic. The feeling was contagious. Beads of sweat broke out over Wesley's body.

Another exhale. Travis's breath washed over Wesley's face. It had a faint sour tinge. "I'm not doing this very well, I'm sorry. It's been a while." He swiped his hand over his jaw. "Would you please go out on a date with me, Wesley? To dinner or a movie or something?"

Wesley's heart began to pound in his throat. It leaped right up from his chest and into his throat, making it nearly impossible to breathe, let alone actually speak. He nodded, rather stupidly. He thought he might have tried to say yes, but nothing came out. He nodded again.

The smile that broke over Travis's face was both ecstatic and terrified. If Wesley could have formed a complete thought, he might have laughed. "Good." Travis nearly panted. "Pick you up Wednesday? Six?"

Still unable to form words, Wesley nodded.

"Great. See you then." Travis turned and, without so much as a look behind him, walked out the door, making sure not to bang it this time.

Wesley watched Travis's hulking form through the window as he walked to his truck, pushed Dunkyn over from where he'd apparently been curled up in the driver's seat, hopped in, and then drove way.

He was fairly certain Travis Bennett had just asked him on a date. He kinda even thought he'd said yes.

He wasn't aware he was smiling until he realized his cheeks were beginning to hurt.

Huh. A date. With Travis.

The Neiman Marcus scarf was forgotten.

THE DAYS leading up to Wednesday passed in a slow blur. A thousand different times, Wesley almost called to cancel the date. He kept his distance from Wendy. The day of the date, he changed outfits at least fifteen different times.

And then he was sitting in the passenger seat of Travis's truck, zooming west down Highway 54 toward Nevada.

There were initial nerves and that spike of thrill as Travis picked him up. God, he was sexy. So manly and big. So red. So....

Then, on the way out of town, all sexiness, dirty thoughts, and twitterpation got thrown out of the truck's window. Travis motioned down a dirt road that angled off the highway. "That's where Shannon grew up. Her folks still live there."

Of course their house was on the way. "Oh." Wesley searched for the appropriate reply. There wasn't one, at least not that he could find.

About halfway through the drive, after deafening silence, Travis turned on the radio. Alan Jackson began whining about something. Wesley didn't mind country music, and had actually liked Alan Jackson until hearing him make some belittling comments about gays when the movie *Brokeback Mountain* was released. He almost asked Travis to switch the station.

No need to make the situation worse. It was just a song.

Music—that was benign. They could talk about music. Wesley knew enough about country music that he could at least drag a few minutes out of the topic. "I hope they play that duet by Taylor Swift and Tim McGraw. I love her." He glanced over at Travis, forcing what he hoped was a casual smile. "Do you have her new album?"

Travis glanced at him, then returned his attention to the road. "No. No, can't say I do. I bet Avery will be asking for it for Christmas, though."

The drive to Nevada only took twenty-five minutes. At least that was what the clock said. Wesley was certain they'd both aged a year by the time Travis pulled off the highway and headed into the small town. Soon after, Travis came to a stop in the parking lot of the Golden Corral. Wesley turned toward him, getting ready to laugh and make some comment about how funny it would be to actually have a first date at the Golden Corral.

Travis was already pulling the keys out of the ignition and had thrown open his door to get out.

Wesley glanced over at the restaurant, then back to Travis.

Before shutting the door, Travis smiled nervously. "This place has a great buffet. Shannon and I came here for her senior prom."

With an ever-increasing sinking feeling, Wesley exited the truck and joined Travis in walking across the parking lot.

What. The. Hell.

What the hell had he been thinking? The next time he needed to swear off men, he was going to move to Antarctica. Apparently a small hick town wasn't even enough to stop his stupid, slutty ways that enabled his poor decision-making. Although Antarctica probably had men too, somewhere, and knowing him, he'd sniff them out. Was the Isle of Lesbos a real place? He should check into that. If he were ever going to give himself the time to just be Wesley, it would have to be there. Lesbians… they'd have lots of cats and horses he could help. Way to stereotype. Seriously, though, if he couldn't stay away from men in a small town with more churches than any other business—save for used car lots, perhaps—*while* living in his grandparents' old house, there really wasn't much hope for him.

And of all the men, he chose this one. A father of three. A man who was still mourning his dead wife. *Wife!* A man who was apparently recreating prom night with his dead wife.

God, he was an idiot. What the hell was wrong with him? He deserved every bit of awful this date could dredge up.

TRAVIS POINTED at his cheese-covered baked potato with his steak knife, then motioned with it over his shoulder. "Did you see the potato bar back there? They have about everything you could imagine on a baked potato."

Wesley started to simply nod but then realized it was the first thing Travis had said that didn't somehow tie back to his dead wife. Better grasp for straws while he had the chance. "You know, I did. I'm kinda just a butter and sour cream guy."

Dead air. Again.

Wesley twirled his fork inside his cheese-free baked potato. He deserved this. He did. He'd brought this torture on himself.

He searched desperately for a way to get the conversation going. He glanced around the generically decorated chain restaurant.

Old people.

More old people.

Then he saw it.

"I noticed there was a soft-serve ice cream bar. It looked like it had nearly as many toppings as the baked potato bar." Ice cream. Who didn't enjoy talking about ice cream?

Somewhere, Todd was fucking his little twink and laughing at the top of his lungs.

Travis nodded his agreement. "You're right. It's pretty good. Plus you can choose vanilla, chocolate, or, if you pull the middle handle, it does them together in twist."

"Oh, that sounds good. I might have to give that a try." Wesley fiddled with the button on the cuff of his olive green shirt. Apparently *he* didn't enjoy talking about ice cream.

Crickets. Wesley could have sworn he actually heard crickets. Couldn't have been. It was November.

"You know"—Travis didn't look up at him from across the table, keeping focused on something that fascinated him about the fake candle between them—"when we came here for prom, I tried to feed Shannon a bite of my ice cream cone and it dripped on her dress." A laugh seemed to emerge from somewhere in the distance. "Man, was she ever mad. I was pretty sure she was gonna make me take her home."

"Oh." What was he supposed to say to that exactly? "I... can see how that would be stressful. Especially on a prom dress."

Travis shrugged. "She was a smart one. Just took off her wrist corsage and pinned it right over the stain."

"Yeah." Wesley cut off another bite of the thin steak. "That is pretty creative."

Travis nodded, a flush growing over his checks.

Within moments, the pink hue over Travis's skin had blossomed to full-blown scarlet. Wesley had almost found himself getting angry. He thought Travis had to be continually bringing up his dead wife on purpose. But the sight of the big man's silent confession of embarrassment washed his irritation away.

Maybe Travis was trying. What did Wesley know about the guy? Good-looking—though Todd wouldn't think so. Loving father. Protective. Hurting. And he obviously was more than he first appeared to be. Or at least gayer than he first appeared to be.

For the past two days, Wesley had tried to figure out what Travis wanted from him. If it had just been sex, Travis wouldn't have needed to ask him for dinner. Although maybe he didn't know that. He hadn't hooked up with a guy in years.

The only thing Wesley could come up with was that Travis must have some sort of feelings for him. Emotions had definitely been there when they'd kissed.

Wesley kept coming back to the theory that Travis simply felt indebted to Wesley for helping Dunkyn. Dramatic as it might seem, and misguided as well, Travis might feel like Wesley had saved the dog from cancer. Those feelings of gratitude might have gotten twisted into some sexual tension and then combined with all the residuals around his wife's death and made the poor man think he had feelings for the man who cured Dunkyn's "cancer."

In his less rational, more emotional, teenage-girl moments, which he'd thought were dead, Wesley couldn't help but play with the idea that Travis actually did have some homosexual desires and that those feelings were directed at him. More of a hope than an idea, really, and a stupid hope at that. Even if it were true, he was once again back to the most basic of all gay rules—you don't date a newly out man. Ever.

But he had seen it. He'd seen it the night Travis kissed him, that look that only another gay—or, at least, gayish—man could give....

And now, that blush. It seemed to make Travis look like nothing more than a big embarrassed kid. That blush told the tale, didn't it? It had to. While Wesley wasn't sure how deep they went or why they were there, he was certain of two things. Travis Bennett had feelings for him, however abstract or fleeting they were. And Travis was in over his head—he had no idea what he was doing, and he knew it and was embarrassed by the whole thing.

The least Wesley could do was keep trying.

"So do you know why Nevada says its name like it does?"

Travis looked up at him, a rather desperate relief showing at the subject change. "What do you mean?"

"Well, why it's Nevada, with a long *a* in the middle instead of just calling it Nevada, like the state?" Maybe not the best conversation starter, but it was something Wesley had always wondered. And surely it couldn't be tied back to Shannon.

Travis shrugged. "I dunno. Never really thought about it. I guess the same reason we all say El Darada, instead of El Dorado, like it's spelled."

Success! No dead wife in sight. Wesley leaned forward. "Actually I've always wondered about that too, and the fact that you all say El Darada when you use the full name, but El Do when you shorten it."

Travis's brow furrowed in thought. "Huh. You know, I've never even realized we do that."

"Yeah, and my grandparents always said worsh instead of wash. 'Put the clothes in the worsh-machine.' 'Go worsh your face, Wesley.' 'If you say *suck* one more time, I'm gonna worsh your mouth out.' But if they were talking about the president or the state, they'd always say Washington. It never made any sense."

Oh my God. Someone kill him. This was worse than talking about the weather. Worse than talking about baked potato bars and Shannon's prom dress.

Wesley glanced over at the tables beside them, searching desperately again for some escape, some new topic. Nothing. "Mom would get so mad when I'd come back from a long weekend with Grandma and Grandpa and I'd have picked up part of their accent. She said she'd worked long and hard to get rid of her own accent and no child of hers was going to pick it back up." Dear God, he couldn't stop. The horrible conversation just kept going and going.

He was about to jump into how his grandparents had butchered the words Pinocchio, pliers, and dinosaurs, but then Travis jumped in. *Thank God!*

"That always drove Shannon crazy too. The whole worsh thing. She never noticed it until we went to college, and then someone made fun of her about it. I bet she and your mom would have gotten along real well."

Just when it couldn't get any worse, when it couldn't become any more awkward and agonizing, a man of semiquestionable sexuality suggested that his dead wife meet the mother of the gold-star homosexual whom he'd kissed while his three children of the aforementioned dead wife slept in their beds only a few hundred feet away.

What the hell was he doing?

And there was that blush. Again.

Dammit.

CHAPTER SIXTEEN

TRAVIS HAD never been so thrilled to pay a tab and leave a restaurant in his life. From the looks of it, Wesley felt the same way. The vet nearly sprinted out the door into the parking lot.

All the stress about this date, or whatever it was. All the inner turmoil. All of, well, all of everything, from the feelings of twenty years ago to now. All for nothing.

When Wesley had opened the door for Travis at his house, he had to admit he felt exactly the way he had when he'd picked Shannon up for dates—maybe not exactly the same, but close enough to know what the feelings meant. He'd made the right call. Things were going to be good. The date was the right choice. Wesley was handsome, standing in his doorway waiting for Travis to pick him up. Manly and pretty, all at the same time. His nervous smile and the questioning yet knowing glint in his eye had only made Travis all the more certain he was doing the right thing.

And then it had all gone to shit.

He was almost pissed at her. Actually if he were being honest, he was pissed off at her. This was her fucking promise that got him in this mess. The least she could do was throw him a bone. Give him something to say that didn't revolve around her. No such luck. Shannon might've been enjoying the show of Travis on his first date with a man, but he sure wasn't, and he was certain Wesley wasn't enjoying it either.

After slipping into the driver's seat, shutting the door, and putting the key in the ignition, he just sat there, searching desperately for what to do, what to say. Pleading with Shannon, God, whoever, to help him know what to say.

Travis could feel Wesley's eyes on him, but he couldn't bring himself to look at Wesley.

"Travis? Are you okay?"

Travis nodded, his throat tight.

The silence returned for a few more heartbeats before Wesley spoke again, sounding equally nervous and concerned. "You don't seem all right.

We don't have to do this. Like I said at Simone's, we can just pretend this never happened. No harm, no foul."

Goddammit, he was fucking this up. He wasn't even sure what *this* was, but he was fucking it up. Actually that was part of it, wasn't it? He *was* sure what this was. He just wanted to pretend he wasn't.

He was attracted to the vet. He was attracted to Wesley. It was high time he quit thinking of him as *the vet*. He liked the guy. There was something about him he respected. And there was something his body responded to. It had been a while since he'd felt that, at least in person.

He was fucking this up. Travis looked away from the steering wheel and turned toward Wesley. The right side of his face was illuminated from the red light of the Golden Corral sign.

He really didn't want to fuck this up.

Travis let out his breath. "Can we go on a walk or something?"

Wesley's eyes widened in surprise. "Travis, we don't have to. We can just go home. There's no pressure. Like I said—"

"No." Travis cut him off, finding his voice. "I want to. Really. I know I'm not doing a good job of this. I do realize that. I just… I don't know. Maybe if we're outside. If we walk."

Wesley inspected him for a second. Travis didn't look away. He respected that Wesley seemed unafraid to say what he really thought and wanted, which probably meant a big fat no was coming Travis's way.

"Sure. Okay. Let's walk." Wesley reached for the truck's door handle.

"No. Not from here." Travis reached out and grabbed Wesley's arm. He nearly pulled his hand back when he realized what he was doing. "There's a really beautiful pond. Shannon and I used to go there and walk around sometimes."

Wesley inspected Travis's hand on the crook of his arm, then lifted his gaze to meet Travis's. "Are you sure you want to take me to another place you and your wife used to go?"

A mist of calm sank over him. A familiar, loving presence surrounded him. "Yeah. Yes, I'm sure."

IT WAS the right call. The few minutes it took to drive from the restaurant to the pond were just as silent as the rest of the night, but as soon as the two of them got out of the truck, everything felt more natural.

"Have you been here before?"

Wesley looked around but shook his head. "I think I might have played at that park we passed a few blocks back when I was kid. I swear that huge slide looks familiar. I thought the one in El Do was big, but it's nothing compared to that thing. But I'm pretty sure I've never been here."

"The kids love that slide. Any time we come to Nevada to go to Walmart, we have to go to that slide. Mason gets a little scared and will only do it sitting on Caleb's or my lap, but Avery seems to think it's the best thing ever invented." Travis paused and motioned back toward the truck. "Are you gonna be warm enough? I think I've got an extra jacket in the back of the cab."

Wesley looked out at the treelined pond. "No. I think I'm good. Thank you, though. It's pretty cold, but most of the snow has melted, and there's no breeze."

"Well the pond is kinda long and narrow. The path around it winds in and out of the trees, so we'll be pretty well protected, even if the breeze picks up."

They walked in silence to the edge of the pond, and this time the quiet feeling was more relaxed and serene.

Travis hadn't been to the pond since before Shannon had gotten sick. He and Wendy had brought the kids to the park, but he'd avoided going any farther. Actually now that he thought about it, he and Shannon hadn't been to the pond since before she'd been diagnosed with cancer. The place held no bad memories. He could still feel her here, but more like a lingering sweetness around the place, instead of the rather unnerving sensation of having her watching him and Wesley over his shoulder.

"I wish you could see this place in the spring and summer." As they walked, Travis pointed toward the right, guiding Wesley down the longer path option around the pond. "It's really something. The trees are so thick and green, and half of the pond is taken over by lily pads. And in the evenings, the frogs are croaking so loud it's like they're singing only for you, and the lightning bugs are everywhere. I swear it's one of the prettiest places in Missouri."

Silence fell again, and Travis looked over at Wesley. The man was staring at him, a strange expression on his face.

"What?"

Wesley shrugged and then grinned. "I don't know. I've just never seen you smile like that. And I know I haven't seen you all that much, but still. You looked so peaceful. So young."

"You saying I look old most of the time?" He gave Wesley a wink, then realized what he'd just done. After a split second, he also realized he was okay with it.

Wesley laughed. "No. Definitely not old. You just looked, I don't know... well, you looked like Caleb, actually. When he was telling me about his chickens and how he's hoping to breed an award-winning bull."

And there it was. Besides the physical attraction to Wesley, there was that. The man seemed to see Caleb. Just like he'd seen Dunkyn. Suddenly Travis realized he was staring. "So, uh. Tell me something about yourself."

Wesley stiffened, suddenly seeming nervous. "Like what?"

Travis shrugged. "I dunno. Doesn't matter, really. It feels like you know quite a few things about me by this point. I don't know much more about you than that you're a vet and you know how to cut out dog teeth. And that you're good-looking." Had he really just said that? He glanced away, looking out over the starlight reflected on the surface of the pond.

"Uhm." Wesley cleared his throat nervously. "I... ah...."

"Why El Do?" Travis looked back at Wesley. The only nervousness left was the butterfly kind in the pit of his stomach. It was both surprising and rather great. "Why did you choose to come here?"

"Well, because this is where my grandparents lived. I have good memories here."

Travis waved him off. "No. Not that. I know that. That makes sense, but that's not why you're here. Why does a gay man in the prime of his life come to some Podunk town where there aren't any other gay men?"

Wesley cocked an eyebrow.

"I know, I know. I asked you to dinner. We're here on a... date." Okay, maybe still some nerves. "But why are you here?"

"You go for the big guns quick."

"Yeah? Touched on a story, did I?"

"Like you said, why would a gay guy move to El Do?" Wesley paused to inspect him.

Travis stood still, letting him.

"You want the quick, down-and-dirty version or the PC one?"

"Oh, fuck that shit. Never pull that PC crap with me. Hate it. Shoot it straight."

A low crack of a laugh escaped Wesley, cutting through the peace of the night for a second. A bird screeched somewhere across the pond. "Shoot it *straight*, huh?"

Travis couldn't suppress a grin. "Shut up. You know what I mean."

Again, Wesley considered how to tell his story, then slowly continued down the path.

Travis matched him step for step.

"Okay. Here it is. One hundred words or less. After Todd left me, which I already told you about, I kinda had a meltdown. I'd just gotten my veterinarian degree and was all set to open my own practice, and then he left me for that twink. I spent the next twoish years partying. Drinking and whoring with every guy I could find." He paused in his walking and looked over.

Travis kept his face impassive. He forced himself to give a nod.

They started walking once more. "Well, finally, I started to pull my head out of my ass. Somewhere in all the mess, I kept thinking about the house my grandparents left me in El Do. I had such good memories of the place. Of the park and bandstand and everything. So Americana or something. Something so pure about it, which was an aspect I was sorely missing. So I called Dr. Fisher to see if I could intern with her, and she jumped at the chance." He shrugged. "So here I am."

Travis considered before he spoke again, the crunching of the twigs under their shoes somehow soothing. "So you came to El Do to what? Get away from sleeping with guys?"

"Yeah. Basically. I just needed to find myself. I've been kinda lost. You know?"

Did he ever. "You came here, to El Do, to get away from guys, and then I kissed you in the barn and asked you for a date, and you said yes."

Wesley glanced over and grinned. "Yeah, that pretty much sums it up. Guess I'm not doing too great on the staying-away-from-guys thing."

Out of the blue, an image of Wesley naked underneath him in his bed rose unbidden in his mind. He tried to shove it away, but it wouldn't quite dissipate. "Have you, ah, had any luck refraining from sleeping with guys since you got here?"

Travis thought he saw a shadow pass over Wesley's face, but then it was gone. Of course, considering it was nighttime, it might have only been an actual shadow.

"El Dorado has been fairly bleak on the available men front, like I'd hoped. Although there weren't supposed to be any dates either."

Travis wasn't sure how to respond to that.

"Do you mind if I ask you a question now?"

"Nope. Go ahead."

"Okay. You all right if it's a hard-hitting one like you asked me?"

Travis shrugged. "Go for it. Ask whatever you want." He wasn't really sure he meant that.

For the next twenty to twenty-five steps, Wesley remained silent. Travis decided he wasn't going to ask after all. Then suddenly Wesley stopped and turned toward him. "Why did you ask me out?"

He should have expected that one. It was the most obvious question for the man to be wondering. He could barely understand why himself; how was he supposed to answer it for Wesley?

"You know, I don't have a good answer for you. I just know I haven't been able to get you out of my mind. I wasn't expecting to kiss you the other night." Travis forced himself to keep going. It had taken Shannon years to get him to be able to talk about his feelings. It had never gotten to where it felt natural to him, but he'd learned how nonetheless. "I knew I was attracted to you, but I didn't really want to admit it to myself. It had been so long. Then, in the barn…." His voice trailed off, despite his resolve to be blunt.

Wesley looked away from him, staring down at their shoes. "So the first guy you have feelings for and I turn out to be a big whore. I can only imagine what you must be thinking now."

Travis had known they would have this conversation at some point, if conversations kept happening, but he hadn't really seen it coming so soon. To his surprise, considering he'd never spoken to anyone besides Shannon about this before, it didn't feel strange to admit it to Wesley at all. "I can't say I understand the whole open thing like you said you and your ex had, but I'm not going to judge you on whoring around." Yep, he was really going to say it. "For about a year in college, I was fucking guys left and right."

Wesley looked up, his eyes wide, his jaw hanging open in shock. "You what?" Before Travis could reply, Wesley leaned forward questioningly. "Wait a minute. In college? I thought you and Shannon started dating in high school."

"We did." God, he really did hate telling this. "During our junior year, I started fucking guys behind Shannon's back, during one of our breakups.

We would fight and get back together a lot in those days. I'd always known I had some attraction to other guys, but I'd been able to pretty much ignore it. Until I didn't. Later, after Shannon found out—" He let out a sardonic laugh. "—and after breaking up and getting back together again, she said as long as it was other guys, she thought she could handle it."

"Wait." Wesley flung out his hands. "What?"

"Looking back, it doesn't make sense to me either. I think we were both just so desperate to make it work. We really loved each other." Wesley looked like he was about to interrupt, but Travis spoke again before he could. "Long story short, that didn't work either. It hurt her too much."

Wesley considered him. "So you haven't had sex with another man in over twenty years?"

Travis felt his cheeks flush, and he was glad it was dark out. "I've webcammed a couple of times in the past year or two. Not often. I feel like shit every time. I just had to get some… release or something."

"Oh my God." Wesley gaped at him. "You're completely blowing my mind right now. I don't even know what to do with any of this. I just never expected…." His expression changed suddenly, and his voice grew wary. "Did you feel like that after we kissed the other night?"

"Like what?"

He shrugged. "Like you did after you webcammed? Like shit."

"No. Not like that. I've been confused and sort of a mess. Well, no 'sort of' about it. But no. It was nothing like that."

The expression on Wesley's face made it evident he didn't entirely trust Travis's words. "I'm not sure what to do with all this."

Travis was certain Wesley was going to ask to go back to the truck, end the date, and for Travis to take him home. Panic flared in him at the thought. He shouldn't have such a reaction. Hell, that should be the very thing he should hope for. Then it could all go back to how it was—no more confusion, no more drama.

Back to how it was. Shannon was gone. She wasn't coming back, no matter how many starry nights he spent with the buffalo. So what was it he was wanting to go back to? Endless nights of loneliness? Jerking off to a webcam every few months, then feeling like a dirty old man the next day? Being half a man for his kids?

Travis reached out a hand and gripped Wesley's shoulder, his hold firm but nonaggressive. "Please don't freak out. I know I'm not good at this. I do wanna be here with you."

Wesley continued to stare at him with narrowed eyes. "Why?"

Oh fuck. Travis glanced around, finding what he sought, glad it was still there. He motioned up the path, toward the edge of the pond. "There's a bench up there. Wanna go there and sit for a bit?"

"Sure." Even that Wesley made sound questionable.

Travis's mind raced during the all-too-few steps it took to get to the iron-and-wood bench. How was he supposed to explain things he didn't understand? How was he supposed to express feelings he couldn't even name?

They sat, the bench small enough that, as they turned toward one another, their knees touched. Neither pulled away. So close to the pond and a few feet out of the tree line, the night seemed a little brighter. Stars, both overhead and reflected on the pond, illuminated them.

"Is this going to be too cold?" Travis noticed a small snowflake drift between them, and his gaze followed it momentarily. After a second, he refocused on Wesley.

"No. It's cold, but I'm fine. Honestly I'm not really even noticing any of that right now." Wesley made an unpleasant, scrunched-up face, then shook his head. "I know I'm not supposed to ask something like this, but I'm just gonna. So are you gay or bi? Like, what are you?"

The mist-like snowflakes could have turned to hail and Travis wouldn't have felt them against the instant pounding of his heart. God, he hated that question. He'd asked himself that same thing a billion times. Every time he'd fucked a guy in college. Every time he'd gotten off with someone on the webcam. He could hear Shannon's angry young voice asking the same thing.

Wesley kept talking before Travis could even begin to form an answer. "There's no judgment on anything you might say. I just want to understand. I mean I've met plenty of straight guys who just wanna hook up with another guy from time to time, I guess. Is that what you're looking for here, and you just didn't know how to ask?"

The question fucking hurt Travis's feelings. Was he becoming a goddamn girl now? Why hadn't he practiced this conversation in advance? What the fuck was he thinking? Practice a conversation? He was becoming a girl.

"No. I'm not wanting that. As pathetic as this sounds, I'm not just trying to get off here. I can do that on the computer. I hate it. I feel more alone every time I do it."

Wesley gave him a halfhearted smile. "Well, Travis, it would be a little different if you were doing it with a real person."

"Is that why you said yes to tonight? You thought we'd just fuck or something?"

"No. Although I wouldn't turn you down if that's what you wanted." Wesley shrugged. "I don't really know why I said yes. You're hot and I've had you stuck in my head since I met you that day you brought Dunkyn that first time. I guess—"

"You think I'm hot?" Travis had to remind himself to shut his mouth, not to let his jaw continue to gape open. He wouldn't have admitted it to anyone, not even Wendy, maybe not even Shannon's grave, but he hadn't been able to picture Wesley being even partially attracted to him. Though Wesley's response to the kiss had suggested otherwise.

Wesley cocked his head questioningly at Travis. "Are you serious?"

Travis motioned down his body. "Yeah. You're all fancy and shit, and I'm… this. I got this belly. I'm all hairy—" He stopped abruptly, realizing Wesley didn't know about his hairy chest and stomach. God! He was forty-three, for crying out loud; why did he suddenly feel like he was back in junior high?

"All right, no more details like that right now, or I might undress you on this bench." Wesley glanced up at the thickening clouds. "And if we're gonna hook up, I don't want it to be with shrinkage."

And just like that, Travis's cock came fully awake and aching in its smashed denim confines.

Luckily Wesley hadn't seemed to notice. "And… and *that's* what you focus on? That I think you're hot?"

Travis couldn't suppress his smile. He was smiling. Actually smiling. Huh. "Well, it's nice to hear. I doubted you'd look twice at someone like me."

"And that brings us back to you. Someone like you. So you're saying that you didn't ask me to dinner just for a hookup. That you, what? Have feelings for me? Are wanting a relationship? That you actually are gay now? That you've always been?"

Travis held up a hand. "Whoa! Too much. I don't know, Wesley. I can't answer all those because I don't know." God he wished he did. How this reminded him of that conversation with Shannon the first time she'd found out he'd fucked a guy. Except they'd had nearly four years together under their belt at that point.

"Sorry." Wesley placed his hand over Travis's, letting it hover momentarily, giving Travis a chance to pull away. He didn't. "I'm not trying to get you to define everything. I know that's maybe not fair. I'm just trying to understand."

It was an active force of will to refrain from sighing at Wesley's touch. Just the feel of Wesley's warm hand touching his made Travis's world tilt. It made him want to run screaming. Made him want to feel every bit of Wesley's body on his.

This time the silence between them was filled with tension, but also anticipation. Wesley's thumb started to make small circling motions over the back of Travis's hand and wrist. They would look at each other and then look away after a moment or two.

The entire time, Travis's heart threatened to beat right out of his chest.

"Wesley, I can't tell you that I am straight or gay. Shannon said I was bi. Maybe I am. I know that I loved her... that I love her. That she was beautiful and that I didn't want any other life than the one I had with her. I also know I really loved having sex with other guys. There were times in our marriage that it took all my power to block those feelings, but I did, or at least didn't act on them, because I loved her."

Travis looked away, eyes stinging, and stared out over the pond. He was thankful when Wesley gave him that time in silence, letting him sort through the emotions. What did he want? Why had he asked Wesley on a date? Why had Shannon been adamant in making him promise all those things?

After a minute or two—it felt like hours—Travis's heart quieted. He knew what he wanted. He wanted Shannon. He wanted what he'd had with Shannon. He looked back to Wesley, encouraged by the patient, hopeful expression on the man's face.

"I can't answer all your questions, Wesley. I'm not sure of most of them myself. Here's what I do know." He paused, taking a deep breath and then exhaling slowly. He couldn't believe what he was about to say. He took another breath, playing the words over in his mind. He waited for guilt. He waited for a sense that he was betraying his wife. Neither came. He took a third breath, and then he spoke. "I know that you're the first person I've kissed since Shannon left. The first person I wanted to. You're the first person I've been attracted to. The first person to make me feel... to make me feel—" He fluttered his hand in front of his chest. "—like this."

Wesley's lips curved into a crooked smile. His voice was soft, an edge of excitement discernable. "I feel it too."

Travis nodded. "Okay." He exhaled. "Good. So let's just go with it?"

"Yeah." Wesley paused, his second confirmation sounding more certain. "Yeah. Let's do."

"Okay." Now Travis was grinning.

"So you gonna kiss me again?"

CHAPTER SEVENTEEN

THE SHADOWS slithered over Mason's bedroom wall. He pulled the covers up over his eyes, then quickly brought them back down, just enough so he could peer over the edge. It was better to see what they were doing. If he covered his eyes, they might make their way onto his bed.

Sometimes the gloomy visitors were nothing more than frolicking calves over meadows. Other times, he could make out Dunkyn and Dolan coming to visit him before he fell asleep. When they bounded over his walls, he would often giggle, although quietly. Aunt Wendy didn't like it when he or Avery stayed awake past their bedtime.

His favorite times, though, were when the shadows merged together into a solitary silhouette. Though he couldn't remember her, he knew it was his momma visiting him, watching over him. Mason recognized the long, flowing hair in the outline of her shape, even if he couldn't see the color. He'd stared at her pictures so many times he'd know her anywhere.

It wasn't his momma who moved over the walls tonight, though. It wasn't the dogs or baby cows. Mason didn't know what the shadows were, but he knew they'd get him if he wasn't careful. If he closed his eyes too long. If he fell asleep.

He looked at the night-lights perched on the bedside tables. First he checked the blue dolphin, curved like a crescent moon. Someday he was going to swim with dolphins and maybe find a mermaid. Narrowing his eyes, he inspected the light quality. No flickering. Seemed okay. Before turning toward the other side, Mason looked back at the sinister shadows. They were still coasting along his walls, but no closer to him. Not yet. He pretended to look away, but instantly jerked his gaze back to the shadows. Yep, still where they had been. That was good.

Satisfied, he turned toward his favorite night-light, the frosted glass unicorn head. He'd begged his daddy for her. Daddy hadn't wanted him to have another night-light. One was enough. He was a big boy. Avery didn't have a night-light, and she was fine. Then, for his sixth birthday, the unicorn had been in one of his biggest packages. It was so big he had to lift it with both of his hands.

He hadn't been scared of the dark for weeks and weeks and weeks.

Maybe he needed to ask Daddy and Aunt Wendy for a third night-light. The shadows had been coming more lately, ever since Dunkyn got sick a few weeks ago. He didn't even care what the night-light looked like. Although he'd seen one shaped like a heart the last time they'd been at Walmart. It was pink. Surely that color would keep away the bad shadows. He'd pointed it out, but Avery had said it was for girls. Aunt Wendy had told her that boys and girl both have hearts. Hearts were what kept us alive, so the night-light could be for boys or girls.

Mason's gaze zoomed away from the unicorn and found the slinking shadows just in time. He was pretty sure one had been right next to his bed. Maybe that's what the shadows wanted. Maybe they could hear his heart beating so hard. Maybe his heart was calling to them. Even he could hear it. He couldn't a few minutes ago, but he could now.

Maybe the shadows collected hearts.

Mason whimpered.

Maybe they *ate* them!

A slice of light cut into the room as his bedroom door suddenly creaked open. Mason yelped and pulled the covers fully over his head.

"Hey, buddy. You shouldn't be awake. Are you okay?"

Mason nearly fell for it. He almost uncovered his head.

He wouldn't. They couldn't trick him.

A heavy pressure pulled at the sheets from the corner of his bed, the weight pinning his toes as his mattress creaked. He bit his lip to keep from crying out. Maybe they'd leave.

Please leave. Just leave.

"Mason, what's going on, my little man?"

The sheet was pulled off his face, and his daddy looked worriedly at him.

"Daddy?"

His daddy smiled gently. "Yeah, bud. It's me."

Mason sat up, letting the blanket fall to his waist. He yanked his left foot. His dad was sitting on his big toe. His foot slid out of its sock and was free. "Daddy!"

Big warm arms wrapped around Mason's back as he crawled into his daddy's lap.

Mason peered at the walls over the sleeves of his daddy's fancy blue shirt. The shadows were still there. Still slithering, but slower. They'd stay away as long as he was safe in his dad's lap. He rested his head on the muscled chest. Aunt Wendy had told him that he'd be as big as his daddy one day. She said Caleb and Avery were more like their mom, but he took after his dad. Mason liked the idea, but he didn't believe it. There was no way he'd ever be as big as his dad. Daddy wore great big boots. He could hold Mason up in the air with one hand while holding Avery up with his other one. Daddy wrestled buffalo. No way he'd be as strong as his dad.

"Why are you awake, my man?" His dad's big hand stroked over Mason's spiky hair, the calluses rough and familiar against his scalp.

Mason didn't answer.

"Shadows?"

Mason tried to figure out whether his dad sounded angry about the shadows. He didn't think so. He nodded against his dad's chest.

The big arms wrapped around a little tighter. "You're okay, buddy. You're safe."

Sometimes, after Caleb read a bedtime story to Avery and him, Wendy would sing him to sleep. Avery never needed her to. Mason loved hearing Wendy sing, but this was better. Once in a while, Daddy would hum or rock back and forth a little, but most of the time, Daddy just held him still. Making everything safe.

"Daddy?" Mason made sure to keep his voice as quiet as possible. The shadows shouldn't hear.

"Yeah, Mason?"

He paused for a moment. He'd almost asked. But if he did, Dad might get mad and leave him alone in the bedroom. "Did you have a good meeting tonight?" He pushed down what he was really wondering.

"I didn't have a...." His daddy paused, then sighed. He smiled, his cheeks flushing pink even in the dim light. Daddy hardly ever smiled. "I did. It was a good meeting."

Mason just nodded. He was glad the meeting had been good, but tears stung his eyes. He shut them tight, scrunching them up so no tears would fall. He was going to be big like Daddy. He wasn't going to cry.

"Hey, Mason." His daddy's voice was soothing, which only made him have to squeeze his eyes tighter. "Buddy, look at me."

Mason shook his head, trying to bury deeper into his daddy's chest. He could hear his hair scrape against the fabric of his dad's blue shirt.

The arms wrapped even tighter. "What's wrong, buddy? Why are you sad?"

Hot tears dropped onto his cheeks, and then he was sobbing, crying so hard that within seconds he was hiccupping.

His daddy pulled him closer, one big hand returning to his head and securing him safely against his chest.

Daddy didn't speak again until Mason's hiccups had stopped and his tears slowed. Leaning back, his dad wedged his hand into the pocket of his jeans and withdrew a white handkerchief. "Here, buddy. Blow your nose."

Mason blew. And blew and blew. Then he wiped his nose on the sleeve of his flannel Nemo pajamas.

His daddy chuckled, then with a finger gently guiding Mason's chin, tilted his head so he had to look up into his daddy's eyes. "What's wrong, Mason?"

Mason felt his lower lip tremble. He wasn't going to ask. He was afraid what his dad would say. He wasn't going to ask. And then he did.

"Are you mad at me?"

Tears instantly filled his daddy's blue eyes. "Oh, Mase, no, of course not. Why would you think that?"

Mason stared at the tear that made its way down his dad's cheek and got lost in his red stubble. The sight made him quit crying. He looked back up to meet his dad's face. He'd never seen Daddy cry before.

Though there were no more tears, Mason's voice trembled guiltily. "You've been really sad lately. Kinda grumpy. I'm sorry if I've been bad."

And there it was. Another tear down his dad's face.

And then he was smashed back against his dad's chest, wrapped in a bear hug so tight it almost hurt.

"No, Mason. You haven't done anything wrong. I'm not mad at you. I'm not mad at you, Avery, or Caleb."

"Aunt Wendy?"

It sounded like Daddy laughed, but it was a strange, cracked sound. "No, Mason. I'm not mad at Wendy either."

Daddy loosened his hold and leaned back so Mason could see his face again.

"I promise, buddy. I'm not mad at you, and you haven't done anything wrong. I've just been worried about some grown-up stuff. I haven't been sure what I'm supposed to do. It's made me... grumpy, I guess."

"Are you better?"

His daddy smiled, and though no more tears fell, his eyes sparkled wetly in the light of the glass unicorn. "Yes. I'm better. Got it figured out. Things are gonna be good. I can feel it."

Mason just stared at his dad. Making sure. "You're okay?"

Another smile. "Yeah, buddy. I'm okay."

"And you're not mad at me?"

"No, my sweet boy. I'm not mad at you at all. I love you."

Mason smiled up at his dad, satisfied. "Okay. Good."

Daddy lowered his head, giving a quick kiss to Mason's forehead. "Now, you've got to get some sleep. You have school tomorrow, and you should have been asleep hours ago."

"Okay." Mason allowed his dad to help him get back under the covers. Another kiss and Daddy walked over to the bedroom door before looking back. "Are you going to be okay tonight? You want me to leave the door open?"

Mason glanced at the shadows that formed next to the doorway, so close they nearly touched his dad.

The slithery shapes had evaporated, and in their place Mason could see a silhouette. Long hair seemed to blow, as if in a soft breeze.

Mason looked back at his daddy. "You can shut it. I'll be okay."

PART TWO
WINTER

CHAPTER EIGHTEEN

FIVE DAYS had passed since Ashley Mei-Lien had given Caleb his first kiss. Granted, she'd warned him about two minutes before the actual act itself. She'd said she wasn't going to bring in the New Year without being kissed.

Maybe it didn't really count since they'd been surrounded by the rest of the youth group. Could you really get your first kiss between the countdown to midnight and an extralong prayer to usher in the New Year?

He'd choked. Everyone had yelled, "Happy New Year!" Ashley leaned into him, her eyes closed and lips pursed. Caleb had started to kiss her, tried to match her expression, but he couldn't bring himself to shut his eyes, and then she was right there—so close, so beautiful.

What if he did it wrong?

What if his breath smelled like the seven-layer dip he'd been scarfing a few minutes before?

What if she laughed?

Ashley's right eye cracked open, and then her lips were on his, warm and wet.

The kiss had lasted a grand total of two seconds, maybe less. Caleb had replayed it over and over and over again so those two seconds felt like the world's longest make-out session.

She'd waved good-bye to him when her grandmother came to pick her up from the party less than half an hour later. That was the last Caleb had seen of her.

His heart felt like it was going to explode. He could literally feel it smashing into his ribcage. He tried to take a deep breath but couldn't remember how to inhale properly.

Pushing his shoulders back, he shoved the front door open and walked into the school. He made it about three feet before they slumped once more, and his gaze found the yellowed linoleum floor.

He was being ridiculous, and he knew it. He wouldn't see her before physical science, which was fourth hour. If he kept this up, he wouldn't make it through the first day back after Christmas break without hyperventilating.

Not only was he being ridiculous, but he was also being a baby. He was a freshman, for crying out loud. Technically, since the year was now officially half over, he could start thinking of himself as a sophomore. He shouldn't be freaking out about his first kiss. And that was the problem— he was nearly a sophomore and had just had his first kiss. There'd been a couple of kids who had been having sex since they'd been in the sixth grade—granted, not many, but by now he was fairly certain most of his class was. Of course, nearly all the kids in the youth group had taken a purity pledge and swore to Jesus that they'd remain virgins until their wedding night. Caleb was willing to bet most of them had been lying. He knew for a fact Jenny Smith was lying. On Halloween, Jacob Wiseman had shown him a picture on his phone of Jenny flashing her breasts. Maybe that didn't mean Jenny had already had sex, but it made sense that if she'd let Jacob have a picture like that, she'd probably do a lot more than lift up her shirt. And here he was, scrawny redheaded Caleb Bennett, tweaking out over his first kiss. *Lame.*

But Ashley Mei-Lien—how was he supposed to stay cool about that? She was gorgeous and smart and funny. She was sweet to the twins. She wasn't in FFA, but she'd told him she liked to ride horses. She was perfect. *Perfect!* And she'd chosen to kiss *him.*

Four hours. He had four hours until physical science.

Was he supposed to mention the kiss?

Maybe he should ignore her until she approached him.

There was the Valentine's dance coming up....

WHEN THIRD hour rolled around and it was time for PE, the day had already taken decades to get through. Caleb didn't remember one clear moment of literacy his first hour, just the incessant droning of Mr. Bird. At least he sat in the back of the room, and Mr. Bird never called on him, which was just the way Caleb liked it. However, second hour had been Ag, hands down his favorite class of the day, with his favorite teacher, Ms. Hungerford. She was the same age his mom would have been and had even taught with her a few years before she died. Ms. Hungerford was one of the few adults who had known his mom, outside of his family, who didn't treat him like some poor little orphan.

Over Christmas break, Caleb had decided he might take Dr. Ryan up on his offer and shadow him at the veterinary clinic. He was going to ask Ms. Hungerford if he could write a paper about it for extra credit or something, but the thought hadn't crossed his mind once he was in class. Ms. Hungerford even held Caleb back after the other kids left the room to make sure he was doing okay. She'd said he seemed a little off. For one terrible moment, Caleb almost told her about Ashley. He almost asked her advice about what he should do. Thank God he hadn't done that. She probably wouldn't have squealed like Wendy if Caleb had asked her, but still. You *did not* ask your teacher for girl advice.

While PE had never been his favorite class, it actually sounded good. Coach Benn had told them they were going to start with a mile run around the track. In the snow. Any other day, that would have been the ultimate definition of torture, but at the moment, Caleb thought it might be just what he needed: sweat, get the heart rate up, breathe some cold air. After class was over, he could shower and be fresh for when he saw Ashley. Who knew? Maybe running would clear his head enough that he could figure out whether he should ask her to the Valentine's dance or if she'd think that was lame.

As it turned out, he hadn't needed to stress about it at all. Fourth hour wasn't going to be an issue.

CALEB CHANGED into his running shorts and T-shirt. He tossed his EHS Bulldog sweatshirt on the locker-room bench, then sat down to tie his tennis shoes.

"You trying to see up my shorts, Ginger?" A deep voice echoed from the other side of the locker room.

Caleb tensed instantly, causing his fingers to fumble with his shoelaces. He didn't look up. He'd know Dustin Jackson's voice anywhere. Ever since the asshole had been held back in fourth grade, he'd done nothing but torture all the other boys. Things had gotten worse at the beginning of their freshman year when Dustin had turned sixteen. He'd already thought he was better than everyone else, but now he truly thought he was hot shit.

Back in fourth grade, Caleb had done his best to try to be friendly with Dustin. The older kid had seemed so sad, like a dog that bit people because it had been beat on when it was a pup. Dustin seemed to love to pick on him the most. Caleb assumed it was because of his red hair—at least most of the taunting revolved around that. He had never mentioned it to his folks. He hadn't wanted to bother them. His mom was starting to get sick and his dad was completely stressed out. It wasn't as if he had time to tell them anyway. As soon as Caleb got home, he had to help his dad with the twins, the animals, and taking care of mom. Some nights, after the twins were asleep, Caleb would do homework. Sometimes he wouldn't. His teachers had started to call home about his dropping grades, which had only stressed his mom and dad out more. The last thing they had needed was to worry about some jerk teasing him about the color of his hair. What if hearing more bad things made his mom sicker? He could handle Dustin Jackson on his own.

And for the next four and a half years, that was exactly what Caleb did. Actually, after a while, it barely took any effort. Even if he was more of an ass to Caleb than most, Dustin was mean to everybody. Teachers too. Caleb didn't take it personally. Even when Dustin started making fun of him for his mother dying, he bit his lip and just kept walking. By sixth grade, Caleb even quit crying about it in the boys' bathroom.

There was a lot worse in this world than Dustin Jackson and those like him.

So he got his hair made fun of, was called a fag or a retard, got shoved into a wall every once in a while—big deal.

Let the big dumbass do his thing, spew his insults for a moment. If you didn't respond, he'd move on to the next moron who couldn't figure out how to keep his mouth shut.

Caleb managed to get his right shoe tied, but when he switched over to his left foot, Dustin shoved his shoulder. Hard. Hard enough that thanks to Caleb's bent position, he fell off the bench and landed smack on his ass.

He looked up from his place on the tile into Dustin's pimpled face.

Dustin lifted his leg.

Caleb flinched, expecting to be kicked.

With a sneer, Dustin brought his foot down on the bench, positioning his leg so his crotch was right above Caleb's face. "Go ahead, fag. If you're gonna try that hard to see up my shorts, go ahead and take a look."

The locker room was instantly silent, the air thick with tension. No one laughed or joined in. They all liked Caleb, and they all had been on the receiving end of Dustin's attention.

Caleb forced himself to keep from rolling his eyes. He waited a moment to see if Dustin had more coming. When it seemed he didn't, Caleb scooted backward the foot or so to the locker and pushed himself off the ground.

Though not as filled out, Dustin was nearly as tall as Caleb's dad, and as he took a step toward the locker, he was like a tower looming over Caleb's thin five-foot-five build. "Did you like what you saw?"

Any thoughts or worries over Ashley fled Caleb's mind. Dustin's taunting had a different feel, a tone Caleb hadn't ever heard directed at him. He'd heard the boy use it with other kids when they stood up to him or had the nerve to call him a name. Now Caleb's heart was beating frantically for an entirely different reason, one that had nothing to do with Ashley Mei-Lien.

Dustin took another step, bringing Caleb within arm's length. "I asked if you liked what you saw."

How was he supposed to answer that? Unintentionally he met Dustin's green stare. He glanced away quickly.

Dustin shoved Caleb in the chest. The reverberating clang of Caleb's back smashing into the metal lockers startled him more than the actual pain of it.

"Answer me when I'm talking to you, Ginger."

Caleb glanced over Dustin's shoulder, past the cluster of boys gathered around the locker room's perimeter. No sign of Coach Benn. He wasn't sure why he even checked. Coach always took at least five minutes to go to the bathroom and refresh his coffee while the boys got changed.

Maybe reading Caleb's mind, Dustin laughed. "What do you think Coach would say if he found out you were looking up my shorts, fag?"

Just look at the floor. Look at the floor.

"I asked if you liked what you saw, queer bait. Don't make me ask it again."

Most of the time, Dustin tormented him about his hair color or at least jumped around between insults. He seemed to have picked a theme.

Just keep looking at the ground.

The left side of his white shoestring was stuck underneath the tongue of his shoe.

A second shove, harder, sent another echo through the room and a sharp stab of pain down Caleb's spine.

He looked Dustin in the face, forcing himself to not look away. An unusual, angry heat began to build. "I didn't see anything."

Dustin jutted his head toward him, raising his hand to cup his ear in a mocking fashion. "Sorry, what was that, little faggy?"

Goddammit. Caleb couldn't help it; he lifted his chin in defiance. "I said I didn't see anything. I wasn't looking up your stupid shorts."

Caleb wasn't sure if he actually heard a couple of the other boys gasp or if the room just got even more still.

Even Dustin's eyes grew wide. "Excuse me?"

"I said, I didn't look up your *stupid* shorts." Caleb could feel his ears burn. He knew they were bright purple against his red hair. For some reason, the knowledge made him even angrier. He stepped away from the locker.

Dustin didn't budge, of course. However, an excited glint crept into his eyes.

Caleb mentally cursed himself. He should have kept his mouth shut. He knew better.

Just keep your goddamn mouth shut. You were supposed to keep your mouth shut.

Dustin's next words were almost a whisper, but the room was so still it didn't matter. "So, then, you're *not* like your father?"

All the building fire within Caleb instantly turned to ice and melted down his body. "What?" His voice cracked.

The grin that spread over Dustin's face was one of unadulterated joy. There wasn't an ounce of his typical expression in it. He looked like Caleb had just handed him a late Christmas present.

"They're saying nowadays that gay shit is genetic. That it runs in families." Dustin raised his hand and shoved his fat finger in Caleb's face. "So, if your dad's a fag, you must be one too."

Oddly, it flashed through Caleb's mind that it surprised him Dustin could say the word genetic, let alone know what it meant. Another synapse fired and the thought was gone. A string of synapses flashed, and puzzle pieces that had started to gather around the edges of his mind over the past month came into view. For a split second, the locker room was a whiteout as flash after flash and puzzle piece after puzzle piece locked into place.

Slack-jawed, Caleb stared up into Dustin's face.

Dustin's grin faltered, then returned with a smirk. "With your mouth open like that, you might as well get down on your knees. Your dad's taught you how to suck cock, right?"

Another blinding flash of light exploded behind Caleb's eyes, and chaos enveloped him.

THANKFULLY, IT was Wendy who showed up to get Caleb. He wasn't sure he could look at his dad.

There was no doubt he'd come out the loser—he'd gained a cut on his cheek, blood gushing from his nose, and a large chip out of one of his front teeth. Still, the waste-of-space Dustin was gonna have one helluva shiner.

Maybe if Coach Benn hadn't arrived and pulled them apart....

Wendy had been unusually silent as she listened to Principal Eslinger explain the two-day suspension. Caleb couldn't look at his aunt when the principal relayed what had started the fight.

He cringed as the principal spoke anew the claim Dustin had made about his dad. Caleb hadn't repeated what had been said. Maybe Dustin or the other boys had.

Wendy didn't offer an explanation or apology. Nor had she reprimanded him while they were in the office.

After they walked out the front doors of the school, Wendy stopped him with a gentle touch on the shoulder halfway down the sidewalk. "Are you okay?"

He couldn't look at her. He just nodded.

He was anything but okay. His face felt like it had been beaten with a brick, and his tooth throbbed. His mind kept shuffling the puzzle pieces, trying to make them form a different picture.

"Wanna tell me about it?"

He shook his head.

Wendy swiped a lock of his damned red hair off his forehead. "Tell me later?"

He hesitated.

"Caleb." Her voice had a warning edge to it. One she typically reserved only for Avery and his father.

He nodded.

"Good. I don't think fighting is ever an answer, but I know you, and I don't blame you for defending your father. I wish I'd been there to help. Maybe hold him down for ya." She turned and started back down the sidewalk.

God, he loved her. "Wendy?"

She paused and looked back at him.

"Did you bring Dolan with you?"

She smiled a knowing smile, her long earrings sparkling in the January sun. "Well of course I did."

SURE ENOUGH, as they approached Wendy's car, he could see his dog pounding his front paws against the passenger window, trying to get to Caleb. He couldn't help but grin at the way Dolan's extralong tongue smashed into the window in his exuberance.

Suddenly he realized he didn't have to worry about what to say to Ashley for another three whole days.

CHAPTER NINETEEN

TRAVIS CHECKED his cell a little after one. He had three messages and already felt a little guilty. When he'd left Cedar County Feed at eleven, he told Jason and Krissy he'd be back within an hour.

He should have known better. He'd promised himself he was simply going to stop by Cheryl's, say hi, steal a quick kiss if Wesley was between appointments—if there were other people in there, he'd make up some excuse about needing to buy dog shampoo for Dunkyn and be on his way. Turned out, Wesley had a two-hour free window.

A quick kiss became an out-to-lunch sign, a locked front door, and a round of sex in the back examination room…, which then became two rounds of sex.

Dunkyn ate two rawhide bones while he waited. He was starting to like Cheryl's.

The F-350 was pulling out of the veterinary clinic's parking lot when the first of the messages sounded in Travis's ear.

The high school, Caleb expelled for fighting, please call back.

Travis pulled the truck over to the side of the road. His insides grew cold.

Krissy was the second message, letting him know the school had called CCF but didn't give any details. She also wanted to know if he would like Jason to pick him up anything from Simone's, and to please call back quickly and say he wanted her to order from Pogo's Pizza. She and her growing baby simply couldn't handle another cheeseburger.

Even in Travis's growing dread, he bristled at his new receptionist's use of that fucking acronym. He might as well give up and change the sign on top of the building.

The last message was Wendy. She'd picked Caleb up from school and had talked to the principal. Travis didn't need to rush home, Caleb was fine and already out with Dolan taking care of the cattle. And she didn't want him to freak out, things would be fine, but Caleb knew.

He knew.

Somehow his son knew.

Blind panic filled him for a moment. He could go back. Undo it all.

No one would have to know.

He glanced in his rearview mirror, the clinic still visible in the distance.

If he hadn't wanted people to know, the random visits to the clinic probably should have been more subtle.

Did you all see Travis Bennett's truck outside Cheryl's the other day? Yeah, it was weird. Just that truck and the yellow Miata in the lot. Yep, the one with the fag rainbow sticker on the back. There was an out-to-lunch sign on the door. For hours! What do you think was going on in there?

God, he'd been an idiot. *Idiot.* He was acting like a seventeen-year-old idiot, thinking with his dick and letting the stupid, giddy feelings short-circuit his brain. It had been one thing when he and Shannon had been in high school. He hadn't been forty-two, hadn't been a father of three—and she'd at least been a girl.

And now Caleb knew and got kicked out of school for fighting. Hmm, wonder what that was about?

Maybe it wasn't too late. He could explain things away. He and Wesley could end things.

Or do a better job of hiding it.

Or....

He found Cheryl's in the mirror once more. He didn't want to end it. He'd actually been talking to Wendy about telling the kids, though the thought made him sick. His stomach churned at the idea of having *that* talk with the kids. He'd thought the sex talk a few years ago with Caleb had been painful. That was nothing compared to this.

So, he'd tell the kids a little sooner than he'd planned. Hell, Caleb already knew, and he was the one Travis was most worried about anyway. Problem solved.

Right, problem solved. Travis might be acting like a teenager, but he wasn't stupid.

"SO, IS he gonna be our new mommy?"

Travis gaped at Avery. She hadn't said anything for the entire conversation, which was unheard of. She just sat rebraiding her My Little Ponys' tails, then handed them to Mason to tie a ribbon on the ends.

For his part, Mason had stared wide-eyed at Travis as he spoke about caring about Dr. Ryan. "Caring about"—that's what he and Wendy had decided would be the best way to explain it to the kids. She'd tried to get him to say love. That he loved Dr. Ryan.

Considering he hadn't even told Wesley that yet, he thought it best to avoid the L-word. The thought made him want to reconsider the possibility of going back, finding a way to undo it all.

Wendy leaned toward the girl, still keeping one hand on Caleb's knee, where he sat beside her on the living room couch. "No, honey, even when two men lo—" She looked toward Travis, then back to the girl. "Even when two men care about each other, neither one of them becomes a mommy."

Avery considered her aunt's words. "Is he moving in here?"

"No, Avery. Nothing's changing." As Travis spoke to his daughter, he was watching Caleb. He didn't miss the skeptical expression that crossed his son's face. He waited for Caleb to say something. Caleb didn't. He hadn't said anything the entire time.

Actually, the only one who had said much at all had been Wendy.

By the time Travis had been able to force himself to man up and go home, Wendy had supper nearly ready. They'd eaten and the kids talked about their day, which meant Avery told about everything that happened to her, reducing Mason to his typical sidekick status. She'd made a couple of comments about Caleb looking strange with his broken front tooth, which she quickly stopped after Wendy threatened no dessert.

For his part, Mason seemed nearly as anxious as his father and brother. His typical, easygoing, calm demeanor was unable to disguise the tenseness he felt. He kept looking at Travis, then Caleb, then back once more.

Travis had hoped to feel some relief at telling his children about Wesley.

He didn't.

The longer he paced the living room, the sicker he felt. He couldn't help but feel that more than anything, he was just being confusing. What were Avery and Mason supposed to do with the information that he *cared* for Wesley? So what? Like Avery had unintentionally alluded, maybe it would mean something if he was announcing that he and Wesley were getting married, or that they were dating, or something. What were first graders supposed to do with their father saying he *cared* about someone? Big deal.

This was why he hadn't wanted to tell them yet. It was too soon. It didn't make any sense to them.

Yeah, *that* was why he hadn't wanted to tell them.

Suddenly, he made up his mind. As he spoke, Travis kept his attention focused on the twins; he didn't want to see Caleb's reaction. "Dr. Ry—Wesley will be here sometimes. You'll be seeing him a lot more." He hadn't talked that over with Wesley. Of course, Wesley didn't even know about the events that had happened at Caleb's school earlier in the day.

Travis had gotten a text an hour or so ago and hadn't responded.

"Wesley will be coming to dinner?"

At her words, Mason looked toward his sister, then back up at his dad.

If only this were about dinner. "Yes, Avery, Wesley will be coming to dinner."

Wendy's eyebrows rose expectantly when Travis didn't offer any more explanation.

He could tell it was taking all her willpower to refrain from rolling her eyes.

She lost the battle, giving an exasperated look at her brother before focusing again on Avery. "Wesley will probably hang out at our house sometimes too. Maybe we can all watch movies together. Play some board games or something."

Avery's hopeful tone brightened. "Will he play with me with my dollhouse?"

Wendy grinned, a laugh behind her words. "Yes. I'm certain Wesley would enjoy playing with you and your dollhouse."

Travis continued to focus away from Caleb. He definitely didn't want to see his reaction to *that*.

What else was he supposed to say to his six-year-olds? What else could he say? He addressed the twins. "It's getting close to bedtime. How about you both get in your pajamas and I'll read you a story?"

Avery's eyes went large. "Caleb reads us our bedtime story."

Ouch.

Caleb didn't look at him. "I'll still read you the story, Avery. Go get into your pajamas."

On their way out of the living room, Mason looked back toward his dad. "Will you tuck us in?"

"Of course, little man."

AFTER TEETH were brushed, big brother story time enjoyed, blankets tucked in, and good-night kisses kissed, Travis found himself out in the barn with Caleb and the dogs.

The early January night was bitter. It hadn't snowed in a few days, and the top layer was more a crackling layer of ice than the wet, heavy flakes it had originally been. Even the tree branches were covered in sparkling layers of ice. The clouds that settled in when the snow had fallen continued to linger, blocking out the stars just as they had shadowed the sun.

Travis pulled the barn door shut after Dunkyn waddled through. "Turn up the heat for a bit, okay?"

Without responding, Caleb crossed the barn floor and adjusted the thermostat behind the ladder to the loft. It had been installed a couple of years before, another kickback from the feedstore. It had alleviated the nightly check of the chickens' water supply.

Keeping the lights dimmed, Travis walked over to the trough forming the barrier to the lean-to. He pushed away the memory of Wesley leaning against it as they'd kissed the first time. It felt strange to think of it when his son stood so close.

He'd hoped things would be more natural between them when they were alone. Though they were never overly talkative, the silence between them was always comfortable and almost soothing at times. Both men were content to simply be together and work with the animals, few words needed between them.

He balked internally at the thought as he looked over to where Caleb sat on a small bale of hay, dutifully scratching Dolan's belly as he lay with his front legs pawing the air. Travis had just thought of Caleb as a man. Huh. When had that happened?

Long ago, probably. Way before the fine hairs on his son's lip made the announcement. Caleb had been equal part man and father to the twins by the time he'd been ten. When Travis hadn't been.

The boy had grown up overnight, losing his constant chattery ways the same night he lost his mother.

Travis continued to stare, transfixed by his son, seeing him in a new light though no revelation had occurred, at least none of Caleb's making.

The boy had slept on the floor in the twins' room for weeks after Shannon's death. Avery and Mason had still been sharing a room at that time. In the few moments Travis had been able to focus on anything besides his own torment, the sight of Caleb's thin form keeping watch over his brother and sister had cut through him even deeper.

Heartache over what his children had lost.

Anger at what they would have to face.

Worthlessness at his inability to be strong for them.

On one of his more lucid days, shortly after Wendy moved in, he'd taken Caleb to the breeder where Shannon had purchased Dunkyn and let him pick out a puppy.

As he watched his son lavish distracted attention on the dog, Travis thought it might have been the best decision he'd made in the past four years. As mentally limited as he might be, Dolan had saved Caleb in ways Travis would never have been able to.

Travis flinched when he realized Caleb was looking at him, watching him as he stared.

"What did you want, Dad?"

He wasn't sure if the lack of emotion in Caleb's words was good or not. At least he didn't sound angry or disgusted.

He didn't sound like anything.

What *did* he want? "I just wanted to tell you...."

Caleb waited, expression expectant.

"Oh, Caleb, I don't know what I'm supposed to say." He closed the distance between them and motioned toward the other hay bale next to Caleb. "May I sit?"

His son shrugged, turning his attention back to his dog. "Sure."

Travis sat, feeling a thousand years old. Transitioning from feeling like a seventeen-year-old to Methuselah in a day wasn't pleasant. Guilt weighted him down.

Guilt? Why exactly did he feel guilty? He wasn't religious, after all. He wasn't worried about heaven or hell. He definitely wasn't concerned about some rules the God who'd taken Shannon away may or may not have babbled eons ago.

Still, there were more reasons outside of church walls that dictated why two men weren't supposed to be with each other.

He wasn't some horned-up kid in college any longer.

"I'm so sorry I caused this today."

Caleb turned and looked at him in time to notice Travis's motion toward his bruised face. He shrugged again. "No big deal. Dustin Jackson is a jerk. Way before Dr. Ryan moved to town."

The name sounded vaguely familiar to Travis. Another wash of guilt flooded over him. From Caleb's tone, there was no doubt that Travis should be much more familiar with the other boy's name.

Before he could figure out a way to begin to remedy that situation, Caleb spoke, keeping his attention firmly trained on Dolan. "Why didn't you tell me?"

Travis opened his mouth to speak but then stopped, uncertain of what Caleb meant and not wanting to say too much. Better safe than sorry. "Tell you about what?"

"Why didn't you tell me you liked guys?" Caleb said, still working hard to keep from looking at Travis's face.

Oh God. How was he supposed to answer that? How much were you supposed to share with your teenage son? What damage could he do?

"Bud, I didn't think it would be an issue."

Caleb looked at him then, an accusing glint in his eyes. It wasn't an expression Travis was used to seeing on his son. "You didn't think it would be an issue with me, or you just didn't think I'd find out?"

This was horrible. He'd rather change Cedar County Feed's name than have this conversation. "I didn't think it would matter. I didn't plan on there ever being another guy in my life like that."

Caleb sat up straight, Dolan suddenly forgotten. "There are other guys?"

Fuck. "Not for years. Not since your mom and I got married."

A horrified expression covered Caleb's face. "You had a boyfriend before Mom?"

Dolan propped his front legs up on the hay bale, shoving his nose in the crook of Caleb's arm. He went unnoticed.

"*Boyfriend?* No, I've never had a boyfriend. That's not what we did. That's not what I meant."

Travis would have given anything for Caleb to look horrified again. That had been so much better than the expression he traded it for. "Ah, Dad! Gross. I so don't want to know this."

Travis held out his hands, whether in an act of surrender or pleading for mercy, he wasn't sure. "Caleb, I'm doing a horrible job at this. I'm sorry. I don't know how to explain it to you."

Caleb's face darkened. "Did Mom know?"

Again, what was the right answer, what would hurt Caleb the least? He wished Shannon were here; she'd know how to handle this. Maybe he should have asked Wendy to join him.

"Yeah. She knew."

Caleb continued to stare at him. Travis felt sure he'd never forget the expression pasted on his son's face.

"Caleb, I loved your mom. I still love your mom. I've never stopped and I never will. And she loved me. I couldn't have asked for a better wife." His throat closed, and he had to take a moment to speak again. "I miss her every second I'm awake. Hell, every second, period. Even when I'm sleeping."

The expression on Caleb's face changed.

He wasn't able to identify it until he realized what Caleb was staring at. Travis wiped the tear off his cheek.

They stared at each other.

Travis couldn't read the thoughts behind his son's eyes, but he prayed Caleb could see how desperately Travis loved him.

After a moment, Dunkyn padded over to Caleb and joined in with Dolan, pushing his nose against Caleb's palm.

Caleb looked down at the two dogs, a small smile breaking over his face. He began petting them. His left hand on Dolan's bobbing head. His right hand ruffling Dunkyn's long fur.

"Caleb." Travis waited until his son looked back up at him. "I'm so sorry that I'm causing you trouble at school. I wasn't thinking about this affecting you there, though I know I should have. I was just worried about you finding out in general, I guess. And I wasn't planning on having to talk about it so soon." Again the truth seemed best, as much as he wished he were lying. He really hadn't thought about how this could affect his children outside of their own home. He'd been so caught up in his own fear about it all and his own budding feelings for Wesley.

What kind of father was he? He knew what high school was like, what it had been like for the effeminate kids when he'd been in school. It was one reason he'd never acknowledged the attractions he'd felt, not even to himself.

Caleb shrugged. "Whatever, Dad. I'm not worried about that."

"You don't have to be tough, bud. You don't have to spare my feelings. I'm so sorry that this is affecting you. I will talk to Wesley, and we can—"

Luckily, he didn't have to finish that sentence, as he wasn't sure what he was about to say.

Caleb waved him off. "Seriously, Dad. Don't worry about that." He motioned toward his face. "Dustin's an ass, and, if anything, he probably will quit picking on me now that he knows I'll fight back if I have to."

Will quit picking on him. The words cut at Travis. More confirmation that he had missed so much, *was* missing so much.

Caleb continued, his typical soft tone remaining, but sounding more assured than normal, more adult. "I'm sure I'll get teased some, but nothing big. I've got good friends. And there's a couple of gay kids at school. Maybe this will help them."

There was Shannon, shining out of Caleb. In addition to seeing her slight frame, Travis could hear her sense of fight and compassion in their son.

"Things probably aren't like when you were in school, Dad. Most kids don't care much. That Darwin kid who graduated a couple of years ago…." Caleb's brow rose in question. "Do you remember him?"

Travis nodded, though he had no clue.

"He was gay, and he was one of the popular kids. Kinda. He pops into youth group every once in a while."

There was a gay kid in the Holy Church youth group? If Caleb had been the kind, Travis would have sworn he was making it up.

"Will you tell me if things get bad? If you're getting threatened or teased because of me?"

Caleb hesitated before answering. "Dad, it's nothing I can't handle. I've been doing fine."

His sweet son was beating his heart to a pulp. "I know you have. But, will you tell me anyway?"

After a second or two, Caleb nodded.

Again, silence fell. This time, though, it felt more familiar, akin to what had always existed between them. They were still tense, still wary, but Travis was pretty sure they were headed to a good place—maybe even a better place than they had been.

"Caleb?"

His son looked back up at him.

"I'm proud of how you stood up for yourself today."

Caleb only nodded. When he did speak, his voice was barely more than a whisper. "I did it for you."

And if that didn't bring more tears to his eyes…. He wanted to rush to his boy and wrap him in his arms and sob.

He stayed where he was.

"I'll make an appointment to get that tooth fixed. You got three days outta school. Might as well put them to use."

"Am I getting in trouble for that, by the way?"

Travis couldn't remember the last time Caleb had gotten in trouble. The boy was perfect, which, now that he thought about it, was probably not a good sign. Still, he laughed. "Are you kidding? Taking on an asshole like that? Boy, I'll take you to the stock show and buy you a new cow."

Caleb's head jerked up once more, his eyes wide. "Are you serious?"

He hadn't been. It had just been an expression, kinda. But if he'd ever heard of a kid who deserved something more, he couldn't remember it. "Yeah, Caleb. I'm serious."

His son beamed, as innocent and carefree-looking as his younger sister.

Silence fell once more, each man lost in his own thoughts. Travis was blown away by the change in things, marveling at how much of his son he'd been missing and vowing to remedy that. Caleb was probably dreaming of the perfect prizewinning steer.

"Dad?"

Travis looked up, pulled out of his reverie, concerned at the caution in his son's voice. "Yeah, what's wrong?"

Caleb hesitated. Nervous. "I'm not gay."

Travis tried to refrain from cringing at the word, and at the implication that *he* was. He was fairly certain he succeeded. "I know that, Caleb."

More hesitation. "I don't think I'm ever gonna be."

Thank God. "Caleb, that's fine. I'm not expecting you to be."

He could tell Caleb wanted to say something more. Like him, his son needed time to process certain things before he spoke. Travis waited.

After a minute or two filled with ponderous attention lavished on the dogs, Caleb addressed Travis again. "Once my tooth is fixed, I think I'm gonna ask Ashley to the Valentine's dance."

That name he remembered, thanks to Wendy's meddling on Halloween, though he still hadn't seen the girl. "Oh yeah? That's the Mei-Lien girl, right?"

"Yeah."

Travis leaned his back against the wall and crossed his arms in front of his chest, relaxing into this moment he hoped would go on forever. "What's she like?"

As Caleb spoke, telling his father everything from how pretty the girl was, to the clubs she was in, to how good she was with the twins—even Avery—Travis was reminded of the talkative, animated little boy Caleb had been once.

No tears fell as Travis listened; he speckled Caleb's descriptions with questions, just to keep hearing his son's voice.

Though there were no whispers, he knew Shannon was beside him. Listening.

CHAPTER TWENTY

SNIFFLES CHEWED on Wesley's fingers, his baby teeth sharp and rather painful. Wesley managed to pull his fingers out of the puppy's mouth without losing skin and distract the little guy by vigorously rubbing his sides. Little was a misnomer. The nine-week-old was massive. Making sure to keep his hands far from Sniffles's gnawing mouth, Wesley looked at the pretty, fortysomething, WASPish woman on the other side of the examination table. "Ms. Michaels, you are going to have one massive dog, even for a Saint Bernard. Judging from his paws and how big he is already, I'm guessing he'll be around one hundred and seventy pounds or so. Maybe more."

The woman smiled adoringly at the dog. "That's fine by me, more to love."

Wesley eyed her petite frame. "I would suggest starting puppy training pretty soon, especially with how big he's going to be. Walking him will be a nightmare if he's not well behaved."

She waved him off. "Oh, don't you worry, we'll teach him some manners. And my husband, Craig, is rather huge. Sniffles won't be able to jerk him around. And he's rather particular. Sniffles will be the most polite little, or not so little, guy you've ever seen."

Wesley eyed the pup. If Mr. Michaels was all that particular, a Saint Bernard wasn't the right choice, especially with how big Sniffles was going to be. Nothing under four feet was going to be safe from constant drool. Wesley gave Sniffles a final tousle, then lifted him off the metal table and placed him on the floor. He returned his attention to Sniffles's adoring mother. "If you'll just follow me up front, I can get you Sniffles's papers to show he's all caught up on his shots. And we can make an appointment for about three weeks, when he'll be due for his rabies shot. We can also do a Lyme vaccine, which I'd certainly recommend."

"That sounds great." Ms. Michaels hooked a jeweled leash onto the dog's collar, then followed Wesley out of the room. "When did you say Sniffles needed to get neutered?"

"When he's about six months old, give or take." Wesley stepped behind the computer in the front office and began typing in Sniffles's information.

After paying, setting up the next two appointments, and collecting all of Sniffles's papers, Ms. Michaels headed for the door, then turned back to Wesley, hesitantly. "Dr. Ryan, may I ask you something?"

Something in her tone made Wesley pause. Up until this point, Ms. Michaels had been casual and bubbly. The sudden somber switch made him wary. "Certainly, Ms. Michaels."

"You can call me Carrie, if you'd like." She started to walk back toward him, but Sniffles had sat down and pulled on the leash with his teeth. She glanced at the dog, then back to Wesley. "Do you mind if I put Sniffles in his carrier in the car? I'm not sure of your schedule, but it would just be a minute or two of your time."

"Of course. I have a little bit before my next appointment." He tried to not let his mind go crazy as he watched the woman through the window. He probably should have offered to help with the dog. It was snowing again, and Ms. Michaels was visibly struggling lifting the squirming dog.

There was really only one thing it could be about.

Since Travis had told him about what had happened to Caleb at school a couple of days ago, Wesley had been expecting villagers with pitchforks to show up at the clinic's door.

Before he could slip into full panic mode, Ms. Michaels was back, dusting snow off her hair. She let out a small groan. "Goodness, it feels good in here. It is freezing outside." She walked back toward Wesley, who remained behind the counter. "I just can't seem to get used to these Ozark winters. They're just bitter."

"Oh, I didn't realize you weren't a native." That made him feel a little more at ease, like he wasn't starting off at such a disadvantage.

"Oh, no. We moved here—" She did some mental figuring. "—six or seven years ago. Craig is the supervisor at the shirt factory. I'm a city girl, and, honestly, I'm ready to get back."

Wesley was feeling better already. Maybe this had nothing to do with him and Travis. "I'm from Kansas City. My family is still there. It's actually been more of a challenge to get used to being here than I anticipated. Though we get the same kind of winters there. But they do a better job keeping the roads cleared."

Ms. Michaels glanced out the window toward her SUV. "I should probably make it quick. I don't want to leave Sniffles out there long, actually."

That worked for him. "What can I do for you?"

Despite her press for time, she hesitated, glancing nervously around the main office, finally looking at him again. Her brown eyes were kind and full of concern. "This may sound strange, and if I'm overstepping my boundaries, just say so." Another pregnant pause. "I just wanted to make sure you're doing okay here?"

"That I'm doing okay?" It looked like it probably had something to do with him and Travis after all.

Ms. Michaels hurried on, her cheeks flushing. "Well, I've heard rumors about you. That you are, um, dating"—there was a question in her tone—"the gentleman who owns the feedstore."

Though he wasn't going to hide anything, neither was he going to confirm anything for her. She seemed kind enough, but the town had felt less friendly the past couple of days. Wesley wasn't sure if that was the reality or just his perception.

When she realized he wasn't going to respond, she continued. "I just wanted to offer a kind word I suppose." She twisted her hands in front of her. "I guess that seems silly."

Wesley relaxed somewhat. "Oh, well… thank you. That's nice of you. I… ah…." This was beyond awkward.

Ms. Michaels placed both of her hands on the glass counter, leaning in toward him, her words coming quicker. "You see, my son, Darwin, is gay. He's doing great now, but it was hard for a while." Her eyes clouded over momentarily, lost in some memory. "It got bad enough that he attempted to take his life. I swore that I would never…." She seemed at a loss for words. "I'm not saying you're feeling that way or anything. I just wanted… well, I just wanted you to know."

All reservation melted away, and his heart broke for the woman and what she'd gone through. And he was touched at what she was attempting to do. Giving in to the impulse, Wesley walked around the counter and wrapped her in his arms.

She hugged him back instantly, her small frame trembling in his much larger arms.

After a few moments, Wesley pulled back, giving her a little space. "Thank you, Carrie. Thank you for trusting me with that. Your son— Darwin, I believe you said—your son is better now?"

She wiped at her eyes and smiled. "Oh, yes. He's doing well. He's a sophomore in college and is quite happy." Her smile brightened, pride radiating through her emotions. "He's at peace with who God made him to be."

Wesley wasn't sure what that meant. He'd heard of kids having gone to religious camps to make them straight or some such nonsense.

Carrie continued, answering his question before he could figure out how to ask. "There was a fellow in our church who was…." She fumbled for words again. "Well, I guess you could say he was a guest speaker at the youth group when Darwin was in high school. His name was Brooke, and he talked to the kids about his experience being gay." Tears filled her eyes once more. "He saved my son's life."

"He saved your son? He was there when Darwin tried to hurt himself?"

She shook her head. "Oh, no. Not like that. He simply let Darwin know that he was okay. That he was exactly how he should be. Brooke and his husband were the first people Darwin knew who were gay, and"— she shrugged again—"they took the time to love him. Craig and I owe them so much."

Wesley had no idea what to say. If Carrie hadn't been so emotional, he would have thought she was making the whole thing up. A church in El Dorado Springs had a gay guest speaker talk to their youth group? And his husband?

"I know you're not a teenager, Dr. Ryan, but I've also learned how lonely it can seem. I'm not sure how you've gotten along since you've moved to town. I know what it's like to be an outsider here and to have a gay son. I just wanted you to know, so that you…. Well, I just wanted you to know."

Wesley hugged her again, immensely thankful for the tiny woman. "I'm so glad your son is okay. I hope I get to meet him one day."

She smiled at him when they separated. "Oh, I'd love that! Maybe when he comes back during summer vacation, I could bring him by, or we could all go to dinner or something."

Wesley grinned. "Absolutely. You can count on it."

"Wonderful. And in the meantime, Sniffles and I will see you in a couple of weeks." Carrie squeezed his arm and walked toward the door.

"Carrie?"

She looked back him. "Yes, Dr. Ryan?"

"The guest speaker, Brooke, are he and his husband still in town?" How would he not have heard of them? Surely Wendy would have mentioned it, or Travis, if he had known.

Her smile faltered. "No. Things were pretty hard for them here. They moved a couple of years ago. Right around the time Darwin graduated. They keep in contact with him, though."

Of course they'd left. *Things were pretty hard for them here.* Wesley's heart sank at the implication.

WESLEY WAS glad he had a little bit of time before his next appointment. He wasn't sure how to process Ms. Michaels's story. On one hand, it was nice to have a friendly face show up out of the blue, someone who wasn't connected to Travis or Wendy. Though nothing had changed since Travis had told him about Caleb and that word was out that Travis and Wesley were connected, Wesley felt like every eye in town was on him. No one had said anything, but Wesley could feel it, though maybe it was his imagination. He'd begun to feel like the town leper. But if Ms. Michaels wasn't closed-minded, maybe there were others. Maybe she and Darwin had sort of paved the way with the help of that Brooke guy and his husband—although they'd apparently hightailed it out of there. That didn't bode so well.

Truth be told, he was exhausted. He was relieved he and Travis didn't have to be as careful anymore, not that they'd been careful enough. They'd made it about two months before the shit hit the fan, but in a town as small as El Do, Wesley figured they couldn't have expected much more.

He wasn't worried about what the town would think or say. He really didn't care about what anyone else thought. Until realizing that Caleb had gotten into a fight because of him, at least by default, he hadn't really considered the implications outside of his own turmoil, selfish though that might be.

Everything with Travis had been a whirlwind, and that included sex. He was having some of the best sex of his life. Things with Todd had been good, though Todd had always been rather predictable when it came to sex, except for the whole leaving him for a twink factor. Sex with others had been fun, dirty, and frequent—well, maybe frequent was an understatement.

But sex with Travis? Holy hell. The man was an animal, just as much a bear when they were fucking as he looked like he'd be. Wesley hadn't expected it. With the man's trepidation about the whole gay thing, and his pain around his dead wife, Wesley had been prepared to have to be patient with the sex, taking things slow and staying about as vanilla as possible.

He needn't have worried. Once Travis had given in to his attraction to Wesley, the floodgates had opened, and many times Wesley had to concentrate on walking normally the rest of the day.

He loved it!

And therein was the problem, wasn't it? He was falling for the redheaded brute. Wesley truly had intended to spend the next year or so solely focused on regaining his equilibrium, figuring out his next steps, and using the time to get grounded before moving on.

Instead, he was having sex with a father of three. Travis had just brought up the possibility of Wesley spending time with the kids. That added a whole different level to their relationship.

When he'd gone back to Kansas City to spend Christmas with his family for a couple of days, Wesley had expected to be able to take a breather and get some perspective. He expected to realize he'd been caught up in emotion, the intensity of new sex, and doing nothing more than rebounding, two years later. If nothing else, he'd give in to his mother's snide comments about El Dorado, some of which he could understand, now that he'd been there a few months.

No such luck. He'd missed Travis. After only two days.

It wasn't just the sex or the butterfly feelings and excitement of something new.

He'd missed Travis. The man. His quiet humor. His awkward attempts at flirting. His fondness for overuse of the F-word. The way he spoke about his kids. How gentle he was with Dunkyn. The strange mix of intense masculinity and tender compassion.

He did not want to fall in love with the man. He didn't want to get trapped before he'd figured everything out. And Travis wasn't alone; he came with three kids and a sister Wesley truly did love.

And what if he did fall in love with Travis? What if he gave in and went for it? Sure the past two months had been amazing, but they'd been living in secret. You were never supposed to date a guy who'd just come out, and Travis hadn't even come out, not technically.

Wesley was setting himself up for greater heartbreak than he'd experienced with Todd, and he knew it. He needed to walk away quickly before greater damage could be done, before Travis realized he couldn't face his friends and the people who did business with him. It was one thing for Wesley to be the new gay vet in town. He might have been able to pull that off. But for Travis, one of the good old boys, to suddenly switch teams was not going to be fun.

Nor was it going to be fun to be the one who'd corrupted the good, upstanding father of three. He'd be the faggot who had taken advantage of the man's grief, stolen his soul, endangered his children's lives.

WESLEY HAD worried before, but he'd done his best to slough it off as being dramatic. It didn't feel that way now that people were finding out, now that Caleb had gotten beaten up, now that the prospect of being with Travis as a couple in front of the kids, as a family, loomed in front of him. The concerns didn't seem dramatic at all. They were so huge that the only absurd factor was that he'd not acknowledged them before.

It didn't matter that Travis was older. He was newly out, although not really. He was just discovering all of this, or rediscovering it, at any rate. He might as well be a teenager. Wesley should have been the strong one, the wise one. He knew better, but he'd ignored the warning bells and all the stop signs along the way. That was so typical.

If he wrote down the pros and cons, the answer would be obvious, which was exactly why he'd refrained from doing so. On one side, the list of reasons to cut and run would take pages. On the other side, he could only write, *but I love him*, and it would be written in whiny-twelve-year-old-girl voice, in glitter pen.

God, he hated himself for that.

Wesley didn't just have feelings for the guy. He wasn't just having killer sex. He was falling in love with Travis. Two months or not. Newly out father of three or not. Small Podunk town or not. And all the baggage Todd had left him with or not.

It shouldn't be possible—not this soon, not knowing everything he knew, not with everything he'd already gone through.

He wasn't falling in love with Travis.

He was already in love with him.

And he was just fool enough to keep going, to stay in it.

He was going to look back and see all the exits he could have taken. All the should've, could've, would've.

He was going to hate himself when this was all over and he was left even more broken and bleeding than he had been. He knew it. It was unavoidable.

So be it.

ABOUT TWENTY minutes before his scheduled appointment to check a hamster with a potential eye infection, Iris came rushing through the clinic's front doors, Horace hacking and wheezing in her arms.

Still lost in his increasing stress, Wesley jumped at the sight of them. It only took him a moment to focus on those in front of him. Actually, it was a relief to get out of his own head. He only needed to take one look at Horace. "What did he try to eat this time, Iris?"

In her typical floral muumuu, this one a smash of brilliant lime green and orange, with her massive breasts swaying with each undulation, Iris Linley provided quite the image as she swept across the lobby. Her long, flowing coat did nothing to suppress the mishmash of colors.

Wesley had to bite his lip to keep from smirking.

"Oh, Sister Hill came into the flower shop. It seems there's some impromptu event at the church today and she needed an arrangement of lilies. Of course I told her I can't just whip those out of thin air. I would need to place an order."

Wesley lifted his eyebrows questioningly.

"Well, she settled on a nice bouquet of silk begonias. Nice."

No matter how hard he bit his lip, Wesley couldn't suppress a chuckle. "Iris, what did Horace try to eat?"

Iris rolled her eyes. "Well, Sister Hill may be the pastor's wife, but the woman is an idiot. She set her purse on the floor and poor Horace was curious." Iris plopped the sputtering cat on the countertop, freeing her arms to flail about as she ranted. "I mean, seriously, you'd think the woman would have more common sense."

Wesley began to reach for the cat, but remembered the claw marks Horace had left him with the last time. He pulled out the lower drawer of the cabinet behind the counter and withdrew a pair of long gloves. "So, you're not certain what he might have gotten out of her purse?"

"Oh, no. I'm certain. She had extension cords." She placed her hands on her hips. "Now, I ask you, what kind of woman carries around extension cords?"

With the gloves in place, Wesley picked up Horace, who increased his choking, though he might have simply been protesting being held by Wesley. "Just follow us, Iris. I imagine you remember the drill."

SURE ENOUGH, Horace had attempted to ingest slivers of the extension cords. With long tongs, Wesley pulled out a curling slice of the cord's brown plastic coating.

Horace was instantly able to breathe better and proceeded to object to being back at the vet's by yowling loudly.

Wesley had to raise his voice to be heard over the obnoxious cat. "Iris, I have another appointment coming in soon. However, I'd like to take some X-rays, make sure that Horace hasn't ingested any more of the cords. Would you be comfortable leaving him here? If everything looks fine, you can pick him up later this evening."

Iris's watery eyes widened. "Will he be all right?"

"I'm certain he will be. I'd just like to make sure we keep it that way. That's why I'd like to be certain we aren't leaving anything behind."

She was on the verge of tears. "Well, if you think that's necessary."

"I promise, as soon as I finish with this next appointment, I will get right to work on Horace and call you as soon as the X-rays are available."

Iris nodded slowly.

"Let me just get Horace situated, and I'll meet you up front."

Wesley once again gathered the hostile cat in his arms and carried him to one of the kennels in the back.

Back at the front counter, Horace could be heard squalling through the entire clinic. "From the sound of him, I think he's going to be fine, Iris."

"I hope. I do love him so." Iris's eyes were red-rimmed, and her cheeks were blotchy. She dabbed at her eyes with a yellowed handkerchief.

"I'll take good care of him, Iris. I promise. I'll call you soon."

Instead of leaving, Iris continued to stand in the middle of the lobby, staring at Wesley.

"Is there something else that you need, Iris?"

She cocked her head, for all intents and purposes looking like a rather ponderous turkey dressed up as a tacky peacock. "I heard you are having relations with Travis Bennett, Wendy's brother."

"What?" Wesley nearly choked. He was suddenly more sympathetic toward Horace. "Having relations?"

She made a squishy face. "Well, I don't know what you boys call it. Dating, I suppose."

Wesley just stared at her, awestruck.

"Well? Are you?"

If it had been anyone else asking in any other way, Wesley would have been able to avoid the question or play it off. But she, Iris Linley, had completely thrown him. "Yes. I guess you could call it that."

Iris's eyes narrowed. "Are you certain you're not trying to get a job at the church?"

What was this woman's hang-up with that? Wesley shook his head, still mostly slack-jawed. At this rate, he might start drooling. "No. I'm not."

She nodded and smiled. "Very good. I can't say I would have felt this way until recently, but I will say I hope you two are happy. You're both nice men, and those Bennett children need a mother."

Before Wesley could even attempt to try to sort out her meaning, Iris turned and headed to the door, slipping back into her long coat and waving over her shoulder. "Please do call quickly. I will be worried about poor Horace."

She had to pause at the door to let a young mother and a little boy through, and then she was gone.

Wesley continued to stare after her, watching her through the large window.

"Are you okay, Dr. Ryan?"

He turned away from the window with effort and focused on the two people in front of him. "Oh, yes. Sorry. You must be, ah, Ms. Miles, with the hamster."

The little boy held up a small wire cage with a trembling rodent trying to hide in a corner.

"What is that noise?"

Wesley looked at the woman in confusion for a moment. "Oh! That's Horace. He's in the back. He's fine, just unlikeable." He looked at the hamster again. Poor little guy. No wonder he was shaking. "Why don't I just take a quick—"

The telephone rang.

Good God. The clinic was turning into total chaos.

He tried to smile at the woman and child. "One second, please. Let me get that."

Wesley walked the three feet to the landline phone and picked up the receiver from the wall. "Cheryl's, this is Dr. Ryan. How can I help you?"

Though Wesley hadn't thought of the man in nearly two months, he knew the voice instantly and was transported back to that stormy night as John Wallace spoke into his ear.

"Got my final clearance from animal services today. I wanted to let you know that you and that shit Bennett you're fucking can suck my cock. You're not getting my land. If you try that shit again, it will be the last fucking thing you do."

CHAPTER TWENTY-ONE

IT HAD been all over town, no matter where he went.

Wendy kept telling him it was in his mind, that he was projecting.

He wasn't.

He was willing to bet Wendy had heard enough gossip at The Crocheted Bunny that she knew he wasn't as well.

Travis had first noticed it when Jake Thurston filled up his tank at the Sinclair. When the kid was washing the F-350's windshield, their eyes met for a moment. Jake blushed and looked away like he'd been caught with his hands in his pants. Even as Travis paid, Jake had kept taking sidelong glances at him. Maybe that had been Travis's imagination, and maybe it hadn't. Jake was a junior in high school, though, so it made sense that he would have heard the rumors since Caleb and that thug Jackson had gotten suspended.

Then Betty Glover at the Tastee-Freez barely spoke when she handed him his chocolate malt through the drive-through. Truth be told, it was an improvement. The woman never shut up. She'd stand there waving the ice cream through the air like it was just a prop to help her tell whatever boring event she was attempting to relay. There was no way she was paying any attention to the high school gossip—Betty Glover was one hundred and fifty years old if she was a day.

When Travis stopped by the hardware store to pick up a new three-eighths-inch drill bit, Charles Maxwell handed Travis the bit, his change, and a receipt, and asked him if he was feeling like his normal self lately. When Travis responded that he was, Charles just grunted. Unlike Betty, the man rarely strung two sentences together, so that interaction might not have meant all that much.

When Travis got his mail at the post office, Peter Holtz mentioned that they hadn't gotten any junk mail addressed to Shannon in several months. Travis had stormed into the post office late one afternoon a few months after Shannon had passed, and ranted and raved about them delivering mail that was addressed to his dead wife. The details of that afternoon were hazy—he'd had a few beers that day—but he still felt justified. How hard was it to make sure you didn't deliver a man's dead wife's mail? Each letter or advertisement that arrived was one more declaration of her absence. No one at the post office ever mentioned the incident, and Travis never got any other mail with Shannon's name on the envelope. It made no sense for Peter to bring it up nearly four years later, and Travis was fairly certain there had been an accusation in the man's tone.

The twins had brought home a pamphlet—just tucked inside their Friday folders, mixed in with all the work they had done over the week—about how changes in home life and relationships could cause stress and how to best avoid subjecting your child to undue anxiety. He'd never been overly fond of Ms. Welton, and upon seeing the fucking thing, Travis had been ready to rush to the school and demand her resignation. Wendy had reminded him that with one child recently suspended, the school probably wasn't too keen on any advice the Bennetts might have to offer—that, and she was certain the pamphlet had gone out in all the students' folders.

Yeah, right.

Even Shannon's parents had been unusually distant when they'd crossed Travis's path as he visited her grave. They still hugged him and asked about him and the kids, but there was a guardedness that hadn't been there before. They had to know. They had to. Travis almost asked them point-blank, but couldn't, not right there by Shannon's grave. Still, they had to know.

It seemed everyone knew.

JASON HAD been resentful of Travis offering Krissy a job before asking for his input. The first day or so she was there, the tension was so great Travis had begun to consider whether he'd made a mistake. If it didn't work out at Cedar County Feed, Travis decided he'd ask Krissy to be a nanny to the kids or pay her to work at Wendy's store. But then, miracle of fucking miracles, Jason and Krissy bonded... over their shared love of giving Travis a hard time.

It was almost cute, if it hadn't been so annoying.

For weeks, anytime the two of them were in the same room, there was cackling and juvenile humor. Travis reminded Jason that Krissy was the teenager, not him. It didn't do any good. At moments, Travis caught himself feeling jealous of the two. It almost felt as if his best friend had been stolen away.

For the past several days, though, Cedar County Feed had been quiet. Not only were there fewer customers, but Jason and Krissy were oddly silent. However, it seemed like things were normal until Travis walked into the store, and then the two of them would instantly clam up.

Wendy swore this was all in his mind as well.

The final straw came when Travis was bringing in an order from Simone's. This time, he actually had only stopped by Cheryl's for a moment. There had been clients there.

Travis had intentionally been as quiet as possible when he shut the door of his truck. As he walked up the sidewalk, he could hear Jason's barking laugh a good ten feet from the door. No sooner had he turned the doorknob than the two of them fell instantly silent, both fiddling unconvincingly with papers on the counter.

Travis swung the door closed with a swift backward swipe of his boot, walked over to them, and plopped the white paper bags on the counter. "Okay, you two, out with it!"

They both looked at him, wide-eyed, full of forced innocence. Then each of them simultaneously focused elsewhere, Jason thumbing through a stack of papers too quickly to actually be reading them and Krissy staring at the computer screen, one hand dropping to her expanding belly.

"Seriously?" Travis looked back and forth between the two.

Krissy was suddenly enthralled by something on the computer screen.

Jason glanced at him for the briefest of seconds. Amateur.

Travis waited.

Still nothing.

He sighed. "Just ask already."

Jason didn't look up. "Ask what?"

"Oh for fuck's sake, Baker. You're being—"

"Fine." Krissy looked up at him, her other hand coming to rest on her stomach as well. "Is it true you're dating the new vet? The guy who was with you the day you offered me this job?"

Jason whipped his head around to stare at her in surprise.

Despite telling them to ask, it was Travis's turn to freeze. Terror surged through him. The emotion surprised him, though it probably shouldn't have.

When he didn't answer, Jason turned to face him. His eyes narrowed.

Travis wasn't sure what the expression on his best friend's face was. Not hate. Maybe disgust.

"Is that a yes, Travis?"

Travis continued to stare at him before he could find his voice. "What if it is?"

Jason cocked an eyebrow. "*Seriously?*"

Travis cleared his throat. "Um. Yeah. It's true."

Yep, Jason flinched. He definitely flinched.

Krissy grinned and looked at Jason. "See? Told ya. We're ordering from Pogo's all next week."

Travis gaped at Jason. "You actually placed a bet against me?"

Jason squared his shoulders. "I bet *on* you. I told Krissy she was nuts, that all the talk was just that: talk. I bet *for* you."

He'd known it wasn't going to be easy, that it wasn't going to stay a secret. He'd known there was going to be talk. Somehow, despite knowing, he'd managed to convince himself otherwise, even after Caleb's altercation. Travis had always been a master at self-deception.

Shannon would be fine if he slept with guys. She'd said so.

His attraction to guys would go away.

Shannon wasn't going to die. The doctor swore she'd be fine.

He wasn't drinking too much. He was a grown-up; he could do what he needed to do.

He could do this thing with Wesley. It wasn't going to be a big deal.

Travis and Jason stared at each other, neither speaking.

"Oh, get a grip, you two." Krissy's voice was flippant, almost an assault to the tension between the two men. "So Mr. Bennett likes guys now. So what? Have you turned on the TV lately? Not such a big deal."

Travis looked over at her. Somewhere in the back of his mind, he knew she meant well. He even realized she was defending him. "Krissy, why don't you head on home? Take the rest of the day off. I'll still pay ya."

She blanched. "I'm sorry, Mr. Bennett. I wasn't trying to stick my nose in anything. I won't say anything to—"

He waved her off. "Everything's fine. Looks like everybody knows." He pulled apart the stapled bag and removed her chili dog, then slid it across the counter. "Just head on home. We'll see ya tomorrow."

Krissy looked skeptical but picked up her lunch, jacket, keys, and purse and walked to the door. Before she opened it, she turned back to them. "Really, Mr. Bennett. It's not such a big deal. And Mr...." She circled her hand in the air, searching. "The vet's real cute. You could do a lot worse."

It took effort for him to keep from groaning. He wanted to dig a hole in the middle of the floor and then crawl in and die. "Will you flip over to the closed sign too?"

She rolled her eyes and complied before letting in a cold rush of air as she stepped outside.

After she left, the tension increased. He and Jason stood where they were—neither moving, neither speaking.

A full two minutes passed.

Travis was the one to crack. He motioned toward the bag of food. "I know you wanna eat. Go ahead before it gets cold."

Jason didn't even look at the food, which told Travis just how serious this was. His friend opened his mouth, looked like he was getting ready to say something, and closed it.

"Oh, just say it, Jason. Whatever you're gonna say, just get it out already."

Again Jason made to speak, but no words came. Not a sound. He just looked away.

"Fine, Baker. I'll do it. What? Are you disgusted? Are you grossed out? You gonna tell me I'm not a man?" Travis had started out calm, his voice almost sounding soothing; however, with each syllable his volume grew, the last words spewing in anger. "Are you gonna tell me how it's a sin? Please do. I'd love to hear about my sins from the biggest man-whore in the tristate area!"

When Jason spoke, his words were more of a guttural groan than anything else. "I don't even know who you are."

Travis didn't flinch. "That's shit. You know exactly who I am. We've been best friends for twenty fucking years."

Jason nodded. "Yep, and now there's this. All of a sudden you like fucking guys."

"What, you jealous I didn't try to fuck you? Can't believe someone wouldn't actually want to get in your disease-ridden pants?" Even as he lashed out, Travis wished he could take the words back. But he couldn't, and he felt more coming. There wasn't even beer to blame.

Grimacing at the comment, Jason shook his head in distaste. "Is this just some new part of missing Shannon? You just lonely or some shit? I get that. You just need to get off or something?"

"This has nothing to do with Shannon!" Travis slammed a fist on the counter.

"You bet it doesn't. She'd be sick to know what you're doing."

Travis let out a warning growl. "She knew."

This time Jason flinched. "That is fucked up, dude. I can't believe you'd disrespect her, talking like that."

"She. Knew. She knew before we ever even got married."

Another flinch, then a pause. Sadness fell over Jason's features. "Like I said, I guess I don't even know you."

Travis's anger fled, leaving a panicked desperation in its place. "Is it really so bad, Jason? I know you really don't give a shit what all those Bible-thumpers say."

"Fuck that. You know better." Jason's tongue darted out, wetting his lips. "You're just not who I thought you were. I've always looked up to you. Always admired you. Thought of you as a brother."

"We are brothers, Jason."

Jason just shook his head. "Nah. I was wrong."

The times Travis had allowed his brain to travel down the roads of what-ifs of this discussion with Jason, limited though they were, he had honestly believed Jason would just laugh and shrug it off like he did everything else. Jason was nothing but live and let live. "You seemed fine with Wesley. You even defended him against that shit Wallace."

"This ain't about Wesley. I'm fine with him. Even kinda like him. He is what he is. I don't have a problem with fags. I just...." Jason's voice trailed off.

Inside his head, Travis screamed at himself to keep silent. "You don't have a problem with fags, but what? You just what?"

Jason looked him full in the eye. "I just didn't know you were one."

They stared at each other; then Jason nodded, turned, and walked around the counter.

For a moment Travis thought his friend was coming to punch him in the face. Then, stupidly, he thought Jason was going to hug him.

Jason did neither. He just walked past Travis and out the door.

CHAPTER TWENTY-TWO

WESLEY COULDN'T get enough of running his hands over the bulky muscles of Travis's chest. Travis had complained about how pale he was in a self-conscious manner on a couple of different occasions. Wesley loved it. It was so different from his own naturally sun-kissed skin. Even in the dim light slanting through his bedroom window, the freckled skin gleamed. The way Travis looked in these moments, sweaty after sex…. God, there was nothing sexier—damp red hair covering his heaving chest and belly as his breathing returned to normal, his fat cock glistening and growing soft on his hip, the subtle scents of musk, hay, and sun.

There wasn't much in the way of sex in which Wesley hadn't indulged, and while he'd definitely been with more experienced partners, he'd never been with one with such hunger, such passion. It wasn't a romantic passion necessarily, at least not in a sweet way, but it was all-consuming—the grunting, the force, the sweat—the pure animalistic nature that came over Travis while he was fucking.

Wesley curled his fingers into the hair covering Travis's belly, giving a light tug. "You are one bear of a man."

Travis snorted. A flush of embarrassment rose on his cheeks, visible even in the shadowed room.

Wesley gave another tug. "Well, you are. My big red bear of a man."

A self-conscious smile played at the corners of Travis's mouth.

Wesley was glad Travis didn't try to cover his belly and didn't look uncomfortable at Wesley's possessive term of endearment. If anything, it seemed as though Travis enjoyed the compliment. It was times like these that he struggled with refraining from professing his feelings.

Maybe Travis wouldn't freak out if Wesley said the L-word, but he didn't want to risk it.

Of course, there was a good chance he'd freak out himself if he used the L-word.

It was too soon.

Too new.

Still, in the dead of the night, when Travis came to Wesley's house after his kids had gone to sleep, when he was naked and sweaty in Wesley's bed, no other word seemed to suffice.

Sure, maybe "at first lust" would have been appropriate. Not anymore, though lust was still there in spades. Thank God! But there was more.

At times Wesley was pretty sure Travis was on the edge of saying it as well, sometimes even when sex was nowhere close to being in the picture.

He was pretty sure when Travis caught his gaze over dinner, or across the room while they watched a movie with the kids and Wendy.

He was pretty sure when Travis nervously put a large hand over his leg as they were driving to Nevada or Collins for a *date*—Wesley still felt like a teenager every time Travis asked him if he wanted to go on a date.

He was pretty sure when he was on the living room floor of the Bennett house playing with Dunkyn and Dolan and would look up to see Travis watching him.

He was pretty sure when Travis was beside him in bed, having just shot his load or dozing off. Wesley couldn't help but fantasize about sleeping in *their* house, in *their* bed.

Maybe he really was a teenage girl.

Wesley no longer wanted the white picket fence. He didn't want commitment or promise, nothing that could be broken. He didn't want a marriage, legal or otherwise.

He didn't want it.

Actually, he'd thought he didn't want it. However, with Travis beside him, he did.

God, he was screwed.

Travis was sexy as hell. Sweet and kind, in his own way. Great in bed... *great*... it was no wonder the man had three kids. He was just this manly combination of things Wesley found irresistible.

He was dangerous. He was going to break Wesley's heart.

"You okay?"

Wesley looked over, seeing Travis looking at him. "Huh?"

Travis's brows creased in concern. "Are you okay? You got really tense all of a sudden."

Wesley exhaled, trying to make his voice normal. "Oh, yeah. I'm totally fine." *I'm scared shitless.*

"Did I hurt you?"

Despite his stress, Wesley laughed. "No. Well, no more than I like." He reached down and patted Travis's limp cock. "You're a big boy."

Travis's chest swelled in an adorably sweet, proud way.

"Don't get cocky."

"I'm ready to go again, if you want."

"Give me a minute to recover, but I'm not gonna turn you down." Wesley ran his hand up over Travis's body, relishing the pure mass and strength the man radiated. "For a man in his forties, you've got the libido of a twenty-year-old."

Travis reached out and pulled Wesley closer to him, causing Wesley to groan at the touch. "If we get to a place where we don't have to use condoms, it will get even worse. I'd forgotten how much I hate those things."

God! The thought of Travis inside him raw—it took everything in Wesley not to throw caution into the wind and take that next step now. There wasn't any real danger. He'd been tested and Travis hadn't been with anyone besides Shannon in two decades. Still, it wasn't time. Not yet.

"That wasn't me pushing." The teasing tone left Travis's voice. "Really."

"Oh, I know. I just wish we could. That sounds so good."

Travis lowered his head, bringing his lips to meet Wesley's, his stubble scraping over Wesley's already tender jaw.

They kissed for a while.

Wesley again battled to keep from saying something that would ruin everything. He'd promised himself he was going to wait for Travis to say it first. He was certain he saw Travis's true feelings. He would have bet money Travis loved him. However, he *wasn't* willing to bet their relationship on Travis not freaking out if Wesley said he loved him. It seemed Travis didn't feel as though he was cheating on Shannon, but that might change if they labeled this as love.

"You're looking stressed again."

"Sorry. My brain is just working overtime tonight." Wesley smiled, or at least tried to.

Travis's face was perfectly framed by the moonlight pouring through the bedroom window. "Wanna tell me about it?"

"Nah. I'll be fine." Wesley shook his head, then successfully forced a smile. "Did I tell you that Iris Linley came into the clinic the other day? Horace had been eating extension cords."

Travis rolled his eyes. "She's something. Drove Wendy crazy when she opened up the store. Complained about everything Wendy was doing. She was a lot more patient than I would have been. Shannon never cared for her, either, always felt like she was nothing but a gossip."

The first few times Shannon's name had come up in casual conversation, Travis had gotten tense and Wesley knew their time together was about to be cut short. He took it as a good sign that Travis was able to talk about her without triggering the need to flee.

"Iris is a little strange, no doubt, but she's been nothing but friendly to me. Once in a while it seems forced—" Wesley repositioned himself, raising up to his side, propping his elbow on the pillow, matching Travis's position. "—but I'd rather that than her being a bitch about it. Even if she's uncomfortable with the whole gay thing, at least she's making an effort."

"She's my least concern."

Wesley grinned inwardly. Travis hadn't even flinched at the word gay. *Baby steps. Baby steps.* "I kinda like her, actually. I can't stand her mean cat, but she seems pretty harmless. She's asked me twice now if I am planning on working with the kids at church. As if!"

Travis's expression darkened. "She goes to the Holy Church. Same place Wendy takes the kids. I know there was some incident with a gay youth pastor or something there a few years back. It was before Caleb was old enough to be in the youth group, and it was around the time Shannon was getting sick. I didn't pay much attention, to be honest." His brows furrowed again. "I think there was even something in the paper about it, possibly from Iris, actually."

"Hard to imagine a gay youth pastor. I can't even fathom that in Kansas City, let alone here in El Do. I've heard about a gay-friendly church in KC, but I never went."

"No. Not my thing either." Travis's carefree expression was quickly evaporating. "My folks burnt me out on that as a kid."

Picking up on the change in Travis's demeanor, Wesley tried to switch to something more positive. "Actually, I'd kinda forgotten already, but there was another lady in, right before Iris…. Carrie, I think, and she'd mentioned something about that too. She was nice. She knew I was gay and said that her kid was. Mentioned about us getting together when he returned from college."

Wesley's words had the opposite of his desired effect.

"It seems like everyone is talking about us. Wendy keeps telling me I'm imagining it, but I'm not. People are treating me differently. Even Shannon's folks are acting strange. If people are actually coming into Cheryl's and mentioning it, then there's even more proof."

"I thought Caleb hadn't had any more drama around it."

Travis shrugged. "Well, he hasn't been back long after his suspension, but I don't think he'd tell me even if there was more drama. He's trying to protect me."

Wesley slipped his hand into Travis's, giving it a little squeeze. "It's so easy to see how much he adores you."

Travis hesitated, looking as though he was struggling to find words.

Wesley waited.

At last Travis motioned between them with his free hand. "I feel selfish about this. And stupid. I guess I was just fooling myself to pretend this wouldn't affect my kids."

Wesley's heart sank. He'd worried about it long before anything had happened to Caleb at school. So many odds were stacked against him and Travis, but he doubted any were larger than how their relationship, *or whatever it was*, would affect Travis's children. "I'm so sorry, Travis. The last thing I want to be is a source of stress or cause you pain. You or the kids."

"I know." Again Travis paused, searching.

The first few times Wesley had jumped in, attempting to provide feedback or his own thoughts, trying to help Travis. However, he'd quickly realized the other man simply needed time to process his own thoughts.

"You know, part of me thinks this might be good. That it's what I need to give my kids. Let them see you need to be strong enough to be who you are. Not give a fuck about what anyone else thinks or says. I'm so crazy proud of how strong Caleb proved himself to be the other day."

Wesley nodded. He'd been amazed when Wendy had told him about it, touched at the emotion Travis showed when he'd relayed the story later. Wesley had already really liked the kid, but his admiration had skyrocketed hearing about what Caleb had done. "He's an amazing kid."

Travis smiled, but it was a sad, forced kind of smile. "Yeah. He really is. I'm lucky Caleb's my son. And the twins are lucky he's their brother. If it hadn't been for him and Wendy, I'm not sure what would have happened to them."

It had been hard hearing Travis speak about the year or so after Shannon's death—his drinking, his angry outbursts, how he'd basically abandoned his children as he got lost in his own grief—he was there, but not there at all.

Wesley couldn't blame him. Hell, he'd been the same way after Todd left him and that had just been a breakup, without any kids involved. The shame that radiated from Travis the few times it had come up was agonizing.

Wesley searched for the right thing to say, something supportive that would validate Travis's feelings, but wouldn't harm their relationship. There was no more dangerous ground than this, and he knew it.

Travis didn't give him a chance.

"I really do feel that way, like I'm giving them an example of living life how they see fit. Not to cave to other people's expectations. And honestly, I don't give a shit what anybody thinks. As long as the kids and Wendy are okay with us"—again he motioned between them, and Wesley's heart soared back up at the implied suggestion of their pairing—"I don't give a fuck what anyone else says. Not even my parents or Jason."

Wesley wondered at the specific mention of those two choices. Travis hadn't said anything, but he was willing to bet there was a reason he used them as an example.

Travis had kept fairly consistent eye contact throughout the conversation, but as he continued, he seemed to focus on something on the wall behind Wesley's head. "I'm starting to wonder if I'm just using that as an excuse, though. A reason to justify what I want. Maybe I'm telling myself that so I can be selfish. Letting my kids face whatever teasing or... prejudice or whatever, so I can be with you."

The thoughts raced in Wesley's brain. What the hell was he supposed to say to that? If he validated Travis's fears about his kids getting teased, which they would, he might as well tell Travis to get out of his bed and never come back. However, if he pretended otherwise, he'd be showing Travis just how selfish he wanted to be. And in that vein, the thought that screamed the loudest was the thrill of Travis referring to them as a unit.

"I can't figure out what I'm supposed to do, Wesley. Wendy says the kids will be fine. That if I'm happy, they'll do better, and they'll grow up strong enough to be whoever they are."

Wesley smiled. Thank God for Wendy. "She's right. They will."

Travis raised an eyebrow, waiting.

Feeling like he was being tested, Wesley pushed on, saying what he did not want to say. "Travis, I really do think what your sister is saying is true. I really do. I also think that your concerns are true too. I'm sure some jackass will say something about their dad being... about you and me. But I also think kids get teased all the time. If it's not one thing, then it's another."

"Yeah, I know. But it's different if it's about *me*. If my kids are getting teased because of something I choose to do."

Let's move away. Let's move to California or New York, where it won't be a big deal. Let's escape this town. Go somewhere we can be a family.

Wow, Wesley. Move fast much? And talk about selfish—suggesting the kids give up their home so you can be with their dad is the definition of selfish.

"I wish I knew what to say, Travis. I feel like anything I say is going to be wrong."

Travis smiled, looking at Wesley again. "That's exactly how I feel too."

They looked at each other for a long time. It took everything in Wesley's power to keep silent, to keep from begging Travis not to leave him. It was difficult enough to make him feel pathetic.

Yeah, that was helpful.

When Travis spoke again, his words were whispered. "I don't want to lose you. I don't want to stop this. I also don't want to hurt my kids. But, I lo—"

Wesley felt his eyes grow large, and he tried to keep his expression stable. He was certain that he failed. Was Travis about to say what he thought he was?

Travis's body tensed for several moments, then slumped, almost as if in defeat. He met Wesley's gaze, his expression direct and confessionary. "I love you. I feel silly saying it. Like it's too soon or some shit, but I do. I've only felt this one other time, so I know what it is. I love you. I even told Shannon several days ago."

Before knowing Travis, the idea of some guy telling his dead wife that he loved him would have sounded creepy and just plain weird. However, now that he was in it, Wesley couldn't imagine anything better.

The fact Travis had "talked it over" with Shannon made it more real than just about anything he could imagine.

Wesley couldn't keep from beaming. "I love you too, Travis. So much. It scares me how much I love you."

Travis smiled back. Gentle, if not a little sad. "I know you do."

Wesley waited, wanting to pull Travis to him, to kiss him and have him inside again, this time without the damned condom. Something in Travis's expression held him back.

"I love you, Wesley." Travis's hand squeezed Wesley's, their fingers still intertwined between them. "Honestly that makes it so much harder. I think I would know what to do if I didn't love you. I could end it. Chalk it up to really great sex or something. But I do. I love you."

Wesley wanted to hear why. He wanted to have that romantic exchange of each of them listing all the things they loved about the other and sharing the exact moment they realized they loved the other. He wanted giddy. He wanted sweet. He wanted full-out, hot and heavy sexy. He wanted… something besides this tension-filled declaration of love.

"I feel like I'm supposed to say I'm sorry for making you love me or something. I feel like it's bad." He hadn't meant to say that out loud, but he couldn't deny the truth of his words.

Travis leaned closer and kissed him before pulling away. "I don't want you to feel like that. Not at all. I just wish it were easier. That it wasn't so… complicated."

"I'm willing to do whatever I can do to help make it better." Wesley fished for ideas. What in the world could he do? Though Travis had lived in El Do longer, he was new to the whole being gay and out thing. Although now that he'd thought of it, Travis actually hadn't gone quite so far as to say that. Whatever. It was just a label. Meaningless.

Wesley caught the expression that crossed Travis's face—the one Travis seemed to quickly try to erase.

"What? What is it, Travis? I can tell you thought of something. What can I do to make it better?"

Travis offered a forced smile and shook his head. "No. Nothing. I think I'm just desperate. I'm sure we can figure it out. Right?"

There was that naivety. Wesley wasn't so sure they could figure it out. But there was nothing he wasn't willing to do to give it a try. "Just tell me. Please."

Travis hesitated again, making Wesley think he was going to refuse.

"Well, maybe…." He cleared his throat. "Maybe you could butch it up a bit?"

Wesley flinched. "What?"

Travis looked at him, desperate pleading in his eyes, his voice full of apologetic defensiveness. "You know, just be a little more manly about some things or something? Maybe that would make it a little easier on people…."

Wesley tried to not be hurt. He really did. He also tried to stuff down the flare of anger. "What do you mean? Do I embarrass you?"

Travis rushed forward. "I don't mean you'd have to change much. You know. Just maybe dress a little more normal."

"*Normal*?"

"Not so fancy. Maybe less purple or something." Travis still wasn't meeting his eyes. "Maybe walk a little straighter?"

"Walk a little *straighter*?" Wesley cringed inwardly at the squeak in his voice.

"Well, you kinda swish at times."

"You want me to be *straighter*?" There was that new shame. Maybe he was experiencing life backward. Wasn't shame supposed to be early on, when you were figuring yourself out? Not after two decades of being an out and proud gay man. But it was there, and it was greater than the shame John Wallace had ignited, yet it was brought on by the man who'd just claimed to love him.

He was not going to cry. He wasn't going to. He wasn't sure if the tears burning his eyes were from anger or hurt, but they were there, blurring Travis's form.

He was not going to let them fall.

He turned onto his back, letting his head lay against the pillow, and stared up at the dark ceiling.

Travis reached out, trying to take the hand Wesley had withdrawn. His voice filled with an apologetic tremor. "I'm sorry, Wesley. I shouldn't have asked it like that. Just forget I said anything."

He wasn't going to make it. Wesley felt a tear roll down his cheek. Thankfully it was on the side of his face away from Travis. His voice cracked as he spoke, betraying the tears he kept hidden. "I think you should go now."

He felt Travis's body freeze beside him. "Wesley, really, I'm sorry."

"Just go. Please."

CHAPTER TWENTY-THREE

THE BULL'S gaze bore into his back as Travis unloaded the feed from the bed of the truck. He turned, looking the buffalo in the eye. The nearly two-thousand-pound animal didn't so much as bat an eyelid, just stared with an accusing glare.

"Really, Jarrod? You've got to give me shit too?"

As if in confirmation, the bull blinked and continued with his silent indictment.

Travis looked down, meeting the brown eyes of Dunkyn, who looked rather insignificant next to Jarrod. Dunkyn too leveled a judgmental stare at his master. "Yeah, I've heard it from you all day, Dunk. Go chase the buffalo."

Dunkyn didn't oblige.

The buffalo and corgi weren't the only ones to pass judgment on Travis Bennett. He'd felt it ever since he'd gotten up that morning, though he'd only managed an hour or two of sleep after coming back from Wesley's.

He'd heard it in the way Wendy slid his huge thermos of coffee across the kitchen counter.

He'd seen it in the way Mason smiled gently up at him as Travis woke him for school, and in the way Avery thanked him for braiding her hair with the gold ribbon woven into the strands.

He'd felt it when Caleb looked over his shoulder as he walked up the school sidewalk and told his dad he'd see him after work. Travis could hear the undercurrent, the resounding question of why his dad would screw things up with the vet when Caleb had defended him at such a great cost.

Dolan's licks were less frantic and more repulsed in nature.

Krissy knew her boss was a prick. The way she showed him her progress toward her high school diploma reeked of accusation. From somewhere in her belly, the baby found time between dividing and multiplying cells to mock him.

Even Wendy's fucking rabbit had glared at him when he'd stopped by The Crocheted Bunny to bring Wendy a cheeseburger at lunch. Nutmeg had stared at him with her creepy pinkish red eyes and called him a coward. A coward and an asshole. A coward and an asshole and a hypocrite.

Only Jason didn't lay blame on him. Of course, Jason wouldn't even look in his direction. To him, Travis was nothing more than an invisible ghost, something he had to walk around and give great effort to avoid, but a ghost, nonetheless.

Travis turned his back on Dunkyn and Jarrod and the entire herd. He could feel some of the females staring at him from deep in Mr. Walker's woods. He continued to unload the feed, ignoring the animals' judgment. As it had all day, his body shifted to autopilot as his mind pondered his guilt.

Guilt was too strong a word, really. It was just a matter of timing. He probably shouldn't have said he loved Wesley and then immediately asked him to man it up a bit. In his defense, Travis reasoned, he hadn't been planning on asking Wesley to change anything. Of course, he hadn't exactly planned to confess his love, either. Sure, he'd told Shannon, but he hadn't been ready to take that step with Wesley, not yet. However, as soon as he'd said it, though scary, it had felt right.

He did love the man.

He'd known with Shannon quickly too. Of course, that had been the knowing of a teenage boy. It had grown, just as he and Shannon had grown. If anything, though, that fact gave him more confidence in his feelings about Wesley.

He'd known love—true, undying love. The breakup, fight, argue, changing the babies' diapers, morning breath kind of love. The kind of love that remains after the lust disappears, when the manners wear off, when you wanna strangle the other person. The kind of love that allows the lust to reappear, even with all that other shit mixed in.

Too soon or not, Travis Bennett knew love. And he knew he was in love with Wesley Ryan.

He also knew he was in lust with Wesley Ryan.

And he knew he loved that combination.

He and Shannon had been through a hell of a lot worse than asking the other to change a couple of things. For fuck's sake, Shannon had loved him in spite of him fucking other men!

Wesley was just too sensitive.

Maybe it was just a gay thing. Maybe because Wesley was more feminine than himself. Shannon was sensitive too. She'd come unhinged when Travis had told her she acted like a bitch sometimes when she was on the rag.

Man, had she screamed. She'd even thrown something at him. What had it been? Not a plate....

A pang shot through his chest as he realized he couldn't remember.

Whatever it had been, they'd fought, they'd yelled, they'd gotten over it. She didn't get all quiet and then tell him to leave.

Wesley was just too goddamned sensitive.

The eyes burned into his back. He couldn't tell if it was Jarrod or Dunkyn. He refused to look and continued to toss out the feedbags.

Plus, Wesley had asked if there was anything he could do to help. Travis hadn't just pulled the request out of his ass. The man had asked how to help make things easier on his kids.

Was it really that much to ask? To not wear some damned foo-foo designer jeans and Easter-colored shirts? Maybe a scarf wasn't always necessary anytime it was below fifty degrees. Was it really that hard to move your shoulders instead of your hips when you walked?

Maybe Wesley just needed to wear a pair of boots.

Drive a different car.

Not play with the fucking Barbies every time Avery and Mason wanted to. Or at least not *ask* to play with the Barbies with them.

However, he kinda loved watching Wesley play with the dolls. It wasn't like Travis hadn't spent countless hours playing with the Barbies as well.

He loved the fuck outta Wesley's guts for driving that pansyass car with a fucking rainbow sticker around town.

As far as being able to move that ass? He didn't remember any of the guys in college being able to get fucked like that.

Travis tossed the last bag of feed out of the back of the truck and hopped down, then stripped off his jacket and threw it over the side of the truck bed. Though it was still snowy, the afternoon sun was warm. Travis glanced over toward the field. Jarrod had wandered off toward the females, but Dunkyn remained where he'd been, though he'd sat down in the snow.

They stared at each other.

"Fine, Dunk. You win. I'm an asshole. Got it." He patted his thigh, and the dog bounded over the snow, pausing to lower his head into the powder and burrow toward Travis for a few moments before popping his head back up. Travis chuckled. "I might be an asshole, but you're the dumbass."

Dunkyn padded the final few feet up to Travis, only pausing when he was beside him and looking up, expectantly.

Obliging, Travis bent and scratched the dog's ears. "All right, let's get this shit moved into the barn."

Though Emmitt Walker had more money than God, Travis hadn't been able to convince the man to upgrade any aspect of his barn, even though he offered to sell him the items at cost. Mr. Walker liked things traditional. Travis had taken him to his own remodeled barn in hopes of convincing him. Mr. Walker had taken less than three minutes, didn't even let Travis finish showing him all the bells and whistles, before proclaiming that Travis had gone soft, that he might as well have turned his barn into a spa.

In truth, Travis enjoyed both extremes. There really was something more satisfying about working at Mr. Walker's farm, even if Travis was able to be more efficient at his own. In addition to wanting to keep things *authentic*, Mr. Walker was also a perfectionist and a bit of an elitist. Or at least he didn't share well. It was fine for him to drive his trucks and tractors into the barn, but God forbid Travis back his truck into the barn to make unloading easier.

Travis didn't really mind this either. Mr. Walker, though unwilling to share his toys, paid much more than Travis felt was needed for the work he did. Travis had said as much, but Mr. Walker always waved him off. More than any of it, though, Travis didn't want to lose the buffalo, or his access to the property. There were too many memories here. Too much of the past two decades—times with Shannon by the pond, summer picnics with the kids, teaching Caleb how to fish for catfish. Mr. Walker's farm felt as much like home as his own house did.

Dunkyn stayed by Travis's side, walking back and forth from the pile of feed by the truck to the barn as Travis transported the bags inside. As he often did, Travis spoke to the dog, bouncing his thoughts off his old friend.

"I guess, if I'm being honest, I'm the one who's afraid of what people will think. I want my kids to be brave. To be whoever they want to be, no matter what the fuck anyone else says."

Dunkyn looked up as Travis paused with two bags over his shoulder and peered down at the dog.

"Is it teaching them to be brave to be with Wesley, or am I just being selfish? Is all the brave shit just spin?"

Trying to wag his quarter-inch tail, Dunkyn only succeeded in waddling his butt back and forth in adoration.

"Caleb was for sure brave with the fucking Jackson kid. And Wesley doesn't even seem to think twice about what people think about him. He moved from the city to here to take over someone else's business and didn't even try to hide what he was. Takes guts, right?"

Dunkyn continued to wag, this time adding a tongue loll or two just to show support.

"And Shannon… well, I know what she'd tell me to do. And she'd have loved Wesley."

The slamming of a door caught Travis off guard. He hadn't heard anyone else drive up. Letting the feed down off his shoulders, he left it on the concrete of the barn floor and walked toward the open door.

Emmitt Walker was walking toward the barn, his truck parked just on the other side of Travis's. Though never overfriendly or demonstrative, the man looked even more cantankerous than usual. He looked up and paused when he saw Travis in the doorway. "Hey, Bennett."

Travis stepped out of the barn and walked toward the other man. "Hey yourself, Mr. Walker. How ya doing today?"

Mr. Walker didn't answer but bent down to scratch Dunkyn's head as he waddled up to the older man. Mr. Walker hadn't taken to Dunkyn when Shannon had bought him for Travis. Like Travis, he'd considered the smaller dog a substandard excuse for what a dog should be, until he saw Dunkyn darting in and out of the buffalo's hooves, herding them effortlessly. From that moment on, he'd been a die-hard fan of the dog.

Travis waited until Mr. Walker and Dunkyn's bonding moment had passed and Mr. Walker stood back up.

"I saw your truck down here from the window." Mr. Walker gestured up the hill toward his small mansion of a house.

As Travis was there every day, sometimes twice, he knew there had to be something special about Mr. Walker's appearance, especially considering the reactions he'd been getting all over town, whether Wendy wanted to admit it or not. "Yep, just unloading some more feed. We're still good on hay and such. Probably won't need more until next month."

Mr. Walker grimaced, a distasteful sound in his voice. "Well, we made it longer with what we harvested than I thought we would, truth be told. I'm gonna have to get me a new farmhand if Dana Jenkins can't do better than this next year."

"Dana's a good guy, Mr. Walker. I'd say he's the reason we've been able to last as long as we have. We didn't get half the rain last season we normally got."

Mr. Walker's eyes narrowed, and he leaned forward, such a small amount it was barely perceptible. Travis could feel it more than see it. "You don't need to tell me about how much hay we should or shouldn't be able to pull in during drought years. I've been doing this longer than you've been alive, boy."

Travis started to reply, but Mr. Walker kept going.

"It's actually why I came down here, Bennett. I gotta question for ya. There's been some talk over town, and you know I don't put no never mind to gossip, so I thought I'd just come down here an' ask."

Gruff though he was, Travis had always liked Mr. Walker's bluntness. The world would be an easier place if everyone played by Mr. Walker's directness. Or at least, that's what Travis had always felt. Mr. Walker's next words made Travis question that notion.

"Talk is that you and that new vet fella have been—" Mr. Walker uncharacteristically faltered for words. "—have been havin' relations."

Travis tried to keep any expression from crossing his face. He wasn't sure if he succeeded or not.

"Well?" Mr. Walker raised gnarled fingers and scratched his nearly translucent hair.

"Dr. Ryan is my…." Travis cleared his throat. He thought he was going to be able to come out and say it. He thought he could be as blunt and direct as Mr. Walker himself.

Apparently not.

And what was he supposed to say? His boyfriend? He was forty-two years old. He wasn't supposed to have a boyfriend or girlfriend or anybody.

Travis looked away from his employer. "I actually don't see how that is any business of yours, Mr. Walker."

God, that didn't feel good.

"Don't pull the political correct bullshit on me, Travis Bennett." Mr. Walker thumped his fist against the open tailgate of the F-350. "I asked you a simple question, man to man."

Dunkyn let out a warning growl at the clang of the fist against the truck.

Travis looked down at the dog. Even Dunkyn was showing more guts than himself.

He looked back up, meeting the older man full in the face. "Wesley Ryan and I are together, Mr. Walker. Is that a problem?"

To his relief, Mr. Walker didn't push for more details on what it meant to be "together." Though his eyes did widen in surprise.

Travis wasn't sure if the man was taken aback that the rumors were true or that Travis didn't deny them.

Nearly a full minute passed before Mr. Walker spoke again, his tone uncharacteristically cautious. "Well, now. I can't really say. It might be a problem."

Anger and loss raged simultaneously. Every bit of him wanted to tell the man to fuck off, but the thought of losing his right to care for the buffalo and have access to Mr. Walker's farm was painful. It would be one more way he'd lose Shannon.

Travis stuffed his fists into the pockets of his jeans, willing them to stay where they were and for his mouth to keep shut while he was at it. If Mr. Walker started spouting about religion and God, Travis was going to lose his cool. He and the older man had done more than their fair share of knocking all the shit that went on at the churches throughout town. If he dared to pull the God card….

"You see, Travis, this job, taking care of buffalo and the farm, taking care of the barn, being trustworthy enough to respect the land and care for it, well, that's a man's job. It seems like you may not be up to the task."

Knuckles cracked as Travis clinched his concealed fists tighter. His words were surprisingly clear through his gritted teeth. "Mr. Walker, I've done this job for nearly two decades. If I wasn't man enough to take care of it, you'd have figured it out by now." *Shut up.* He should shut up. "Unless you're dumber than I thought you were."

Mr. Walker's milky eyes flashed. "You best watch how you're speaking to me, boy."

Travis stood straight, making him realize how he'd begun to slump. "You're the one calling my manhood into question, Emmitt. It occurs you may wanna watch how you speak to me."

"You're the one changing, Travis. Not me."

"Nope. Same man I always was."

Mr. Walker shook his head. "Nah. You're not. Not if you—"

Travis took a step closer, shoving his fists even deeper, thankful he hadn't popped open either of the beers on the floorboard of his truck. "Who I'm fucking has nothing to do with how much of a man I am, or affect how I care for your animals."

Mr. Walker flinched at Travis's crassness, as if he hadn't said fuck half a million times over their years together.

Travis suddenly found he didn't give a shit what anyone thought. He'd believed that was true, but as the sensation of freedom washed over him he realized it hadn't actually been. It was now.

"I love this job, Mr. Walker. And I'm damned good at it. You know as well as I do, you'd be costing yourself a whole lot of time and effort to train someone else to take care of everything around here. And you also know they wouldn't do as good of a job as I do."

To his credit, Mr. Walker hadn't stepped back against Travis invading his space or in the face of Travis's visible anger. Or maybe he really was dumber than Travis thought.

At last he gave a curt nod toward Travis. "Fine. I'll keep you on."

Travis started to speak, but was cut off.

"For a trial basis."

Travis guffawed. "A *trial* basis? Are you fucking kidding me? I've done this job for twenty years."

Mr. Walker stood taller, at least as much as his bent spine would allow. "You tell me you haven't changed. I wanna see that. Take it or leave it."

Travis wanted to show Emmitt Walker exactly where he could shove this job. He didn't need the money. Not a bit of it. This was all because he loved the work and loved the farm, which was the problem, wasn't it?

A movement behind Mr. Walker caught Travis's attention. At some point, Jarrod had wandered back out from the trees and was staring at the scene. He met Travis's gaze.

It wasn't about the money. It hadn't been for nearly fifteen years. He'd do the job for free, just to stay with the buffalo and to keep that tenuous connection to Shannon.

Another moment of eye contact with Jarrod, and Travis looked back to the old man in front of him.

Travis nodded.

CHAPTER TWENTY-FOUR

"I'D HAVE at least four years of undergrad and *then* four years of vet school? That means…." Caleb did some quick finger calculations. "The soonest I'd be done would be when I'm twenty-six!"

Wesley glanced away from the X-rays he was inspecting. "Plus, you'd typically need two to five years of internships or residencies. And, it can take a bit to get accepted into a college of veterinary medicine. I didn't graduate until I was thirty-one, because it took me a while to get accepted into the University of Missouri. And then I still had a couple years of residency at the zoo." He didn't want to discourage Caleb, but neither did he want to gloss over the experience. With how he'd left things with Travis that morning, Wesley had been surprised when Wendy had dropped Caleb off at the clinic after school as they'd planned so he could shadow for the afternoon.

"Good God! You didn't even get started until you were thirty-three. All that work and you're already close to retiring."

Wesley let out a burst of laughter. "Not hardly!" He decided not to mention the two years spent floundering between graduation and taking over the clinic. He didn't really get started until just a few months ago at thirty-five. Pathetic.

Caleb fiddled with a pair of forceps. "Maybe I should just start out as a field hand and work until I can own my own ranch or something one day. Dad doesn't have a degree like that. He just got some normal four-year thing, and he's fine. He wouldn't really even need that to own the feedstore."

"True. You have to really want to be a veterinarian if you're willing to put in all the effort that's required, but there are other ways to work with animals." Wesley pointed to the backlit X-rays. "See that fuzzy line there?"

Caleb closed the distance between them and stood behind Wesley's shoulder. "Yeah. That means it's broken."

"Just a fracture, actually." Wesley spoke to Caleb but continued to inspect the X-ray, more for the boy's comfort rather than any need to attain more information. "You did a really good job with that dog, getting him calmed down and soothing him as I took his X-rays. You're a natural."

There was no false modesty, nor any boasting. "Yeah. I've worked with animals my whole life. Same with Mom and Dad. It would be weird if I weren't a natural."

"Well, don't let the amount of school throw you off if you decide you want to be a vet. If it's something you want to do, it's worth it."

Caleb was silent for a little too long, causing Wesley to unclip the X-ray and look back at the boy. "I would be more than happy to help you search for scholarships and such when the time comes, if you'd like."

Confusion passed over Caleb's face but quickly faded. "Oh, no. That's not too big a concern. I just, well, I'm not sure if I want to do college at all."

"What? Not do college? Why?"

He shrugged, then glanced to the door as if expecting someone to come in. He looked back at Wesley, his expression serious. "I know you're dating my dad and all, but are you okay just keeping this between us?"

A momentary shot of panic flashed through Wesley. He didn't even know if he and Travis were still dating. Travis hadn't texted or called since Wesley had asked him to leave that morning.

Not all about you. He brought his focus back on Caleb. "Um, yeah, it can stay between us. I mean, as long as it's not something unsafe your dad needs to know or something."

It seemed Caleb wasn't concerned about that possibility. "It's just that college takes a long time. Just the normal college is four years, and that's not even if I do the vet thing. That means I wouldn't be home for that long. Maybe summers and some long weekends or something, but that's different than actually being at home."

Wesley waited for the problem, but it looked like Caleb was done speaking. "So…. You're not wanting to leave home?" The thought made no sense. Wesley had loved his family, but leaving for college had been one of the best days of his life. Freedom!

Caleb looked away and began to slowly pace around the room, a finger tracing over counters and examination equipment as he moved. "The twins will be nine when I graduate high school, and that would mean they'll be thirteen by the time I returned. And if I did the vet thing, I wouldn't be back until it was time for them to graduate high school."

"Well, like you said, you would still come back during summers, and I'm sure your dad and Wendy would bring them to see you wherever you chose to go to college."

The frustrated expression on Caleb's face left no doubt that Wesley wasn't even close to understanding. He stopped pacing and looked Wesley straight in the face. "Avery and Mason need me. Wendy and I are like a mom to them, and sometimes like a dad too. I won't abandon them."

Wesley stared at the boy. He knew he shouldn't, but he couldn't help it. He'd heard Travis's guilt over his absence in his children's lives that first year after Shannon died, but it was different seeing the evidence of it from his kid. Although, Wesley corrected himself, Caleb wasn't really a kid or a boy. He might look like one, but he'd grown up a long time ago, taking on a role too large for his still-narrow shoulders. Wesley spoke before he paused to think. "You're really something."

Caleb looked nervous. "What do you mean?"

Wesley searched for words—adult words, therapist words, father-like words.

He gave up. "You're just kinda freaking cool. You stand up to some bully at school, defending your dad about dating me, and you're afraid to go to college because you don't want to leave your brother and sister alone."

A blush crept over Caleb's cheeks, making them nearly match his hair.

"No, Caleb, I mean it. When I grow up, I wanna be like you. Dang. You're awesome."

And the hue of Caleb's cheeks surpassed his hair after all.

"No wonder your dad is proud of you."

Caleb looked up and locked his gaze onto Wesley, suddenly looking like a starved man seeing a feast. "He told you that?"

"Yeah. Of course he has." Maybe Travis was different with his kids than Wesley thought he was. "Hasn't he told you he's proud of you?"

Caleb shrugged. "Yeah, but dads are supposed to say that."

Wesley smiled, trying to infuse it with as much reassurance as he could. "Well, he's not just saying it. He's crazy proud of you."

Wesley was fairly certain he saw Caleb begin to tear up, so he turned away, unconvincingly distracted by a set of retractor tools. He busied himself with straightening up the counter, organizing the disposable materials by the sink in an effort to give Caleb space.

Maybe he'd been too hard on Travis. Maybe he'd been selfish.

It wasn't just about the two of them. There were three kids to think about, two of them young and one of them already sacrificing so much. If butching it up would make it easier for Travis's kids, then it was a pretty small request.

"Wesley?"

Wesley jumped slightly, startled out of his thoughts, and looked back over at Caleb, who, though flushed, looked under control. "Yeah, Caleb?"

"Are you and Dad breaking up?"

Wesley flinched. Were they? "Why do you ask?"

"I dunno. He seemed different before I left for school this morning." Caleb waved a hand in midair, searching. "He seemed sad. Like he used to be all the time."

It really wasn't just about the two of them. While the thought added another level to his stress around his and Travis's relationship, Wesley was pleasantly surprised at the surge of protection that swept through him as he looked at Caleb. He wasn't sure how to answer him, though, so he asked what he'd been wondering for weeks. What he probably wouldn't have gotten the nerve to ask before this moment. "How do you feel about your dad and I dating?"

Caleb looked up at him, his blue eyes wide, and then he glanced quickly away. "I dunno. It's kinda strange, I guess."

God, he didn't want to ask this. Regardless of anything beyond the other issues he and Travis had to face, Caleb being okay with their relationship was going to be vital. He was more certain of it than ever. And while Caleb seemed to have defended them at school, it could have been nothing more than a boy taking up for his dad and might not imply he was okay with the whole gay thing at all. "Strange as in bad?"

Another shrug. "It kinda freaked me out, honestly. For a bit."

For a bit. That was encouraging. Wesley paused, hoping Caleb would keep going.

He did.

"I just didn't think about Dad being gay. I mean, I'd kinda thought about it. I guess it sorta crossed my mind when I saw you two together. There seemed to be something, but…."

Wesley tried to smile but was too nervous to be certain he'd actually pulled it off. "You've been nothing but kind to me since we've been together more. You and the twins. You've all been supersweet."

Dear God. *Supersweet.* It was no wonder Travis wanted him to butch it up.

Caleb shrugged a third time, his shoulders seemingly the only part of his body still working. "Well, Wendy loves you. She'd been raving about you way before Dad. And, now Dad is… happy, I guess. At least more than I've seen him since I was little. Even the house feels better, you know? Less… depressed, maybe?"

All good signs, but not actually coming out and saying he was okay with it. Wesley really needed Caleb's approval. For a factor he hadn't seen affecting him directly, outside of the stress it caused Travis, it was suddenly vitally important what Caleb thought of him. "Would you rather I not spend time with your dad and your family?"

The question felt weird once the words were out of his mouth. At once inappropriate, giving a child that type of power, and also rather pathetic, like Wesley was begging a fourteen-year-old to like him.

Caleb cocked his head skeptically, suddenly making him look more the teenager he was. "If I said I wasn't okay with it, would you stop dating Dad?"

Well, he'd asked, hadn't he? Why would he have asked what the kid wanted if he hadn't planned on adjusting what he did based on the response?

Would he stop seeing Travis if Caleb didn't approve?

So much for the afternoon being about Caleb shadowing him and helping Caleb decide if he was interested in the veterinary field. For a man who was realizing his relationship was so much more than just about him and Travis, he was sure making it all about him.

The two eyed each other. Not in hostility, just with an inspecting curiosity.

In addition to gaining even more respect for Caleb Bennett as more than just Travis's son, Wesley realized the boy truly was pivotal. There were no guarantees things would work between him and Travis, even if Caleb loved the idea of his dad having a boyfriend. However, their relationship was doomed if Caleb was against it. No doubt. And maybe rightly so—Wesley wasn't sure. Not that it mattered at the moment—things with Travis were what they were, and Wesley wasn't at all sure what that was.

"Yes, Caleb. I would stop seeing him if you weren't okay with it." What had he just done? Damn him.

Caleb cocked his head, looking reminiscent of Dolan in the motion. "Do you love my dad?"

Considering he and Travis had only said that once, less than twenty-four hours ago, promptly followed by what seemed to constitute their first fight, it seemed rather wrong to announce it to Travis's son.

"Yes. I do. I love your dad."

"Then why would you leave him just because I'd tell you to? That doesn't seem like love."

The answer came automatically. "Because he loves you more than me. And he always will." Wesley hadn't thought of it quite like that before, but hearing the words in his own voice, he suddenly realized the truth behind them. He was kind of surprised that he was okay with the realization.

The small smile that curved over Caleb's lips wasn't in victory or satisfaction. Maybe it was a smile of relief.

"Like I said, Dad's happier than I've seen him since Mom died. I didn't think I'd ever see him like that again. And the twins have never seen it."

Wesley's neediness peeked its head out in that moment, wanting Caleb to declare that Wesley had brought his dad back to life, that he was the answer to a prayer the boy had been waiting on, that he wanted Wesley to be his second dad.

Caleb nodded slightly. "Yeah, I'm okay with you spending time with my family."

WENDY PICKED up Caleb, obviously using every bit of restraint she had to refrain from asking questions—if Caleb had wondered about the status of Wesley and Travis's relationship, Wendy definitely had. By the time Wesley finished shutting down the clinic, it was past seven, and was long past sunset.

It was going to be the first night in weeks that Travis and Dunkyn hadn't come over late in the evening. Before that, Wesley had finally gotten to a place where he liked sleeping on his own. After two years of an endless string of one-night stands, the solitude had been rather refreshing. Honestly, he hadn't been ready to give it up.

And here he was again. No sooner had he claimed some strength from being alone than Travis had crawled into his bed and into his heart, making the thought of the lonely night ahead seem endless.

Maybe this was how it should be. If there was a time for it all to fall apart, this was it. Before he completely fell in love. In love with Travis, in love with the kids, in love with the dogs.

The kids.

More than ever, it was crystal clear he hadn't just been dating Travis. He'd been dating the entire family. To date Travis meant he was implying he was ready to jump into a parental role when the time came. Maybe he could look at it as nothing more than a hook-up with feelings attached.

If he hadn't been spending so many dinners at the Bennett house.

If he hadn't spent endless hours playing with Avery and Mason and their vast assortment of dolls and toys.

If he hadn't taken the kids to the park while Wendy closed up The Crocheted Bunny.

If, if, if….

But he had, unbeknownst to him, subconsciously or not, been dating the entire family.

The idea of kids was daunting. Wesley couldn't even take care of himself. He used to be able to easily, but the past few years had proven he could barely keep himself sane, let alone care for not one other person, but four.

But….

There was always a but.

Actually, no, there wasn't. There hadn't been a but in two years.

And the only buts with Todd had been along lines of…

…*but at least he's not abusive.*

…*but at least there's someone to sleep next to.*

…*but at least I'm not alone.*

The buts with Travis? The ones that came after "I'm not ready for all of this," and "he's got three kids and a dead wife," and "he wants me to butch it up."

The buts for all of those?

…*but I used to want kids, before Todd.*

…*but I am happier than I can remember when he's near.*

…*but I love him.*

THE YELLOW Miata hadn't even pulled into the driveway before Wesley had his cell phone in his hand, trying to figure out what to say to Travis—how to make it right, how to apologize for not seeing the bigger picture.

When the phone buzzed in his hand, Wesley slammed on the brake, causing the car to lurch and the tires to screech in protest against the pavement.

THEN THE STARS FALL | 233

He looked down and swiped his thumb across the screen to open the text from Travis.

Can I come over tonight? I'd like to talk.

Well, that wasn't cryptic.

Not knowing if he should be relieved he was going to see Travis after all or prepare himself for the it's-not-your-fault-I-don't-wanna-be-with-a-Nelly talk, Wesley forced his shaking thumb to type back a yes.

THE HEADLIGHTS of the F-350 flooded through Wesley's grandparents' living room curtains sometime after eleven. *His* living room curtains. Wesley had spent the last few hours doing nothing more than pacing and sweating, playing out entire conversations, gesticulating as he wandered throughout the house. He'd exhausted nearly every scenario, from breakup to makeup sex. All it had really accomplished was to further stress him out and make him feel insane.

Wesley threw open the front door before Travis had a chance to knock—nothing like playing it cool.

Travis and Dunkyn stood on the front porch, awash in the yellow light spilling out of the house, frozen patches of snow smattered across the tar-pit darkness of the yard. Dunkyn looked up at Travis, then peered over at Wesley, issuing a whine.

Wesley just stared at them—well, at Travis. He looked like he'd aged ten years since that morning. His eyes had huge bags under them, and his typical ruddy stubble was more akin to a beard than any five-o'clock shadow. Like Wesley, Travis's skin had a sheen of sweat. "You look terrible."

At that, a smile broke across Travis's face, and he snorted out a breath of air. "Thanks a lot. You don't look so great yourself."

Wesley lifted his hand to his face, realizing he'd not shaved that morning either. He couldn't remember the last time he'd let himself go ungroomed.

"Can I come in?"

"Oh God, yes! Sorry." Wesley stepped back, making room.

Travis entered, closely followed by Dunkyn, who chuffed and shoved his nose into Wesley's shin.

Wesley shut the door and bent to pat the corgi's head. He wanted to plop down on the floor and wrap his arms around the dog. He'd thought he'd be able to read whatever Travis wanted to say in his expression. He couldn't. It would be so much easier to pay attention to the dog and block out whatever shoe was about to drop.

He didn't. He was a big boy, after all. After a moment, long enough to attempt to force his breathing to return to normal, Wesley straightened and faced Travis. Come what may.

"Listen, Wesley," Travis began before Wesley could think of what to say, "I am so…." Travis's voice wandered off as he inspected Wesley's face. His large fingers grasped Wesley's jaw and carefully tilted his face toward the light.

"What?" Wesley wasn't sure what to do. None of the scenarios he'd practiced had begun like this.

Travis grinned, suddenly looking younger. He tilted Wesley's head a bit more, then let go, looking Wesley in the eye. "I never realized your beard was red. You've always been so close shaven."

"Yeah, I don't like being unkempt." He rolled his eyes, realizing how queeny that sounded. "Although I guess you know that already."

Travis's grin broadened. "It's red, Wesley. Just like the rest of us."

Wesley lifted his hand and ran his fingers over his stubble. "Oh. Yeah. I hadn't thought of that, actually." Was that a good thing?

"I'm sorry."

Travis's words caught Wesley completely off guard, even though an apology had been in one of the enactments. One of the better ones. "I was going to say that to you."

Travis's smile faltered. "Why? You didn't do anything you need to apologize for."

He hadn't? "I overreacted. I was only thinking about me and my feelings. I wasn't thinking about how… I'm perceived, I guess you could say, could affect your kids. I should have been more open to the idea."

"No, Wesley. I owe you an apology. Not the other way around. I want my kids to be exactly who they are. *Whoever* and *whatever* they are. Why should I want anything less for you?"

"Because it could make things harder for your family. Your kids have been through enough. *You've* been through enough. I can try to—"

Travis cut him off, once again taking his jaw in his hand, this time with his thumb resting over Wesley's lips. "Don't you dare. You be who you are. You are brave, and you are unlike anyone I've ever known. The thing I loved the most about Shannon was how alive she was and how she was Shannon. There was no one else like her. And though you're different, that's exactly how you are."

Wesley had definitely missed some scenarios. Not even the best one had gone like this.

Travis kept talking, his low voice even softer than usual. "I love you. I love you, Wesley. I hate that the first thing I did after telling you that was ask you to change. I don't want you to change. I want you to just keep being you. To keep being here, with me. With us." He pulled his thumb away from Wesley's lips only to cover them with his own.

Tendrils of fear tickled the back of Wesley's mind as he sank into Travis's kiss. The moment to flee mostly unscathed was passing. Now that he was more acutely aware that so much more than he and Travis hung in the balance, he had to decide. If he was going to escape, this was the moment.

While Wesley couldn't sweep those tendrils away, he did ignore them. He allowed himself to get lost in the kiss. It was far from the first one he and Travis had shared, but unlike any of the ones that had come before.

At last, and all too soon, Travis pulled away, though he didn't lose contact with Wesley. "Will you forgive me? Are you still in this?"

Screw the tendrils. "Oh, yeah. I'm in this."

The crooked smile on Travis's face made him look nearly childlike, or as close as his thick, rugged features would allow.

"I love you, Travis."

"Good. That makes me a lucky man." The look in Travis's eyes shifted. "Can we go fuck now, please?"

"Oh hell, yeah. And no more condoms."

Travis groaned. "Fuuuuck…. And I thought I was tired *today*. Tomorrow is gonna be rough. We're not getting *any* sleep tonight."

CHAPTER TWENTY-FIVE

SALT OF the earth. Norma and Willard Bennett were salt of the earth people. That's how Norma would describe herself and her husband.

Through the hour-and-a-half drive south from El Dorado, Travis felt himself flashing back to childhood as he prepared to face his parents. He remembered showing them a bad report card, admitting he was the one who broke his mother's pie plate during a late-night fridge run, confessing that he'd dented the truck coming home buzzed after one of the home games, enduring his mother's disappointed, long-suffering expression and his father's belt, and, later, his father's lectures.

He'd had it easy. He'd been the favorite child. He might have a few childhood scars, but not many, and nothing most other kids of his generation didn't have. His sister, on the other hand, had been able to do nothing right.

Travis had always been easygoing and quiet, and he liked to fly under the radar.

Wendy was boisterous, questioning, and spirited—everything a girl wasn't supposed to be.

Travis might get in trouble at times, but it was expected. Boys would be boys.

Neither of them had a bad childhood. Not at all. Norma and Willard had been caring parents and loved their children. They might have been a little undemonstrative and militant, but both he and Wendy knew they were loved. They also knew what the expectations were and the consequences should they not be met.

When Travis had told Wendy he was going to drive to Neosho and spend the night with their folks, catch them up to speed, Wendy had just grinned at him wickedly. "Looks like after thirty-seven years, I'll finally be the favorite."

She was probably right. While their mom had been devastated when her daughter had the selfishness to abandon her husband, surely that was better than her son trying to find a husband of his own.

Was that what he was doing? Husband?

Travis shoved the thought away. He was nervous enough without all of that in his head.

Several miles outside of the city limits, his childhood home grew larger as the F-350 made its way down the long dirt road. The late-January day was bright and clear. All the snow had melted, but ice was in the air. He could feel it. He'd checked the weather. Things were supposed to stay mild for the next couple of days. If he saw so much as a snowflake fall after he'd spoken to his folks, though, Travis was going to jump back in the truck and hightail it home. Big four-by-four or not, no way was he taking the chance of getting iced-in for days with his parents after confession time.

Travis remained in the cab of his truck for a few moments after parking in front of the faded green house. He was certain his parents knew something was amiss. Sitting outside their house wasn't going to help much.

WISHING THAT he prayed, Travis exited the truck, pausing to lift Dunkyn to the ground, and then made his way up to the house. One step up to the porch, and Travis began to pray anyway.

He was a man in his forties, for crying out loud. He shouldn't be this fucking nervous seeing his folks. Oops—he'd have to watch his language. He hadn't slipped up by cursing in front of his parents since high school. As off-balance as he was today, he might slip. That was the last thing they needed.

Proving that they were aware of his presence, Willard opened the front door before Travis had a chance to knock. Travis stared at his dad behind the mesh of the screen door still between them.

Maybe he felt like he did because his dad still dwarfed him. Though both he and Wendy had inherited their sturdy build from their father, neither had managed to surpass him. At nearly seventy, Willard had retained most of his six-foot height, and though most of the tons of ranch-earned muscle had shifted into fat, he still struck an impressive figure. Travis never felt small next to anyone except his father.

Willard motioned to the screen door. "Well, come on in, boy."

Travis forced his hand to move; he reached out and pulled open the door, and then nothing stood between them.

Automatic movements began to return, and Travis stepped through the doorway, Dunkyn at his heels.

Willard took his son's hand and gave two firm shakes. "It's good to see you, Travis. We didn't expect to see you again until spring." While they never accepted Travis's offers of monetary help, they did allow him to buy them bus tickets to come visit the grandkids a few times a year.

Norma emerged from somewhere behind her husband and padded up to Travis. He bent and wrapped her gently in his arms for a light hug. She was as small and frail as Willard was large. She looked so much older than her sixty-three years.

Not for the first time, *cancer* screamed through Travis's mind as he held her fragile body. He tried to shove the fear away, but he wasn't quite successful. Her touch was so fleeting Travis barely felt it.

She pulled back, her sun-weathered face peering up warmly at Travis. "It's good to see you, son. Such a nice surprise. Christmas already seems like so long ago. I do wish you woulda brought the children. I'm sure they've already grown so much in the past month." She stooped to touch Dunkyn's nose with her fingertips.

"Soon, Mom. If you all wanna come up before spring, you just say the word."

Willard shut the door, causing the room to darken slightly, though afternoon sun sifted through the yellowed lace curtains of the living room. "Might as well tell us what you got to say. Your mom and I are worried, gotta say. Somebody sick?" He'd never been one for small talk.

"Willard, stop. Travis hasn't even got a chance to sit yet. Give the boy a moment." Norma shooed him with a flick of her veiny hands. "You men sit, and I'll get you some tea. And some pie. I baked one of my gooseberry pies I had frozen in the icebox when you said you was coming, Travis. I know they're your favorite." She turned toward the kitchen, then paused, her fearful eyes meeting her son's. Her voice was even more fragile than usual. "*Is* anyone sick? Are the kids okay?"

It seemed Shannon's sickness had done a number on them all. Though she'd always been too loud and outspoken for Travis's parents, too much like Wendy, they'd grown to love her, especially after Caleb's birth.

"No, Mom. We're all well and healthy."

She sighed, her hand coming to rest over her chest, the strength pouring out of her at her relief. "Praise the Lord."

Travis moved toward the kitchen with her. "Let me help you, Mom."

"No. Now you git." She shooed him away again. "You sit with your father. Let me do my job."

Travis obliged, knowing it would do no good to argue. He took a seat on the orange sofa next to his father's recliner. Both chairs had been there for as long as he could remember, probably even before he'd been born. Dunkyn lay down with a grunt and propped his head on the toe of Travis's boot.

His father nodded at him but remained silent. Now that everyone's health was accounted for, he was content to wait for whatever news was coming.

Travis typically didn't feel any anxiety in his childhood home, not like what Wendy claimed to experience. She always said that the walls started closing in as soon as she stepped back into the house. It was part of the reason Travis paid for their folks to take the bus to El Do. Now, as he looked around the dated but clean furnishings, all so familiar and loved, Travis had a similar sensation.

Unlike Wendy, he'd become a master of shoving things away, even as a child. Out of sight, out of mind. As he sat surrounded by his past, memories tugged at him, this time more emotional than visual. He remembered what it felt like to know he was a little different than he was supposed to be, that something was a little off and that whatever it was needed to be hidden, needed to be smothered.

Norma brought in three iced teas one shaking glass at a time.

Shortly after, three chipped china plates made their way onto the coffee table, pie and fork balanced on each. After the last one, Travis's mom finally sat on the opposite end of the sofa.

Travis realized he'd accidentally taken her spot, the one next to Willard's recliner. He was surprised his dad hadn't motioned for him to move over. "I'm sorry, Mom. I wasn't thinking. You wanna trade places?"

She smiled gently, though the worry seemed to be returning to her eyes. "No, dear, you just sit right there between us." She shifted back to a more supported spot on her new location on the couch. "Would you be a dear and hand me my pie, though?"

He removed the smallest serving of pie from the brass coffee table and passed it to her, noticing how the plate shook as she took it from him, but he pushed the growing worry away.

They ate without speaking for a few moments. Only the watery smacking sound of his father's lips broke the silence. Travis had to control his facial expression at the first bite of the pie. Gooseberry had been his favorite of all the pies his mother used to make. However, the bite was sour, causing his eyes to squeeze shut of their own accord. The past couple of times he'd been home, Travis had noticed his mother's food wasn't what he remembered. She'd always been a terrific cook. Whether it was his slanted memory or her ability, the food had not lived up to what Travis recalled from childhood. This pie was not a result of skewed memory, however. His mother must have forgotten the sugar. All of it.

He watched his father for a reaction as he took a bite. There was none. Either Willard's taste buds were failing or he'd grown accustomed to the change in Norma's food and mastered the art of nonreaction. Travis was willing to bet it was the latter. Though gruff, Willard had always been extremely protective of his wife. The only time Travis remembered getting any consequence from him other than measured spankings with the belt was a fist to the jaw when Travis had cursed at his mother when he'd been in high school.

His father's son, Travis was able to take the next bite, and each one after, without any reaction other than the occasional compliment to his mother. When all that was left was the edge of piecrust, Travis really was able to close his eyes and drift back through four decades. Whatever might be affecting her, Norma Bennett was still able to make the best piecrust in the four-state area.

Travis's dad had been a ranch hand his entire life, until arthritis had taken hold of his joints. A few years ago, he'd been forced to take a job at a factory in Neosho. Travis tried to think of something he could ask that could ease them into conversation but not make his father feel shame over his perceived weakness. On the edge of losing his own farm, his buffalo—*I spend more time with them than Mr. Walker ever does*—Travis was more cognizant than ever of the loss his father must have experienced.

Willard turned his sun-lined face toward Travis, cutting off the need for transitions. "So, tell us. What brought you here, son? It must be big to take you away from the feedstore on a Saturday, and without the kids."

"Ah, Jason's got the store under control. And we hired a new girl to help out, so it's covered."

His mom inhaled a breath and looked at him hopefully. "Is that it? Is this new girl someone you've been seeing?" She clasped her hands together in her lap, over the folds of her skirt. "I've been praying the Lord would send you a good woman to help take away your loneliness, to be a mother to those beautiful children."

Oh dear Lord. "No, Mom. Krissy, the new girl, is in high school. She was just in need of a job."

Norma's face fell. "Oh. Well, that's nice, I suppose."

The room fell silent again. Travis hadn't practiced what he was going to say. He'd done his best not to think about it. Now that he was in his childhood home, sitting between his parents, the terror of truth lay thick over the room.

Willard spoke again, his voice more commanding this time, leaving Travis feeling even more childishly exposed. "Well, come on, boy. Out with it. Just say whatever it is so we can face it together, like a family."

Fuck! "Well, I wanted to tell you in person. I doubt you'd find out some other way, but as more and more people are knowing, I didn't want to take the chance you'd hear it from someone besides me...." Travis glanced out the window, praying to see a snowflake falling behind the lace curtains. No such luck. Maybe he could run for it anyway.

"Travis. Come on." Willard's bark made his son flinch.

"Okay. Okay." Travis sucked in a deep breath and then let it out, shakily. "I ah...." He wrung his hands, his thumbs tracing over the calloused palms. "You see, I've started...." Fuck. This was the hardest thing he'd ever had to do. Ever.

A whisper touched his ear. No clear words, but it was there. This was far from the hardest thing he'd had to do. This was nothing in comparison.

He sat up straight, the couch groaning at his movement. Dunkyn shifted below him, moving away from Travis's boots.

Travis wished he'd changed places with his mom so he could face his parents at the same time and not have to look back and forth.

"Well, it's like this. I'm dating someone. Ah... a man. His name is Wesley Ryan, and he's a veterinarian in town. It's been a couple of months now or so. Wendy really likes him. The kids think he's great. Sh...." He'd almost said Shannon liked him. That would have been... unhelpful, though it felt true enough. "I like him." He cleared his throat, forced his voice to sound more declarative. "I love him."

He'd not been able to face his parents, not fully, as he spoke, but he made himself look at them, turning his head to look them both in the face. His father wore a disgusted expression. His mother showed nothing but shock. Travis suddenly worried about the possibility of a stroke.

Maybe he shouldn't have done this.

"I just didn't want you to hear it from anyone else but me."

Travis turned back to his dad. The disgust on Willard's face was morphing into a look of anger. Travis shifted his attention toward his mom.

Tears were already streaking down Norma's face. Her trembling voice was barely audible. "Travis, grief can do strange things. The devil uses it to sneak inta us. He's using Shannon's death to tempt you. To try to steal you away. You must fight this, son."

God, he hated seeing her cry. Hated the fear in her voice. "Mom. This isn't new. I know it is to you both, but this isn't new. Even Shannon knew about it, even before we got married."

Norma's mouth worked silently.

"I don't care what she knew or didn't know. She was never good enough to be part of this family anyway."

All embarrassment and shame fled as Travis turned toward his father. It was a sheer act of will that kept him seated on the sofa. "Dad, watch what you say about my wife."

Though Travis had never used that tone toward his father before, Willard wasn't taken aback in the slightest. "Well, she wasn't. And I don't need to be concerned with Shannon's memory. You obviously aren't."

Losing the battle, Travis stood, fists clenched and trembling at his sides.

Norma spoke up, her tone pleading. "Please. Let's not fight. That won't solve anything. Let us pray." She turned toward her husband. "Willard, *please*. Let's pray for healing."

Travis tried to keep the anger at his father out of his voice, though he couldn't manage to look away from Willard. "Mom, this isn't something we can pray away. I'm sorry, but I didn't bring this up to get help with it. I simply wanted you to know."

"But the children, Travis. Think of them. Think of the example you are to show. Lead them in the paths of righteousness. This… sin… will corrupt their souls." At the tears in her voice, Travis turned away from his father. The years Norma had aged in the brief moments since hearing his truth ripped at his heart.

Travis knew there was no hate behind her words. She was terrified and panicked for their souls. Travis could see the image of him and his children burning projected from behind her eyes. He wished he could take that away for her.

Of all his fears about loving Wesley, hell was not one of them.

"I don't want to hurt you, Mom. I don't believe it's wrong. Not like you do."

She leaned forward, struggling to rise, but she wasn't able. "That's what sin does, Travis. It blinds us to the truth. It smothers out the voice of God. Makes us believe the lie."

Travis moved toward her, reaching out to take her hands, a mix of frustration at her stubborn beliefs and the desire to comfort her in her fear waging within him.

"Don't touch her."

Travis turned, angling himself cautiously against the anger in his father's voice.

Willard shook with fury of his own. "You are a disgrace to your family. We raised you better."

Travis was far enough away from his dad that he didn't have to look up into his face. He'd known they'd be upset. His mother's reaction was exactly what he should have expected. He hadn't anticipated such anger from his father, though—confusion and arguments to be sure, but not this.

Willard stepped toward him, one of his knees letting out a loud pop at the movement. "Are you determined in this?"

Travis glanced back at his mother apologetically, then faced his father once more. "If you're asking if I'm going to pursue this relationship, then the answer is yes. I don't know where it will lead, but, yes. I am determined."

Norma let out a pitiful moan from behind him, but Travis didn't look back, though it killed him.

"You are no longer welcome in this home."

Travis flinched again. "Dad."

"Willard." Norma's shaking voice called out from a great distance. "There is redemption. There is—"

"Quiet, Norma!"

Travis had never heard his father use that tone with his mother. It had been reserved for his children and unruly cattle.

"You are no longer a son of mine. You are no longer a man."

Travis felt something in his chest begin to crumble.

Then a whisper. An affirmation.

Travis looked his father full in the eyes. He saw the blue eyes that stared out at him from his own reflection. From the face of his sister.

Travis and his father stared at each other. Neither flinching. Neither wavering.

After a moment or years, Travis broke the connection and looked down at his mother. He attempted a smile. Something to impart love, comfort, encouragement… something. He wasn't sure if he succeeded.

The screen door banged against the doorframe behind him as Travis took the one step off the porch and walked stiff-backed to his truck, Dunkyn by his side.

He refused to look into the rearview mirror as he drove away. He would not consider the possibility of his father changing his mind, nor would he ponder what it would mean if this were truly the last time they would see each other.

At some point as he drove through Neosho, Travis pulled off at a hotel by the highway. He would stay there for the evening. He would return home the next afternoon.

He needed a night to think. A night to himself. A night of quiet. A night not to think.

CHAPTER TWENTY-SIX

THE HOLY Church looked as if it had been lifted out of Kansas City and dropped accidentally in El Dorado. The mini-mega church had none of the small-town charm Wesley would expect from this little town and, apparently, it wasn't done growing. A new offshoot of construction was jutting out in the corner of the parking lot. It was definitely not like the church he had attended with his grandparents.

Wesley had stared at it several times as he'd driven by, thinking how out of place it seemed with small neighborhood houses on three sides of it and Travis's buffalo field on the other. It was easy to see the original structure. While no shrinking violet itself, it made a charming picture. Wesley was fairly certain he could remember what it looked like before it was devoured by the expansion. He glanced over at Wendy, who had just opened the car door for Mason. Caleb was doing the same for Avery on the other side of the car. "You sure this is a good idea?"

Wendy adjusted Mason's cap so his ears were covered from the morning chill. Satisfied, she turned her attention on Wesley. "Yes. Nothing bad is going to happen, Wesley. I promise. Everyone is friendly. They've all been supportive of us."

He read between the lines. Wendy had told him, when the kids weren't around, how accepting they'd been of her when she'd moved in with Travis after Shannon's death. After her parents' reaction, Wendy had been afraid that her divorce would only alienate her. No one seemed to mind. Of course, no one had known her in El Do before the divorce, so that might have helped some.

Wesley couldn't help but be irritated at his nervousness. He didn't use to feel like a freak show everywhere he went, but that was changing. And he wasn't as naive as he'd been only a couple of short months ago. People were talking about the new vet dating one of their men. It didn't matter that Travis never went to church. His kids and sister did. His dead wife had. And now, his boyfriend was entering the doors.

What the hell was he doing?

"Caleb, would you please take the twins into children's church?" Wendy grinned at her nephew. "It seems I need to do a pep talk with our resident veterinarian here."

Caleb took Mason's outstretched hand. "Sure, Wendy." He smiled earnestly at Wesley. "It's gonna be fine, Wes. I'm sure things have settled down now, and we won't have to move. Just be you. They'll love ya."

At his words, Wendy looked at him, a shocked expression on her face. Caleb didn't seem to notice, only gave Wesley another encouraging smile before turning and walking up the steps toward the church with the twins. Mason craned his neck to look over his shoulder, giving Wesley a small wave.

Wesley waved back, a moment of adoration cutting through the nerves at the sight of Mason's tiny, wiggling fingers and Caleb using his new nickname. After the boy had shadowed Wesley at Cheryl's, he'd started referring to him as Wes. Wesley had always hated that name and corrected anyone who'd tried to shorten his full name. Coming from Caleb, though, it sounded like acceptance, and was possibly the best thing he'd ever heard.

He turned from the kids' retreating forms and looked at Wendy, who was intently staring at her reflection in the car window as she fixed her red curls, a little too concerned about them to be believable.

"That's not convincing, Wendy."

She peered over at him, her voice sounding innocent. "What do you mean?"

He put his hand on his hip. "Really? I'm supposed to believe there's not a story there somewhere? *We won't have to move?*"

Wendy dropped the pretense and turned from her reflection, pulling her Western-style woven jacket tighter about her. "Well, I didn't know Caleb knew about that. He was young enough when it happened that he wasn't really aware. I guess he's heard things now that people are talking again."

"What things?"

Wendy waved at a car pulling into the parking lot a few rows over.

"Wendy...."

She sighed. "Fine, if you're going to get all huffy. Though I really think it would just be better if we went in and started fresh."

Wesley continued glaring.

She lifted her hands, rings flashing in the sun. "Fine, fine!"

He waited, but Wendy still didn't speak. "Oh good God, Wendy. Whatever it is, now I'm twice as freaked out about it."

Wendy rolled her eyes. "You don't need to be freaked out. It's not about you in the slightest. Don't be a drama queen."

Wesley thought he was going to have to prompt her again, but after another sigh, Wendy launched into the story.

"Well, you know that gay youth pastor a few years back. The one Carrie told you about?" She didn't wait for him to confirm. "Well, and this is before my time.... Actually, it all happened right after Shannon's death. When I started coming with the kids, the new pastor had just started. So I missed all the drama, and Caleb, like I said, was too young back then for the youth group, so it didn't affect him at all."

At her pause, Wesley arched his eyebrows at her.

"Oh, fine. It seems that the preacher who brought in the gay youth pastor, I don't even know his name...."

"Brooke." There was no way Wesley could have forgotten the guy's name from Ms. Michael's story.

Wendy gave him a surprised look. "Oh, right. Brooke. Well, the preacher, Brother Bron, I believe his name was, I never met him, was new to the church at the time too. I guess when he asked the gay youth pastor, Brooke, to be part of the youth group, well, shit hit the fan, as you can imagine."

Wesley snorted. "Yeah. Duh. Sounds like a dumb move to me. I can't imagine people being okay with that. Not here."

"Exactly. Not saying it's wrong, obviously, but it seems like a pretty... bold move from a new preacher. Anyway, I guess at that same time, the preacher's daughter got pregnant by Brooke's cousin, who also worked with the kids."

"Oh. Not married, huh?"

Wendy shook her head. "Nope." She waved her hands in a fluttering gesture. "From what I've heard, there was all kinds of drama around it, and the end result was Pastor Bron was asked to step down, though I think he was here a little over a year or so before that finally happened."

Wesley waited, but it looked like Wendy was done talking. "Ah... what about the whole moving thing?"

She rolled her eyes again and gave him an exasperated grin. "You're like a bulldog that just won't let go of something. Fine. Due to the whole mess, the entire family moved. All of them. Not just the preacher, but the whole mess of them. I think their names were Durke or something. I'm pretty sure I remember something about the mom being Sue Durke. They had just left when I started at church. I never met any of them, but it seemed that the family was one of the pillars of the church, so they say. People were pretty upset and torn about the issue."

"And, you thought this wasn't pertinent information before bringing me to church? That because one of their family members was gay, a whole family had to move out of town?" Despite the biting cold, sweat was trickling down Wesley's sides.

"I'm sure there's more to the story than that. A lot has changed. And, it was years ago."

"You moved here *four* years ago, Wendy. We're not talking decades here."

"Well, you're not planning on getting a job at the church." Wendy bugged her eyes at him. "Iris has already made sure about that, hasn't she?"

"I don't think I can do this. I don't think we *should* do this. We should have at least asked Travis. After everything that happened with your folks yesterday, this is the last thing he needs to drive home to this afternoon."

She shook her head. "No, this is exactly what he needs. We need to start making this normal. You're not trying to influence their kids or preach about God. You're taking care of their animals. And the more they can put your face with all the rumors, the more they will see you as just another person. That's what Travis needs. That's what you need. And the kids. For this"—her hands fluttered between them, including herself with him—"to be normal."

Wesley wasn't sure church was the way to do it, especially after Wendy's story, but he couldn't argue with the logic of it. There wasn't a more social place in El Do than church. Maybe she was right. Maybe if they saw he was just another person, like them, that he was normal, it might make it easier for his and Travis's relationship. In the back of his mind, he heard Travis suggesting he butch it up.

"Fine. Okay, Wendy. Let's do this." Wesley pulled the rust orange scarf from around his neck. "Can you open the car so I can put this back in there?"

Wendy narrowed her eyes. "Why?"

He sighed in exasperation. "We're gonna be late, and the last thing I want is the entire church turning around to watch us walk in."

She didn't relent. "Don't you dare leave that scarf in the car, Wesley Ryan!" She motioned down to her ever-vibrant ensemble. "Look at me—I am who I am, and they have no problem with it."

"You're a girl."

She lifted her chin. "You be who you are."

Though he was past wanting to discuss anything, Wesley loved her protectiveness over him. He softened his tone. "I will, Wendy. However, a scarf doesn't make or break me. Let's ease these people into this. Maybe the Durkes wouldn't have had to move if they'd gone a little slower."

Her blue eyes darted back and forth as she searched his face. "Fine. But if you walk in with a cowboy hat tomorrow, we're gonna have a talk."

Wesley laughed. "Deal."

Wendy opened the car door long enough for Wesley to toss the scarf into the front seat, then relocked it.

As they walked up the steps the kids had taken a few minutes earlier, a voice called out from behind them.

"Dr. Ryan!"

His nerves spiking, Wesley turned toward the voice. Carrie Michaels was walking across the parking lot. Speak of the devil. A gorgeous mountain of a man walked beside her, holding her hand.

Wesley waved, and he and Wendy waited for them to catch up.

Carrie's smile was bright and genuine. "Dr. Ryan, I'd like you to meet my husband, Craig."

Wesley took Craig's outstretched hand, doing his best to keep from staring. The man was even better looking up close. *Way to go, Carrie!*

"It's nice to have you here, Dr. Ryan. Carrie tells me we're slated to get together for dinner when our son, Darwin, comes back from school." Though Craig's expression wasn't as open as his wife's, his greeting seemed genuine.

"Yeah, that sounds great. And you can call me Wesley." He motioned toward Wendy. "Do you all know Wendy?"

"Of course. Though we haven't ever done more than small talk after a church service every once in a while." Carrie reached out and gave Wendy a quick hug. "We'll have to remedy that."

Wendy smiled and shook Craig's hand as well. "I'd love to."

From above, the chimes of the church bells cut through the air, which seemed to be getting colder by the moment.

"And we're late, apparently." Wesley had started to feel a little less nervous as they spoke to the Michaelses, but the bells sent another spike of adrenaline through him.

Carrie piped up, her voice excited. "Would you guys like to sit with us?"

"Um, sure." Wesley glanced over at Craig, uncertain the man would have the same feeling as his wife.

He smiled with a nod. "Please do. It's good that you're here."

For a moment Wesley wondered if Craig meant it like it was good for heathens to come to church, but he seemed genuine enough.

Wendy settled the matter. "That would be great. Thank you. Let's just get out of this cold already."

DESPITE THEIR lateness, few people turned around at their entrance. As they walked up the aisle, a motion caught Wesley's eye. Turning slightly, he saw Iris Linley waving at him, a friendly smile on her sour face. Wesley gave a small wave back before he and Wendy sidled in beside Carrie and Craig several rows up from Iris. He wasn't sure how he could have missed her. Her church muumuu was even more audacious than those she used for everyday wear. This one had lace around the collar, nearly causing the eye to water as it battled with the floral print underneath.

As they settled in, Wesley felt more at ease. The music was upbeat and pretty. A six-person worship team led the congregation in an assortment of contemporary choruses. They even had a small orchestra off to the left. It didn't have a small country-town feel at all.

Actually Wesley realized that, as far as church went, he kinda liked it. The space was vast and modern, and the vaulted ceilings seemed nearly limitless. Things were clean and sleek. Even the podium was a minimal design of glass, an open Bible showing through the clear structure.

The crowd was a good mix of old and young, and despite the vastness of the sanctuary, it was surprisingly full. Whatever the Holy Church was doing, it seemed to be working. Add to this the killer youth building on Main Street and he could see why families with school-aged kids would want to be there.

When the music ended and announcements had been made by a dynamic, well-spoken woman—Wesley would have placed money on her being lesbian—a large older man waddled up to take his place behind the glass pulpit.

The groan Wendy let out beside him was loud enough to make Wesley turn toward her.

She looked at him guiltily and leaned toward him to whisper. "I'm *so* sorry. I don't know how I forgot. Pastor Carver is out of town today." She motioned toward the pulpit with her chin. "This is Pastor Thomas. He was the preacher before the guy I was telling you about in the parking lot. I hate when he preaches. Actually, when I remember he's doing a service, I skip it."

Great. Wesley started to turn away, but Wendy pulled him closer.

"See that woman over there? The one with the dyed-black beehive hair?"

Wesley found the thin woman on the far right of the sanctuary, seated primly in the front row. She looked more like a crane perched on the edge of a pond, searching for small fish to devour, than an actual woman.

He nodded that he saw her.

Wendy put her lips to his ear. "That's Brother Thomas's wife, Twyla. That woman is a *biiiitch*."

He whipped his head around to glare at her. His whispered admonition was louder than he'd intended. "Wendy!"

She shrugged. "Well, she is."

Wesley shook his head and turned his attention back to the preacher. It took all his resolve to not look away. He would have given anything to trade the sleek glass pulpit for an oversized wooden block. Brother Thomas was a huge man, rolls of fat visible from his too-thin shirt and overhead lighting. Sweat was already pouring down his face and wetting his shirt, causing it to be even more transparent.

It was tragic.

His amplified voice cut through the silence. "Open your Bible to Revelations, chapter six."

There was a brief period of rustling as people turned in their Bibles, despite the scripture being prominently displayed on the screen behind the stage.

Without so much as a transition, Pastor Thomas launched into his sermon, his fist rising in the air from the first word. "The first part of the chapter reveals the opening of the first five seals and entrance of the four horsemen. The slain righteous calling out unto God for vengeance. For retribution to fall upon those who do not follow the Lord your God. Read with me at verse twelve." His voice rumbled, rising and falling with each inflection of the words. It reminded Wesley of the stereotypical televangelist. He remembered hearing Jerry Falwell a couple of times on the TV as a kid. He loathed that monster.

"And I beheld when he had opened the sixth seal, and, lo, there was a great earthquake; and the sun became black as sackcloth of hair, and the moon became as blood; And the stars of heaven fell unto the earth, even as a fig tree casteth her untimely figs, when she is shaken of a mighty wind. And the heaven departed as a scroll when it is rolled together; and every mountain and island were moved out of their places. And the kings of the earth, and the great men, and the rich men, and the chief captains, and the mighty men, and every bondman, and every free man, hid themselves in the dens and in the rocks of the mountains; And said to the mountains and rocks, Fall on us, and hide us from the face of him that sitteth on the throne, and from the wrath of the Lamb: For the great day of his wrath is come; and who shall be able to stand?"

Pastor Thomas's voice rang out with passion, like a cry to war as he read. His sweat increased as if the fires of hell were licking at his back. "Those who do not follow in the ways of the righteous will cry out for death, for mercy, for relief. It. Will. Not. Come!" His fervor hinted that he was just getting started.

Wesley gaped at Wendy in astonishment.

She shrugged again. "See why I skip when *he's* up there?"

CHAPTER TWENTY-SEVEN

HE DIDN'T plan it, but Travis changed course from the road that led to his home as he exited the cemetery early Sunday afternoon. Of course, what had he done that he *had* planned lately? Life seemed to be unfolding one second at a time. That was better than where he had been, he supposed—stuck in the past, buried in a grave as surely as Shannon.

HE'D WOKEN up before the sun, as always, although momentarily confused by the sparse hotel room. He'd gotten used to waking up in Wesley's bed, Wesley's lithe chest rising and falling in sleep, Dunkyn curled up over the covers at their feet. At the sight of the unfamiliar alarm clock, the events of the day before came back to him, along with the pang of a headache when he moved to sit up. He glanced down at the brown shag carpet below the bed. Empty beer cans.

Oh, right.

He barely remembered stopping to pick up the six-pack before checking into the room. Well, whatever; being disowned by your parents entitled you to tie one on.

And if it didn't? Fuck it anyway.

With another groan, he pushed himself out of the bed and stumbled in the dark toward the bathroom.

Dunkyn made a similar noise as he carefully jumped off the bed.

After flicking on the light, Travis stood in front of the toilet and emptied himself of at least four of the cans. As he groaned for a third time, this one in relief, he caught sight of his naked reflection in the full-length mirror across from the open bathroom doorway.

Still pissing, he rubbed a hand over his hairy belly.

Wesley claimed he thought Travis's body was manly and sexy. Travis didn't really believe that, despite Wesley's body's reaction to him. He should lose a few pounds. Maybe have one less pitcher of beer on bowling nights. Oh, shit, he'd forgotten the Old Bulldogs were meeting later that evening.

He narrowed his eyes in accusation, peering at his reflection again. He flexed his heavy triceps as he shook his cock after the stream ebbed. He hadn't thought about his body or appearance for years.

Bowling. Two nights of beer in a row.

He flexed again.

He was fine. Shannon had always said she liked him bigger as well.

What the fuck was wrong with him? He was staring in the mirror worried about his body, and he'd accused *Wesley* of being too gay. Fuck.

A chicken-fried steak skillet and two pots of coffee accompanied him as he watched the sunrise from the window of a Village Inn on the outskirts of Neosho. If he'd gotten up earlier, he could have watched the view with the buffalo. That would have been better.

He'd taken his time driving back to El Dorado, meandering down appealing country roads that paralleled the highway. His thoughts didn't come in words or clear images. His mind just felt heavy and tired.

So much loss—Shannon, the life they'd planned, the image he'd built of himself, friendships. Jason had become all but a stranger. He'd probably lose Cedar County Feed. It wasn't just his imagination that business had dropped off. The books didn't lie. He'd just lost his parents, but he probably should've seen that one coming. Even the loss of Shannon felt different lately—not less, just different, and even that change was a loss.

By the time Travis had arrived back in El Dorado, it was a little before noon, which meant most of the town would be in church. He'd planned on going to Mr. Walker's farm to tend the buffalo, but he should've known better.

Realizing what Travis needed more than he did, the F-350 had pulled into the cemetery. Then he and Dunkyn were in front of Shannon's grave, the knees of Travis's jeans growing damp from the frost covering the brown grass.

They stayed there for over an hour, undisturbed. Not even birds or squirrels chattered in the massive tree branches overhead.

Travis didn't say anything. He didn't need to. Shannon knew it all already. He just needed to be with her, to sit with her, to trace her name.

He waited. Some small part in the back of his brain, or soul, or something, grieved—for her, their children, his parents, everything. But, mostly, he just sat. Quiet. One thumb endlessly traced her *S*, the other hand continually passed over Dunkyn's warm fur.

He waited.

Quiet.

Still.

Cold.

Numb.

He waited. He waited until he felt her whispers. Until he could hear, if not understand them. He waited until he felt somewhat like her Travis again. Caleb and the twins' Travis. Wendy's Travis. Wesley's Travis.

Travis Bennett.

AFTER THE cemetery, instead of his home, Travis pulled up behind Patsy and Glen Pope's old Mercury. After parking the truck, he and Dunkyn exited and walked up to the front door of Shannon's childhood home.

He rang the bell and could hear old-fashioned chimes call from inside.

After some moments and some shuffling, Glen opened the door, his face momentarily surprised to find Travis and his dog waiting on the porch. Glen looked past them, confused. "The kids with you?"

Travis shook his head. "Nah. Just me." He glanced down at Dunkyn. "Us."

Glen stepped backward, making room to squeeze by his expansive belly. "Well, come on in, boys." As Travis and Dunkyn entered, Glen called out toward the kitchen. "Hey, Patsy. Travis is here, put out another plate."

Patsy's thin face poked out from the kitchen doorway, her blue eyes bright behind her glasses. "Well, what a nice surprise." She shuffled out of the kitchen toward Travis.

He closed in on her quickly, not wanting her to have to put in more effort than necessary. Shannon's parents were nearly a decade older than his own. Shannon had been their one and only miracle child, when they'd given up ever having a baby.

Patsy allowed him to place a tender kiss on her cheek, then waggled her spotted fingers down at Dunkyn in greeting, not attempting to bend, before looking at Travis. "Are the kids alright?"

"Oh, yes. They're fine." Travis forced a smile. "I would imagine they are at church with Wendy. Although, if your church is out, theirs probably is as well."

Patsy tilted her head ever so slightly, eyeing him. "You look like you need some love. Come sit down. Pops and I were just getting ready to sit down to some sandwiches. We had some leftover turkey from the Lions Club meeting the other night."

Patsy retrieved a third plate from the cupboard while Glen got a glass and looked over at Travis. "Beer?"

He shook his head. "Oh, goodness, no. Water, please."

When all was situated and the three of them were seated around the table, Glen offered up a brief prayer.

It was Patsy, outspoken like her daughter had been, who broached the subject. "I suspect you're here to talk about you and that vet fellow who took over at Cheryl's."

Travis had been certain they already knew. He could tell from the way they'd acted the past couple of times they'd seen each other. That, and it seemed the whole town knew. Still, hearing the words so directly took him momentarily off guard. Though nervous, he couldn't help but smile at her. She was so Patsy, so Shannon. "Yeah, that's why I'm here." He wanted to ask who told them, but that was beside the point. "I'm sorry I didn't tell you sooner. You should've heard about it from me."

Glen nodded his agreement, though not unkindly. "That would have been preferable."

Patsy rushed in. "But we understand. You probably needed time to figure things out. Try to understand…." She fumbled for words. "Well, to understand."

He looked back and forth between them. He hadn't been expecting an outburst or screaming; that was never their style. Patsy might have her daughter's direct approach, but not her temper. Still, the two of them looked almost commonplace, like they were discussing the weather. Well, almost.

"You two don't seem that surprised. Although I'm not sure how long ago you heard it, I guess." God, he hated this, hated having to discuss his personal life. This was his sex life, kinda.

Patsy and Glen exchanged a look, a silent conversation passing between them. When they returned their attention to Travis, the beginning of a grin played at the corner of her wrinkled mouth—a grin, an actual grin. "I've known for about twenty years or so."

Travis's face fell, and he nearly dropped his sandwich. "What?"

Glen just nodded, looking uncomfortable, and the expression on Patsy's face was no longer just a hint of a smile.

Then Travis did put down his sandwich and leaned toward them, the weight of his elbows making the table groan. "What?" He couldn't seem to make his brain form any other thought.

"Shannon told me during one of your breakups, a bit before you got married." Though her smile didn't completely fade, she didn't quite meet his eyes. Nor did she look at her husband. "She asked me to keep it secret. I didn't even tell Glen until recently. When people started talking."

Glen leaned back in his chair and crossed his arms. "I can't say I was expecting that. Or that I appreciated the secrecy, either."

Travis tried to form a thought, a reply, something. But nothing came, other than complete astonishment. Patsy had known? This whole time? And Shannon had told? He didn't think there was anything Shannon had kept from him.

It took a moment for Travis to realize what the feelings were that began to curdle in his gut. He was hurt, and kinda angry at Shannon, his dead wife, which then added a shot of guilt to the party as well.

She'd told.

Reading his expression, Patsy placed one of her paper-thin hands over Travis's suddenly clenched fist. "Don't be mad at her, son. Shannon needed to talk, to figure it out. She needed her mother."

Travis met her eyes then. "What did you tell her?"

Patsy laughed, her smile returning. "Oh, you know Shannon, and I'd learned long before that little announcement that she didn't need or want to hear what I thought she should do. She just needed to talk and have her mother listen. So that's what I did."

Travis suddenly wondered about the miscarriage. They hadn't told anyone, or at least that's what he'd thought. He almost asked. God, he wanted to ask. He needed to know it had been their secret. He opened his mouth to ask, but stopped.

He thought there had been a whisper, but it had been so soft he might have imagined it. But, maybe.

Shannon had loved him. She'd loved him so much that she'd accepted him for exactly who he was, even when he couldn't really do that for himself. She was the strongest person he'd ever known.

Travis met Patsy's pleading gaze and thought of his mother's fear-filled eyes from the day before. He unclenched his fist and placed his other hand over Patsy's. "I'm so glad Shannon had you."

A tear spilled down Patsy's cheek.

Travis looked over at Glen, not releasing Patsy's hand. "Both of you." He suddenly felt like he had to explain, like he had to convince them.

"I loved Shannon. I loved your daughter with all of my heart. She was my best friend, and I still ache for her."

There were tears, then, on all three faces around the table.

"I still love her."

In a rare affectionate move, Glen placed his hand for a moment over the top of the tower of Patsy's and Travis's hands before pulling it away once more. "We know, son."

TRAVIS LEFT Shannon's parents' home with a strange mix of sorrow and relief. Shannon had given him the world. She'd even given him her parents.

Maybe his own would come around. Maybe they wouldn't.

On the way to his house he texted Jason, telling him he wouldn't be at bowling that night. Jason didn't text back, and Travis shoved that particular hurt from his mind.

Tonight he needed to be with his family—with his and Shannon's children, Wendy, the dogs, and the stupid rabbit. He needed to be with Wesley.

All of them. Together.

Without giving himself time to reconsider, he called the Popes less than five minutes after leaving their house.

If the family was going to be together, they needed to be there too.

THE COVERS had worked their way off Wesley's back at some point during the night. The faintest hint of sunrise crept through the slit in the curtains, highlighting a strip of soft golden skin. It was an act of strength for Travis to keep his fingers from reaching out to trace the glowing section. Even without the contact, his body responded, demanding he end Wesley's sleeping.

It had been a short night. After being with the family, waiting for the kids to fall asleep, then the extended rounds of sex, you would have thought he'd been gone for a lot longer than one night. He and Wesley hadn't fallen asleep until the wee hours of the morning.

What little sleep he'd gotten had been filled with dreams, a constant shifting of faces—his parents, Wesley, Shannon, the kids. Every fucking face in El Do. He'd given up sleeping nearly half an hour ago.

This was better.

Though he wasn't allowing himself to touch, this was better.

Wesley was beautiful. So blond and tan. Such a strange mix of masculinity and beauty.

The swell of his muscles, the glow of the red stubble across his cheek. His gentle temperament, his soft laugh, his almost mothering nature.

He'd known he was in love with Wesley, known it was too late to back out and avoid more risk of loss.

The events of the past two days had cemented the fact. There were no longer aspects of his feelings for the man that were abstract or fuzzy. If he let his mind try to wade too deep into the future, terror began to take over. But maybe that was normal. He tried to believe it didn't mean things were destined to shatter, that Wesley wouldn't leave, wouldn't get sick.

He tried to believe it didn't mean that he, himself, wouldn't get freaked out and flee.

That fear was easy to dispel, easier than the rest. He wasn't going to leave. The hard part was over. People knew. The shoe had dropped.

"You gonna hold me, or just lie there staring creepily and breathing like a stalker on the phone?" Wesley didn't move.

Travis chuckled, embarrassed at being caught. "Thought you were sleeping."

"Hard to sleep when someone's drilling holes into my back."

"Sorry."

"Don't be." Still he didn't move. "So, you gonna hold me or what?"

Wordlessly, Travis slid over, eliminating the space between them, wrapped his arms around Wesley, and pulled him closer so his back was flush against Travis's chest and stomach.

They both let out involuntary sighs at the contact. Then laughed.

"Man, you feel good."

Wesley arched his back, making his ass push against Travis's erection, eliciting a groan.

"Feels like you didn't get fully satisfied last night."

Travis wrapped Wesley tighter with one arm and let his other hand slide down to encircle Wesley. "Kinda feels like that for you too."

"I don't think I'm ever gonna get my fill of having you inside of me." Wesley placed his hand over the arm Travis had wrapped around his chest, giving it a little squeeze. "I so want to be enough for you."

The sound of fear in Wesley's voice more than the words themselves cut through Travis's growing arousal. He paused, ceasing the stroking motion over Wesley's length that he'd involuntarily begun. "What?"

Wesley let out a forced laugh and shook his head against the crook of Travis's arm. "Nothing." After a moment, he halfheartedly pushed his hips forward against Travis's cupped hand. "Keep going. That was heading to promising places."

Travis pulled his hand away. "Hey. Look at me."

Wesley didn't. "No. Come on. It's nothing. I wasn't trying to ruin the mood. Just keep going."

He scooted back a bit, making room, then tugged gently on Wesley's shoulder. "Wesley, look at me."

After another moment's hesitation, Wesley sighed and shifted, causing the sheets to tangle as he twisted to his other side. He looked at Travis for a second, then glanced away.

Travis didn't like what he saw. Maybe not all the shoes had dropped. "What is it?"

Another shake of his head. "It's nothing. You know me. I tend to overthink things." Wesley leaned in and kissed Travis's lips.

He placed a hand on Wesley's face before pulling away. Then he waited until those warm brown eyes finally looked at him again. "Wesley, talk to me."

For a moment it looked like Wesley was going to cry. He didn't. Nor did he speak.

"For fuck's sake, Wesley. You're freaking me out here." He didn't want to say those next words, but he couldn't stop himself. "Are you getting ready to leave?"

The pause before Wesley spoke didn't help matters. "No. No, Travis. I'm not thinking about leaving. That's not what I'm worried about."

"You're worried about *me* leaving?"

Wesley's mouth opened like he was getting ready to speak, but then he closed it. He nodded slightly.

"Why the fuck would I do that?" Even Travis couldn't deny the panic in his own voice.

A bitter laugh escaped Wesley. "Why wouldn't you?"

"Are you kidding?"

Wesley pulled back, putting space between them as they lay facing each other on the bed. He pulled the sheet up, partially covering his chest. "Am *I* kidding? You're losing everything. Your parents. Your best friend. People are talking about you all over town: big, strong Travis Bennett fucking that pansyass faggot."

Anger filled Travis at the tone in Wesley's words and the shame he could hear as Wesley spoke that last word. He was going to kill his parents. Jason. Everybody.

Then guilt flared and consumed him.

That had come from him. *He'd* called Wesley a faggot. *He'd* asked Wesley to butch it up.

"Wesley…." What the fuck could he say? How was he supposed to fix the damage he'd done? "I don't give a fuck what anyone else says. And I don't want you to change. I love you. I'm so sorry that I—"

"I'm not Shannon!" The words burst from Wesley, nearly a yell.

Travis flinched. "What?"

Wesley seemed to cave in on himself; it was agonizing to watch. His voice was barely audible. "I'm not Shannon, Travis. I never will be."

He wanted to reach out to touch Wesley again. He didn't. He tried to keep his voice calm, tried not to panic, tried not to get angry. "I know that. I'm very aware that you're not Shannon. I'm not asking you to be."

"Really?" There was no accusation in Wesley's tone, just sadness.

Travis did reach out then and wrapped his fingers around the fists clenched tight over the sheet. "No. I'm not."

Tears ran down Wesley's cheeks, heavy and slow. His eyes fixed on the pillow under Travis's head. "Maybe not. Maybe not in words. But you need me to be her. Even if you're not asking it."

He searched Wesley's face, trying to understand. He tried to figure out the right reaction, the right thing to say. He waited for a whisper. Something.

He waited too long.

"I'll never be Shannon, Travis. I can't be everything she was. I can't make her come back." Wesley's gaze finally met his again. "She's always going to be here. You're going to be constantly looking for her. I won't ever be enough."

Still no whispers, but Travis suddenly understood. This wasn't the first time he'd had this conversation.

He was finally able to get his hand between Wesley's, still in their tight grasp. "When Shannon was pregnant, the first time. Before the miscarriage…." His throat closed up suddenly. He'd never spoken of this, not even with Shannon. It had been said aloud that one time, then done.

"It's okay, Travis. You can't help—"

"No. Let me finish. Just wait, okay?" Travis refused to look away, or to let go of Wesley's hands.

Finally, Wesley nodded.

Travis took a couple of deep breaths, then tried again. "We'd just gotten back together after she'd caught me fucking some guy in my dorm room. She'd gotten mad and had some fit, for the billionth time that week. Not that I blame her. She kept saying she wasn't going to be enough for me. That I was... she said I was bisexual." He forced himself to not look away. To stay grounded on Wesley. "I hate that word." Travis took another breath. "She said I wouldn't ever be able to love her completely because part of me would always be wanting something else. Wanting a man."

He waited for Wesley to nod, to smile. To get it.

He didn't.

"Don't you see?"

Wesley shook his head. Though lessening, the tears still fell.

"This is the same. Just the opposite. You know I loved Shannon, that I love Shannon with everything in me, right?"

Wesley nodded. "Of course. That's what I'm—"

"I do. I always will. But do you think my desire to fuck guys ever went away when I was with her?"

Wesley didn't respond, but the look in his eyes seemed to alter.

"It didn't, Wesley, and she knew it. And I know it hurt her. Sometimes a lot. Other times, it was just what it was. It was just me. Just my shit. We've all got our shit." Travis unlocked his fingers from Wesley's hand and pressed his palm against Wesley's cheek. "I will always love Shannon. She will always be a part of me. And, Wesley, without her, I don't think I would have ever had the courage to love you. Because of her, I know that what I feel for you isn't going to leave. Even if you do."

He was crying now. The truth of his own words cut Travis's heart and filled him with surety of his feelings for Wesley and terror of the truth of it.

"Even if you get out of this bed and leave, I will love you for the rest of my life. Shannon left. And I'll never quit loving her."

Travis could no longer see Wesley clearly through his tears. "I will never stop loving you, Wesley. Not ever. Even if you leave."

He sniffed, a snotty, disgusting, broken sound, but he forced himself to look at Wesley once more. "Please don't leave. I can't lose you both."

CHAPTER TWENTY-EIGHT

FEBRUARY BROUGHT more cold and ice.

It brought a frigid midnight house call to check on a mare quarter horse that'd gotten a laceration across its flank from an exposed nail.

It brought another visit to the Holy Church. Travis couldn't believe Wesley was going back and adamantly refused to consider attending. With Pastor Carver preaching, Wesley found the sermon much more palatable. Still, he wasn't sure he would keep going. It was probably worth it every once in a while. It gave him another chance to bond with the kids, and two of the church people had become clients, the quarter horse being one.

It brought a solitary rose and a box of chocolates from Travis on Valentine's Day. Wesley hadn't thought Travis would even think about the holiday, and hadn't wanted him to feel bad, so he hadn't done anything. He'd more than made up for it when Travis came over late that night.

It brought decisions.

He was going to buy Cheryl's. At the risk of putting the cart before the horse, Wesley decided it was time to leap, time to live. It was time, even if it seemed too soon. He also decided he was going to keep the name. It had been Cheryl's willingness to give him a chance that had brought so much good into his life. It seemed wrong to cut her out of it.

His mother nearly had a conniption—a gay man owning a veterinary clinic named Cheryl's in that Podunk town? Her son had to be insane.

She was probably right. However, he wasn't insane enough to have the families meet. Not yet. Soon, maybe, but not yet.

SOMEHOW MARCH brought even more ice and snow than February. The weather wasn't all that different from the weather in Kansas City, a mere two hours away. Still, it all seemed so much more drastic in a small town, more limiting.

It was a Saturday in the second week of March that the sun broke out from the mattress-thick layers of clouds. The afternoon was actually warm, at least compared to previous weeks. There'd been no scheduled appointments at the clinic, so Wesley had left his contact information on the door, in case anyone needed him, and had gone to The Crocheted Bunny to honor a long-standing promise to help Wendy set up a website, both for her store and for a new business of the same name, a line of crocheted stuffed animals she'd been creating. The website looked great, and was nearly ready to go live and start accepting orders. It had taken some convincing to make her increase the prices, but he knew some rich Kansas City housewives who wouldn't look twice at designer stuffed animals unless they had the price tag and the label to match. Wendy was talented enough that she could make her label worth it.

It seemed the warmer weather was not only keeping people from stopping by Cheryl's but also keeping people from shopping at The Crocheted Bunny. By three in the afternoon, Wendy decided she'd had enough of website design, would do a little more paperwork, and then close up shop. She sent Wesley over to the park to entertain Avery and Mason so she could move quicker.

Truth be told, Wesley was still somewhat nervous when it was only him and the twins. When Caleb was with them, he stepped into the father role and Wesley could just follow his lead. However, Caleb and Dolan were somewhere romancing Ashley Mei-Lien, so Wesley was on his own.

It wasn't as challenging as Wesley kept worrying it would be. All he really had to do was let Avery do her thing, and he and Mason just went along for the ride.

Today Wesley and Mason were sidekicks as Avery reenacted every Disney heroine she could think of. Actually, that was every day. One moment Wesley and Mason were two of the three bear brothers to Avery's Merida. The *Brave* character was Avery's favorite because of her red hair. Similarly, Avery often pretended to be Ariel. It was only a matter of theme if she wanted her two gentlemen servants to be friendly Sebastian and Flounder or villainous Flotsam and Jetsam. However, on this afternoon, probably due to the patches of ice here and there over the playground, Mason was reduced to Olaf the snowman and Wesley was to be Sven the reindeer.

Avery, in full Elsa splendor, zoomed down the slide at breakneck speed, her red hair whipping behind her as she bellowed "Let It Go" at the top of her lungs. Avery caught Wesley's grimace at her screeching high note. He quickly gave a poor whinny imitation, in an attempt to cover his expression.

Standing up at the end of the slide, Avery placed both hands on her hips. "Wesley! That is a horse sound. You're a reindeer!"

"Oh, right." Wesley opened his mouth, then stopped. "What sound do reindeer make?"

Avery scrunched up her face as she considered.

Mason hopped off the swing he'd been using. "Reindeer eat carrots."

"Right!" Avery pointed her finger at Wesley. "Sven, eat carrots!" She hopped off the end of the slide and began to run to climb back up the ladder before pausing to admonish him again. "But don't eat Mason's, I mean, Olaf's nose. And, Mason, Olaf waddles. You need to waddle."

Obediently, Mason began waddling back and forth, more like a penguin impersonation than a brainless snowman, but it seemed to satisfy his sister, who nodded, then continued on her journey up the slide.

A few more waddling steps brought Mason to Wesley's side. He whispered in a barely audible voice, "I'm tired of that song, Wesley."

Wesley laughed but looked up to make sure Avery wasn't overhearing. "Me too, buddy. Should we try to get her to switch to Cinderella?"

Mason shook his head. "No. I don't wanna be a mouse today."

God that kid was cute. So serious and sweet. "What do you wanna do?"

He shrugged. "I dunno. Caleb said we could play *Plants vs. Zombies* tonight."

"Oh." Wesley struggled to keep up. "On his school iPad?"

Mason nodded, his eyes wide with excitement. "Yeah, we just got the double pea shooter and the one that breathes fire!"

"Really? That's awesome. You'll have to show me." Wesley had no idea what the kid was talking about.

"Olaf!" Avery stood at the top of the slide, pointing down the steps. "Olaf!"

Wesley leaned closer to the boy. "Mason, that's you, buddy."

"Oh, right!" Mason turned and walked toward his sister. At her glare, he began a fast-paced waddle.

Satisfied, Avery shook her long hair behind her like the movie star she was. "Olaf, Hans is trying to break into my ice castle. Come get rid of him!"

Wesley looked up at her in confusion. "Am I Hans?"

She rolled her eyes, looking much more like a sixteen-year-old than a first grader. "No, Wesley. You're the reindeer, not Hans." She motioned in irritation at whatever invisible villain was at the bottom of the ice castle disguised as a slide. "You just stay there and eat carrots!"

"You got it, Avery. And hold on to the handle, sweetie. You're really high up."

"I'm Elsa, not Avery!"

"Oh, right. *Elsa*, would you please hold on to the handle?"

Obediently she gripped the curved bar at the top of the slide, then turned back to bossing her snowman brother around.

Forgotten for the moment, Wesley watched the twins play together. While he could see Travis in all three of the kids, he enjoyed watching Mason the most. The stocky little guy was basically Travis's clone. At first, when he'd started spending more time with Travis's kids, he thought Avery was rather a spoiled princess, and not in a good way. And she was, but when he took the time to really observe, Wesley noticed how she was constantly adjusting to Mason, just as he was to her. She was definitely the leader, but clearly loved her twin. She was also possibly a little more advanced than her brother in a few ways. She often stopped to help Mason tie his shoe or guide him to where missing puzzle pieces ought to be placed. Wesley's brother Josh's two oldest kids, Vanessa and Kaylee, fought like harpies. Of course they were teenagers, but they'd always been rather combative. While there were small arguments from time to time, Travis's children genuinely seemed to love each other. It was almost strange. And watching Caleb parent the twins endeared him to Wesley. He was probably the greatest kid Wesley had ever met.

Kids. The thought still terrified him. He was in this. He was in love with Travis, and he had fallen in love with all three of the kids. While the thought of the added responsibly of children made the relationship that much more daunting, it also made the risk of hurt so much worse. The breakup with Todd had nearly been more than he could handle. What if things didn't work out with Travis? He wouldn't lose just a boyfriend. He'd lose the kids and Wendy. He'd lose an entire family.

Even the couple of times he'd spent with Shannon's parents had made them begin to feel like family as well.

It was too much, and it was too messy.

Maybe that's what was making it better than anything he'd ever experienced.

It was why he really didn't see any other option than buying Cheryl's and why he didn't want any other option. He wanted this to work. He needed this to work.

It was going to work.

After another twenty minutes of playing with the twins, which included a brief transition into *The Lion King* where the twins were Simba and Nala, and Wesley the dreaded Scar, Wesley and the kids walked back through the park. They paused at the spigots to drink the frigid, rusty spring water, then continued to Main Street and walked, rosy cheeked, in to The Crocheted Bunny.

Though he hadn't heard the voice in months and hadn't thought of the man in nearly as long, Wesley felt like ice water had just been poured over him instead of stepping into the heated store.

"Missy spent hours on this crap, and it came out looking like shit. She followed every damned direction." A loud bang on a wooden surface reverberated up to the tin ceiling.

Though Wendy's voice was strained, Wesley could hear her effort to remain cordial. "Mr. Wallace, I've already said I'd give you a refund. I'm not sure what else you expect me to do."

There was another slam on the wooden counter. "I want the time Missy spent on this to be reimbursed."

In the racket, the two of them hadn't heard Wesley and the twins enter the store. Forcing his voice to be calm, Wesley bent to whisper to Mason and Avery. "You guys go to the playroom; take Nutmeg with you if you want, okay? Everything is going to be fine. I'm just gonna help Mr. Wallace leave."

His small chest puffing up bravely, Mason nodded, grabbed Avery's hand, and pulled her toward the opposite side of the store where Nutmeg's little farm was hidden. For a moment, it looked like Avery was going to protest, but with another tug from her brother she turned and followed after him.

Wesley was only a few feet from the counter when Wendy noticed him, her eyes widening in relief.

Midyell, John Wallace turned to look over his shoulder, following Wendy's gaze. When he recognized Wesley, his words trailed off.

For a moment, Wesley couldn't identify the expression that crossed over the pockmarked face. Whatever it was vanished before he could name it, anger filling the man's features once more. "Well, if it isn't the town faggot. Imagine seeing you out and about. I didn't figure you went anywhere without Bennett's cock up your ass."

Wendy's face flared in anger. "You listen here—"

Wesley rushed forward, that strange voice rising up within him as it had that night in the Wallace house. He reached for John's neck once more but was able to force his hand back down before making contact this time. His whisper was low enough to be clear to Wendy and John, but not loud enough to carry over to the twins. "Now, you listen here, you fucker. There are kids in here right now. You'll watch what you say, and you'll also be careful of how you treat this lady." The protectiveness that surged through him was surprising. He gave himself over to whatever the feeling was. "You need to leave. Now."

John cowered for a second and looked like he was going to comply, but only for a second. "You don't have your *boyfriend* or his other fuck buddy like you did at the feedstore. What are you gonna do, pussy?"

Wesley took a step closer—somewhere in the back of his mind, his old self cringed and tried to get him to slow down. He pushed it away with barely any effort, letting that other voice in him take over. "Travis and Jason weren't in your house that night either. And it wasn't me who pissed on the floor."

John's face darkened, and he glanced over at Wendy before glaring back at Wesley. "You shut the fuck up, faggot." His words didn't have the same conviction they'd had moments before.

Wesley closed the space between them and looked down into the shorter man's face. They were close enough he could smell John's sour scent. "Get the fuck outta here, or I'll tell everyone in town about that night."

John's lower teeth bit into his lip, and he glared.

"Try me." To his own disbelief, Wesley wished John would. That he would try to do something to him right then and there.

A second longer of glaring, maybe seeing the determination in Wesley's eyes, and John shoved past Wesley and walked, stiff-backed, out the front door. He swung it open so it crashed into the wall and swayed on its hinges. From somewhere in the back of the store, Wesley heard Avery's startled yelp.

WESLEY REACHED for the carved name, then paused a hairsbreadth away. The edges of the S were slightly smoothed out over the marble.

Shannon Avery Pope Bennett

He let his hand fall. He couldn't bring himself to touch her. It felt sacred. It felt like Travis.

Hell, it felt like Shannon.

He'd never met the woman, but it felt as if she was always there. He knew her as surely as if they were best friends—best friends in love with the same man.

Wesley knelt on the ground, the hard layer of snow crunching and instantly making the denim wet.

He continued to stare at her name. Seeing it carved in a headstone seemed abstract. It didn't really make sense. She was real enough to him that it felt peculiar to see her death spelled out before him. So irrefutable.

There wasn't a sense of loss. It would have been strange if there were, although he felt guilty that the sensation didn't come. Her death had caused so much pain for the people he loved, for a man and children they both loved.

Despite Travis's assertion that he loved Wesley as much as Shannon, Wesley didn't believe it. He believed Travis believed it, but that didn't make it necessarily so. How could he? She was the mother of his children. She was his childhood sweetheart. They'd spent... how long together? How could Travis feel anything even remotely similar for him?

How could he ever?

I will never stop loving you, Wesley. Not ever. Even if you leave.

A scraping noise caused Wesley to look up. Overhead, a squirrel scampered over one of the twisting branches of the old oak. Wesley squinted at the animal's progress in the brightness of the dying sun. He watched until the little animal disappeared inside a crack in the trunk.

When he returned his attention to the grave, it suddenly seemed like what it was—a grave, a marker of death. He was a mere six feet from Shannon's bones. From what was left of Caleb, Avery, and Mason's mother. Of Travis's wife.

Please don't leave. I can't lose you both.

Would Travis love him if Shannon had lived?

If Travis could choose, if he had to choose, would he bring Shannon back and let Wesley go?

What was wrong with him? How could he ask such questions? How could he even allow himself to think such things?

How selfish could he be?

And, really, what difference did it make?

Shannon was dead. Travis couldn't bring her back.

Wesley was here.

He was second best. But he was alive, and he was here. And he loved Travis. And Travis thought he loved him.

Even if you get out of this bed and leave, I will love you for the rest of my life.

That wasn't fair, was it?

Travis did love him. Wesley knew it. He could feel it. He could see it.

It wasn't a competition for first or second place, or any place at all.

Maybe it was even pathetic to question it. Travis had done more than prove that the love he claimed to feel was real. He'd chosen Wesley over his parents and his best friend, over what was easy and expected.

Travis chose to love him.

I will never stop loving you, Wesley. Not ever. Even if you leave.

Wesley did believe him. He really did.

And by God, he loved Travis back. Enough to stay in this town if need be. Enough to put up with whispered looks and being known as a faggot.

Actually, that word was already losing its effect. Shame was leaving. The next person who called him that was going to find out Travis hadn't fallen for some pathetic queen who was afraid to break a nail.

Scarves, swishy walk, and fancy clothes or not, if one more person called him a faggot, he was gonna smash a tiara onto his head and show whoever it was that he wasn't going to take it. He'd done it with that asshole Wallace just the other day. He'd do it again.

His own laugh startled him as it broke through the icy silence of the graveyard. Wesley couldn't suppress a grin as he addressed Shannon's headstone. "You're not gonna be the only one with a temper."

The past two years aside, he wasn't a wimp. Goddamn fucking right, as Travis would say. Wesley Ryan was no wimp.

He'd come to this town to get his life back under control. To be himself once more.

And here he was–Wesley Ryan.

He was a veterinarian, and a damn good one.

He was over that douche bag of a cheating boyfriend.

He was over taking shit from anybody.

He was in love with Travis Bennett and his three kids.

And he was secure enough to love a man who would always be in love with two people. At least he was going to be.

Wesley reached out and touched Shannon's name, feeling the love he saw in Travis's eyes for his wife and feeling the love he saw in Travis's eyes for him.

"You must have been truly amazing to have someone love you as much as Travis does." His eyes burned, but he refused to let the tears fall.

He didn't speak it out loud. It seemed both prideful and rather disrespectful to do so. He felt it, rather than thought it. Shannon had been amazing to inspire such love. What must that say about him that Travis now loved him as well?

Wesley traced the S of Shannon's name, knowing his finger mapped a pattern the man he loved had traveled countless times.

"I will love your children with everything I have, Shannon. I will die for them if the need arises." The tears were hot over his frozen cheeks. "I will love Travis for the rest of my life, and we will be a family. Your children and your husband will never be without love. Ever. I will believe that you will watch over us, that you approve of what you see." His voice broke and caught in his throat.

"Thank you for giving them to me. All of them. Thank you."

A cool breeze washed over him, chilling his tears.

Though not clear, Wesley heard and understood.

CHAPTER TWENTY-NINE

IT WAS the twenty-third of March, and Iris Linley closed up Rose Petal's Place an hour early, just like she did on the twenty-third of every month. After choosing the best flowers from her stock, she made her way to the cemetery, the two bouquets resting on the passenger seat. Like she did every month, she parked her car outside the wrought iron gates that marked the cemetery entrance. True, there were gravel paths for cars between the rows of graves, but if Iris had her way, vehicles would be struck from the hallowed grounds.

Trudging past the gates, her rubber boots crunching through the crusty layer of snow, Iris made her way through rows and rows of graves. Down one rolling hill, up another, and then down the second, stopping halfway. As always, she passed Vern's grave without more than a second glance. She had waited until he died to move his burial plot. There was no way she was going to have him spend eternity resting beside their boys, and one day, herself. He'd been a lousy father and an even worse husband. His constant philandering was the least of his flaws. Other than leaving their house quieter, the day he died had been one of the most freeing days of her life.

The sun wouldn't set for a couple more hours, but the day was already growing dark with heavy clouds rolling in. Probably meant more snow, but hopefully not ice. Iris pulled her thick yellow jacket tighter around her girth. She'd never been a small-boned, waifish thing, but after the boys, well, food was good. It helped her forget. Vern had chosen the bottle and women; both those were sins. Of course, he'd chosen those sins long before they lost the boys.

Iris knew gluttony was a sin too, but, well, God had to give her something. He'd taken everything else.

God forgive her thoughts. Please.

She laid the bundle of lilies at Jack's grave and an arrangement of baby's breath and roses in front of Dean's tombstone. No matter what other flowers she chose, Dean always got baby's breath. He was her baby.

Iris didn't cry. It had been years since she'd cried by their graves. She couldn't even remember their faces. She gotten rid of every photo in the house in a rage after… one of their funerals… she couldn't remember which one. She remembered the fire in the backyard, and Vern screaming at her. Finally hitting her.

Wasn't that horrible? That had to make her a horrible mother. She couldn't remember her children's faces or voices or laughs. None of it. She was horrible.

They came to her in her dreams, Dean more often than Jack. She would be able to see them at times, right after the dreams ended and she woke up. If she didn't open her eyes right away, they would stay with her for a bit. She would remember them. But then they were gone.

They'd died exactly three months apart, to the day. Jack had gotten into a fight in jail on the three-month anniversary of his little brother's suicide. Iris knew it had been intentional. Though not by his own hands, Jack had killed himself as surely as Dean had.

That she remembered. Maybe she couldn't see Dean's face anymore, but she could still see her son's sixteen-year-old body hanging stiff from the branch in their backyard. He'd strung the rope up right next to the tire swing he and his older brother used to play on. She couldn't recall his face, but she could see *that*, the way the rope cut into his neck. She didn't even have to close her eyes. She could still hear the screaming, though she didn't always remember that she'd been the one doing the screaming.

No longer did she speak to her sons. Just stared at their names, at the dates of their coming and going. She would look at the empty spot beside them, the one with the blank tombstone. She'd be sixty soon—not nearly old enough, not nearly close enough. Maybe the food would help her lie next to them quicker. As she always did, she pushed that thought away promptly. It was a sin to kill yourself. She pushed that one away even faster.

The clock had a funny way of moving when Iris Linley spent time with her boys. The world did too. Everything faded away. Thoughts and smeared memories played in loops in her mind, but for the most part, she was just there, but not there too. It would seem like minutes, and then Iris would realize she was hungry or cold, or it had become night, or she needed to pee. Hours would go by, and she wouldn't sense their passing.

Maybe it was the cold on this particular twenty-third. Maybe it was that the screaming somewhere in her past was louder than usual. Maybe it was God, though, to be honest, she didn't really believe in him anymore, not since standing by that tree.

No.

No, God.

She pushed that away too.

That was a sin.

Whatever it was, time returned to her sooner than was typical. Not saying good-bye, she turned and walked back up that second hill, then down, then started up the first hill. Near the top, while she was still shadowed by one of the massive, leafless oaks, she heard a voice.

She'd not earned the title of the town gossip back in the good old days for nothing. Iris recognized the voice instantly. It was that Dr. Ryan fellow. The queer who had saved her dear Horace.

While philandering and drinking were sins—and suicide and maybe gluttony—eavesdropping definitely was not.

Careful to make no further noise than she might have already, Iris placed her gloved hands against the tree and peeked cautiously around.

Thankfully, his back was to her, so the vet wasn't aware he was being watched. For a moment, when he grew quiet, Iris was worried she'd been found out.

Then he continued.

Iris was quick. She could put the pieces of a story together quicker than any reporter. The pieces she couldn't find, she easily made up. She was a good judge of character, and she was certain the bits of her own making were as close to the truth as truth itself.

On this occasion, though, Iris didn't require that particular skill. It was all spelled out clear as day.

The vet was kneeling in front of Shannon Bennett's grave. And though he whispered, in the still, frozen air of the evening, his words carried easily.

Iris listened as Dr. Ryan spoke to the dead woman.

He told Shannon how much he loved her husband.

He told her how much Travis still loved her.

He told her about her children and how much he loved them.

He told her he would love the children as if they were his own.

He told her he would love Travis with everything he had.

He told her he would take care of her family.

Iris leaned forward, almost to the point of losing her balance, but not quite. She squinted, bringing the vet into sharper focus. It was the strangest thing. The man was tilting his head, lifting his ear to the side. He looked like he was listening.

Iris strained.

She heard nothing.

A branch snapped under her foot.

Dr. Ryan flinched, then looked around.

Iris's first instinct was to whip back behind the tree, but she doubted it was thick enough to conceal her. Instead, she stepped back out into the open, forcing an innocent expression on her face.

The vet raised a hand in greeting, but left it suspended in midair, looking panicked.

It was clear he'd been crying, and Iris felt a touch of guilt for intruding. Betrayed by stepping on a twig. She'd lost her touch somewhere along the line. "That was a real beautiful thing to say to Ms. Bennett, Dr. Ryan. Real beautiful."

Dr. Ryan's hand fell back to his side, and his cheeks flushed pink.

Iris couldn't tell if he was embarrassed or angry. She motioned behind her. "I was just here visiting my boys."

He looked past her and back again. He seemed to be searching for words. "I'm—" His words caught and he cleared his throat. "I'm sorry for your loss, Iris."

She only nodded, not acknowledging the sentiment. "If the Bennetts can't have their mother, they're real fortunate to have someone like you to love them instead."

Dr. Ryan's shade of pink deepened. "Um, thank you, Iris." He looked back at his car. "I should, um, I should go." He looked back at her. "Do you need a ride?"

She shook her head. "No, dear. I like taking my time. You go on. Your pant legs look mighty wet."

Without confirming, Dr. Ryan offered her a forced smile, then turned. He walked to the end of that row, got into that prissy yellow car and drove off. He might have waved over his shoulder, but Iris wasn't certain.

When she was sure he wasn't returning, Iris left her spot beside the oak and moved to stand in front of Shannon Bennett.

The two women had never gotten along. Shannon had been too full of herself in Iris's opinion, always acting like she was better than everybody else.

Still. It was sad. Children without their mother—almost as bad as a mother without her children.

Iris tilted her head, assuming the same position Dr. Ryan had previously taken.

Nothing. She heard nothing.

She almost spoke to the gravestone, nearly told Shannon the vet was a good guy. She didn't.

On her way out of the graveyard, though she didn't pause, she nodded at Dionysius Durke's grave.

She asked for God's forgiveness, and she was going to show God's love this time whether she understood the ways of Dr. Ryan and those like him or not. He really was a good man.

She would show God's love.

Even if there was no God.

She pushed that thought away before she passed back out of the wrought iron gates.

PART THREE
SUMMER

CHAPTER THIRTY

THE OLD Bulldogs consisted of four El Dorado Springs natives. Three of them, Jason Baker, Charlie Mumock, and Squirt Daniels, had played on the football team in high school. Jason couldn't remember Squirt's actual name, if he'd ever heard it. Their senior year, the three of them had taken the Bulldogs to state, or three games away from it at any rate. Close enough for El Do. Belinda Friar was an Old Bulldog, too. She had been on the cheer squad. Considering she'd fucked nearly every guy on the football team, she might have been the most responsible for the team's close brush with greatness. She still slept with Jason and Squirt from time to time. Charlie was married. So was Squirt, but Charlie actually acted like it. Only the fifth member, Travis Bennett, wasn't an actual Bulldog. However, Jason had vouched for him when the team was formed. Now, twenty years later, he doubted Charlie, Squirt, or Belinda even remembered that Travis hadn't graduated with them.

Sunday evening had always been Jason's favorite night of the week. It was filled with old friends, greasy food, and endless beers—perfect. Oh yeah, and bowling. That was pretty fun too.

Actually, Jason loved every aspect of his life. He had a cake job that he loved where he got to hang out with his best friend every day. He and Travis had built CCF up so that, as long as they didn't go crazy, they were set on the money front. He was handsome, still had a killer body, and was charming. And he knew it. He had an endless supply of pussy.

Fuck. He was living every guy's dream—up until the past few months.

It had started when Travis hired Krissy. Jason didn't have any problem with the girl. But Travis hadn't even asked for Jason's opinion. Granted, CCF belonged to Travis. However, the place felt as much his as it did Travis's, at least most of the time. If Travis had asked, Jason wouldn't have had to even think twice. He would have hired Krissy in a minute. Hell, Krissy'd had her baby a week ago and would be out for a couple of months to spend time with… Jacob. Yeah, Jacob. It had only been a week, and Jason already missed her snarky, irreverent sense of humor. He loved the girl working there. She'd blended in perfectly with Travis and him.

But Travis hadn't asked.

Even more than being hurt about Travis's lack of inclusion, Jason was upset that he was upset. It made him feel like a pouty little bitch.

He would have gotten over it. He had gotten over it.

Then the other shoe dropped.

Travis a fag?

A *fag*?

Jason had no problem with Wesley Ryan. Up until he'd realized the vet was fucking his best friend, Jason had really liked the guy.

Jason also didn't have a problem with fags, for that matter. He'd had more than one threesome in which he was not the only naked body with a dick. *Never* in town, or anywhere close, and there'd never been any real gay shit. Just casual contact as he and the other dude double-teamed the chick.

If a guy liked fucking dudes, what did it hurt Jason any? He didn't give a fuck.

But Travis—a fucking faggot?

Travis was his best friend. He was family, *more* than family. They were brothers, more than brothers. They loved each other.

Jason was enlightened enough and intelligent enough that he'd considered the possibility that he was so upset about Travis and Wesley because he had some unrealized feelings for his best friend. He'd done more than just consider and push it aside.

He'd tried to jack off to Travis's picture. He'd had to put it facedown on the bed to finish. He didn't feel a thing. He loved the guy. Fuck, he'd die for the guy and his kids, and Wendy too. But he wasn't in love with him, not like that.

He'd come to the conclusion that he, Jason Baker, was a little bitch. He was butthurt that his best friend hadn't told him about such a big part of himself. There was nothing Travis didn't know about him. Nothing. Jason even told him when he'd fucked that married chick in Collins several years ago and then paid for her to have an abortion. Travis knew *all* his dirt. Everything. It was part of the reason Jason loved him so much. Travis might call him an idiot or call him on his shit, but Jason knew he could trust Travis with anything.

Apparently, that hadn't been a mutual feeling.

To make it even worse, Travis didn't tell him even after he and the vet started fucking. He did, but not till after half the town was already talking about it. Jason had been defending the dude. Saying there was no way Travis liked cock. He would know. He was the guy's best friend. He'd even joked to Squirt that if Travis had a craving for dick, he'd be choking on Jason's meat and nobody else's.

The thought of that made him cringe.

Jason missed his best friend. He missed the ease that had existed between them. Jason didn't do well with conflict, never had. He was ready to end this awkwardness and get things back to normal. He wanted Travis back. He wanted the whole Bennett clan back.

He missed his family.

He just didn't know how to go about it.

He'd almost thrown his arms around the big redheaded moron when Travis had walked into CCF last week, just to end it and get things back to normal. He just couldn't make himself.

He needed to fix things. He just didn't know how.

Then he got his chance.

He, Belinda, and Charlie didn't give a shit about how the Old Bulldogs scored. It was bowling, for fuck's sake. It was a big ball you rolled down a plank of wood so you could get trashed on cheap beer. He knew Travis felt the same, though Travis was actually pretty good at the game, better than Jason and Charlie, that was for sure.

Squirt felt differently. He lived and breathed bowling. He often said if the finger holes in bowling balls were wet, he'd rather fuck them than pussy. And that was saying something for Squirt, who had even lower standards than Jason. Squirt was on a more competitive team that met on Tuesdays; he only stayed with the Old Bulldogs because of their friendship. He always got more belligerent during the third game, when all five of them were toasted and everyone besides Squirt was playing worse. There wasn't a Sunday that passed where Squirt didn't threaten to leave the team. Belinda always told him to not let the door hit him on the way out, and that he would be using the bowling ball because her pussy would be off-limits to him.

Jason loved it when girls said pussy. So did Squirt.

They were four frames from the end of the game. The bowling alley's air-conditioning was out and, even though the sun had set an hour or more ago, the June day had been stifling. The bowling alley was stuffy and miserable. To make up for it, the Old Bulldogs had ordered a couple extra pitchers of beer.

They were sweaty, loud, and trashed.

Travis was up. Even drunk and on their third game, Travis had still been playing well. Probably better than usual. However, whatever the reason, as he threw his ball, it went askew, tipping into the gutter before it reached the pins.

"What the fuck!"

Travis turned around at the yell with a sheepish look, until he saw the expression on Squirt's face.

The scrawny man rose off the orange plastic bench and took a step toward Travis. He looked like a chipmunk challenging a bear.

Jason grinned. Squirt got on his nerves a lot of times. It would be fun to see Travis tear into him.

Squirt's voice was so loud the entire bowling alley turned at the noise. "What? Now that you're a faggot you've lost the ability to play like a man?"

Travis flinched.

The entire space went silent.

None of the Old Bulldogs had mentioned anything about Travis, at least not in front of him. After a couple weeks of strained awkwardness, it had all gone back to normal, save for the silence between Travis and Jason.

The team had adopted the motto "out of sight, out of mind"—at least, up until now.

Squirt went from angry to irate so quickly that it took Jason a moment to realize he wasn't just fucking around or trying to push buttons.

"You shouldn't even be on this team. You shouldn't even be allowed in this building or the fucking town." Squirt closed the distance between himself and Travis and shoved a finger in Travis's massive chest. "We oughta round up all'a your kind and get rid'a ya. You shouldn't exist."

Apparently Travis was having a similar reaction to Jason's. Maybe it was the haze of the beer. His expression transitioned from shocked to confused.

As Jason watched, he was able to identify his best friend's flash of emotions. For a second he saw embarrassment cross over Travis's features and then the flush of crimson that announced Travis was ready to explode in anger.

Squirt was such an ignorant idiot he didn't even realize the danger he was in.

Without realizing he was moving, Jason stood as well and strode toward the pair.

Squirt was in the heat of things and oblivious to Jason's approach, as well as the furious trembling of Travis's clenched fists. "We're gonna run your little faggot-ass vet outta town, and then you. Fuck that. We're gonna string him up the nearest tree and make you watch. He's gonna be—"

Jason's fist smashed into Squirt's temple, sending the man crashing to the ground.

Letting out a cry, Squirt covered the side of his face with both hands. "What the fuck!"

Bending, Jason brought his left fist down in an arch, smashing into the unprotected side of Squirt's face.

Squirt scuttled backward, his bowling shoes squeaking on the wooden floor.

Jason went after him.

Before he could kick him in the crotch—the fucker had his legs splayed, just asking for it—a death grip pulled him back. "Let me go, you fuck—" His words dropped off as he met Travis's blue eyes, now more shocked than angry.

The two men stared at each other, neither paying attention to the whimpering curses at their feet.

Jason looked at his best friend, his brother. Even in his drunken anger, he felt himself grin at Travis. "Looks like the Old Bulldogs are gonna be short a member. Think your fag boyfriend might wanna join?"

CHAPTER THIRTY-ONE

"I WAS thinking it would be nice to remodel the kitchen before Caleb arrives." Shannon rubbed her hand over her extended belly.

Travis gave a mock groan. *"Seriously? We have less than two months before the baby is born and you wanna remodel?"* Fuck, she was beautiful, the sun lighting up the vibrant red of her hair. The last month or two, both of them had been able to let go of the fear of miscarriage. Even if the baby came early, there wasn't any huge danger. It was one of the last days of summer, and they'd decided to have a picnic by the pond. Over her shoulder, he could see the herd of buffalo grazing by the grove of trees.

Shannon rolled her eyes. *"Yes. There is plenty of time. More time than what we'll have after he's born, that's for sure. When we had Wendy's party in June, she mentioned that it would look really good if we put in larger windows in the kitchen, looking out over the barn. It would really brighten it up."*

"Did she? I love how my sister has ideas of how to spend our money."

Shannon ignored him. *"While we're at it, I've been looking at house magazines. It wouldn't be too much more work to knock out a couple walls, open the kitchen up to the living room. Make it into an open concept kind of deal."*

"And we're supposed to afford this on a teacher's salary?"

She shrugged. *"Cedar County Feed just expanded. You think Mr. Bland might turn it over to you in a couple of years. Business is good."*

"Nothing like counting chickens before they hatch."

Another shrug. *"So, we take out a second or something."* She took a bite of the lemon squares her mother had made. Powdered sugar dusted her nose. *"No time like the present."*

Travis reached across the blanket and swiped his thumb across the tip of her nose. *"And if I say yes? What do I get in return?"* He waggled his eyebrows suggestively.

"Whatever you want." Shannon matched his expression.

"What if I want it now? In advance?"

Shannon made her voice sound shocked. "What if the buffalo notice?"

"Jarrod has a whole harem. He'd understand."

"And if Mr. Walker should show up?"

He leaned toward her, close enough that he could feel her breath on his lips. "Don't try to make me lose the mood."

Her eyes twinkled. "And I'm so fat!"

"You're gorgeous." He kissed her. "And you know it."

She kissed him back.

SWEAT POURED over Travis's back, not that it mattered. He was drenched. It was barely eighty-five degrees, but the humidity was thick and muggy. And it was only June. It was gonna be one scorcher of a summer. He rested the wooden plank against his thigh and motioned toward the ground a few feet away. "Would you hand me that, please? I guess I dropped it."

Mr. Walker swiped a red bandana over his forehead before bending to pick up the hammer and pass it to Travis.

Taking the tool from him, Travis repositioned the board again so he could hold it steady while hammering in the nail. "I swear the fence was fine yesterday. Dunkyn and I stood right here and watched the buffalo last night." He didn't mention that Wesley had been with them.

"I'm bettin' it was those Smith boys. I caught them messing around in the field a couple of weeks ago." Mr. Walker let out a disgusted breath. "That fat one probably broke the fence trying to crawl over."

"Really? You didn't mention they'd been in."

"I don't owe you explanations, Bennett."

Travis brought the hammer down harder than he needed to in order to keep from saying something he'd regret. "Well, I'll swing by their folks' house on the way home. Jarrod's been getting kinda cranky, even with me. We're lucky he didn't charge at them."

Mr. Walker grunted. "Serve 'em right if he did. They've no business trespassing. And you mind your own business. I've already called their no-account parents. It's their own problem if they can't keep their kids in line."

Travis bit his lip. He was seriously getting sick of walking on eggshells around Emmitt Walker. There were moments it wasn't worth it. But then, times like the night before, Wesley's naked body in the moonlight, the screeching of the katydids and toads loud in their ears, made him continue to play submissive to his boss.

Another couple of swings and the new board was secure. Travis stood straighter, his back popping. Lifting the bottom of his shirt, he tried to dry off his face. No use, the shirt was soaked.

Mr. Walker cleared his throat. "So I heard there was some excitement over at the bowling alley last week…."

Travis kept his voice measured and his attention fixed on the fence. "Oh yeah? People sure do love to talk."

"Yep. Sure do." The man spit a brown stream into the grass. "Hear ol' Squirt might be pressing charges."

Travis laughed, genuinely. "Not a chance. Jason and Wally Sinclair are drinking buddies from time to time."

"Still, a police chief has to do his job."

Travis looked over at Mr. Walker. "True, but it doesn't help Squirt's case that Sinclair caught him screwing his wife a while back."

Walker's brows shot up. "Oh, didn't hear about that."

From somewhere in the field Dunkyn barked.

Travis ignored it. "Yep. Why do you think he divorced her?"

Mr. Walker chuckled. "I like that Jason Baker. He's a scoundrel, but a good guy."

Travis refused to look away from the other man. *Shut up. Don't push it.* "Even if he's best friends with a fag?"

Mr. Walker opened his mouth to reply, but was distracted by Dunkyn's increasingly insistent barking. He looked toward the sound. "What the hell's the matter with your dog?"

Travis followed the sound, searching for the corgi. He was hard to see through the tall blades of grass. Dunkyn stood at the edge of the pond by one of the female buffalo. Travis squinted, trying to make sense of what he was seeing. "Oh shit."

"What?"

Travis started climbing the fence. "If I'm seeing things right, Jane is giving birth, and she's standing in the pond." Jane was the only cow left to calf this summer. It was her first breeding season.

"Ah, for fuck's sake." The older man followed Travis's lead and climbed over the fence as well. He jogged after Travis, who was running full speed toward the pond.

As Travis ran, he realized Jane wasn't in the water but simply close to it. As she lay down, the calf was already halfway emerged.

By the time Travis reached the water's edge, Dunkyn's hysterical bark was nearly hoarse. Just a few feet away, Jane gave a bellow, and a final push freed the baby buffalo, its slimy form slipping from its mother. Before Travis could reach it, the calf rolled down the small slope and into the pond.

"Walker! Hurry up!"

Without pausing, Travis rushed past Jane, who was struggling to stand, and into the pond. The calf was already submerged, but the water splashed from where it struggled.

Even as quickly as Travis sloshed through the water, the calf had already slid six or seven feet from shore. The water came midway up Travis's thigh, but as he slipped his arms under the wriggling form, the weight of the calf forced his legs deeper into the muck, sinking him up to his waist.

The newborn was only forty or fifty pounds, less than the bags of feed Travis tossed around without extra effort. Still, with the kicking legs and his position in the mud, it was several moments before Travis could get a decent hold on the animal. Finally he was able to secure the calf to his chest, slipping his arms around the calf's forelegs and keeping its head and upper body out of the water.

"Wipe off its face, Bennett."

Travis heard Mr. Walker's yell, but couldn't make out the meaning over the splashing and the pounding of his own heart.

Emmitt's second yell got through to him. Locking his left arm into a tighter grip, Travis swiped his right hand over the calf's snout, clearing away the birthing membrane, allowing the animal to breathe. At the motion, the calf slipped, and Travis buckled, momentarily allowing the calf to plunge beneath the surface of the water. With a yell, Travis managed to regain his hold under the foreleg, and he reared backward, the motion causing him to sink even deeper into the muck. He managed to get the exhausted calf's head above water.

"Fuck."

Travis glanced toward the cursing and saw Mr. Walker attempting to sludge through the water toward them. He took a breath and yelled at the man. "No. Get back. I got it. You go get the truck."

Mr. Walker only hesitated a moment before following the directive.

Luckily, the trailer had already been hitched to Travis's truck, so all Emmitt had to do was shove the tools off the trailer and then drive the truck through the gate.

Within four minutes, Mr. Walker had backed the truck to the pond, allowing the trailer to dip into the water. Using ropes, he was able to secure the calf to the trailer while Travis continued to keep the baby's head above the surface. A few minutes later, he drove the truck forward. For a second the tires spun in the muck, but they caught hold and pulled the calf free of the pond.

Emmitt had the calf untied, off the trailer, and lowered onto the grass by the time Travis was able to free himself from the pond.

Mr. Walker squinted at him in the sun. "You lost your boots."

Travis gave an exhausted laugh. "Yep. The catfish can keep 'em." He walked closer and stood above the heaving calf. "It's okay, you think?"

"I imagine. Or will be. What a way to enter the world, huh?" Mr. Walker motioned with his chin to Dunkyn, who was sniffing at the calf. "Good thing for your dog."

Travis grinned. "Yeah, he's a good one." He looked around the field. "Where's Jane?"

Walker looked up, searching. "Oh, for fuck's sake. Dumb bitch."

Travis followed his gaze. Jane stood with the rest of the herd at the edge of the trees, grazing like nothing had happened. "Huh. She might not take to the calf after all that. Might need to bottle-feed this one."

Mr. Walker nodded. "Yep, bet you're right." He looked up at Travis from where he knelt beside the calf. "You mind asking that vet of yours to come take a look at this one?"

The request caught Travis off guard. "Um, yeah. You bet. I'm sure Wesley wouldn't mind checking him out."

Emmitt nodded, turning back to the calf. That was as much thanks as Travis was going to get.

"Mr. Walker?"

He looked back up at Travis. "Yeah?"

"I reckon my *trial period* is over. Don't you?" If the man gave the wrong answer, he could go fuck himself. Pond and buffalo and memories be damned.

Mr. Walker studied him for a minute before giving a slow nod. "Yeah. I reckon so."

CHAPTER THIRTY-TWO

"WHAT *IS* it with you Missouri hillbillies and your blue cheese enchiladas? It's not real Mexican food!" Wesley gave an exaggerated shudder.

Travis smirked and took a large bite, intentionally speaking with his mouth full. "Real or not, either way, they're delicious. And that's the second time today you've called me a hillbilly. You developing a new kink I didn't know about?"

"Oh come on. Like you didn't deserve that." Wesley picked up his cell, and after tapping the screen a couple of times, turned it toward Travis to show him the picture Wendy had sent that morning. "You wore boots with your shorts to tend the cattle. Boots. Shorts. Together."

Travis shrugged. "What's wrong with that?"

"Nothing, if you're a fourteen-year-old girl. Otherwise, you're a redneck."

"I thought I was a hillbilly."

Wesley gave him an exasperated stare. "And a hick too. A hick with pasty white legs."

Travis lowered his voice and leaned closer. "You like my pasty white legs. Thick. Hairy. And you like how they lead up to—"

"Shut up!" Wesley glanced at the tables around them, unable to keep his grin in check. No one seemed to be listening.

Travis leaned back in his chair, smiling in satisfaction. Something caught his attention and he looked over, raising his hand.

Wesley followed the motion.

Shelly took her time walking over to their table. "Yeah, Travis? Whatchu need? 'Nother beer?"

He nodded. "You know me well, darlin'."

"Yep. Sure do. Knew your wife too."

Wesley glared at her back as she walked off toward the kitchen.

"You might wanna put that knife down, Wesley."

He looked down at his hand. His knife was still safely tucked below the lip of his plate. "Very funny."

"Well, you looked like you were thinking about it."

Wesley was surprised at Travis's smile. He'd expected Shelly's comment to have shaken him. "Not a bad idea, now that you mention it. She's always kinda a bitch."

"Nah. Let her be. People are gonna say what they're gonna say." Travis took another bite of the blue cheese mush.

Breaking off an edge of his taco salad shell, Wesley considered Travis for a moment. "When you blindfolded me and told me it was an impromptu date night, I was expecting a candlelit picnic at the Walker farm or something."

"Are you kidding? A candle in a field with as dry as it's been the past couple of weeks?"

Wesley rolled his eyes. "You know what I mean."

Shelly returned and unceremoniously plopped the can of beer in front of Travis and swirled away before any other requests could be made.

Travis took a swig, then let out a sigh. "So, what? You saying Gringos isn't special enough for date night?"

"No, it's not that. I like Gringos, except for that thing you're eating. Just a blindfold didn't really hint at another dinner at Gringos."

Travis's eyebrow rose. Mockingly or teasingly, Wesley couldn't tell. "Were you expecting a ring?"

"Shut up." Wesley wished that thought hadn't crossed his mind. He hoped he wasn't blushing and giving away the truth of Travis's guess. From the heat in his cheeks, it seemed he was failing.

Travis put down his fork and propped both elbows on the table, again leaning in toward the middle. "You're a smart, educated man, Dr. Ryan. You telling me you can't figure out what's special about this dinner?"

They'd been to Gringos at least a couple times a week in the past few months. It was Caleb's favorite restaurant. Blue cheese enchiladas for him too. Again Wesley looked around at the other tables. A few of the patrons were glancing at the two of them out of the corners of their eyes from time to time, but for the most part, few were paying them any attention. Wesley didn't see anything different about the place. He turned back to Travis. "No. I can't say that I have any idea."

Travis looked genuinely disappointed. "We've never been to any restaurant in El Do by ourselves on a date. We always go to Nevada or Fort Scott or Collins."

It was obvious Travis had put thought into this date and Gringos meant something special to him, but for the life of him, Wesley had no clue. It made him feel like an ass. "Sorry, Travis. Spell it out for me."

"Fine. Guess I don't remember how to be romantic." Travis sighed. "Every other time we've eaten here, we're with the kids and Wendy or Jason. We don't stand out too much. But now, with it just being you and me, with all the talk around town. Well...." He shrugged, as if that explained everything.

Wesley thought he was beginning to understand. "And the reason you told me to wear a scarf. In eighty degree weather...."

The look in Travis's eyes was deadly serious, almost challenging. "I want to make it clear to everyone that you and I are together—" He took a breath. "—and I want to make it clear to you that I want you *exactly* how you are. That I love you."

Wesley's throat constricted with emotion, but he didn't cry. He was not going to cry, dammit. Neither could he speak.

Travis took another draft of beer, swallowed, and refused to look away. "Clear enough for you?"

Wesley nodded.

"After this, we're going home, and when the kids are asleep, there's another part to this date." Travis waggled his finger at Wesley's face. "And, no, there's not a ring in that part either."

Mocking. Definitely mocking.

WITH THE kids in bed and Wendy working on her online orders, Travis, Wesley, and Dunkyn walked out of the house under the night sky.

"The rest of the date is in the barn?"

Travis slid his thick fingers between Wesley's and gave a little yank. "I'm gonna start thinking you're high maintenance if you keep complaining about our dates."

"I'm not complaining. I'm just confused."

From somewhere out in the shadowy field, a cow bellowed. An owl screeched in response.

"Just go with the flow. Trust me a bit." Travis continued to lead him.

Upon reaching the barn, Travis unlocked the sliding door and pushed it open.

Without waiting, Dunkyn trotted inside. Wesley followed his example.

Once they were in, Travis turned and slid the door closed once more. Without flipping on the lights, he grabbed Wesley's hand again and led him over to the ladder that went up to the hayloft. Pausing, he bent down and rubbed Dunkyn's head. "You're staying here for a bit, bud. Don't wake up any chickens." He looked back at Wesley and motioned up the ladder. "After you."

Even with Travis's assurance there wasn't going to be a ring, Wesley's heart hammered as he climbed up the rungs of the ladder, which was stupid. He didn't want a ring. It was too soon for a ring.

Who was he kidding?

As his head rose above the floorboards of the hayloft, Wesley gasped. Like a silly schoolgirl, he gasped.

Across the expanse of the hayloft, the large square door for hay was open, exposing the sky full of stars. In front of the door, the hay had been swept clean in a massive circle. A large patchwork quilt was spread over the boards. Around the quilt's perimeter, several clusters of lanterns were lit and glowing, filling the space up to the slatted rafters with flickering warmth.

Not speaking, Wesley climbed the rest of the way into the loft and stood to the side while Travis joined him.

Travis looked at him, a questioning expression on his face.

Wesley had to clear his throat before words could form. "Travis, it's beautiful." Was he supposed to say thank you? That felt weird.

"Good. Glad you like it."

Wesley looked around again, securing the sight in his memory. There was a bottle of wine, two wineglasses, and three cans of beer. A laugh burst from him. "Are you drinking wine?"

Travis shook his head. "Nope. But I'll drink my beer outta a wine glass, if you want."

Wesley laughed again. "You're ridiculous." He motioned toward the lanterns. "And I thought you were worried about fire."

"Well, it's not like they were burning all through dinner or anything. Wendy came out here and lit them for me while we read to the kids." Travis stepped toward the blanket and paused. "But this was my idea. She just helped."

"I love it." Wesley closed the little distance between them. He cupped his hand over Travis's scratchy cheek and lowered his head the few inches it took to kiss him.

Their kiss was tender, almost nervous. Almost like the first one so many months before, below where they stood at the moment.

Travis pulled away, but kept hold of Wesley's hand, then led him toward the blanket. "Here, it's almost time."

"Time for what?"

Travis smiled. "You'll see."

Instead of pausing at the blanket, Travis walked over it, still guiding Wesley. "Sit there." He motioned toward the square door that opened out onto the field.

Wesley, afraid of heights, hesitated. He was not going to ruin this. Not when Travis had gone to this much effort. He got as close as he dared and sat down, crossing his legs underneath him.

"Not like that. Scoot up to the edge. Let your feet hang over the side."

Wesley leaned forward a bit, peering over the side. "That's got to be at least forty feet down."

Travis laughed. "Not hardly. Go on. Scoot up. I won't let you fall."

Hesitantly, Wesley did as he was told, scooting with his hands and butt until his legs dangled over the side of the barn, like he was sitting in a chair. Travis sat down behind him, his legs securely around Wesley.

His fear forgotten, mostly, Wesley leaned back and rested against Travis. "God, you feel good."

"So do you." Travis encircled Wesley in his arms while caressing Wesley's chest.

Wesley let out a sigh and let his head fall back to rest against Travis's collarbone, his fear of heights fully forgotten in the sensation of Travis's touch. He let his hands slide up and down Travis's thighs, the denim soft under his palms. "So what's it almost time for? Please tell me sex."

Travis's voice was soft and gravely in his ear. "Not yet, but soon. And out here in the barn, we can be as loud as we want." His finger slipped inside Wesley's shirt, straining the fabric as he reached for his nipple.

"I thought you told Dunkyn not to wake up the chickens."

Travis chuckled. "Sadly, I think the chickens are not going to have a restful sleep this evening." He pushed his finger in farther, then withdrew.

Lifting his other hand from where it had started to lower past Wesley's waist, Travis started unbuttoning Wesley's shirt. "Let's get this off."

Within moments, the warm night breeze brushed against Wesley's naked torso. He leaned back against Travis and paused. "Take yours off too."

From behind, Travis began tugging at his own shirt, the motion forcing Wesley forward.

Wesley gripped the edge of the doorway. "Whoa! There's not gonna be any sex if I'm nothing but a squished pile beside the barn!"

Travis chuckled again. "You're cute when you're dramatic."

Then the next second, Wesley's bare back was against the thick hair covering Travis's chest and belly.

Travis instantly began to roam his hands over Wesley's body. His erection pushed against Wesley's back. "I should have planned this better. Shoulda had us take off our pants before we sat down."

Wesley readjusted himself so the fold of his jeans was less constricting. "I bet we can remedy that."

"Actually, no, we can't. It's time." Travis pointed out into the night.

Following his gesture, Wesley looked out to the field, at first not seeing what Travis meant. Then he did.

Travis's whisper was a mixture of lust and wonder. "I heard there was going to be a meteor shower tonight. Thought this would be a good way to watch it." As he spoke, he slid his hand down Wesley's stomach, fiddled with Wesley's jeans, easily unfastened the button, then moved his hand underneath the material.

Wesley didn't even attempt a reply, just groaned and pushed back into Travis.

They sat there, bodies silhouetted in the hayloft's door, while glittering trails streaked through the stars.

CHAPTER THIRTY-THREE

THE TWINS helped blow out the thirty-eight candles covering the bunny cake. Wendy clapped, then kissed each of them on the cheek in turn. "Thank you, sweets! Two more years and I won't even attempt to blow out the candles anymore."

"I want the nose! I want the nose!" Avery stretched her fingers toward the button of pink frosting.

Wendy grabbed her little wrist. "Rudeness, lady."

Avery glanced up at her aunt, a pleading look on her face. Blue eyes wide.

Wendy laughed. "Oh, girly, you know that look doesn't work on me. I'm not the wimp your father is."

Travis ruffled his daughter's hair, earning himself a look of annoyance. He probably shouldn't, but he loved that expression. It was just as much Shannon as when the child threw back her head in laughter. He bent and stage-whispered, "Just tell Wendy how young and beautiful she looks, Avery. She'll give you the whole cake."

Jason piped up from his place across the table. "Or just place an order for one of the most expensive stuffed animals this side of the Mississippi. That will work too."

"You two hush up. It's my birthday. You gotta be nice." She wasn't able to maintain her forced sternness. "And, you, Jason Baker, should be ordering on a weekly basis with as many little bast—" Wendy's eyes widened as she glanced at the twins. "—with as many little Bakers as there probably are out in the world."

Travis laughed at the genuine panic that passed across his best friend's face as he glared at Wendy.

"Don't you dare curse me with that." Jason shuddered and began mumbling to himself.

Wendy leered at him, then turned toward Caleb. "Will you help me cut the cake, and I'll go get the plates."

As Caleb nodded, his girlfriend shot up from her seat. "Oh, you sit, Ms. Bennett. It's your birthday. I'll go get the plates."

Wesley slid out of his chair to stand up. "I'll help you, Ashley. And I'll get the ice cream."

Travis watched as the two of them walked toward the kitchen. He never got tired of looking at Wesley; he was so handsome and... bright. Yeah, that was the word. Wesley was bright. He had that quality that seemed to make life radiate out from him. Just like Shannon.

He couldn't remember the last time he'd felt so content, so perfectly at home, surrounded by his family.

Actually, yes he could, and it had been years ago.

He'd never thought he'd feel it again.

Turning back to the table, he caught Caleb staring after Ashley and Wesley, looking as in awe as Travis felt.

Caleb's cheeks flushed, and he gave a grin and a shrug toward his father. Then he looked down at Mason, who was sitting at his brother's feet, petting Dolan. "Since Avery wants the nose, does that mean you want the tail?"

Mason peered up at Caleb, hero worship plastered over his face. He nodded.

Travis felt his eyes burn. "Excuse me, I'll be right back." He pushed his chair back and left the table. He walked out of the kitchen, Dunkyn trailing at his feet, to his bedroom.

He just needed a minute.

All these feelings were still too new. After so many years of feeling nothing but sadness, or nothing at all, it was hard to find his equilibrium.

He didn't turn on the light, but walked over to the bed and sat on the edge, picking up the framed photo off the nightstand.

Shannon, young and laughing out in the sunshine. Beautiful.

Travis didn't even remember where it had been taken. And while he loved all of the pictures of her with their children, with him, this one had always been his favorite. It captured her. When he looked at it, she was right there beside him.

Not that she ever really left.

Glen spoke a few words behind him before Travis realized the whisper was from an actual person.

"She'd be so happy tonight. She'd love seeing all of the joy in that room."

Travis cleared his throat as he turned toward his father-in-law. "Yeah. She would."

Glen didn't join Travis on the edge of the bed, but he placed his hand over Travis's shoulder. "Did you hear from your folks?"

Travis just shook his head.

He'd called his parents a week or so ago. He'd left a message on their machine, offering to get them a bus ticket to come to Wendy's birthday. Just like they did every year.

They hadn't called back.

He knew their mom had called Wendy earlier in the day, wishing her a happy birthday. From overhearing Wendy's side of the conversation, it had sounded strained and forced. And short.

She hadn't said anything, and neither had he, although it had taken a couple of hours before Wendy had seemed like herself again.

"They'll come around."

Travis looked over at Glen and shrugged. "Maybe. Yeah, maybe they will."

They wouldn't. He could feel it.

It hurt and it made him sad. But not really. He'd already lost so much and had gained so much in return. Travis actually felt worse for his mother than anything. She'd come around, if it were just her. But it wasn't. He knew she was hurting.

He pushed the thought aside, returning his focus to Glen. "It means so much that you and Patsy are here. Really."

The old man smiled. "You're our son—" He gave a nervous laugh. "—and you've got our grandbabies. I reckon there's not much you could do that those three wouldn't make up for."

Travis chuckled. "Well, good to know I have a few free passes."

They remained there for a few more moments, staring at the photo.

Glen broke the silence once more. "Let's get back out there. There's more of Shannon out there than in here."

"Yeah, I know. You're right. Give me another minute, okay?"

Another pat on his shoulder.

"Sure, son."

ANOTHER RUSH of emotion flooded through Travis—so much that he had to steady himself on the doorframe—as he exited the hallway into Shannon's open-concept kitchen and living room. Dunkyn paused beside him.

His house was so full of people. So full of noise and laughter and bright colors, all highlighted by the stretch of the field and barn outside the wall of windows. The cattle were close, visible on the other side of the fence as they grazed in the glow of the late-evening sun.

Travis let the visual sink in.

Patsy and Glen were seated close to Caleb and were chatting with Ashley, going out of their way to make her feel welcome, of course.

Wendy was shooing Dolan away with her feet as he begged for her cake, all the while laughing at something Jason had said.

Avery had poor Nutmeg dangling from the crook of one arm while she shoveled in birthday cake with her other hand.

Wesley was bent over Mason, helping him wipe up punch that he'd spilled over his shirt.

Maybe feeling Travis's attention, Wesley looked up. He smiled, then lifted a questioning brow.

Travis nodded in reassurance.

With a whisper at his back and his dog at his feet, Travis reentered the room and joined his family.

"YOU KNOW, I've been thinking...."

Travis glanced over at his sister from where he was drying the dishes.

The sun had set long ago. Shannon's parents, Jason, and Ashley had gone home. The twins were in bed. Caleb and Dolan were shutting up the chickens for the night. He, Wendy, and Wesley were cleaning up. Dunkyn rooted around under the table, collecting any crumbs that may have been overlooked.

"You know, Wendy, I always get nervous when you have that tone in your voice." Travis stacked another plate on the pile in the open cupboard.

Wendy scowled at him. "Don't be mean because I'm smarter than you."

Travis groaned and Wesley laughed but didn't say anything. Smart man.

She continued before he could offer a retort. "As I was saying before I was so rudely interrupted, *on my birthday*, I might add, I've been thinking. When Wesley moves in here, it would be a little strange with all of us under the same roof. It makes sense if he and I just switch. I take over his grandparents' house and he moves in here."

Travis froze, a glass raised in midair in one hand, a dishtowel in the other. He glanced toward Wesley, who was similarly immobile where he'd been wiping off the table.

Wendy pressed onward, pretending not to notice her brother's panic. "I'm sure it would take some adjusting, as the kids are used to me being here, of course. But Wesley's house is just down the street. It's a three-minute drive. Or, if you jog like Wesley, a ten-minute little jaunt."

Wesley spoke, a warning inflection in his voice. "Wendy, I know it's your birthday, but you might have overindulged on the wine. It appears to be affecting your mouth."

She waved him off, a spray of water flicking off her fingertips. "That's ridiculous. I've had enough cake that all the alcohol was absorbed. And it just makes sense. Plus, your grandparents' house is in need of a serious makeover, and I have some ideas."

A pang of loss cut through Travis. He'd not considered a day when Wendy didn't live with him any longer. Though he supposed he'd been remiss in not realizing it was inevitable at some point.

The stronger sensation was excitement. He'd not allowed himself to think of the next step with Wesley. The idea of him living there, sleeping in the same bed, their bed, every night, and being a parent alongside him brought a wave of excitement.

And pure, unadulterated terror.

His gaze met Wesley's across the room. He looked just as alarmed as Travis felt, although Travis thought he saw some longing in there as well.

Wendy kept on, her voice rising in excitement, betraying her assertion of the birthday cake's effect. "The orders on The Crocheted Bunny's website are really starting to take off. And with the prices Wesley forced me to charge, if it keeps up, I could really make some amazing changes to that house."

Wesley looked away, but not before Travis noticed the corners of his lips turn up into a smile.

Wendy shook her hair over her shoulder as she plunged her hands back into the soapy water. "I'm thinking open concept, of course. And more windows, *obviously*. Maybe adding on a sewing room. I was thinking it might be nice to hire a manager for the store downtown and open another one at my new house. Kind of a home, workshop, store sort of combo. Maybe with a really state-of-the-art rabbit hutch outside where I could raise bunnies. Nutmeg needs a friend. Maybe there could even be a doggy door." Wendy giggled. "Well, a bunny door, in any case."

CHAPTER THIRTY-FOUR

HE WAS proud of Caleb. Maybe that was a strange reaction to seeing his teenage son sneak a kiss from his girlfriend when he thought no one was looking, but that's what Travis felt. Actually, he noticed it twice during the Fourth of July fireworks display. It was perhaps not pride, exactly—more happiness than anything. Caleb really was starting to act like a normal kid, finally. At least more than he used to. Travis had been worried that his and Wesley's relationship might make his son become even more withdrawn and protective of the twins. It seemed to be having the opposite effect, though.

Thank God.

The F-350 and Wendy's car were backed up to their chosen section of the fairground, and right on the edge so they could pull out and avoid the escaping traffic. Mason had fallen asleep before the fireworks had even begun and was curled up in a blanket in the bed of the truck. Between the addition of Wesley and Ashley, the truck wasn't meeting the demand. He'd have to get a van or something.

He'd have to register it under Wesley's name. He was not going to look like a soccer mom.

"Jason, throw me the volleyball setup, would ya."

Jason bent to pick up the bag of equipment and tossed it to Travis with a grunt. "We'd better move faster or we're gonna get stuck behind that line of cars for hours despite our good parking spots."

He shrugged. "No rush. We can wait."

"Maybe for you, but I got places to be."

Wendy called over from where she and Ashley were folding up the quilts that had been spread over the ground. "Whoever she is, you're probably better off right where you are. Don't wanna have to start buying my stuffed animal lines for any of your spawn, right?"

Wesley laughed before Jason could respond.

"You find the idea of me procreating funny do you, Mr. Fancy Veterinarian? Maybe you should—"

"Travis! Wesley!" A loud yell cut Jason off.

Travis flinched and turned toward the voice, searching in the crowded darkness.

Charlie Mumock rushed toward them, panting heavily. His right hand was clasped over his side.

"Travis, I just heard on the CB… I…." Charlie stopped as he reached them, bending over and placing both hands on his knees, his portly form heaving in exertion.

Jason, who was closest, slapped him on the back. "Easy man, don't keel over on us. Your wife would kill me if I let ya die, and I'm not giving ya mouth to mouth."

Ignoring him, Charlie peered up at Travis, sweat pouring down his face. "Wesley's place is on fire, man."

"What?" Wendy dropped her edge of the quilt.

Charlie turned toward her voice, as if just seeing her. "Yeah, Wendy. We just heard on the CB as we were packing up. The clinic is on fire."

Wendy looked from Charlie to Travis. "There must be some mistake. Why would the clinic be on fire? The police or somebody would have called us."

Travis felt a sinking feeling in his stomach and pulled out his cell phone from his pocket. Two missed calls. He'd felt it, but it had been during the last explosions of the show. He hadn't bothered.

He could hear other voices, Caleb and Ashley. Jason. Avery. Charlie. None of them were clear enough to understand.

"Oh shit!" Panic broke across Wesley's stunned expression. "Oh shit! I've got to get there. Horace! I wasn't even thinking!"

"What?"

Wesley gestured in frustration. "Horace. Iris Linley's stupid cat. He's at the clinic." He was patting his thighs furiously. "I don't have my phone on me. I bet they've been trying to call me too."

Out of nowhere, fear washed over Travis, and he glanced over at Mason's sleeping form in the back of the truck, then at Avery's frightened face as she hung on to Caleb's neck as he held her. It was irrational, but he needed to get them out of here. Out of the open.

Reading his mind, Wendy stepped up to him. "I'll take care of the kids. You and Wesley go to the clinic."

He started to nod, but hesitated. "I'm not leaving you all."

"No. Go. I'm sure there's nothing to be done for the cat, but you can't just sit here, waiting. I'll take the kids home. Just keep me updated."

Travis hesitated again, then nodded. She was right; he couldn't just wait around. "Okay."

"Wait." Wesley grasped Wendy's arm as he spoke but looked back and forth between her and Travis. "Take the kids to Glen and Patsy's."

"Why?" Wendy yanked away a strand of hair that had fallen in front of her face.

"I don't know. Just a feeling." Wesley's gaze locked on to Travis. "This has something to do with me. I can feel it. I don't want the kids at home, just in case."

Though Travis couldn't say why, there was truth in Wesley's words, so much that it almost made some strange kind of sense. And he knew who—without a doubt he knew who was responsible. "Wallace. That fucker."

Wendy gasped, but Wesley nodded. "Yeah. I bet so."

Despite the business being on fire, having a face behind it erased any fear, leaving only anger once more. John Wallace. He wasn't afraid of that sniveling asshole, but he was going to kill him.

Then another thought. He whipped toward Jason. "The feedstore!"

"Oh fuck!" Jason snarled. "Goddamned fucker."

"I gotta get out there. Maybe I can get there before he does."

Wendy shook her head. "No. Don't do that. Just call the police. If you go there and he's there—"

Jason put his arm over Wendy's shoulder as he joined her. "Travis, you and Wesley go. I'll take Wendy and the kids to Glen and Patsy's, then head to the feedstore. I'll call Wally Sinclair and tell him to send some of his boys to CCF, let him know what we think is going on." He nodded at Travis. "I'll take care of Wendy and the kids. I promise. You and Wes go."

Wendy looked like she was going to argue, then let out a frustrated rush of air, hurried over to her purse, and pulled out her phone and a set of keys. She glanced at the screen and nodded. She had missed messages too. She held out the keys to him as she walked back. "Take my car. Jason and I will take the truck."

CHAPTER THIRTY-FIVE

JOHN WALLACE had waited for the Fourth of July. He didn't really have any notions about independence or liberation, nothing quite so obvious as that. He'd just wanted to do it while fireworks were going off all over the town. Well, maybe that was obvious as well, but he shoved the thought aside. The time for reflection and planning had passed. It was time for action.

To prove his point, he stuffed the bottle rockets in his back pocket, unzipped his pants, and pulled out his cock.

As he urinated over the glass door of Cheryl's, he stroked himself. Just a little. There was something so satisfying about watching the hot stream arching from his chubby as the splatter from his piss against the glass sprayed against his legs.

Maybe he shouldn't have worn shorts. He might burn his legs.

That was dumb. He wasn't gonna get in the fire.

When his bladder was empty, he stuffed his now-full erection back into his pants. Picking up the plastic tub of gasoline beside him, he began to slosh it over the side of the building. He knew there was an alarm system in the veterinary clinic, so he wasn't going to break a window or anything. There was more to do this evening. No sense running the risk of getting caught yet. He'd just make sure to get enough gas over the place that it would do the trick. He could manage to splash enough of the shit up onto the roof without covering himself in the process.

John checked his watch, squinting in the darkness. Almost nine. Perfect. The fireworks at the ballpark were scheduled to go off at nine. Should give him enough time to get downtown before anyone noticed the fire out on Carman Road.

After working his way around the clinic, dousing every area that looked likely to burn, John returned to the main entrance and placed the gas can on the bench that sat outside the front door. He had two other cans in the back of his truck. This one would help get the blaze really going.

Shit! He'd forgotten the bottle rockets.

Taking another lap around Cheryl's, John stuffed the fireworks in random cracks and wedges in the building.

Fuckin' shit, he was brilliant! Who the fuck committed arson and offered a firework show at the same time? When he'd purchased the fireworks, his first inclination had been to get smoke bombs. He could just picture the blue, yellow, and green smoke pouring out of the fire. He'd been at the counter with scores of bombs when he realized it was going to be night and the colors wouldn't even show. Instead he opted for bottle rockets.

Headlights washed over him, causing him to jump. He whipped around to face the street, but whoever it was kept right on zooming down the road.

Probably hadn't even noticed him.

Turning back around, he gave himself a little shake.

Knock it off, Wallace. You've got this. You're gonna show those faggots.

Taking a final, appreciative glance over his handwork, John pulled a pack of matches out of his pocket.

He dropped them.

After scooping them back up, he withdrew a match, then struck it. He held the tiny flame up to his face and grinned. "All right, you little fucker. Do your shit!" He tossed the match toward the gas can.

Even before the match hit the bench, the flame vanished.

"Goddammit. Motherfuckin' shit." John stomped forward, stopping at the bench to glare at the worthless match.

Withdrawing another one, he struck it once more. This time, he slowly lowered it to the pool of gasoline next to the tank.

It blazed up in a small rush of an explosion.

John flailed backward, barely keeping himself from falling. He swiped a hand over his face.

He might have just singed off his eyebrows. He couldn't tell. Then he looked back at the fire, and he noticed the flames licking at the side of the can.

He turned and ran, nearly falling once more as his feet skidded across the gravel. He'd made it into his truck and slammed the door when the gas can exploded into a small ball of fire.

Instantly a river of flame rushed over the walls of the clinic, and John realized he'd parked entirely too close. Jamming in the key, he turned the ignition. With a roar of life, the truck lurched backward, spraying the gravel, then screamed in protest as John slammed it into drive.

He fishtailed onto Carman Road and zoomed off toward downtown, and as he glanced into his side view mirror, he saw the first of the bottle rockets zip up into the air.

He howled in pure joy and retribution.

JOHN HAD no delusions of getting away with it. None. He wasn't even trying to.

That was part of the glory of it all. Those faggots would know exactly who had ruined their lives.

Besides, jail wasn't so bad. He'd spent a few months there in his late teens. Not a big deal. He figured this time would be quite a bit longer than a few months. He wasn't sure what the sentencing period would be for arson. Especially for three counts, but he didn't care.

Well worth it.

Plus, he wouldn't have to put up with his fat bitch of a wife harping all the time. Hell, if he'd thought about it, he could have set his own place on fire with Missy inside.

Not that he'd really do it. He wasn't a murderer.

Plus, his boy would need his mom with his dad in jail—although being Missy-free was a pretty fucking awesome thought.

As he turned off the highway about three minutes later and onto Main Street, another rush of joy filled him.

They were gonna get theirs. All of their fucking businesses wasted.

The original plan hadn't involved that bitch Wendy's store, but John couldn't shake the image of that fucking faggot vet threatening to spread lies 'bout him all over town. Besides, Wendy's place was right on the way to Travis's feedstore. Right between the two places. Perfect trifecta.

Trifecta.

A perfect, flaming trifecta for the faggots. John laughed out loud, enjoying the crazed tinge he heard in the sound. He couldn't remember where he'd heard that word, *trifecta*.

Who cared? What did it matter?

What mattered was that they were gonna get theirs. All of them.

They'd taken everything and ruined his whole goddamned life.

The original plan hadn't involved fire.

It had been simple enough.

John was gonna go into Cheryl's and fuck the damned faggot vet. Then he was gonna tell everyone in the whole town how the fucker had come on to him, and maybe say something about how Dr. Ryan had bragged about fucking little boys or some shit.

John hadn't really been certain when he was going to do it, but he was going to. Sometime. He hated seeing that fag around town. And he and Bennett flaunting that shit in everyone's faces.

God, he hated them.

He wasn't sure when he was going to march in there and fuck that vet. But he would have. He *would* have. It was just a matter of time.

Then that fucking bitch from animal services did a surprise inspection four days ago.

They'd cleared him. He'd made all the changes they required. Cost him a damned fucking fortune cleaning up his field and getting everything up to code. Whatever the fuck that meant. He'd managed to keep his temper during every single one of their inspections.

He'd been cleared. He'd passed all the inspections.

All that was left was to fuck that prissy vet and get the fucker kicked out of town. Or lynched.

Then that bitch had shown up three months after they'd given him their approval. She showed up on his doorstep with court orders to seize all his livestock. Said she'd snuck in a few days before and hadn't liked how he'd let things deteriorate again. Course the bitch hadn't said snuck. But that's what she did. Fucking snuck right onto his property so she could steal his cattle.

Like it wasn't even fucking America.

He had rights.

Fucking took all the goddamned cows.

God, Missy was screaming. At him.

Course he made her scream for an entirely different reason. He grinned at the memory as he pulled into the alley at the back of The Crocheted Bunny. Served her right. Fucking Missy. Goddamned cunt.

It had actually been Missy who was the inspiration for John's Fourth of July shindig. Well, kinda. She wasn't smart enough to think of anything as grand as this, but it had been during her beating that it had come to him.

It had been strange. In between his fist making satisfying cracks against her face, he saw the vet clinic exploding in flames.

It wasn't until later, with Missy moaning annoyingly in the bedroom, that his real brilliance had taken hold. Not just Cheryl's, but Cedar County Feed too. Both of those faggots. As he played out the scenario in his mind, he realized the route he would drive would take him right past that shit crochet store.

Trifecta.

Fucking trifecta.

JOHN HAD been fairly certain The Crocheted Bunny didn't have an alarm system. Sure enough that he was willing to bet on it.

As he broke the back door open, he wished he'd gone the extra mile and bought a lotto ticket. It was his lucky day—no alarm.

Shit. If he'd won the lotto, he might even have been able to afford a fancyass lawyer to keep him outta jail. And divorce Missy the cow while he was at it.

Wendy's store was easier than the clinic. As full of shit as that bitch had filled the place, he probably didn't even need to waste the can of gas.

Still, he was gonna do things right.

After sloshing the walls with the gasoline, John shoved a shitload of all the crap in the store toward the middle of the space. He doused the pile with the remaining liquid and tossed the can on top.

It rolled down the pile and clattered on the floor.

He left it.

He glanced down at his watch.

Fuck, he'd been in the store over a quarter of an hour. Surely someone had noticed Cheryl's burning by now. He was surprised he hadn't heard sirens.

This time, as he tossed the match, the flame hit the pile and set it ablaze.

He allowed himself just a moment to enjoy the heat and then turned. He walked casually through the store and out the back door.

Glancing back, John realized the flames were already licking up the walls where he'd left the trail of gasoline. It was burning even quicker than he'd imagined.

Perfect.

He jogged down the alley toward his truck and the remaining gas can. Sirens wailed in the distance.

One more stop.

Then… trifecta!

John reached his truck and had the door open when he heard the click.

He ignored it.

"John Wallace, you piece of shit."

Startled, John whipped back around.

At first, all he saw was the rifle pointed at his face.

"You are a pathetic excuse for a man." The rifle moved a step closer. "Or for a human, for that matter."

The voice became clear in John's mind as the woman's face moved farther into the light. Wendy Bennett. Uppity bitch. He reached out to take the gun from her.

"Give me a reason, John. I'm not Missy. I'll blow your fucking head off."

The sirens were getting closer.

John lowered his hand.

Chapter Thirty-Six

PART OF him felt ridiculous for going to the fire. There was nothing he could do, nothing either of them could do, but he'd go crazy waiting.

There was already a small crowd gathered around Cheryl's as he and Travis stopped Wendy's little car on the side of the road. He'd had some stupid vision of rushing into the burning building and rescuing the damned cat. The clinic was already too far gone; there was no way Horace was still alive.

"Oh fuck."

Wesley looked over at Travis's face, the fire casting weird shadows over his features, making him look older. Not like himself.

"Wesley, I'm so sorry."

Wesley looked over from the passenger seat. "It's just a building. Nothing that can't be replaced.... Except for Iris's cat. I don't understand this. It just...." His voice trailed off as he looked back toward his burning business. Suddenly he needed to be closer. Even though there was no chance of rescuing Horace, Wesley needed to be there, to do something. He couldn't just sit and watch. "Come on."

They got out of the car and rushed toward the crowd, then pushed through to the front of the group.

Neither of them tried to go any farther. There was no point. There was nothing to be done. He'd already known, but still....

A solitary fire truck was stationed nearby, and a few firemen rushed about. The water from the hose didn't seem to be making much of a difference.

The clinic was nothing more than flames. Brilliant orange lit what was left of the clinic structure from inside, making it look like a sinister jack-o'-lantern. Thick plumes of black smoke billowed in waves into the sky, blocking out the stars.

Despite the growing crowd of people, it was oddly silent. The roaring and crackling seemed to consume the night air as surely as the fire devoured the clinic. Every so often a firefighter's command would cut through the rush of the flames, but that was all.

Wesley was hypnotized by the fire, watching his business be devoured. This was the symbol of his new life, his freedom, his regaining control. The loss swept over him, making the already blistering heat of the night combust.

Wesley looked over when he felt Travis grasp his hand. Several moments passed before he was really able to focus on Travis.

"Wesley, this was just one man. Not the entire town, okay?"

Wesley just continued to stare at him, unblinking.

"It's just a building or two, all right? Please don't take it as a sign or anything."

Wesley tried to make sense of what Travis was saying.

"Don't make any rash—"

A high-pitched wail cut Travis off. The sound was painful and shrill, cutting through even the roaring of the fire.

The scream seemed to break Wesley out of his shocked stupor, and he looked away from Travis, searching.

Then he saw the source.

Still wailing, Iris Linley rushed through the crowd, shoving people aside in her panic. Over and over she screamed Horace's name.

It was painful to hear.

She ran surprisingly fast for a woman of her size. Breaking through the crowd, she charged toward the burning clinic, the tails of her housecoat flapping behind her. One of her slippers fell off, causing Iris to stumble. She caught herself before she fell and continued her rush toward the fire.

Her trip gave one of the firemen time to reach her. Grabbing one of her outflung arms, the fireman whipped her around, nearly causing them both to fall.

To Wesley's amazement and horror, Iris continued toward the clinic, dragging the fireman along behind her. His heart broke for her.

Wesley started to rush toward them, but before he got more than a few steps, another firefighter caught hold of Iris. Between the two of them, they were able to bring her to a halt. After another moment of struggle, Iris crumpled to the ground in a sobbing heap, her wails increasing.

AS INSANE as the night of the Fourth of July had been, it was nothing compared to the following two weeks. Wesley had never experienced anything like it. With the confusion of who was responsible for what in all the licenses, titles, and insurance documents that had been finalized between him and Cheryl Fisher less than a month previously, it was nothing short of a paperwork nightmare. He was surprised that the insurance company had yet to claim Wesley had some sort of involvement in the fire. It did look a little suspicious. The ink of signatures was barely dry and the place just happened to burn to the ground.... So far, they hadn't. He wasn't too concerned, though. Even if the insurance company put up some type of fight, the details were pretty cut-and-dried when the arsonist was caught red-handed and more than happy to brag about his *victories*.

The fucker.

If John Wallace had been smarter, he could have at least tried to claim that Wesley had set him up to it and get him involved in insurance fraud. Luckily, the man was as big a moron as he was a disgusting excuse for a human being.

Wendy had been covered by insurance as well, and with her holding John Wallace at gunpoint as the police arrived, there was no doubt of her innocence. Wesley would have given anything to have seen that moment. Wendy and Jason had been on their way to take the kids to Shannon's folks when they heard over the truck's CB radio that the cops were headed to The Crocheted Bunny. It seemed that someone had noticed John Wallace moving around in the store and called the police. They had been nearly to Main Street when they heard the announcement, and Wendy had forced Jason to hightail it to her shop.

Travis couldn't stop laughing every time Jason retold how Wendy jumped out the passenger side before he'd even gotten into park, yelling for Jason to take care of the kids, then grabbed his rifle out of the lock box—which had been left opened in the rush to leave the fairground—in the truck bed.

For his part, Wesley could just picture Wendy with the gun trained on John Wallace, the red, white, and blue broomstick skirt she'd worn that night whipping in the breeze as the blaze from the fire caused her red hair to glow wildly in the darkness. His vision was probably more dramatic than it had actually been, but that's how he saw it, every time.

Wendy sighed beside him. "You know, I know I've said it before, but I could seriously get used to this." She leaned against the huge walnut tree at the edge of the playground. "It's like vacation."

Wesley grinned, watching the twins as they played. It seemed Avery had decided to be Snow White. She was unmoving on the merry-go-round, her hair artfully splayed around her. As she lay in death-like sleep, Mason dutiful spun her around. Wesley wasn't sure if the boy was supposed to be Prince Charming or one of the dwarves. "It is pretty nice, I've got to agree. I'm sure it would be different if either of us had a house payment we were worried about, though."

"But we don't, so that's the beauty of it all. We're on an extended vacation." She fluttered her fuchsia-hued broomstick skirt, stirring up a breeze in the muggy humidity. Her boots lay discarded under a nearby picnic table.

A chime sounded from Wesley's pocket. He withdrew his cell and glanced at it. "It's Travis." Swiping his finger across the screen, he viewed the text, then reported to Wendy. "He's dropping off the food to Jason and Krissy, then he's on his way."

"Good. I'm starving." She patted her stomach.

"Seriously?" Wesley looked over at her. "I don't think I'll ever be hungry again!"

"True, but I must say I'm getting sick of casseroles. Not to be unappreciative or anything, but Simone's sounds so good right now."

He couldn't disagree with her there. Both the freezer at his house and at Travis and Wendy's were overflowing with pan after pan of casseroles. They had so much, they'd started sending them home with Jason and Krissy. With all the mouths to feed in Krissy's house, the girl had been nearly ecstatic. It made Wesley feel even more ungrateful, but there were only so many meals with a chicken soup and mayonnaise base a guy could eat. "I still can't get over Iris being the ringleader of that whole thing."

Wendy nodded, not opening her eyes. "You really should come to church. I'm telling you, at this point, you're a minicelebrity."

He shuddered. "As if you could make me want to go any less after last time."

Wendy kept going. "Between Iris making certain everyone in the church got signed up for meal-delivery duty and Carrie Michaels' little speech about acceptance and showing God's love to everyone during last week's prayer meeting, there's not gonna be one person in town who will risk saying a bad word about you and Travis."

Wesley snorted. "Not to mention that you're liable to shove a rifle in their face if they say anything negative."

"I'm going to ignore that unladylike depiction of me." Deigning to open her eyes, Wendy turned toward him, strands of her hair getting stuck on the bark of the tree. "I'm serious, though. Even Pastor Carver requested prayer for you and Travis, well, and me, last Sunday."

Another snort. "Probably to get us saved or to repent from our evil ways."

"I don't think so."

"Well, I'm sure Pastor Hellfire and Brimstone loved that."

It was Wendy's turn to snort. "Who cares what Pastor Thomas and Twyla think!"

Wesley didn't speak for a while, getting lost in the madness of the past two weeks. At last he spoke. "Have you spoken to Iris? Is she okay?"

"Oh, Wesley. You need to quit feeling bad. She'll be okay. If you're worried about her, pop into Rose Petal's Place." She chuckled softly, but not disrespectfully. "Maybe take her a casserole."

"That's not a bad idea, actually. Makes more sense than people bringing us food. It's not like we had a death or anything."

He could still picture Iris tearing through the crowd in front of Cheryl's that night. For some reason, he saw that more clearly than anything else—the sight of her nearly flying into the fire, the sound of her screaming, the struggle of the firemen trying to hold her back. He and Travis had gone to her and helped bring her back toward the crowd. Wesley could still feel her tremble in his arms as he'd held her. She'd been nearly inconsolable.

She'd never blamed him, though he'd expected her to.

The morning of the Fourth, Iris had called him in a panic. Wesley had left the Bennetts, who were preparing for the Fourth of July celebration, and met her at Cheryl's.

Horace had killed a bird and had gotten one of its bones stuck in his throat. Wesley had been able to remove it, but the cat kept wheezing. Upon further inspection, once Horace had quit trying to scratch Wesley's eyes out, he discovered that the cat's throat was inflamed from some previous injury.

Wesley had convinced Iris to leave Horace there overnight. He'd planned to go back in after the kids were asleep and check up on the cat.

Though he certainly understood loving your pet, and he'd seen many people lose their shit over the death of their dog or cat, none had ever had quite as intense a reaction as Iris.

He hadn't expected it from her.

"Do you think it's too soon to get her a kitten or something?"

Wendy smiled gently at him. "I don't know, sweetie. I really think you should just go talk to her."

He wasn't sure why, but he wasn't able to face her yet, especially knowing she was championing them getting at least one home-cooked meal a day.

She was a strange woman, that Iris Linley.

"Daddy!"

At Avery's squeal, Wesley looked over. Travis and Dunkyn were trudging up the sidewalk from the lower park. Travis's arms were loaded with two large white paper bags and a tray of drinks.

Travis nearly dropped it all as Avery crashed against his legs in a bear hug.

Wesley and Wendy walked over to him, each retrieving a bag.

Travis glared playfully at them. "You could have at least met me down by the bandstand so I wouldn't have had to schlep it all the way up here myself."

Wendy gave her best British accent impression. "Darling, in case you weren't aware, Wesley and I are now ladies of leisure. We don't *schlep* anywhere." She switched back to her normal alto. "Since when do you say schlep, anyway?"

Travis ignored her and gave Wesley a quick kiss. "Sorry, I'm so sweaty."

With a laugh, Wesley wiped his forearm over his lips. "Wow, you really are."

"Well, it's hot out here, and I just had to climb up a Missouri mountain."

Mason walked over to them and waved up at Travis. "Hey, Dad."

"Hey, partner." Travis bent down and scooped the boy up in his arm. "Who's your sister making you be today?"

The boy looked sheepish. "The evil queen."

Travis burst out laughing, then shot a withering look at Avery. "Really?"

She shrugged, unconcerned. "Well, someone needed to make the poisoned apple."

Wendy called over from where she was unpacking the burgers and fries and spreading them out over the table. "Mason, don't let your daddy give you a hard time. If he's going to be a queen, you can too!" She paused to pop a wavy fry into her mouth. "Just try not to be evil."

CHAPTER THIRTY-SEVEN

REFLECTIVE CAUTION tape gleamed in the cacophony of colored light from the spinning carnival rides. From where they were perched on top of the Ferris wheel, the burnt-out husk of The Crocheted Bunny looked skeletal and menacing. The rest of Main Street radiated with life. Hundreds of people flooded the streets, and the twang of country music blared from the bandstand.

Travis breathed in deep, loving the smell of the mixture of the summer air and fried carnival food. The Ferris wheel moved forward and jerked to a halt once more as another cart unloaded and filled with more people. With Wesley's fingers warmly intertwined with his, Travis searched the crowd. After a few moments, he found Wendy and Jason in line for the carousel, the twins hopping about excitedly between them. Following his line of sight, Wesley spoke up, breaking the comfortable silence between them. "I promised Mason that we'd do the Tilt-A-Whirl after this ride."

Travis looked over at him. "Are you serious?"

Wesley's brows knitted. "Yeah. Why?"

He shook his head. "I keep forgetting we weren't together last year. The last time we rode that, he threw up all over us."

"Oh. I guess that explains why Avery said she'd never ride that again."

Travis laughed. "Yeah, I can't say I blame her."

"Well, maybe now that he's older it won't affect him the same way." The ride slid forward once more, then halted again. "It feels like we've been loading forever."

"That's okay. I like it up here. Just sitting." Travis let his gaze wander over the town. "El Do looks so small from up here."

"That's because it is."

"I keep trying to spot Caleb, but I don't see him anywhere."

Wesley gave him a skeptical look.

"What?"

"The boy's got a girlfriend. I doubt he's worried about carnival rides. He and Ashley are probably making out in some dark corner of the youth group building."

"Thank you so much for that visual." He grimaced.

Wesley just grinned. "You're welcome."

Though he didn't relish the thought of Caleb making out with anybody, Travis had been relieved at the change he'd seen in his son. Though still quiet and overly protective of the twins, Caleb had actually started to seem like a real teenager and not a forty-year-old soccer mom.

With a final lurch the Ferris wheel began to move, gradually picking up speed. The warm current of air was soothing in the too-hot, end-of-July heat. "You know, Caleb told me last week that he's decided he wants to be a veterinarian."

Wesley shifted to look at him easier. "You okay with that?"

"Oh, yeah." Travis was so much more than okay with that. "I'm glad he's going to go for it. I was worried he would feel like he couldn't get out of this town if he wanted to."

"Are you wanting to get out of this town?"

Travis looked over at Wesley, a shot of panic slicing through him. "Why? Are you?"

"No, I was just curious. We haven't ever really talked about it."

"Oh." Though he was relieved, his heart was still pounding against his ribs. "I don't know. I haven't considered it for a long time. Shannon and I talked about moving for a bit at one point." He shrugged. "I guess I'd like the twins to finish growing up here. Their grandparents are here, their home, everything." He looked away from Wesley, afraid of what he might see in his eyes. "Are you okay with that?"

Wesley squeezed his hand. "Yeah. Surprisingly. I'm gonna need frequent trips to the city, but I like it here. Some parts, I love."

"Like the buffalo?"

Wesley laughed.

Travis loved that sound.

"Yeah, the buffalo are pretty great. I was kinda referring to the man who takes care of them."

Travis forced a shocked expression over his face. "You're fucking Emmitt Walker?"

Wesley shuddered, a true and involuntary reaction. "You're disgusting."

This time, it was Travis who laughed. After a moment, he grew serious again. "So, Jason and I were talking the other day…." Suddenly he was nervous again. That was stupid. There was no reason to be nervous.

"Yeah?"

Travis cleared his throat. "Well, we were talking, and thought it might be time to expand Cedar County Feed again. We thought it would make sense to have a veterinary clinic attached. You know, a one-stop shop kinda deal." He rushed ahead, his nerves getting the better of him. "You know, if you decide you don't wanna use the insurance money to rebuild where you were…."

Wesley's brown eyes searched his face, the lights of the carnival reflected in them. "Are you sure you'd be okay with that?"

So much more than okay. "Yeah, if it sounds good to you."

"I think that sounds"—the smile that broke over Wesley's face said more than any words—"perfect."

Travis never looked away as the Ferris wheel began to slow. "There's one catch, though."

"Yeah, what's that?"

"You've got to change the name to something besides Cheryl's."

Their cart came to a stop at the pinnacle of the ride once more as lower passengers began to unload. Wesley pretended to consider. "What did you have in mind? Something like the Cedar County Feed & Clinic? We could call it CCFC. I bet Jason would like that."

"Shut up." Travis gripped Wesley's chin, holding his face still before he kissed him. "I love you."

CHAPTER THIRTY-EIGHT

"I CAN'T believe you and Jason actually talked me into this."

Wesley grinned over at Travis before pulling his scarf tighter against the unusual mid-September chill. "I think you secretly like it."

"No." Travis shook his head. "Nope. Nope. Nope. And nope."

"Come on, you've got to admit you like it just a little bit. It's got a good ring to it."

Travis looked at him and rolled his eyes. "No. I like you. Love you. But I hate the name. Actually, now that I think about it, there's no way you could ever doubt my love again, after this. You or Jason."

Wesley motioned up at the gigantic metal sign on top of the feedstore. The red chrome capital letters, CCFC, sparkled in the light of the sunset. "I think it's got personality."

"Yeah, that it has. Just definitely not a good one."

Wesley reached out and intertwined his fingers with Travis's. "You could have vetoed it."

Travis forced out a guffaw. "Right. The two of you would never let me hear the end of it."

Wesley just smiled. As nervous as he was about joining the clinic with the feedstore, having so much of his and Travis's lives intertwine, there was an underlying sense of peace about the whole thing. It just felt right. "Come on. Let's go home. I'm sure the others are starving."

"Actually, they're eating on their own tonight." Travis suddenly looked nervous.

"Oh? Impromptu date night?"

He shrugged. "Kinda."

"Awesome. However, if we are going to Gringos, I'm not getting that blue cheese crap. No sense in trying again." Wesley let go of Travis's hand and started to walk toward the truck. He glanced back when Travis didn't follow. "Everything okay?"

Travis hesitated, peering over at the feedstore. "Don't you wanna see what they did in the addition today?"

Wesley inspected the new structure on the side of CCFC. "They just put up drywall yesterday. The most they could have done was some trim and stuff. I'm just excited that we can start installing all the equipment next week. I'm sick of doing house calls all day long. Let's go eat. I'm starving."

Again, nervousness crossed over Travis's expression. "They might have done more than that. Let's go see."

Suddenly Wesley felt as nervous as Travis looked.

Surely not.

He forced out a breath and stepped back toward Travis. "Okay. Let's see."

Travis didn't say anything else as they walked up the steps and entered the original section of the feedstore. However, the sweat beading over Travis's forehead did nothing to calm Wesley's nerves.

After walking through the feedstore, Travis paused outside the newly framed doorway that led into the clinic. He started to say something, then simply stuck out his hand.

Wordlessly, Wesley took it, and they walked through the door.

In the middle of the main room, where the front desk would soon be built, surrounded by walls of drywall and plastic sheeting, sat a square folding table and two chairs. A solitary candle flickered in the center of the table, next to a large white paper bag and two lidded Styrofoam cups.

Wesley's heart rate increased with anticipation and he looked over at Travis, who refused to meet his eyes. "Wendy?"

"No." Travis chuckled nervously. "Jason. If Wendy would have done it, there would have been a tablecloth and the burgers would have been on plates, not left in the fucking Simone's bag."

They stood there, unmoving. Even though Wesley knew what was going to happen, he couldn't quite believe it. He was so terrified he almost hoped he was wrong, that Travis wasn't about to do what he assumed. His heart sank at that thought, betraying him.

Finally Travis pulled him toward the table. "Well, come on, you said you were hungry. And the burgers aren't as good when they're cold, no matter what Jason thinks."

Wordlessly Wesley allowed himself to be led to the table and followed Travis's lead when he sat down across from him.

The tension was so great Wesley was starting to sweat as well. Self-consciously, he tore open the paper bag from where it was stapled shut and began pulling out the burgers and wavy fries.

Travis stood up so quickly his thigh bumped the table, nearly causing the drinks to fall over. "I can't take it anymore."

Within two steps, he was in front of Wesley. Travis shoved his hand into his pocket, pulled out a ring, and dropped to one knee.

"Oh, Travis—"

"No, wait, please. I just need to do this all at once."

Wesley closed his mouth. Where was he supposed to look? At Travis? The ring?

Travis wiped the back of his forearm across his mouth, then looked Wesley in the eye.

"I love you. I know you know that already, but I do." Travis paused, took a deep breath, then started once more. "I didn't think I'd ever be happy again. Not like before. You don't get that... a guy doesn't get that more than once in his life. Most don't even get once. I was done. You know?"

Wesley started to reply, but Travis cut him off with a small shake of his head.

"Sorry, babe, gotta finish." He tried to smile but wasn't successful. "I don't wanna wait anymore. There's no reason to. I want to spend the rest of my life with you, Wesley." He held the ring up between them, blocking Wesley's view of his face.

A simple, thick gold band.

Travis spoke from behind the ring. "Shit, I didn't even ask, did I?"

Gently, Wesley pulled Travis's hand down, lowering the ring. There was no way he was going to miss Travis's face in this moment. Not for anything.

This time Travis's smile was brilliant. "Will you marry me, Wesley Ryan?"

Part Four
The Following Spring

EPILOGUE

AVERY EXAMINED her reflection in the mirror. She tucked a wayward lock of strawberry blonde hair behind her ear. Glancing back and forth between the framed picture on the dresser and the mirror, she decided that Wendy had done a good enough job. Her hair was nearly identical to what her mom's had looked like on her wedding day.

Taking a step back, Avery took in her entire reflection.

She nodded. It was exactly what she'd wanted. It was perfect. From the sparkling silver cowgirl boots to the locket around her neck that had belonged to her mom, it was exactly what Avery Bennett had wanted.

She'd had to fight for it. A few weeks ago, Wesley and Wendy had taken her on a shopping trip to Kansas City.

Just her!

Caleb and Mason had stayed back with Dad.

It had been a *perfect* day.

They'd started at Children's Palace. It was the largest toy store she'd ever seen *and* it was shaped like an actual castle. It had turrets on either side and everything! She'd picked out a deluxe makeup kit for kids. Dad had glared at Wendy when he saw what Avery brought home, but he hadn't taken it away. She'd also picked out a double pack of My Little Ponies. They were twins. One orange and the other pink. She'd known Mason would love them.

He did.

After the toy store, they'd gone out to lunch to this Asian place where they cooked the food right in front of you. The chef had spun an egg on his spatula, tossed shrimp into people's mouths, and made a volcano out of a stack of onions.

That all had been amazing. Amazing!

Avery couldn't wait to move to the city. One day, when she was older, she was going to move to Kansas City and be a movie star. Or maybe a model. Something. Something that had nothing to do with cows or chickens or buffalo or any kind of animal poop.

And then, it had all gone downhill at the part she'd been most excited about. Dress shopping!

That was when Ms. Ryan had shown up. She was Wesley's mom. *Uck.*

Avery loved Wesley so, so, so much, but his mom was bossy. She kept having Avery try on dresses that were pink or yellow. One of them was even red.

Red!

Avery was almost done with second grade, and she knew that redhead girls were not supposed to wear red dresses. And to a wedding of all things.

Avery had picked out a long white sleeveless dress. The whole skirt was covered in lace and little white flowers. As she tried it on, she knew it was the one she wanted.

It even came with a matching headband.

But Ms. Ryan kept saying it looked like a wedding dress, and that wasn't appropriate for a little girl to wear to a wedding.

Even Aunt Wendy had started to irritate her. She hadn't told Ms. Ryan to mind her own business or anything.

Avery had decided she was going to throw a fit. A real one. Not a little kid fit, but one worthy of a soon-to-be third grader. She was going to teach that lady that she couldn't just show up out of the blue and boss everybody around.

Luckily, before she had to do that—*if she had, she knew Wendy would probably take away the new makeup kit*—Wesley had told his mom he thought Avery looked perfect in the dress.

He was right.

Even then Wesley's mom had argued.

Wesley had kissed his mom on the cheek and told her that since there was no bride at the wedding it wouldn't hurt if Avery dressed like one.

Avery really did love Wesley.

She squinted at the mirror again, annoyed. The same lock of hair had slipped out of place. Again! She tucked it behind her ear once more, then noticed something.

She lifted the picture off the dresser with both hands. The frame was a silver metal and it was heavy.

She looked at her mother.

Avery hadn't noticed it before because of all the flowers in her mom's hair. She hadn't worn a wedding dress, but she did have a bunch of white flowers woven into her pretty red hair. Underneath the clump of flowers, her mom had a strand of hair hanging down in front of her ear.

Placing the frame back, Avery looked again at her reflection, pulling the lock of hair free once more from behind her ear.

Everyone told her she looked like her mom. She hoped she did.

Her mom had been so beautiful.

She wished her mom could be there to see Dad get married.

With a lift of her lacy skirt, Avery twisted her foot to see the boot sparkle in the mirror. She was satisfied. She looked every inch a bride. She couldn't wait! There was going to be wedding cake and dancing.

Only a few more minutes and she was going to have to line up with Mason to walk down the aisle.

Mason had a sparkly bow tie that matched her boots.

The only thing she didn't like about the wedding was that Daddy and Wesley had decided to have it in the barn.

In the barn!

Gross.

She and Mason were going to walk down the aisle with Dunkyn and Dolan.

Dolan was going to have a ring tied on his collar for Wesley to give to Daddy, and Dunkyn was going to have ring tied to his collar for Daddy to give to Wesley.

She liked that.

AUTHOR'S NOTES AND ACKNOWLEDGMENT

I KNEW I would return to the world of *The Shattered Door*, the town I grew up in, one day. I wasn't sure when or how, but then Travis and Wesley showed up, asking to be with Dunkyn and Dolan—or maybe it was the other way around. *Shattered* told the tale of the pain, fear, guilt, bullying, etc. that I felt growing up. However, there was another part during those years in El Dorado Springs. Lightning bugs. Thunderstorms. My grandpa's buffalo. My chickens. Friends that I loved dearly. Simone's Drive-in (if you're ever driving on 54 and pass through El Do, you have to stop and get a burger. They're perfect!). Despite the pain I felt a lot of the time, there was so much good, as well. So much beauty and love. I hope I was able to capture that aspect of El Do with *Then the Stars Fall*.

As strange as this may sound, I have to give credit to the 'Red Family,' as I call you, who attend church with Stephen and me. Though I've never spoken to you, I've watched the love you show each other. I've intentionally stayed away so that I didn't accidentally write who you really are in these pages. However, when I needed a family for this story, it was you—a father and three beautiful children. Though I don't know your own story, the love the Bennetts show each other is the love I see you show each other every day. And to Caleb (I don't know your real name), I've never seen a better big brother in my entire life. The two little ones are so blessed to have you!

First off, I'd like to thank all of you, readers, bloggers, and fellow writers of the M/M world. I've never been part of such a loving community before. You all are truly wonderful!

Elizabeth—I will never be able to thank you enough or stop singing your praises. Thank you for continuing to support my attempts to fly!

Desi—I love you more with each book we do together. Thank you for respecting my writing, my characters, and being strong enough to challenge me. I trust you fully!

Anne—I am humbled and honored to have such a classic, beautiful, and moving piece of your art grace the cover of *Then the Stars Fall.* I pray my words embody your masterpiece.

Stephen—Thank you for continuing to walk through this life with me. Thank you for letting your boyfriend disappear inside his own head while this book poured forth. Thank God that you are so patient. I love you with all of my heart!

My family—Mom, Dad, Trenton, and Gavin. I love each of you, and I love how we never, ever give up.

Brandilyn and Ruslana—Thank you for being my betas and seeing this book in its roughest moments. Thank you for your feedback, both the bits I stole from you and the parts I ignored because I'm a bitchy artist. I love you both!

Amber—Thank you for letting Travis have your last name. I just couldn't picture him not being a Bennett for some reason. Love you, lady!

People of El Do, friends, family, and others, yep, even you others—Thank you for raising me my first eighteen years. Through the love, the friendship, and even some of the torture, you taught me to be brave and strong. Thank you for that!

Cheryl—I love being a teacher in the same school with you! Your grace, strength, and humor are unmatched. Though you are so much different than the Cheryl in the book, I love seeing your name scattered throughout. I will never have a dirty martini with blue cheese stuffed olives and not think of you with love.

Dunkyn and Dolan—I told you that your story was coming! Some people might find it strange to dedicate a book to you guys, but luckily, we don't care, do we? You are the best corgis in the world. Dunkyn,

there were many, many dark nights I would not have gotten through without you sleeping by my side. Dolan, you entered Dunkyn's and my world and shattered any illusion we had of serenity. You always show your love and adoration, even when I'm at my worst. I love you both.
—Dad

BRANDON WITT resides in Denver, Colorado. When not snuggled on the couch with his two corgis, Dunkyn and Dolan, he is more than likely in front of his computer, nose inches from the screen, fingers pounding the keys. When he manages to tear himself away from his writing addiction, he passionately takes on the role of a special education teacher during the daylight hours.

Website: http://www.brandonwitt.com
Author Facebook page:https://www.facebook.com/brandon.witt.author
Twitter: https://twitter.com/wittauthor
Youtube

BRANDON WITT

THE
SHATTERED
DOOR

http://www.dreamspinnerpress.com

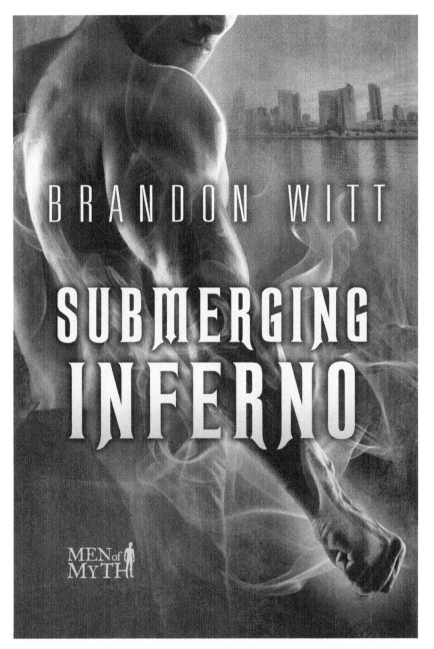

BRANDON WITT

SUBMERGING INFERNO

MEN of MYTH

http://www.dreamspinnerpress.com

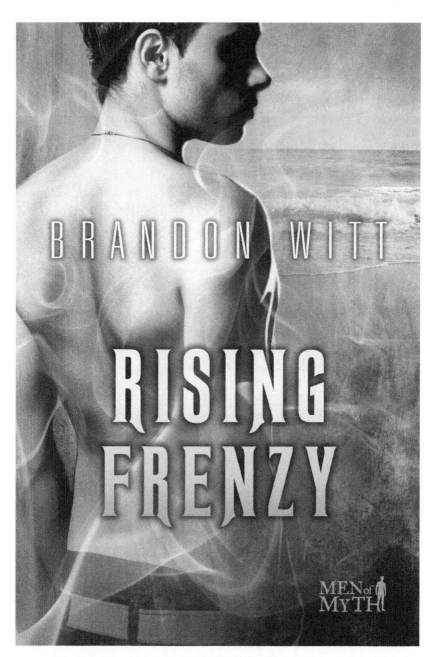

BRANDON WITT

RISING FRENZY

MEN of
MYTH

http://www.dreamspinnerpress.com

BRANDON WITT

CLASHING
TEMPEST

MEN of
MYTH

http://www.dreamspinnerpress.com

CPSIA information can be obtained at www.ICGtesting.com
Printed in the USA
LVOW04s1934300914

406612LV00010B/166/P

9 781632 162588